NO WAY BAC

In a quiet south London suburb violence suddenly
erupts, signalling the beginning of a vicious
campaign of terror, while at the capital's exclusive
Dorchester Hotel the British Security Services begin
a discreet surveillance of someone they know to be
one of the world's most wanted men . . . someone
whose links with the past can destroy them all. Their
target is Hashimi Ross, a highly trained and ruthless
terrorist who is now on a mission of the most
dangerous kind; a personal vendetta to exact
revenge on the men he holds responsible for his
girlfriend's brutal death.

Willie 'Spider' Scott owes Ross his life, and now
that the debt must be repaid he finds himself the
unwilling pawn in a battle of wits when the Security
Services move in to destroy their old adversary and
deem that Scott's own life might be expendable.
Only Detective Chief Superintendent George
Bulman is aware of the top-secret manoeuvres – but
Spider's alliance with Ross has placed both men
outside the law – and a nerve-shattering climax
ensures that for the three of them there can be no
way back.

George Bulman is the star of the television series
Strangers and *Bulman*. *Bulman* was screened most
recently in the summer of 1985 and a new series is
currently in preparation.

THE CRYPTO MAN

'A well-constructed thriller, fast-paced and gripping'

Daily Telegraph

'In this complex, yet tidily plotted mystery the tension rises on a steep curve to a last-minute climax that will leave readers drained, but wanting more . . . memorable entertainment'

Publishers Weekly

10,000 DAYS

'Tough, vivid, to the point'

Daily Mail

'Action-packed . . . delivered in nail-biting prose'

The Sunday Times

**Also by the same author,
and available from Coronet:**

The Crypto Man
10,000 Days
The Mosley Receipt

About the Author

Ken Royce was born near London, and now lives in Hampshire. He served in various regiments during the Second World War, and his main interests are jazz, antiques and travel.

One of Britain's leading writers of suspense, his previous books include THE XYY MAN, THE THIRD ARM, 10,000 DAYS, THE STALIN ACCOUNT and THE CRYPTO MAN. THE THIRD ARM was placed in the Top Six Thrillers of 1980 by *The New York Times* and THE STALIN ACCOUNT was recommended by the *Daily Mail* as one of the best thrillers of 1983.

As well as the *Strangers* and *Bulman* series, Ken Royce's THE XYY MAN was adapted for television and THE WOODCUTTER OPERATION and THE SATAN TOUCH have also both been adapted for Japanese television.

No Way Back

A George Bulman Adventure

Ken Royce

CORONET BOOKS
Hodder and Stoughton

For Stella

Copyright © 1986 by Kenneth Royce

First published in Great Britain in 1986 by Hodder and Stoughton Ltd
Coronet edition 1987

British Library C.I.P.
Royce, Kenneth
   No way back: a George Bulman adventure.
   I. Title
   823'.914[F]   PR6068.098

   ISBN 0-340-41372-7

Printed and bound in Great Britain for Hodder and Stoughton Paperbacks, a division of Hodder and Stoughton Ltd., Mill Road, Dunton Green, Sevenoaks, Kent (Editorial Office: 47 Bedford Square, London WC1B 3DP) by Richard Clay Ltd., Bungay, Suffolk

1

It was nearly midnight, the street almost empty. Hashimi stood close to the windows of the wine shop and gazed at the casualty sign of the hospital across the street; the reflector studs of the sign shone bright in the cold weather. He pulled his coat tighter and wished that he had something warmer on his feet than sneakers, but it was important that he moved quietly.

From the railway station to his right came shouts and abuse from drunks. It was what he had been waiting for. It was Saturday night and with the military garrison of Tidworth so near, Andover was an off-duty attraction to troops. When the pubs turned out it was not unknown for fights to break out among servicemen or tanked-up gangs of youths hell bent on some swaddy bashing.

He pushed back into the doorway, not wanting to be seen. When satisfied that the group was coming his way – the sounds much uglier now – he crossed the street and entered the small hospital's car park, then moved behind the tall hedges lining the front.

The gravelled parking area stretched up the incline towards the dark shape of the single-storey hospital complex. A darker shadow to his left indicated the tarred driveway, and a rising moon reflected on a few parked cars. He waited.

He had no real idea where the body might be. He was not even sure if it were still there; it might have been moved to the main general hospital at Winchester to await a post-mortem.

He wondered about the four parked cars; they were unlikely to belong to visitors at this hour and the doctors normally parked directly outside the main doors well out of sight of his position. The drunks were much nearer. He started to walk up the incline, found the gravel too noisy and crossed to the more exposed tarred drive. Behind him there was a yell of someone in great pain and he quickened his pace. The hospital staff would be used to Saturday night casualties, and were probably dreading the first arrival; some cases would be horrific.

Hashimi Ross was sensitive to every sound, every shadow or change of pattern. Probably the most wanted man in Europe, his experience of evasion was vast. He had been in Portsmouth watching Television South news when it had been announced that the mutilated body of a black girl had been found behind a hedge near some watercress beds in the Andover area and that it had been taken to the local hospital for police examination. Identification had not been made but Hashimi had been satisfied with the description. And he had been near enough to make the journey to find out for sure.

He reached the buildings and took a path that would lead to the main entrance. Peering through the glass he could just make out the tiny reception office to his right. As far as he could see there was nobody in it but his view was partially obstructed. He tried the double doors. The right-hand one was open.

The drunken group was now coming up the main approach, trying to quieten down as they neared the hospital. One man, supported by two colleagues, was whimpering.

The unlocked door was held open while the injured man was helped through. Having quickly taken cover Hashimi caught a glimpse of a face screwed up in pain from the shadows. He heard a good deal of coarse banter which subsided as a nurse approached. Hashimi quickly wrapped a handkerchief round his left hand and sprinted to tag on to the struggling group, but keeping a little distance behind them. With her attention on the badly injured man the nurse barely glanced at him.

She led the way down the corridor to the small casualty station. A bench faced the open doorway of the examination room. The injured man was helped into a cubicle while Hashimi turned back down the corridor. He passed an open ward. From the dimly seen beds came the muted sounds of sleeping patients. He reached a closed door and opened it carefully, closing it again when he heard heavy breathing inside. He struck home on the second attempt.

He could make out the faint shape of a screen but there was no sound at all. He went in, closing the door behind him and groped for the light switch. The light was dim and as he rounded the screen he noticed there were no windows in the room. A shrouded body lay on a trolley. Hashimi had seen too much of

8

death to hesitate; he pulled back the shroud and almost vomited. He stepped back with his hand over his mouth, unprepared for his own reaction. He felt a prickling in his eyes and could not believe he was close to tears.

Choking back his revulsion, Hashimi came nearer to the ravaged corpse. The bullet had gone in at the top of her skull, shattered the head and had torn a vast and ugly exit hole under her chin. He ran a hand lightly down the sleek thigh as if she was still alive but the flesh was so cold that he quickly removed his hand. The smooth, dusky patina of health had vanished from her skin. He fought with his feelings. Death had never disturbed him so much. But Sophie had been very special and she had been killed – and tortured – because she had responded to his need to help a friend. She had died protecting someone else but she had done it for him.

Hashimi pulled the shroud back over her. He let his hand linger momentarily. Without looking back he switched off the light and left the room to the sound of more casualties arriving. His face was a mask as he turned towards the door, but in his eyes was an expression that Sophie would have recognised and feared had she lived.

"There's a sheikh who wants to see you, boss." Charlie Hewitt had closed the door to Scott's office behind him, keeping his voice low.

Scott, peering up from a bunch of files on his desk, noted Charlie's unease and wondered why he had not used the intercom from the reception office counter. "A sheikh?" He grinned slowly. "How do you know he's a sheikh?"

"He's wearing the gear. Night shirt and tea towel round his head. He says he's Sheikh Yamani." Charlie smoothed down his fair hair.

Scott stiffened. "You having me on, Charlie? You're talking about the Saudi Arabian Oil Minister. What's he want anyway?"

"He didn't say, only that it was important."

Scott nodded. From time to time strange people called to see him. And most of them led back to his past one way or the other. He had to be cautious. "Show him in."

When Hashimi Ross entered his office Scott rose to greet him with mixed feelings. He held out a hand, his smile wide and sincere. "Hello, Hash, you must be bloody mad coming here. They're all out looking for you and this place will be like a homing bug to them."

"I've always been mad." The two men shook hands warmly, Scott who was over six feet and proportionately built, towering over Ross. But Ross carried himself well. He was known as the Arab by most police forces and now appeared every inch the sheikh he had claimed to be. He sat down, drawing his robes around him. "Nobody will look for me dressed like this. There are plenty of Arabs in London. So how are things?"

There was so much to say. Scott suddenly realised that he had not seen Hashimi since he had blasted Scott out of Albany prison on the Isle of Wight. It was still a national scandal that nobody had yet been arrested. "I've not had the opportunity to thank you for the breakout," he said weakly. "You saved my life."

"I probably did," agreed Hashimi easily. "But I don't want thanks; I enjoyed it." He paused, his gaze firmly on Scott. "I found Sophie last night."

Scott gripped the desk. "I wondered. God, I'm sorry. I felt things closing in. I warned her. It was too high a price to pay for my breakout. I don't know what to say. She was bloody marvellous to me, looked after me on the run and it was me they were really after."

"I know. But I want the bastards who did it."

"So do I." Scott knew that he was on difficult ground.

"Not in the same way. You'll leave it to your friends in the fuzz. I can't wait for that."

"I have one friend in the fuzz, and he only carries a copper's rank as a matter of convenience. Don't make it sound like I'm shacked up with the whole Met."

"Bulman, you mean? Okay, I hit under the belt. I met him, as you know. I nearly topped him."

"It was as well you didn't. Where you left off he carried on. You sprung me but he got me off the hook. Your efforts would have gone in vain but for him. He put his whole future on the line, possibly his life as well. You and he aren't too different. You even comb your hair forward, same as he does."

"So he's going bald, too. Cut the crap, Spider. Who did it?"

"Leave it to Bulman. He won't give up. And he wants the whole shebang, not just the blokes who actually killed Sophie. Was she the one found down in Hampshire?"

"As if you didn't know. I sneaked into the local hospital before they moved her out. I don't need a post-mortem report. I know what killed her; a soft-nosed four-five slug by the look of what's left of her head. They made her suffer, Spider. If you had seen her you wouldn't be sitting there prevaricating. You'd be after them."

Scott sat silent for some time, then met Hashimi's gaze quite evenly.

"You owe me, Spider. And you owe Sophie, too."

"I know I do. I can never repay either of you. But other people are involved whether you like it or not. And I have to be satisfied that whatever I do won't make it any worse for you."

"Had I heard that from anyone but you I'd have blown my stack. But I'm being polite, Spider. Polite. You're an old and valued friend. But there's a limit to my patience, even with you. All I want is a name or names. The rest is up to me. I don't need your protection." He smiled but it was icy and threatening. "You know damn well that I can look after myself. So tell me, my friend, or make yourself my enemy."

"Balls. And don't be bloody patronising. Even Bulman doesn't know for certain. That's what the post-mortem will be all about; to give Murder Squad some hard facts and some forensic proof. Nobody knows for certain."

"Okay. Just point me in the right direction. Somewhere to start looking."

Scott did not reply. Instead he sat staring at Hashimi, watching the growing blaze in Hashimi's eyes which darted about restlessly. He was constantly aware of what he owed this man; his dilemma was real and his anguish deep.

Then, in seconds, Hashimi produced a gun with no noticeable movement. He held it just above the top of the desk with a steady, experienced hand. "A CZ vz 70," he explained. "Czech. Designed by the Kratochvil brothers. 7.65. Won't make as big a mess as someone made of Sophie but it will do the job. Spider, I have to know. I'd hate to have to use this on you."

"I know you would." Scott's mouth was dry. Hashimi was unpredictable. He kept the fear from his voice. "All the same, you won't do it here. It would make a din, Lulu would poke her head out of her office and young Charlie Hewitt has already seen you. Would you shoot them too?"

"Sure I would. But you can save all that."

"We're talking about innocent people. You'd be defeating your own ends. You'd never make it."

"There's no such thing as 'innocent people'. To me indifference is guilt."

"You're all knotted up, Hash. You've always thought things through before. You're on borrowed time and you know it so why cut short what's left?" Scott was taking a dangerous but calculated risk.

"That was *your* blow below the belt. I know there's no way back for me. I've killed too many people. Which makes it all matter so much less." The gun remained steady; it would always be so with Hashimi.

"Then you'd better shoot me. That way you'll have squared your own account. Save me and kill me. That has to be a first even for you. Dammit, man, whatever you've done before you've at least believed in. There is no point in this. Ask Sophie when you catch up with her. Ask yourself now if she would want it."

"You were always crafty with words, Spider." Hashimi was sweating now. "That's how you got me off the hook all those years ago when we were in Dartmoor together."

"I'm also straight. You would never have sprung me had you not believed that." Scott leaned back in his chair, hearing it creak at the weight. "I want Sophie's killers too. Just as badly as you but not in the same way. Don't you think that if I was face to face with them I wouldn't be tempted to take them apart. Look, Hash, I'll go this far. I don't know precisely who did it but I think I know who was behind it. If I'm right, and if Bulman is right, he's in Brazil or somewhere like that. He skipped because Sophie was only part of the killings. If you find him and take him out you might avenge Sophie but other people who have suffered just as much need him alive for many reasons. The whole thing's a cesspool."

"The cesspool is not my business. Sophie is." Hashimi put

the gun away. He smiled. "I would still have used it, you know. Even on you. But you've done what I wanted; you've pointed me the right way." He rose. "We can't have a drink while I'm in this rig. Muslims don't drink. I saw what it did to my mother."

Scott rose and came round the desk. "Be careful. They could well have their eye on this place."

"Maybe. But you were in prison as Tony Sims, and nobody is looking for Willie 'Spider' Scott. Too many people in high places would be embarrassed, to say the least. They won't pull you in. And if they pull me they can never be sure that I won't implicate you which would take them back to square one. I've got it all tied up." The Midland accent was just discernible.

Scott, who knew Hashimi's background, thought it ironic that the Arab's education had done nothing for him. "Be lucky," he said with considerable feeling as he gripped Hashimi's arm with both hands.

Hashimi punched Scott playfully on his chest. "You, too, old friend." He turned towards the door. "I'm glad you talked me out of it, Spider. I must be losing my touch."

"Or getting more sense in your thick head."

Hashimi smiled. "It's far too late for that. See you." He closed the door quietly behind him.

Scott felt drained. There was no way he could stop Hashimi. Nor could he sit idly by and watch a friend destroy himself.

2

Scott gave Maggie a long hug and kissed the top of her head. "I've given you an extra dribble." She was referring to the two whiskies waiting on the antique mahogany sideboard; they always had a drink together on Scott's return from the office.

He picked up the glasses, handed one to Maggie and raised his own. "Cheers."

Maggie looked at him quizzically. "Well? Who did you run into?"

Scott laughed and lowered his glass. "You never lose the knack, do you? Read me like a book. Hashimi Ross called in."

The soft amusement left her eyes at once. "He's the man who got you out of Albany prison last summer. Called the Arab? But, Willie, they're looking for him everywhere. Isn't that dangerous for you?"

"We'd better sit down." Scott crossed to the settee and they sat at opposite ends of it, half facing each other. "Yes and no," he answered. "Officially the police are looking for him because of his terrorist record. But it's never been confirmed that he was the man who blasted a damned big hole in Albany's visiting room. There's no way they would bring me in for that; George Bulman and I saved too many faces in high places."

"Which could be strongly resented in the same high places. Don't underrate them, Willie."

"I know. You warned me before and you're right," Scott conceded. He drank thoughtfully. "I'm worried about Hash, though."

Maggie reached for his hand. "Your soft touch for villains has landed you in too much trouble. The man *is* a terrorist. And, he's killed people, Willie. Lots of them."

"You don't have to remind me, love. But I think that he's so disillusioned with the terrorist game that he's given it up. He was the best once. I accept that his regret doesn't excuse what he's already done." Scott put down his drink, easing his hand from Maggie's. He folded his arms across his chest, head lowered.

"He wants to avenge the death of Sophie. She was tortured, Mag, and then shot. All because Deacon and his mob wanted to find me. I feel terrible about it. I always will. And I feel deeply obligated."

Maggie looked away. She had never met Sophie. When she had first heard from Scott that Hashimi had arranged for him to hide out with the girl, she had believed him when he had assured her that nothing had happened between them. Sophie had been Hashimi's girl, and judging by a photograph she had seen, the black model had been beautiful. That she had died protecting Scott made Maggie feel sick with despair. And now Scott was saying that Sophie had been tortured before being killed. Yet she had to force him back to his own plight. She said, "Your conscience will be the death of you. Your sense of right is always weighted against yourself. It wasn't your fault. You know it wasn't, Willie, so please don't get involved."

He turned to face her squarely. "You want me to change my nature? Be someone else?"

"You know I don't. How can an ex-cat burglar be so soft?" She stretched her hand out again. "I'm sorry. That was low. Just let the police handle it."

Scott smiled wryly. "You don't really think that I'm going to help Hash to knock off Phil Deacon and his mob, do you? My concern is to save Hash from himself. I owe him. But for him we wouldn't be talking now." He faced her directly. "Is that taking duty too far?"

She shook her head miserably. "No. I know what he has done for you. But I also know what he is. He won't thank you for interference; if he has a blood lust he'll satisfy it. There is no way that you can dissuade him. Don't put yourself in the wrong."

"He did for me, love. It's not something I can forget."

"Partly for you perhaps. But you told me he enjoyed doing it. Anyway, how could you possibly help him?"

Scott rose, smiling slightly. He pointed to her glass. "You want another?" And when she nodded he picked up the glass and said, "I don't know if I can help. But I have to give it some thought even if I come up with nothing." He crossed to the whisky decanter on the sideboard. Over his shoulder he said, "I've already taken one step, but he won't be overjoyed to find out I've given him a bum steer. I told him that the bloke he was looking for had gone to Brazil, which is what George Bulman told me. I didn't mention Deacon by name or tell him that the whisper is that Deacon is back, if not in England then in Europe."

"You helped him when he was in Dartmoor, didn't you?"

He turned to hand Maggie her drink. "He was very young then. It was just before he got into the violent political arena. He was beginning to air his views and he aired them too often to the wrong people. The prison barons decided to close him up. I was able to talk sense to them and to him and kept a friendly eye on him."

"Why, Willie? If he was that brash wasn't he also objectionable?"

Scott sat down and put an arm round her. "He was floundering. We talked a lot. He was split between two religious ideologies. I think he was born in the Lebanon but spent most of his life in the Midlands. Certainly he was educated here. But with a fanatical Islamic father and a staunch Catholic mother he was in trouble from birth. That particular religious mixture is fairly rare. His old man is loaded and close to Gadaffi and encouraged Hash's murderous capers on behalf of Islam. His mother hit the bottle under the strain and nobody knows what happened to her. Some mess, eh?"

"But he's killed innocent people, Willie."

"Yes, but he sees innocence as a matter of definition. If people ignore his cause then they're guilty by neglect. And people don't matter, it's what they stand for. Okay, it's sick but he doesn't see it that way. Anyway, his causes became more varied and he became more confused. Meanwhile he has dug his own grave and he knows it. There's no way back for Hash. He could hide himself among the P.L.O. or some other group but it's doubtful if they would trust him now. He is no longer dedicated to one particular cause, not even a splinter group. But he's better at the game than any of them and they know it. If his latest enemies don't get him someone else will." Scott drank thoughtfully. "I sometimes think that he's willing them to get him. The only future he sees is a death wish."

"Don't you think that your account is square with him? You saved him in Dartmoor and he broke you out of Albany."

Scott grimaced. "I only counselled. *He* blew a bloody big hole in a top security prison to get me out." He pulled Maggie closer. "He's in his mid-thirties and his life is already over. His crimes can't be obliterated. He knows it. He won't go out with a whimper so it will be a violent end. If he goes out knocking off Deacon's mob he'll reckon he's atoned to some extent; done the public a belated favour."

Maggie lowered her head on to Scott's shoulder. "Your liking for him can be dangerous for you."

"There are no rules for liking people, love. You do or you don't. And yes, I like him although it's easier not to dwell too much on what he's done. It's an emotional response and I'm strong on emotion; I can't stand these cold-blooded logical types."

"Just don't get involved, eh? For me." But it was wasted breath and Maggie knew it. Love against friendship was not the issue; it would be what he believed was right.

Detective Superintendent George Bulman felt uncomfortable in his best suit. Hat and topcoat were now in the small cloakroom, the number tag in his pocket. He sat at the crowded, half moon bar, his chunky, rough cast face angled towards the main door so that he could keep his eye on the arrivals. An untouched glass of whisky was in his hand. Bulman was uncharacteristically nervous. He was beginning to suspect his own motives in coming. And when Betty Moorcroft came through the door some moments later he suffered a twinge of warning as he eased himself from the stool and went to greet her.

"Betty, you look great." He took her coat and handed it to the cloakroom girl, holding it clumsily. As he guided her to the bar he wondered why he had not found her so attractive before.

"Gin, I seem to remember." He signalled the white jacketed barman.

"I'll have the same as you, George. But with more water."

"Really?" Bulman placed the order not sure what to do next and wondering what the hell was wrong with him. But he knew what was wrong; he had been thinking far too much about Betty

Moorcroft, and the lady was married. And because his conscience shifted gear he heard himself saying, "Does your husband know you're here?"

Betty smiled over her glass, then put the drink down as she broke into a soft laugh. "My God, George, you've guilt written all over you. When did you last take a woman out?"

Bulman grinned but was flustered. "I'm old-fashioned. A married woman is different." He shrugged uneasily. "It's the way I am."

"You rang me," Betty reminded him mercilessly. When his dark eyes almost disappeared in the folds around them as he screwed up his face, she took pity on him. "Don't worry about Bob. We were shaky before Dad was killed." Betty smiled bitterly. "I won't spin you the one about my husband not understanding me; we understand each other only too well." She sipped her drink. "I'm sorry. I didn't mean to give you that line. It's so boring."

"Not to me. You want to get it off your chest?"

"Not here. Not tonight."

At that Bulman felt easier. Betty seemed to have lost a little weight and had taken care to look good for him. "The table is booked," he said to change the subject. "And we have a little time in hand."

"You said you wanted to tell me about Dad's murderers. Or was that an excuse?"

"I wouldn't stoop that low. But it's off the record. You're a copper's daughter, you'll understand." Bulman was thoughtful. Not for the first time was he stepping out of line but this was different.

"I know you're bound by the Official Secrets Act. So was Dad. I never got a thing out of him. In the end his secrecy got him killed."

"Delayed solving his murder," Bulman corrected. "But he was right." He drained his drink, studied the empty glass and glanced at Betty who was half smiling.

"Don't change your habits for me, George. But I'm okay with this one."

He called for a large whisky. "I did want to see you again," he confessed. "I simply didn't have a chance to ask you before."

18

"A copper's work is never done. I know."

"If you can call me a copper. The reason for your dad's murder will never be published. Although we know who did it, it's unlikely that he'll ever be pulled in. Not for that, anyway."

Betty put down her glass slowly. Very quietly she asked, "Are you saying there's been a cover-up?"

Bulman shifted uneasily on his stool and pulled the fresh drink towards him. He rotated the glass slowly, his gaze fastened on it. Then he cocked his head to look at Betty. "Don't go outraged on me. Don't do that, please. It's difficult enough. I'm breaking all the rules by telling you anything."

"Or trying to appease me so that I won't start ripples or contact the press."

Bulman looked so hurt that she was immediately sorry. "I shouldn't have said that, George."

"You've every right to feel as you do. What stings is the possibility that you might mean it. I've made more ripples in official circles than you could ever dream up. I've put my job on the line to get at the truth. But tonight is not the time I would choose to soft-soap you." He hesitated before continuing awkwardly, "Tonight is important to me personally."

Betty laid a hand on his arm. "I'm sorry. Dad did the same sort of work as you; I should know better." And then she gave him a warm smile. "You really are out of the ark, George. You're out of practice."

His gruff voice became rougher. "I was never any good at chatting up birds, particularly ones as attractive as you."

Betty laughed. "Now you *are* kidding. But keep going in the old-fashioned way." She shifted position, angling her legs towards him. He gazed at them as she chided him, "Come on, George, you haven't led that sheltered a life. You've seen legs before."

"Not so nicely turned as those."

"Out of practice? Well, well. Tell me, George, do I get any more? About Dad I mean."

"We know he was killed because he was getting close to solving a string of political murders stretching back years. I can categorically say that the person behind the killings has paid the price. He's dead."

"But not the actual perpetrators?"

"Right. The complications of pulling them in are enormous. It's not just a political cover-up. Spider Scott's involved. If the truth of his part came out so would everything else. And Spider's suffered enough, and he more than anyone else solved your father's murder. Bring the killers in and you could bring Spider down. Would you want that?"

"That's only part of it, isn't it?"

"An important part. At least to me."

"How can a copper be so protective of an old creeper like Spider?"

Bulman sighed. "It's a long story. Years ago I misjudged him very badly. I guess I've mellowed. He's just the same and I've learned that his word is his bond. He used to have this overpowering impulse to break into difficult places and he was bloody good at it; no fancy tackle. I've seen him shin a rain stack like a monkey. And he's big, as you know. He served time for it more than once. He learned a good deal about antiques and *objets d'art* along the way, so it wasn't all wasted."

"Has he really given it up?" Betty sounded sceptical.

"As long as he has Maggie by him he can cope. With them it's for real. She comes from a good family who didn't like the set-up at all. When Spider finally realised he had kicked the habit they got married. Her parents did not attend the wedding."

"Did you?"

Bulman smiled. "I wasn't going to turn down free booze."

Betty raised her glass in salute. "Here's to you, George. Underneath all that growling I believe you're a pussy-cat."

Bulman grinned wryly. "Many a villain has thought that and then wondered where he went wrong on the way to the nick." He added, "Your father thought the world of Spider."

"I know they worked together once but that's all. Why does Maggie call him Willie?"

"That's his name. He's called Spider by his old pals, villains, and the fuzz, like me; but Maggie wants to forget that part of his life." Bulman's eyes clouded. "He's a natural fall guy. People use him and more often than not he finds it difficult to refuse. Government departments have used his talents and have treated him shabbily."

"Have you used him?"

Bulman hesitated. "Yes. I've kept an eye on him, though. One day they'll try again."

Betty glanced across quickly. "What do you mean?"

Bulman avoided her gaze. "He's expendable. Not to me. Not to his friends. But to others, some of whom your father knew about. And they still find him useful in more senses than one."

"George, you're saying that he's doomed – that sooner or later they'll get him."

Bulman rubbed his face. "Did it sound like that? He has a great knack for beating the system when all the odds are stacked against him. I just sometimes feel that there will come a time when he won't be able to beat it."

"Then you'd better continue to keep an eye on him. Are you going to tell me any more about Dad?"

He glanced at his watch as the head waiter approached. "Looks as if our table is ready. Can we stop talking shop while we eat? I've ordered champagne, if that's all right with you."

Betty gave him a quizzical look as she slipped from the stool. She tucked her arm through his as they went towards their table. Before sitting down she had one last stab. "Is there no chance at all of getting the men who murdered Dad?"

Bulman pulled a chair out for her. She thought his expression was strange as he went round the table to take his seat. "Yes there is. There are some interesting developments going on. The boyfriend of one of the murdered parties is not averse to toting a gun himself; he's apparently on the warpath."

"More violence? More killing?"

"Make up your mind, Betty. Do you want justice or not?"

"Yes, but through the courts. Not a wild justice."

"You won't get it through the courts. Does that rule out the other kind for you?"

Betty was holding the large menu in her hands; the waiter had disappeared while they made their choice. "I can't believe what I hear. Is this a copper talking?"

"A kind of copper."

"You'd stand by and let it happen?"

"I doubt that I would be involved in any way."

"You already sound involved. Don't hedge, George. Not about this."

"I'm sorry. I don't want to upset you. You've asked the questions and I've given the answers. You want me to lie?"

Betty lowered her menu. "You're dead serious. Well, would authority stand by and let it happen?"

Bulman answered slowly. "I don't think authority would stand by."

"That's a devious answer."

Bulman shook his head unhappily. "It's the only one I can give you. Don't let it spoil the evening."

Betty smiled in agreement. But she felt disappointed to feel that for the first time Bulman had deliberately evaded the issue; he knew much more than he was telling her. He had already trusted her with a great deal so it had to be something he judged she would rather not hear. And that frightened her. It frightened her a lot.

Dr Max Blaser carried a city image very well. Above medium height and quite well built, he wore a dark, beautifully cut topcoat over an expensive grey suit. Thick fair hair was held in place by a well brushed Homburg. He was a good-looking man, strong-featured with clear eyes always ready to smile. His gloves were hand-stitched pigskin, his umbrella still immaculately furled in spite of the light fall of rain. He turned into the old-fashioned office block in Northumberland Avenue and, once screened, was escorted up to the office of Sir Lewis Hope.

Hope pressed the button that would ensure the door remained locked, and then came round the desk to shake Blaser warmly by the hand. "You're looking well, Max. Really. Do sit down."

"And you still look as if you've stepped off the bridge of a warship. How do you keep the tan?" Blaser made himself comfortable in one of the leather armchairs as his host returned to his desk.

Hope smiled. "Wind, rain and sun and thirty years at sea. It's impregnated." He sat down. "It's a pity you are unable to have lunch. Another time perhaps."

"I didn't want us to be seen together. Oh, I know our 'friends' will be fully aware of our meeting but it is not the same as being seen in public. As head of State Security in Bonn I would be expected to call on you anyway."

"Not even a coffee?"

"You British," Blaser smiled. "No, thank you. I'm on a tight schedule. I must put in an appearance at the embassy before I fly back tonight. I come to ask a favour of you."

Hope kept his expression blank though he hated being asked for favours. And with this man it would not be a small one or he would not have come personally on a special flight. He clasped his long-fingered hands and sat back to listen.

"There's a man called Jost Kranz over here. At the moment I'm not even sure that it's his correct name but he certainly travels under it. He's climbed on to the Flick exposure bandwagon. Claims that he has hitherto unknown facts about government corruption. Would he be on your files?"

"I can readily find out. I've personally never heard of him." Hope mused. "Flick. That massive commercial empire; how you must hate that name in West Germany."

"It simply goes on." Blaser's English was virtually perfect with the slightest trace of a Boston accent. "Ever since Rainer Barzel resigned the Government has been fighting a rear-guard action. The Greens are revelling in it; they see an enormous increase in support and the Chancellor is clearly concerned. It will take a long time to live down."

"But this has been going on since late '81, as I recall. Didn't it start with a tax-waiver given to Flick for the sale of Daimler-Benz? They made an enormous capital free profit from it."

"Almost five hundred million of your pounds at the then exchange rate. There seems to be no end to it. It would be tragic for the country if the Government fell over this. Corruption comes in many forms, but some are infinitely worse than others in the long run. I'd personally rather have monetary than political corruption. The former can be dealt with, as indeed this can, but the latter is infinitely more invidious and ultimately more destructive. Jost Kranz has made the claim that he has more evidence of government corruption than has yet been shown. He claims that in his own good time he will release information to *Stern* magazine for publication."

"Any specifics?"

"More funds passed by Flick to the Christian Democrats for various concessions than has so far been revealed. More bribery of individual ministers."

"But not only the Christian Democrats were concerned, surely? I understood that Flick's favours covered a wider political spectrum."

"Whoever is in Government at the time takes the brunt. So they must be incorruptible." Blaser paused before saying evenly, "Why have I the feeling that you intend to keep me talking?"

"I must have the background, Max."

"In your position you will already have it, Lewis. However, I am about to ask you a favour. Can you deal with this man Kranz for us?"

"In what way?"

Blaser stared Hope straight in the eye. "Get rid of him."

"Deport him? I must have grounds or I'll have the N.C.C.L. on my back."

"You're being deliberately obtuse. Terminate him, no matter how."

"Good God, what are you saying? The man could be a nut. You don't even know what he has on anyone. And you're asking us to *kill* him."

"He's not a nut. We suspect that he is a highly trained professional. We also suspect that he has made clever use of fact mixed with fiction in such a way that it might be impossible to separate the two. We believe that this is not an authentic scandal but a deliberate attempt to dislodge the Government. If that happened there would almost certainly be a fusing of the Greens and the Social Democrats bringing a Red-Green Alliance. We believe that we can ride out the present storm provided that it is not aggravated. There is a deliberate plot to do just that and Kranz is the focus."

"Who's behind it?"

"East Germany with the usual backing. When a man can forge the Hitler diaries and fool most people for a short time it shouldn't be difficult for someone as enterprising to provide fabricated evidence to last long enough to provoke a political calamity. That is what is happening."

Hope sat forward, hands clasped on the desk. "I don't question your judgment. But you are trying to put us in the front line of one of your own scandals. Why on earth can't you do the job yourself?"

"In your backyard? Would you allow that? It cannot be done at home; it would be too obvious."

When Hope was slow to respond, Blaser added, "The man has gone to earth here. We would have to use your facilities in order to flush him out. Having put the fear of God into certain people, he is merely waiting for the right moment. The original scandal has lost a good deal of momentum. People are forgetting. It must be brought back to the boil and dramatically, if far-reaching results there are to be. If you're willing to give the nod and find him for us we'll do our own dirty work."

"As you pointed out I couldn't allow that. We could finish up with a scandal of our own if he has friends here and he obviously has."

"That's exactly my point. It is easier for you to do and would not be a favour to be forgotten."

Hope slowly shook his head. "You are asking me to sanction the murder of someone we don't even know. I accept your appraisal but you could still be wrong. And you know it."

"I'm not wrong, Lewis."

"That's conviction speaking, not fact."

"That's the name of our particular game, isn't it? We need your help very much or I wouldn't be here. The fate of the whole Bundestag is on the line unless we do something." Blaser felt he was getting nowhere. "We've done favours for you."

"I'm unaware of them. Of this kind, anyway."

"Certainly of this kind. For your predecessor."

Hope did not want to discuss his predecessor and studiously ignored the remark.

Blaser added, "I recall that Sir Anthony Eden convinced the C.I.A. to assassinate Colonel Nasser. And it was set up by the C.I.A.'s Technical Service Division. Only the reluctance of the chosen assassin foiled their plan. But the favour was officially sanctioned. And this is trivial by comparison."

"That was a long time ago and a ghastly mistake. We were lucky it never happened."

"I'm quoting an extreme, a national president. But there have

25

been others. Jost Kranz is a dirty little extortionist who is undoubtedly being very well paid and protected for what he is trying to do. We must teach his controllers a lesson. There is far too much to lose."

"I'll need more than you've so far given me. Much more. Meanwhile I'll help trace this man but I warn you, don't do anything that would upset our countries' relationship."

"Isn't that why I'm here, Lewis? Think hard about it. This will affect more than our country if it turns sour."

Lewis Hope nodded but was clearly not happy. And it was not something he could discuss at ministerial level; no politician would want to hear about it. Hope was on his own, a situation he abhorred.

"I'll certainly give it every consideration," he said.

3

"An Arab? You been at the juice, Sammy?" Rex Reisen held the phone away from his ear as if it had offended him. "A friend of Spider's? How can you be sure? Okay. Look, search the bleeder from toes to bonce. A lot can be hidden in them bathrobes. Let me know when he's ready."

Reisen sat back behind a desk that almost dwarfed him. His thin lined face was full of doubt, his sharp, dark eyes bright with suspicion. He opened his centre drawer and pressed a catch to release a secret compartment. Producing a Beretta he then closed the drawer before checking that the pistol's magazine was full. He pulled back the breech to insert a round in the chamber, cocked the safety catch and put the pistol down on his desk behind an elaborate calendar.

To the side of Reisen hung a large oil painting of the Queen. It was good but worked entirely from photographs, as Her Majesty was unlikely to have posed, even briefly, for the artist Reisen had commissioned. The intercom buzzed. "He's clean? You bloody sure? Show him in." Reisen sat back. Life had never been the same since he had let Detective Superintendent George Bulman into the office; now it was bloody Arabs.

Hashimi Ross entered wearing the same Arab dress. "Thank you for seeing me," he said quietly. "I appreciate it."

"Take a pew. You speak quite good English for a wog."

Hashimi contained himself. "That's because I studied it at Warwick University."

"They let you in to spend our money did they?"

"Why don't you stop being offensive?"

Reisen saw in Hashimi's eyes a sign he recognised. He pulled the Beretta forward. "Don't get stroppy, son. And there's a button by my foot that I can press if you're stupid enough to try anything. You'll be stiff before you leave the chair."

Hashimi gazed thoughtfully at the pistol. "Modello 20," he observed. "6.35 mm. Or 0.25 if you prefer it in inches. Double action trigger. Inertia firing pin. Not very big for such an important man. I helped Spider breakout from Albany; that should make us blood-brothers."

Reisen picked up the Beretta. "You're that bloody terrorist they're looking for. You've got a bloody nerve. Stay where you are."

"I don't have to move to take you out. But that's not why I'm here."

"Waddyer mean you don't have to move to take me out? You're as good as dead, son. You'd better send up a quickie to Allah or whoever's your anchor man."

"I have my hand on what your men took to be an ordinary cigarette lighter. It is in fact a radio control to set off the detonator packed into the explosive around my *kaffiyeh*. My head-dress. The band you see holding it to my head is plastic explosive; the detonator is embedded in it."

Reisen froze. "You'd blow your own bloody brains out, you silly bugger."

"Didn't anyone tell you that we fanatics are willing to die for what we believe? Life is not that important to me. But I must tell you that the amount of explosive I have will wreck this building and send you through that window in tiny, bloody pieces."

Reisen studied the cold eyes watching him across the desk. "Are you having me on?"

"Do you want to examine the band?"

Reisen could not see Hashimi's hands; they were hidden in the folds of his *djellaba*. He suddenly realised that his pressure on the trigger was too tight. Even if he shot the Arab, the death contraction of his hands could set off the radio control.

Hashimi slowly raised his hands to remove the *kaffiyeh*. Making sure that Reisen had full view, he took off the band and tossed it to Reisen who caught it with both hands.

"You bloody fool," Reisen bawled. "That could have set it off."

"Only if the detonator had struck the desk and even then it would be unlikely. You will see the join which is held together by the detonator itself. The plastic has been pressed around it. Pull the two ends apart and you will see what I mean."

Reisen laid down the Beretta, his gaze carefully on Hashimi, and very tentatively pulled at the two ends. He placed the band on the desk and picked up the pistol again. He glared across the desk. "You're bloody crazy."

"That's why I don't care what happens to me. Look at my right hand." Hashimi had it clenched, palm outwards. Slowly he unfolded his fingers and revealed the cigarette lighter, kept in place with his thumb. The door burst open behind him and he said quickly, "Tell them to get out or they get blasted with us. *Now*."

Reisen seemed to shrink inside his jacket. "Out," he bellowed.

"But, boss, you called us." The aggrieved voice was close behind Hashimi's chair but the Arab did not take his eyes from Reisen.

"My foot slipped, you silly sod. *Out*."

The carpet pile was too deep for Hashimi to pick up the retreating footsteps but he heard the door close. "That was close," he said evenly.

"Like I said, my foot slipped. Do we have to go through all this? What is it you want?"

"I don't like being called a wog, Reisen. Just bear in mind that the plastic is now nearer you than me." He showed Reisen the control again. "This is similar to the one I used in Albany to spring Spider. Can we get down to business now?"

Reisen was in a unique situation; he had never before been held under threat in his own office. It was almost impossible to believe. He had even lost face in front of his own men. For the moment shame and anger overcame some of his doubt. How do you deal with a nutter? He was used to seeing the fear of death in victims' eyes before they were put down, sometimes screaming and sometimes too terrified to make any sound at all; he now had an inkling of how they felt. "If it's to help Spider I'll listen."

"No, it's not to help Spider. He has scruples and they sometimes get in the way. It could help you, though. Who do you know in your own line who recently went to Brazil in a hurry?"

"That's easy. Phil Deacon. I think the whole bloody family did a moonlight. There's word that they're back, though. Why?"

"Was Deacon tied up with Spider's last job?"

"Up to his eyeballs. I know that much because the fuzz

29

were sniffing around Deacon. I don't know why and I'm not interested."

"Where does Deacon live?"

"Why?"

"If he's the man I want I'm going to kill him."

"What's he done to you?"

"Are you going to tell me or are you scared of him?"

Reisen laughed; it was the first time he'd had cause to since Hashimi had arrived. "I can take out Deacon any time. I drove him south of the Thames. He has a big terraced pad in Wandsworth. I'll write down the address when you leave, which is about now if that's all you want." Some of his confidence was returning.

"What sort of family has he got?"

"There's Vi, his wife. A hard faced peroxided bitch. Watch her. He has a son, Ted, late twenties, more brain than his old man, and knows how to top someone with style. He's the only one with any gump, but he hasn't the bottle to go it alone; needs the old man as back-up. Is that it?"

"For the moment."

Reisen almost relaxed. He gazed at the Beretta and the head-band. "We could have done this without the aggro, old son. Anyone who is a friend of Spider is a friend of mine."

"Unless he's a terrorist wog." Hashimi rose slowly still holding the lighter.

"Well you took me by surprise. No hard feelings?" Reisen reached for a notepad and wrote rapidly on it. "Deacon's address."

Hashimi realised that Reisen was paving the way to regain face for his men. He picked up his head-band, and wound it round the *kaffiyeh* before putting it on, then allowed Reisen to escort him to the door. As it opened, Reisen held out his hand and Hashimi took it; it was just possible that he might need Reisen again.

Reisen spoke tersely to the three men waiting outside the door. "Show our friend down. Watch out for those stairs; they might prove tricky in that gear." Satisfied that he had regained respect, Reisen went back to his desk. He started to shake. He studied the pistol; it was true that it was too small but it was the only size that would fit into the secret compartment. But the

Arab had shown that he knew a great deal about guns; the model was not common. Just then Reisen wanted to kill Hashimi. He did not take kindly to being made a fool of even without witnesses.

When Hashimi Ross stood on the corner of the Wandsworth street he realised that he did not need the actual house number. Two rows of Edwardian terraced houses faced him, run-down and lack-lustre but still solid, with old fashioned sashcord bay windows, railings and sub-basements. Cars were bumper to bumper down each side of the street.

There was one exception. A solitary house stood out proudly with fresh paint, and plaster on the pillars of the front door portico. The steps were scrubbed clean, the railings bright. If that were not enough to draw attention to Deacon's house, a new Mercedes, and a one-year-old Jaguar were parked outside.

Hashimi had discarded his *djellaba*. He wore an expensive topcoat, necessary with the increasing cold, and warm casual clothes beneath. He was hatless. As he crossed the street he wondered just how many times he had holed up in such places around the capitals of Europe. Even now, in London, he had two safe houses similar to those he was approaching; his father had always been generous in providing for the anti-West needs of terrorism, and at the moment Hashimi had no qualms about calling on his father's financial support. He mounted the steps at the bottom of which a man leaned against the railings and apparently impervious to the cold, said, "Phil's away." Hashimi ignored him and continued up. He rang the bell.

Hashimi knew at once that the hard faced blonde who opened the door was Deacon's wife. He guessed that it was part of her function to protect her husband from unwelcome callers. Her bone structure was excellent and but for her aura of hostility she could have been beautiful.

"Is Phil in?" he asked very softly.

"He's not, but if ever he is who do I say wants him?" Vi had softened slightly, her eyes showing a mild interest in him.

"Oh, I just want to knock him off," said Hashimi with a wide grin.

"You'll have to join the queue, love." She folded her arms across the too-tight pullover, pushing her breasts up, and then leaned provocatively against the door jamb. "You don't look as if you could knock off a crumb from a bird table."

Hashimi laughed. "I just want to ask him a couple of things."

"You should do your homework. He's away. Drop him a line to this address and I'll send it on."

"Perhaps you have the answers. Mrs Deacon, is it?"

"Vi. Everyone calls me Vi. If it's anything to do with his work, I won't have the answers. Now be a good boy and piss off."

"Could I come in and speak to you? It won't take long. It's bloody cold out here."

"No, love." Vi offered an inviting look. "It's maybe a pity but I know which side my bread is buttered. First things first. It's sad really. Anyway, Phil can get nasty if he thinks I've been pestered. And I wouldn't want anything to happen to you. Say goodbye like a good feller and drop that line to him."

"In that case, Vi, you'd better step back inside."

Vi noticed the change in his voice and it was a tone that frightened her. The smile left her face and she was about to slam the door when Hashimi pushed past her. "Do as I say."

Vi looked down and saw the silencer protruding between the buttons of his coat. Her face drained of colour, and before she could react further, Hashimi was in, edging her back and closing the door behind him with a foot. Quietly he ordered her not to scream.

Vi moved further back into the hall as Hashimi brought the gun into full view. Vi had never had a gun pointing at her before and her hard features began to crumble. What was so unnatural to her was his quiet authority. He was not being theatrical. He was deadly. Her lips parted and she held out a hand as if to ward him off.

"Stay where you are," Hashimi ordered. "Is there anyone else in the house?"

Her gaze shot to the ceiling. "No. Not now. But there will be soon."

"Nobody upstairs?"

"No. Really." She could hardly speak, terrified by his coldness and the casual way he held the gun.

"Where can we talk without being interrupted? Think carefully, Vi. If someone walks in on us you are dead."

Vi could not take her eyes from the gun. She nodded dully and gestured towards a door on her left. "In here," she said. Fear brought expression back to her eyes but she saw no sign of compassion from Hashimi.

"Open the door wide and then turn to face it."

Vi turned, not much caring to be side-on to Hashimi where she could not really see him. Suddenly she realised that he was standing behind her and she briefly felt the gun in her back.

"Step in, Vi. Right in."

Vi stood in the centre of the room where he had a clear view of her. Hashimi pushed the door right back until it was flat against the wall, then followed her in. Once sure that nobody else was in the room he closed the door and turned the key in the lock.

They were in Deacon's music room. There were large speakers in each corner, the very best of hi-fi gear, reel-to-reel, cassette decks, turntable with stroboscope, tuner, all contained in one cabinet between the end speakers. The walls were lined with shelves containing tapes, cassettes and records. Two comfortable armchairs were strategically placed for the best acoustics. No expense had been spared.

"No one would dare come in here even when he's away."

"I believe you. I can see it's important to him." Hashimi kicked in the nearest speaker, his face tight with anger. For the first time he broke his control.

Vi retched on the spot as she saw the mess he had made of the speaker. "Oh, my God," she said at last. "He'll go raving mad when he sees that. He'll kill you." She held her stomach, her face contorted as if she were in agony. "Why did you do that? What harm has he done you?"

"He killed my girlfriend. Not only killed her but tortured her first. I saw the body. She suffered. *She really suffered.* Fair retribution would be for me to do the same to you, wouldn't you say?"

Vi groped for the arm of a chair, the change in her dramatic. "He wouldn't do a thing like that; he wouldn't torture anyone, not Phil."

"That's balls, Vi, and you know it. It's the same thing if he got someone else to do it. Who's the most likely?"

"Oh, God, how the hell would I know? I'm his wife not his business partner." Vi lowered herself shakily to the arm of the chair.

Hashimi took some records from a rack and stacked them neatly on the floor. He stood over them and glanced at Vi, but she was not looking. Hashimi aimed the gun at the centre of the pile and fired. The silencer reduced the noise of the explosion but the sound of the shattering records brought Vi's head up sharply.

At first she could not take it in then, when she realised what had happened she rose unsteadily to her feet. She stared at Hashimi in disbelief. "It's taken him years to collect them," she said, trembling. "Some can't be replaced . . ."

"He won't be needing them. Who did his killing for him?"

"Do you think he'd tell *me*?"

"Well at least you don't deny that he has someone." Hashimi piled some more records on the floor. "Who did he kill for? They weren't all gang killings." Casually he shattered the new pile with another round.

Vi gasped. She could see herself on the wrong end of Deacon's temper when he finally came back. Cunning penetrated her fear. "There was a man called Salter who used to call on occasion. They used to come into this room because nobody would dare enter if Phil was here."

"Salter? What was he like?"

"Cold-blooded bastard. Phil didn't like him."

"But he still did business with him."

"Yes. Not very often though."

Hashimi moved towards some tape racks. "You're suddenly very helpful, Vi. I wonder why?"

"I think he's in nick."

"Salter?"

Vi nodded slowly. She was listening for the return of Deacon's son.

Hashimi noticed her sudden concentration. "What did he look like?"

"Stocky, dark, middle forties. Had a bit of a Northern accent. Phil reckoned he came from Liverpool."

"And that's all you know?"

34

"I only know that because he called here. I was never in this room with them. So I never really knew what went on."

"And that's all you can tell me?"

"Yes."

"Even though your life depends on it?"

She faced him with sudden bravado. "I can't tell you what I don't know."

Hashimi moved towards the door. He removed the key. "I'm going to lock you in. I want Deacon to know what has happened here." He levelled the gun at her. "Tell him what I told you. I shall kill him in my own good time."

Vi kept the sneer from her face. Phil would go searching the moment he knew about this. Meanwhile she had a reprieve.

Hashimi opened the door and slipped the key in the lock on the other side. "I'll drop it where it can be found. Don't scream. I've been soft with you for a reason. When Deacon goes, you go. Hang on to the thought, Vi. Meanwhile play yourself some records." He closed the door behind him while Vi stared balefully around her jail. She heard the key turn but was not sure whether it remained in the lock. Just then it made no difference; she did not want anyone to see her just now. She stared at the two piles of damaged records, considered what Phil might do when he returned, then started to sob quietly. She would have to ring him in Paris and tell him about her visitor. Her sobbing increased. Suddenly, life was no longer the same.

4

Bulman saw the memo at once, and called through the open communicating door to Detective Sergeant Haldean. "When did he ring?"

The unseen Haldean called back, "First thing this morning. He said he'll be there up to twelve thirty. Any time before then."

Through the door Bulman could just see one of Haldean's hands moving across the only section of the sergeant's desk visible to him. He pondered briefly on how little he actually saw of Haldean in spite of their proximity; their line of communication had always been by raised voice rather than the squawk box each had on his desk.

He looked at the memo again. It was from Sir Lewis Hope, present head of Security Service. He had not stepped foot in Bulman's office at Scotland Yard since Murison of DI6 had committed suicide a few weeks ago. Hope had come out from that affair badly although he had adroitly covered his own tracks by pointing the finger at Bulman, although it had been Bulman who had, in fact, saved Hope's face.

The two men disliked each other and since Hope had taken over at DI5 Bulman had been forced to recognise the weakness of his own position. In his view Hope should never have been appointed. One of Bulman's many problems was that he was really neither one thing or the other. He still carried police rank and was still paid by the Metropolitan Police but his expenses were met by the Security Service to avoid police comment and speculation; even jealousy. He liked his job; it was more flexible than straight police work and was often more interesting. But the difficulty of his position was that he did not have the backing of Special Branch who saw him as some kind of intruder, nor of Scotland Yard itself whose services he had left, and when the chips were down Security Service had the uncomfortable knack of regarding him as a policeman and not as one of themselves. It had not been like that when Sir Stuart Halliman had been around.

Now Bulman was facing an interview with Halliman's slippery replacement. He screwed up the note and threw it in the waste bin. "Hope can get stuffed," he bawled.

Haldean laughed. "That's the reaction he's waiting for, governor. And, anyway, you should not talk about your superiors like that in front of me, a mere DS."

Bulman grinned wryly. Haldean had a knack of bringing him down to earth. "Okay. I'll go and see him. Probably wants me to make his tea." He cleared his desk, put some papers in the wall safe, and grabbed his coat and hat as he left the office.

"Sit down, George."

Bulman wondered how it was that Hope could use his first name but still make it sound like a surname. He hung his coat and hat on the same stand Dr Max Blaser had so recently used. Even with his back turned to Hope he could feel the chill of formality in the office. He took his time sitting down, then changed chairs to Hope's annoyance. I'm getting as bad as he is, mused Bulman, but he felt a sense of grievance; he could not tolerate injustice particularly when it was created to cover the inadequacy of someone in high office.

Hope chose not to notice the reined-in expression on Bulman's craggy face. Almost amiably he said, "Deacon." Then smiled slightly to show how precise he could be.

In spite of himself Bulman showed surprise. Deacon had not been mentioned since a few days after Murison's suicide. Hope had tried to get away from the whole subject but here he was raising it of his own free will. "Sir?"

"I checked with the Met. It seems that Deacon is back in Europe. His wife's actually back home. What does that suggest, George?"

Bulman took his time wondering what was going on in the devious mind behind the large, government issue desk. "Word has reached him that he's free to come home."

"And how could that happen?"

Bulman despaired. "Deacon must have some contact in the

37

Met. Murder Squad has known all along that they have nothing to pin on him. They know he's actioned toppings but equally they know they can't pin him for it. Not without help from Security Service and it looks as if they're far short of receiving any of that."

"Even if they were told what we know, from a police point of view it's only circumstantial evidence, isn't it?"

"Probably. Salter won't talk and he's the link. And Murison, who could have cleared up the lot, is dead; his minions left the hard work to him so real evidence is sparse. We can probably prove that Salter and Deacon met but not what took place between them. But there is a strong circumstantial case against Deacon and I'm somewhat surprised that Murder Squad haven't pressed the issue."

Bulman was crudely trying to get Hope to provide the real reason but he knew that it would not work. Too much was at stake; too many well known names would be bandied in court if Deacon were pulled in. It was ministerial cover-up from more than one ministry. Hope knew this and he would be one of those involved. Mistakes had been made, not maliciously by the innocents in this case, but the old-boy network had suffered to a highly embarrassing degree and public knowledge of it could be disastrous. Murison's death had been put down to strain after the initial press speculation. Some news sheets had even suggested that Murison had been supplying the Russians. It was laughable but it had effectively taken focus away from the real truth: that the British Establishment itself harboured some rotten apples.

"Is there any way we can get Deacon and his crowd?"

"We?" Bulman was puzzled. "Surely it's a police matter?"

"Of course. I meant in your view."

"I don't think my opinion is worth anything. I handed over to Murder Squad what I have been allowed to in the interest of national security. I haven't been in touch with them since."

Hope forced a smile that was meant to be friendly. The lined face was mobile but the eyes remained chill. "George, you're prevaricating."

"Okay. I don't think there is any chance at all of bringing in Deacon and his murderous mob. Even though we know he is

38

guilty and have the evidence to pass to Murder Squad if we were allowed."

"So he could be used again to kill?"

Bulman felt uneasy. Hope was up to something and his present, almost friendly, approach could only be bad news for Bulman. "By whom?"

"Anybody who needs his services."

"He's not likely to jump at that. He'll have to feel his way when he returns home." Bulman did not like the sudden twist in Hope's thoughts. "Anyway, he's aware that we know that he received large sums of money for his services, whether he thinks we can prove it or not; he won't fall into that trap again so readily."

Hope gazed out of the window towards the dark sluggish currents of the Thames. "Supposing someone were able to convince Deacon that evidence of his guilt was readily available, but could be destroyed if he did one more job."

Bulman had a sudden urge to leave the office. Hope was beginning to talk like a raving lunatic. "If anyone mooted that possibility to him Deacon would top them. He would have to unless he wanted to be blackmailed for the rest of his life. Might I add, sir, that in some ways that suggestion is infinitely worse than what Murison did. At least Murison believed himself to be a patriot, no matter how perverted."

"Surely nobody would approach Deacon with such an idea without first taking adequate protection."

"Have you something specific in mind, sir?"

"Me? Good Lord no. It crossed my mind that if Deacon can't be brought to justice, a rough kind of justice might possibly be brought to him. It would be fair, wouldn't you say?"

"You mean fair to the guy who you want knocked off?"

"Don't overstep yourself, George. There is nobody in mind. It was just a delicious thought."

"Is that why you wanted to see me, sir?"

Hope appeared to pull out of his strange mood. "Actually, no. Ever heard of a fellow called Jost Kranz. German. Could be an alias."

"No."

"See what you can find out about him. Special Branch might

39

have something on him. Arrived here recently. May be holed up with friends."

"Left or right?"

"Extreme left I would guess. I'll send over a description by messenger."

"Right, sir. I'll do what I can. Is he the fellow you want knocked off?"

Hope smiled broadly. "You say some very odd things, George. But as you were obviously joking I'll let it pass. Tidy up your act though, there's a good fellow."

But the look Bulman received from Hope's piercing eyes was anything but friendly. The brief honeymoon was already over.

Hope continued to stare at the door long after Bulman had gone; the Detective Superintendent had been too perceptive in linking Deacon's and Kranz's names. Reluctantly, Hope conceded that he might have been too obvious. But Bulman's sharpness had thrust another idea into Hope's mind; Deacon might be of more than one use. There were thorns in Hope's side more painful and potentially far more dangerous than Kranz could ever be. Hope believed that one of them had just left his office. He would have to think carefully, though. It would not be easy to use someone like Deacon, and such a contact must never be traced back to him. Yet the possibility was tempting; it would need a good deal of thought and alertness for the right opportunity.

When Hashimi Ross called the second time Scott was more prepared. Since the first visit Scott had satisfied himself that the office was not under surveillance. There were few better to judge. He called out to Lulu for some coffee as the two men faced each other across the desk.

Scott grinned easily. "The gear suits you, Hash. Gives you dignity."

"It's the Muslim in me. The Catholic side is less disciplined. I don't know how you suffer this routine, Spider. It would drive me crazy."

"It does me, too." Scott shrugged, his expression reflective. "The alternative is to go back to creeping and that would destroy both Maggie and me. I have my moments." He stopped talking

40

as Lulu flounced in with the coffee. Scott watched her closely; Lulu was his barometer to people and he noticed the way she looked at Hashimi. When she had gone he said, "Lulu approves. What is it you have over women?"

"Maybe they can see my future and feel sorry for me. I saw Vi yesterday."

Scott stiffened. "Didn't take you long to get round to her."

"Well I knew I wouldn't get much out of you so I fell back on other contacts. Salter. Mean anything?"

Scott was worried. "How did you get her to talk?"

Hashimi smiled. "How can you show concern for her? She's the wife of a hood, up to her stone-hard eyeballs in it. As it happened I didn't lay a finger on her. So tell me where Salter is."

"You frighten me, Hash. You'll destroy yourself over this."

"I did that long before anyone got to Sophie. Dammit, she had done no harm to anyone. Her only sin was falling for someone like me and protecting someone like you, and she got hacked up for it."

There was a catch in Hashimi's voice which took Scott by surprise. "Did you discover too late that you loved the girl? Is that what it's all about?"

For a moment Hashimi could not answer but his expression gave little away. Eventually he said very quietly, "Just tell me where he is, Spider."

"He's in Wormwood Scrubs." Scott had thought quickly. Hashimi could not break Salter out against his will, and even he would not try a jail-break so soon after the last spectacular.

"Thanks. He's the one who sanctioned Sophie's murder."

"He was the last link maybe, but Murison, the bloke who instructed him, is dead. You're a fool letting this get to you. It'll sort itself out."

Hashimi gathered his robes and reached for his coffee. Before he sipped it he said, "I've never met your Maggie. But I've heard a lot about her. Tell me, Spider, if she was carved up and topped would you just wait for it to be sorted out?"

Scott shook his head slowly. It was not easy to give an honest answer. "What makes you think they'll get away with it?"

"Oh, come on. Phil Deacon is on his way back. He's been

tipped off he's safe from the law. Vi is the advance party."

In his heart Scott already knew that Hashimi was right. "Would you believe me if I said that my concern is for you?"

Hashimi lowered his cup and stared for some time at Scott who met his gaze comfortably. "Yes, I believe you. You're about the only one I would." He put down the cup. "Can you give me a description of Salter?"

"I never met him. Bulman has, though."

Hashimi smiled again. "You think I wouldn't ask him? I think I'm in the same boat as Deacon; I reckon they're scared to pull me in for fear of what might come out. I never got the full story of that caper from you, Spider."

"You never will. It stank, I can tell you that."

"It still stinks. It's not really dead, is it? A tidying up job has been done. They call me a terrorist because I fight for what I believe in, but there was never any ambiguity about what I did or why I did it. How many were topped before you were planted in stir to help authority?"

Scott stared at his untouched coffee. "I'm not arguing. If it's a question of you against the Establishment, I think you'd win on points on moral grounds."

Hashimi laughed. "Crafty devil. You know you haven't once asked me where I am staying."

"I don't want to know."

"The Dorchester. Now owned by the Sultan of Brunei. One of us. I'd like to see the Drugs Squad break in there to search the rooms wouldn't you? No way. They'll not look for me there. If they're looking at all. Come and have a meal with me one night. Bring Maggie."

Hashimi Ross went back to his suite at the Dorchester Hotel and after placing a 'do not disturb' sign on the door, laid the bag he was carrying on the double bed. He removed two bars of Kit-Kat chocolate from the bag and put them on the dressing table. Sitting down he eased one of the Kit-Kats from its protective paper sheath making sure that nothing was torn. With the aid of a pen-knife he very carefully lifted the silver foil covering making sure not to crease it in any way. When the chocolate-covered wafer bar lay revealed he lifted it by two corners and laid it clear of the foil.

He went to the bathroom where among his toiletries were several bottles of vitamin tablets. He opened a bottle of vitamin A. He tipped the dark orange carotene capsules on to the counter. There were three capsules which were much smaller and of a dark buff colour. He put one of these aside, partly refilled the bottle with the A then dropped in the remaining two odd capsules and completed the filling with the rest of the A. He took the one buff capsule into the bedroom and placed it beside the chocolate.

Hashimi opened the middle drawer of the dressing table and took out a carton of two-inch disposable syringes, and a smaller leather wallet in which were several boxed phials of vitamin B12, easily available at any chemist shop. He placed the capsule in a clean ashtray, pierced it with a pen-knife and squeezed out the minute amount of liquid. He worked unhurriedly.

Taking a box of B12 Hashimi pulled out the small tray to reveal five 2 ml glass phials filled with the vitamin. He lifted out the right-hand phial and broke off its neck. This particular phial did not contain B12. He poured some of the liquid into the ashtray and then mixed it with the liquid already there. He now had a diluted mixture of HCN, a compound from gold and silver ore with a solution of sodium cyanide.

He assembled a syringe and then drew up the liquid. With the utmost care he inserted the needle into one end of the Kit-Kat and very slowly injected the fluid. When he had finished he carefully smoothed the chocolate over the tiny hole. Again, holding the bar by finger tips at two corners he lifted it on to the foil making sure that it was precisely in position before folding the foil back over. It was the most difficult part for the foil must appear pristine. He had some difficulty in getting the bar back into its paper sheath but finally he was satisfied.

Hashimi took the syringe, broken phial and empty capsule into the bathroom, and spent some time washing them out before breaking the syringe in two and throwing it with the new clean phial into the waste bin. The capsule would need to be disposed of more circumspectly. He wrapped it in cling film then slipped it into his pocket. He would dispose of it away from the hotel. He washed his hands several times, finally cleaning them with pHisoHex, scrubbing under his nails. He placed the poisoned bar in a secret compartment in one of his travel cases. Then he telephoned Detective Superintendent George Bulman at Scotland Yard.

George Bulman deliberately arrived at the Savoy Hotel late. He knew the invitation to lunch was not a hoax because he had recognised Hashimi's voice on the telephone. He guessed that the well known venue was to reassure him, which it did a little. But he was extremely wary. He went down the short concourse to the main doors off the Strand, and was being eyed by the top-hatted door-man when Hashimi stepped beyond the reflection of chrome and glass to greet him affably.

Bulman barely recognised him. The Arab was dressed in a Savile Row suit, handmade crocodile shoes, silk shirt and tie. The thinning black hair was combed forward like Bulman's own, but the dark restless eyes were as Bulman remembered. Even as they greeted each other, Hashimi was making sure that the detective had brought nobody with him. They did not shake hands.

Once out of general earshot Bulman remarked, "You've tarted yourself up, lad. Bit different from the old jeans and the Colt I saw you with last time we met."

Hashimi glanced around, but from habit rather than nervousness. "Are you wearing a bullet proof vest?"

"I should be, and a bullet-proof head with you about. I hope you're not carrying a gun under that suit, you'll spoil the shape."

Hashimi tapped his jacket. "You should know better than anyone that the finest London tailors are the best in the world for making undetectable gun space in jackets. Most of the top American Mafia come to London to be fitted. And they don't have to worry about the tailor's discretion."

"Is that a fact?" said Bulman as if he did not know. "Can I get rid of this overcoat?"

As they entered the cloakroom Hashimi said, "When you're ready do you mind if we go straight in? I had difficulty getting a table and you are rather late."

"As long as I can get a large scotch at the table. It's not every

44

day a copper is entertained publicly by a wanted terrorist. I must be off my rocker."

Hashimi led the way to the restaurant. "I knew you'd come just the same."

When they were seated Hashimi poked his head above the menu. "Just how wanted am I?"

"You know the answer to that. But before I take you in I want it on record that you bought me a good meal first. It'll be a bit different from prison grub."

"I've already been in stir. Once."

"With Spider. I forgot. Enjoy this while you can."

Hashimi beckoned the wine waiter. "You disappoint me, Bulman. You know damn well that I won't be pulled in. If I am, I'm going to talk and some top brass will go to the cleaners."

Bulman laid down his menu. "I don't understand most of this; I'll settle for a fillet steak." He wedged the menu between two wine glasses and stared straight at Hashimi. "You don't know a bloody thing. Spider wouldn't have told you anything."

"I know that Spider Scott was in Albany as a police plant and that your police forces are searching for a non-existent guy called Tony Sims who broke out. That's a good scandal to start with, isn't it?" Hashimi's gaze roamed the room, for ever watchful. "Listen, Bulman, you forget my vocation. Part of the survival kit is a thorough knowledge of the opposition. I read the announcement about Murison's death; we know what he did for a living. If we're terrorist bastards what was he? The old double standards game. I can bounce names around and your people know it. So cut the bullshit."

Bulman said carefully, "There are other ways of squaring the account with you, Hashimi."

Hashimi waited until the waiter had taken their orders. "Maybe, yes. Various people have been trying to do it for years. I'd like a description of Salter."

"What for?"

"I'm going to kill him. I'm going to kill everyone who was involved in mutilating Sophie, killing her and dumping her in a watercress bed."

Bulman looked thoughtful. He gazed round the filling restaurant and said, "Where the hell do they all get the money from? How can so many afford a place like this? I have to rely on someone like you to buy me a lunch here, which is not worth that sort of information by the way."

"Do you think I'd try to bribe you with lunch? I was hoping you wanted justice as I do. And it would be justice wouldn't it?"

"Your kind. Anyway, he's where you can't get at him."

"He's in the Scrubs. My guess is that he's still on remand and that charges will eventually be dropped through lack of evidence. He's part of the big cover-up; like me, Spider, Deacon and whoever Deacon used to kill. None of them will be up for trial and you know it."

"You can't blast him out like you did Spider. Spider was willing. He won't be."

"I can wait till he's out. But I'd hate to nail the wrong man because you wouldn't describe him."

"I'm not responsible for any crazy thing you try."

"But you didn't mind me springing Spider to help you off the hook, did you?"

Hashimi stopped talking while the food was served. When the waiter had gone, Bulman said peevishly, "You've already ruined my bloody steak. I was looking forward to it." He ate silently for a while wondering which way to go. Hashimi would find out anyway. And meanwhile Salter could be warned. Hashimi was right, of course; Salter would be released. The terrible thing about it all was that Bulman found himself very close to Hashimi's sentiments on this. Salter was a mass murderer and had probably worked out by now that either the police were being blocked or they simply could not come up with hard evidence.

When he was halfway through his steak Bulman said, "There's nothing to describe. He's Mister Medium. Not tall, or short, fat or thin. His hard face could be any villain's. Miserable looking bugger. Dark hair, grey at the sides, middle forties. Real name is Walter Janeski, son of an escaped Pole who became a war-time ace with the R.A.F. His old man would turn in his grave."

Hashimi stared, small hands poised over his plate. "What made you tell me?"

"I don't know. Maybe it was because you and your Sophie saved Spider's life. There's no doubt that she died protecting

46

him. Maybe it's because I'm a raving lunatic who should never have been a copper."

"You've saved me some work." It was the nearest that Hashimi could come to saying thank you to a policeman.

"Don't get me wrong, Hashimi. I detest everything you stand for. I hate fanatics of every kind; they go through people as if they don't exist. Ordinary, simple people whom you scorn because they aren't the raving lunatics that you are. But in this I have a deep sympathy for the girl. Spider had enormous respect for her and he's not a bad judge."

"If you believe that, Bulman, if you respect his judgment, you should ask yourself what the hell it is he sees in me." Hashimi smiled. "I make no excuses for what I am. I believed in most of what I've done. Maybe Spider can see another side to me that you can't."

"And maybe he has made a rare mistake. Keep him out of it, Hashimi. I know what you've done for him. Don't cock it up now. He's managed to do what you haven't; he's put the clock back. He's straight. You've gone too far over the top to salvage anything from life. Don't take him down with you."

Bulman pushed his plate away. "One last thing. The only reason I'm not nicking you now is because it's more than my job is worth. For the moment you seem to be a protected species in certain quarters, but that will change." He smiled disarmingly. "I'll have another large scotch. I need it."

Behind the bravado Bulman was a worried man. He knew that he would have to be armed if he were to stand any chance of arresting Hashimi. Even if he succeeded, he would not be thanked for it. The fact that he was with the Arab at all in such circumstances would go against him if it were known. He was in a no-win situation and he wondered why he had agreed to meet like this. Yet he had learned quite a lot, even if all he could see ahead was trouble. He smiled across the table at Hashimi who was watching him silently. He would have given a lot to know what the Arab intended to do next. An uneasy conviction lingered that it would not be too long before he found out.

5

Walter Janeski was ushered into the visitors' room. A loner by nature, he instinctively chose an unoccupied table. He was not popular with fellow inmates, his surliness resented, but there was that about him which made them keep their distance. Bulman had been right in his description; Janeski was Mister Average in build and appearance until one looked closer: then the hardness really showed up.

When Janeski had received a letter a few days ago from a Karamali Dossa stating that there was news about Janeski's uncle in Poland, he had known it was false. Janeski had no interest in his Polish ancestry. He had never had pride of race like his father. And if he did have relatives there then that was where they should stay. But he was intrigued enough to apply for a visitor's order which he had sent to the Bradford address on the letter. Janeski did not know who to expect. Certainly not the slightly built Sikh who was ushered through the safety doors and who threaded his way round the tables towards him.

Hashimi Ross wore the turban expertly. The rest of his clothes were western, not too grand. Beneath an open raincoat the lapels of the suit jacket were slightly wrinkled. The huge beard and moustache which had taken him a long time to put on completely hid his features. He sat down opposite Janeski and gave a friendly greeting. "Karamali Dossa," he introduced himself.

"Really!" Janeski smiled cynically. "What's the con?"

"It saves time that you know there is one. It's all about money for services rendered. Tea or coffee?"

"I don't need either. What do you want?"

"Make it look right first." Hashimi turned to glance at the refreshment bar.

"Coffee. But don't bugger around. I want quick answers."

Hashimi pushed back the chair. "Do you think I'd go to this trouble if it wasn't important to us both? Relax for God's sake." He rose and fumbled in his raincoat pockets as he went to the

48

tea bar, then ordered two coffees and two Kit-Kats. He had trouble finding his money but finally paid. To cope better he slipped the two Kit-Kats in his pocket and picked up the coffees, one in each hand. He carried them over to the table, the cups rattling slightly in the saucers, then placed them on the table, slid one across to Janeski and produced the Kit-Kats.

"I don't want the chocolate," said Janeski sourly.

"That's okay. Would you rather have biscuits?"

"What I'd rather have is less bullshit and more information."

"Well, take it back in with you; you might get peckish in the night."

Janeski glared. "You trying to be funny? We are stripped and searched once we're through that door."

"I'm sorry. I didn't realise. Well if you don't eat it I probably will." Hashimi gazed round the room. In a low voice he said, "When you are out I would like you to do a job for me. Money no object. I hear you're good. The best."

Janeski slowly stirred his coffee, his gaze fixed on Hashimi. "You must be mad to come here for that. And stupid, too."

Hashimi appeared surprised. "Why? Is there a safer place?"

Janeski made a check of the warders at each end of the room. "Who have you been talking to?"

"You don't expect me to answer that. The information didn't come easily." Hashimi began to tear off the wrapper of his Kit-Kat. He slowly opened the foil so that the four fingers of chocolate wafer lay exposed. He snapped one finger off but left it lying there.

"Difficult or not, someone has a big mouth."

"It was easy enough for me to find out why you're here. Mass murder."

"Keep your bloody mouth shut." But Janeski was intrigued. He watched Hashimi chew at the chocolate finger. "Anyway, if that's the case you have a helluva wait before I'm out."

"You'll be released while still on remand. And you know it. They dare not bring a case against you." Hashimi slowly licked the chocolate from his fingers and then snapped off another section.

"You know far too much," said Janeski picking up his Kit-Kat.

"Whatever I know can't hurt you. I know far less than the

49

authorities and they're afraid to bring you to trial. So why worry?"

Janeski thoughtfully undid the wrapper. "I don't need money. I'm not short."

Hashimi dabbed his mouth with a handkerchief. "In the first place you haven't heard the fee. And secondly, once you are out they can't afford to let you roam loose. *You* are the one who knows too much. You'll have to get out of the country and you'll need all the help you can get. You'll also need some contacts abroad. I can supply them."

Janeski sat back thoughtfully, his gaze hard and suspicious. "They wouldn't dare top me; it would be too obvious."

"You used Deacon and he specialised in toppings that were anything but obvious. Deacon is on his way back but it would be too soon for you to use him again." Hashimi bit into another finger of Kit-Kat and took his time before continuing. "I must also point out that Deacon comes under a different heading where danger to the State is concerned. He's a straightforward killer: a mobster who had no idea of the motives for the murders he did and cared only for the money. You were much nearer the actual link. If you don't know exactly who was behind the killings you instructed Deacon to do, you can certainly guess. They couldn't take a chance on you. It's as simple as that." He slipped the rest of the chocolate finger into his mouth.

Janeski's features had tautened. "You sound like a bloody police spy. Where did you get all this?" He broke off some chocolate wafer.

Hashimi burst out laughing. "I've never been called that before. That's good. Are you interested or not?" He studiously kept his gaze from the chocolate now disappearing into Janeski's mouth and promptly munched his own.

"Who's so important that you come in here like this? And how much?"

"The answer to your first question will come later." Hashimi licked his fingers again and then sipped his coffee. "Twenty thousand."

Janeski grinned as he broke off some more chocolate. "Petty cash. I paid out more than that myself."

"That would be for you. You organise who you like; that's

what you're best at. Whatever you have to pay out will be on top of the fee."

Janeski shook his head and swallowed. "No. You're out of touch. And you are naïve and that makes you dangerous. How would you know I wasn't ripping you off? I can't deal with a man who doesn't think things through."

"What the hell do I need you for but to do my thinking for me? Name your own fee. I don't want to know how it's done or who you use."

"If it's someone up the tree, a politician or someone like that, fifty grand overall."

"Forty."

"Fifty. Take it or leave it." Janeski sat back and finished his Kit-Kat. He frowned. "That bloody chocolate was stale, bitter."

Hashimi blew out his cheeks. "Okay. But I don't want a butcher's job like that done on the black girl. And it mustn't come back to me."

Janeski's eyes narrowed at mention of the girl. "I don't even know who you are, so how can it?"

Hashimi thought he saw Janeski wince and realised that his own nerves were on edge. He pushed his chair back. "Fine. Your problems will soon be over. As soon as you're out I'll contact you." He rose and looked towards the warder at the visitors' door.

Janeski spoke hastily. "You won't know where to find me."

Hashimi gave a glance of assurance. "I'll know. I'll be in touch." He gazed at the two empty chocolate wrappers and the screwed foil. "Be lucky." Then he turned and moved away, hearing Janeski push his chair and walk the other way.

Janeski died on the way back to his cell. He suddenly doubled up and clutched at his chest as his heart muscles contracted. He fell to his knees in agony. At first the warder with him thought Janeski was trying something on until the prisoner rolled on his side doubled up, face contorted with pain. The warder knelt down but refrained from giving mouth to mouth resuscitation due to a refusal by all prison officers after a recent Aids scare in the prison. It would have made no difference. Janeski writhed in agony for the last time, gave a terrible croaking gasp as he clawed at his chest, and died. By the time the doctor had taken a look at Janeski, Hashimi Ross was well away.

The wheels were quick to turn once it was established how Janeski had died. A quick post-mortem revealed the cause and the way it was administered. All stocks of Kit-Kat were checked in the visitors' room, but long before then the awful suspicion had dawned. Janeski had been murdered in prison under the full view of his warders. A nation-wide call went out for Karamali Dossa. The Bradford house was found to be empty, almost derelict.

Accusation and counter accusation started between police and prison staff. The police were supposed to check on visitors' applications if requested by the prison authorities, but that usually meant checking if the visitor had a criminal record; there had been no such record against Dossa. There had been nothing, ostensibly, to cause suspicion.

The Home Office were quickly notified. One junior minister realised the truth. Apathy on a large scale had set in over Janeski's detention. Murder Squad had realised that they had not been given the full details about his crimes by the Security Service and had soon accepted that they would get nowhere with the inquiry while some sort of cover-up was going on. They were frustrated and angry and had lost interest in the certain knowledge that Janeski would soon have to be released through lack of evidence and official intransigence. When Janeski died some senior policemen were even pleased that the job had been done for them. A rough justice had been done. But the prison staff were badly mauled by most of the press who saw only a blatant example of lawlessness in Her Majesty's jails.

What made it worse was that Karamali Dossa had disappeared off the face of the earth. A few people guessed what had happened. George Bulman was one, and he was shaken to his roots. He had believed that Hashimi would wait until Janeski's release. Too late, he realised that he should have known better. Spider Scott, too, realised what had happened and it came as no surprise to him. But it worried him considerably. The Arab would now go all the way.

The seriousness of the murder was further emphasised when Sir Lewis Hope called on Bulman, the first time he had done so for weeks. Hope strode over to the communicating door and asked Sergeant Haldean if he would leave the office for a few minutes. When Haldean had gone Hope closed the main door behind him and waved a newspaper at Bulman who was still seated. Hope paced in front of the desk. "My God, George, we've got to find out who did this."

Bulman did not need to be told what Hope was talking about. Straight-faced he said, "It's not our business. It's in the hands of Murder Squad. It's been their exclusive pigeon from the moment I was forced to hand over to them."

Hope glared. "This isn't time for a private war. Janeski has been killed under our noses. Questions will be asked and we don't want them coming our way."

"You can deal with that, sir. The Home Office won't raise questions; they dare not."

Hope gazed round, found a chair and sat down. He crossed his long legs, weathered face taut, screwed up eyes steely. "You don't think this Arab fellow did it, do you?"

Bulman immediately felt on the defensive. Only Scott and himself knew that Hashimi had blasted Scott out of prison. "Why would he do that? Is there some connection between the two?"

Hope tried to read the lie into the words but Bulman had spoken convincingly. "It was always assumed that Hashimi Ross sprung Scott from prison. And Scott was indirectly tied up with this Janeski thing."

Bulman nodded. "That was all newspaper talk. Only Scott knows the truth and he will tell no one. And it wouldn't be wise to pressure him into it."

"Are you saying he didn't tell you?"

"I'm the last person he would tell; I carry a policeman's rank. And, anyway, to be brutally honest, hasn't whoever killed Janeski done us all a favour? A few people in high places will sleep easier."

"Well I certainly won't. I need to know who did it, George. Keep your ear to the ground. Did you get anywhere with Jost Kranz?"

Bulman suddenly thought he saw a connection between the two issues. "Nothing. He hasn't registered into any of the known hotels or boarding houses. He's probably staying with friends. We have to wait."

"Here's a photograph of him." Hope took from his pocket a folded print and passed it over.

Bulman saw at once that it had been wired through. From where? Germany, presumably. He gazed at lean, slightly supercilious features. A dark-haired, good-looking man in his late thirties. "You want me to give copies to S.B.?"

"Naturally. But I want all reports to come to me through you."

Phil Deacon gazed unbelievingly into the two cardboard boxes which contained the remnants of the records Hashimi had destroyed. He was not particularly big but appeared to be powerful and had the petulant features of a bully; piggy eyes and jutting lips set in an orange-peel face. His big restless hands groped round the two boxes with surprising sensitivity.

Deacon went to an expensive tailor but his beautifully cut suits were ruined by his failure to let the tailor finish the job properly. His interference showed now in the too-broad shoulders and the waspish waist of his otherwise smart light fawn suit. The suit matched his tan. Everything had been fine abroad and he had relaxed under the Brazilian sun and then on the French Riviera. Having received the nod from a contact in the police his return to London should have been one of immediate celebration. But now he was staring at the evidence that it was not.

He held one of the boxes in his strong hands and felt tears of frustration prick his eyes. The music room door was closed and Vi stood at the far end by the untouched speakers; Deacon had yet to see the smashed-in speaker behind his back. With a catch in his voice he asked, "Do you know how long it took me to collect these? Hawkins, Hines, Beiderbecke, Bechet and the others. Jesus, they're all bloody dead now. I won't be able to replace them, not the early ones." He turned, still holding the box almost as if it were a baby. "Why the hell didn't you stop him? How hard did you try?"

"He had a bloody gun on me. I keep telling you for Christ's sake. He was going to kill me."

"Balls. He wouldn't have dared. You just stood there and let him do this." Deacon was almost beside himself with fury.

Vi had dressed specially for him; a sexy bra beneath the tight silk blouse and a pencil-line black skirt. She doubted that he had noticed. All he could think of was his bloody records. For a moment she was glad they were broken.

Deacon suddenly stepped forward and sent her reeling with a massive backhander that carried all his pent-up fury. She collapsed between the speakers, blood gushing from her mouth.

Deacon dropped to his knees, suddenly repentant. Vi's shapely legs were immodestly apart with her skirt ruckled above her knees and stretched tight across her thighs. One high heeled shoe had come off. He put a hand behind her head and supported it while he wiped the blood from her lips. "Vi. Vi. Look, I'm sorry."

But Vi wasn't sure that the moment was ripe to show consciousness. She groaned a little.

"Oh, Vi." Deacon held her head against his chest. He stroked her hair quite tenderly. "I'm sorry, love. Come on, let me get you up."

Vi didn't make it easy for him. She staggered and groaned then leaned back against one of the speakers while he supported her.

"Stay there, I'll get you a drink." Deacon moved away from her.

"I don't want a drink. Look, that Arab said he'll kill you. And then me." She did not have to work at slurring her words; her head was still spinning and her jaw ached. "We've got to do something."

Before Deacon turned back to face her he noticed the smashed speaker. At first he had to grit his teeth to hold back his temper. Behind him, Vi saw his powerful back stiffen, realised why and spoke quickly, "You can replace that, it's no problem."

Deacon unwound and faced her again. "Yeah. Well tell me what happened in detail."

Vi went through it again and believed that this time he was listening carefully, his records temporarily forgotten. When she had finished she stretched out her stockinged foot for the loose shoe and wiggled her foot into it. "You shouldn't have hit me.

I've done no wrong." She would make him pay for the blow.

"I said I was sorry, what more do you want?" He glared at her. "You say he said I topped his girlfriend?"

"Tortured her first."

"Would I do a thing like that?"

"Ted would. Ted's a vicious little bastard." Ted was Deacon's son by his first wife who had died in a road accident some ten years earlier. Vi didn't like him and the feeling was mutual.

"Wash your mouth out, Vi. Ted will do only what I tell him."

Vi had the sense not to reply but her uneasy gaze made Deacon uncomfortable.

Deacon's expression suddenly changed and he exploded, "Jesus Christ. That must have been *The* Arab."

"Who's he?"

"Don't you read the papers? The terrorist. Wanted all over the world for hi-jack jobs and embassy killings. You name it, he's wanted for it." Deacon had almost forgotten. When Salter had told him to lean on the Arab's girlfriend in order to find Scott there had been no direct contact with the Arab. "It wasn't Ted," he said tersely. He had used West Indians outside his own organisation so that there could be no connection with him. So how had the Arab found out?

Deacon had his answer when he read the next day's newspapers and learned that the man he had known as Salter had been killed in prison. Even then he would have made no connection, as the name printed was Janeski, but one paper carried a photograph. As Deacon gazed at the print his blood ran cold. This was war and the Arab had given warning in a most dramatic way.

"What's the matter? You just seen a ghost?" Vi asked across the breakfast table.

Deacon passed over the newspaper. "I didn't take it seriously enough. I thought he'd just put the fear of God into you and broke my records and that was it." He rose quickly, leaving his bacon and eggs untouched. "I must call a family meet. And you don't leave this house without one of the boys. Understand? We've got to fix this Arab before he fixes us."

Vi did not need telling. She had seen the look in the Arab's eyes when he had made his threat to her, but it was not something she could adequately explain to Deacon; all he saw in people's eyes was their fear or pain or greed. Vi had never seen him quite like this before. Shortly after he left the room she heard him call out, the front door banged and the house fell silent. There was going to be big trouble; she pulled her silk dressing gown more tightly around her and gingerly tongued the damage to her lips.

They met at what was left of Streatham Common in south London. Croydon lay south and Brixton to the north. They took the middle course and walked away from the bus stops up the slight incline of the common, beyond the big old tree that countless boys had climbed and swung from over countless years. "I need some shooters," Deacon said brusquely.

Sammy Tanner showed surprise. He was shorter than Deacon, bald and badly dressed in spite of his wealth from arms deals. His run-down appearance was a joke among those who knew him; friends referred to his shabby garments as his tax inspector clothes. However, he had one weakness which was always a giveaway; he could not resist handmade shoes and at the moment was wearing turtle. Hands in the pockets of his topcoat – he never wore gloves – Tanner glanced up at the bull-like face of Deacon and said, "Someone upset you, Phil? You're tense." It was a warning; Tanner did not enter lightly into any deal however small, and this one, in the scheme of things, seemed that it would yield petty cash.

"Unmarked," Deacon went on remorselessly.

"Oh, those sort of shooters. They cost more."

Deacon stopped walking and watched a young girl chase a poodle carrying a lead in its mouth. "Have I mentioned money?"

The shrewd Tanner watched Deacon closely, eyes narrowed in his long sallow face. "Is it Reisen again?"

"No, no. Nothing like that. All I want . . ."

"Only you seem pretty desperate," Tanner cut in. "Not your usual self."

"Jesus." Deacon passed a big hand over his face. "I've just got back from Brazil. I'm clear here. No problem. Except one that has just come up. It's not the fuzz and it's not someone trying to cut in. It's personal. I just want to settle it." He stared down at Tanner and saw the dealer trying to read his mind. "Look, Sammy, I know this is piddling but I've done you some favours. I don't want to go to a small time dealer. I want to be sure that the goods are untraceable. And I know they will be from you. Okay?"

Tanner accepted that Deacon had paid him a compliment and inclined his head. It was cold standing on the common. He started to walk again. "I just want to be sure, as you do, that nothing comes back to me. You usually have plenty of shooters around."

"There's been no need since Reisen. They are never used twice for any job. They finish up in the North Sea. But it's an old-fashioned way of dealing with things. I haven't found the need. These are for a little self-protection."

"How many?"

"I'd like half a dozen automatic pistols, and one ladies' pistol. Something that can be easily carried. Two machine pistols. Two rifles with night sights. I don't want any revolvers. I can't stand the bloody things; they're too clumsy and awkward to carry."

"More reliable, though."

"But not so accurate. Can you do it?"

"No problem, but this sounds like a gang war and I don't like that."

"What difference can it make to you if they're untraceable? And it isn't gang war. Those days are over unless somebody is stupid enough to try my patch." Deacon paused. "There's one more thing, Sammy." He stopped walking again. "I want a meet with Paddy O'Dwyer."

Tanner rocked on his heels, all blandness gone. "That's a lot more difficult than the weapons."

"Come off it. You've been supplying the boyos long enough. You must know how to contact him."

"That's not what I said. He'll want a bloody good reason before he risks a meeting with you. He has to be seen to follow the straight and narrow."

"He owes me one. I holed up one of his boys once."

"If he paid you he'll consider the debt settled."

"I'm not stupid, Sammy. He owes me."

Tanner took his hands from his pockets and smoothed the sparse hair at the sides of his head. "I'll have to give him more than that."

"I just want some information I think he can give me."

Tanner sighed in exasperation. "You know bloody well that won't do. He keeps too low a profile. I don't like the sound of this. He's a client of mine. Give me something or forget it."

Deacon conceded. "It's about the Arab."

"*Hashimi Ross?* You're not going to tangle with him?"

"Just tell him. I can help Paddy, too. Tell him that."

"You're mad, Phil. Leave it alone."

"Tell him. Or he'll get nothing more from you."

"You threatening me?"

Deacon grinned. "With bodily harm? Don't be daft. We all need you. There are other ways. Think about it and tell Paddy to get in touch. Oh, and tell him I'll pay well for the help. After the money the Irish Government lifted from them they need all they can get."

Tanner nodded. "I hope you know what you're doing. I'll tell him. And God help you." He paused before speaking again. "Cash on delivery, Phil."

Deacon ignored the insult and was about to head towards the London Road when Tanner added, "I don't like this at all. There's a bloke keeping an eye on us over by the bus stop. What the hell's going on?"

"Don't worry. He's one of mine."

Tanner caught Deacon by the arm. "You need a minder? You're beginning to make me nervous."

"Just do what I say or you'll have something to be nervous about, Sammy. And that *is* a threat."

6

Sir Lewis Hope, as Director General of the Security Service, had a meeting with the Home Secretary about phone tapping. He had that morning personally tried to get a phone tap on Willie 'Spider' Scott on the grounds that he might lead to Hashimi Ross who Hope and others still thought was responsible for the Janeski killing. It was still not Hope's aim to bring Hashimi to trial; there were other ways of disposal but not until the peculiar talents of the Arab had been exploited. However, much to Hope's annoyance, his request for the phone tap had been refused.

Hope did not need Home Office clearance to carry out surveillance, though. The snag with such measures was that Scott had inbuilt vision against them and if he so much as suspected a tail he was in a position to cause political havoc. It was annoying about the tap but it had been pointed out to Hope that in no way could Scott be considered a subversive; on the contrary, he had often helped the State, albeit reluctantly.

Hope was in a foul mood by the time he ran into Martin Holmes, a minister at the Home Office.

"You look troubled, Sir Lewis. Let me get you a drink."

As Holmes led the way to the members' bar in the House of Commons, Hope replied, "Not troubled. Bloody annoyed." After finding a secluded table he told Holmes what had happened in the belief that he might persuade the minister to help get the Home Secretary's decision reversed some other time.

Mention of Scott was enough. The placid brown eyes beneath the heavy dark brows hardened. Holmes wanted nothing to do with Scott who, with Bulman, had brought him within an ace of enforced resignation over the Murison business. Somehow, he and other politicians involved, had scraped by but it had been touch-and-go. And all because they had been misled by a high ranking intelligence officer who had used his position to eliminate those he saw as enemies of the State: his trust in some of those around him had been shattered, Sir Lewis Hope included. Had Holmes known that in Bulman's opinion Hope had been a bad choice for Director General of the Security Service, he would have agreed with him. As his recent past tumbled across his mental vision, Holmes said shakily, "There is no way I can help you, Sir Lewis." Best to keep it formal was his unspoken resolution.

Hope gazed into his sherry as if it were a crystal ball: the pale fino kept its secrets. "It's strange," he murmured as if speaking to himself. "I command a large organisation which has very efficiently infiltrated those areas which are dangerous to us. We have our tabs on all those who can cause most damage. We have a splendid record of assessment, analysis and surveillance. In fact our house is very much in order and most of the time runs smoothly. Yet time and again I find the whole structure under threat by two men neither of whom really belong to the organisation. How can this possibly happen?"

Holmes thought it prudent not to mention that the high efficiency of DI5 was due to Hope's predecessor, that in his opinion there was a grave risk of efficiency being eroded unless a change were made at the top. "You are talking of Scott and Bulman, of course. Well, surely, the answer is easy. Send Bulman back to full-time police duties. By doing that you effectively side-line Scott."

He studied his sombre-looking companion, recognising that he was on delicate ground; Hope only wanted him as a sympathetic listener, but Hope out-ranked him and Holmes was treading warily. But when Hope did not immediately reply he could not resist adding, "Of course, awkward or not, you'd be losing a good man, an individualist with considerable flair. A non-committee man. And, let's be honest, a man who with Scott's help, got us off a very nasty hook when they exposed Murison. Can you afford to be without him?"

Hope had asked himself that question many times. Bulman was a thorn who could not be categorised. There was no convenient pigeon hole into which he could be pushed. Hope's association with him was ostensibly ludicrous. Normally there was very little chance of someone in Bulman's position even brushing shoulders with the Director General of DI5. But the pattern had been set before Hope had taken up his appointment. Bulman had acted as a loose head for Hope's predecessor and there were advantages in having someone as effective as Bulman set apart from the main crowd of operatives. Bulman's competence, and the unorthodox way he worked, had shown up some of Hope's own weaknesses, and this too rankled. When it came down to it he was secretly afraid to take the irrevocable step of having Bulman removed. Hate him or not, Bulman had saved his face. "I'm concerned about Hashimi Ross," he said finally and at a seeming tangent.

Holmes hid his bewilderment. "Ross? Why so?"

"I still think it was he who arranged Scott's escape from Albany."

"That's generally accepted, I thought. But it's something we would rather not know, isn't it? We can't bring him in – even if we could find him there are grave political risks in doing that. Wouldn't it be better to let some foreign police force find him on their territory and to charge him with crimes that don't affect us?"

Hope suddenly looked up as if only just realising where he was. The members' bar was filling up, the afternoon parliamentary schedule flickering on the screen. He uncharacteristically swallowed half his sherry in one gulp. "I've taken up your time," he said more positively. "I must get back." He finished his sherry and rose abruptly. "You are right, of course. About Ross, I mean. My mind wasn't operating in quite the way you assumed. Thanks for the sherry; things seem to have improved in here."

Holmes thought that the DI5 chief was slowly cracking up; the sherry had not changed. He also wondered what Hope had in mind for Hashimi Ross but on brief reflection decided that it was best not to know. He did know, though, that of necessity Hope could be devious. And he would have to be if he had anything in store for the Arab.

Bulman gazed up at the ceiling and belatedly realised that it needed redecorating. Betty Moorcroft lay beside him in the bed, her head on his bare shoulder, her arm across his adequate waistline. He gave her a squeeze: "I'm sorry, Betty. It's been a long time. I really need a book of instructions."

She laughed into his chest, running a hand over it. "I could tell it had been a long time, George. As for the instructions, I could have sworn that you had written them."

He tried to look down at her but her face was averted and he could only see her ruffled hair. He kissed her head. "I couldn't have been that good, I've too much of a conscience."

She moved her position to look up at him and smiled. "I'm not fooled, you know. You keep putting yourself down. All this bumbling apologetic stuff is a trap. You're crafty, my darling. So helpless. Is that how you lull your prisoners?"

"I don't make love to my prisoners. I can't think of any I fancy." He paused, an impish smile on his face. "Not even the women."

She prodded his ribs and he gasped. Eventually they sat up, happy and content but she knew that there was something on his mind. She reached up and kissed him and they grappled passionately for a while.

When they had cooled down Bulman said, "If you read about this bloke Janeski being murdered in prison, he was the one who finally sanctioned the trigger man to kill your father."

Betty stiffened and pulled the bedclothes up around her. For the moment the loving had stopped. "Killed by this Arab fellow?"

"The Arab. That's how every police force in the world refers to him. There is absolutely no proof that he did it. But he had the motive and he's about the only one who could pull off a stunt like that. It's his M.O. I thought you should know."

"Why? It won't bring Dad back."

"You complained about being kept in the dark. I'll get drummed out for telling you this but a man called Murison sanctioned your father's killing. He was an over-zealous un-balanced patriot high up in DI6 who had a private slush fund which he used to finance the destruction of those he saw as enemies of the State. Your father was getting near to the truth and Murison found himself threatened. When you told me that you didn't believe your father's death was an accident Spider Scott and myself carried on from where your father had left off. This meant us sending Spider to prison as a plant to make contact with an old lag your dad had used. Through his contacts at the Home Office Murison found out and tried to have Spider killed while he was inside. Spider managed to contact the Arab who blew a bloody great hole in the prison's visitors' room. Spider then escaped and holed up with the Arab's girlfriend Sophie. Murison used Janeski to hire killers who tortured Sophie in an effort to try to find Spider. When they failed they killed her. A whole chain of people were affected, and when we finally got to Murison he committed suicide. Politicans innocently involved through neglect or security naïveté saw their heads rolling unless they could arrange some form of cover-up."

Betty gripped Bulman's hand so fiercely that he was surprised by her strength. "Thanks for telling me. At least I now know what Dad died for. I think I can see why the Arab worries you so much."

"He'll try to kill everyone involved in the murder of his girlfriend and that could be a lot of people."

"I have a good deal of sympathy for him."

"It could create problems. We don't want to bring him in but if he goes on like this we will have to. That could be very awkward, Bett."

Betty moved closer, pushed her leg against his, but it was comfort she needed just then. Her father was dead but everything about his death was suddenly very much alive again: it was as if he was operating from the grave. She was very aware of his presence and knew that he would not approve of her being in bed with George Bulman while she was still married. Tom Moody had been straight all down the line. "I've developed some of your guilt," she explained.

He put his arm round her, sensing her unease. "If I've raised ghosts I'll tell you no more. I thought it might be important for you to know."

"It is, George. But you glibly talk of bringing this Arab in when – as I understand it – no police force has managed it so far."

"The French did once. He shot his way out. But he's never operated like this before. Usually it's one job then out. This time he's taking on opposition who'll shoot back. He'll show himself. He's bound to. I can't see even the Arab taking on a big chunk of the London underworld and getting away with it."

"And you can't stop him?"

"I doubt it. The Arab loved the girl too much and that has to be a first with Hashimi. There's only one way to stop him and even then a great deal of luck will be required."

"What's your real worry, George?"

Bulman smiled bitterly. "You're getting to know me too well. I think that along the line some innocent people are going to be killed. There's going to be one hell of a mess with no solutions."

Betty clung tightly to Bulman. "Are the men who actually killed Dad still alive?"

"So far as I know."

"Will they be on the Arab's list?"

"That depends on whether they were involved in his girl-friend's murder. You're hoping they were, aren't you? Don't get too bitter, Bett."

"If the law won't operate against them, then I have to hope the Arab will. I'm sorry, George, but that's the way I feel."

"I know. I can't blame you. It's the aftermath that frightens me. I have this terrible feeling that innocents will be dragged in. And you won't want that. But some scheming bastards will."

Maggie left her office early and was able to meet Scott at his agency. A fierce little wind had sprung up and she clutched her coat collar to her throat while Scott locked the agency door. Arm in arm they strolled towards Trafalgar Square and the wheeling pigeons. "Let's eat out," she suggested. When he did not reply she gazed up to note his preoccupation. She quietly slipped her arm away from his and at first he did not notice. "That's charming," she said. "I didn't realise I had such a devastating effect on you. What's on your mind?"

He pulled himself round. "Sorry, love. Did you read about that prison killing?"

"Dreadful business. What do you . . . it wasn't . . ."

"I reckon it was Hash. His style."

Maggie slowed her pace. "You said that as if it was a merit. It was cold-blooded murder, Willie. How can you be friendly with such a man?"

They turned into the Strand. Both traffic and pedestrians were congested. People hurried down the subways like termites scurrying into the base of an ant hill. The wind was now blocked as they changed direction and Maggie released her collar and hooked her arm back through Scott's.

"We've been through all that," he said. "I can't expect you to understand." When he gazed down and saw her degree of concern he added, "Don't waste sympathy on Janeski; he was a killer."

"What's happened to you, Willie? How can you defend such a thing?"

"I'm not defending it. What worries me is that Janeski won't be the last. He's only the first in a long, bloody line."

Maggie slowed her pace. Very carefully she said, "Keep right out of it, Willie. I don't care what this man has done for you. This is like a gangland killing. Don't get involved, I beg you."

"I don't intend to get involved. But before you are too critical just remember that we would not be walking together now but for him. More likely you'd be taking flowers to my grave. If I'd been found."

"If you do get involved, Willie, then you'd better face the possibility that I might still be doing that in the near future."

He had rarely heard her so bitter.

The locals could not believe what they were seeing. The one house in the whole district which had always been safe from the ravages of vandalism and break-ins, was Phil Deacon's. His muscle was too strong for anyone to tangle with. The local children not only would not dare touch the cars parked outside his house but they virtually stood guard over them and even polished them. What had now happened was that the Jaguar had been moved to make room for a Chubbs van. A team of security experts were fixing burglar locks on every window and door and a complete alarm system was being installed; a mixture of passive infra-red and audio equipment. A small crowd had formed a semi circle outside the house to watch the operation; who would be stupid enough to try to break into the Vicar's pad?

Rumours started to flow. Onlookers recalled seeing suspicious strangers around. These stories were strengthened by the personal supervision of the work by Deacon himself. Chubbs might be the security experts but few knew the villain's mind better than Deacon himself.

Deacon had insisted on having a sound detector in the attic but it had been pointed out to him that the gurgle of water pipes could set the system off: infra-red would be better. Furthermore, the front door was having a steel plate fixed to its inside and all the locks were being changed with the addition of a deadlock on each outside door.

With men and wire and equipment all over the house, Vi had lost her patience: the constant sound of drilling had finally driven her out to shop. Even then she could not escape the net of security that Deacon was casting and which went well beyond her home. One of Deacon's men went with her; he was armed and he was alert.

Vi had difficulty in deciding which was worse: to stay put and tolerate the intrusion, or listen to the monosyllabic utterances of the minder by her side who looked the thug he was. In exasperation she finally made him keep a constant few paces behind.

There was a funny side to all this which Vi would normally have appreciated, for she did not lack a sense of humour. But beneath all the considerable inconvenience, the forced change of routine, the disruption of her normal life, was the continuous undercurrent of menace. Her bodyguard may not have been the brightest creature on earth but she knew his reflexes to be good where they mattered and he was quick and deadly with a gun. He had recently given her lessons in an old warehouse which Deacon had long ago converted to an indoor range.

Vi had taken the lessons seriously because her husband was not a man to get worked up about false dangers. She had been surprised at how quickly she had improved with the small, .22 automatic pistol she now had in her handbag. Even so, the very presence of it was more than sobering. She had been brought into the practical side of Deacon's work and she did not care for it. And in spite of her bravado she was scared; very scared indeed. What was so particularly menacing was the fact that all the precautions sprang from the threats of one man. Somehow, that made it more terrifying.

Hashimi Ross, dressed in jeans, sweater and wind-cheater, carried a duffle bag over his shoulder as he turned into Highbury Grove, which was within walking distance of the Arsenal Football

Club. He went up the steps and unlocked two locks on the heavy front door of one of the large houses, many of which had been converted to boarding houses or flats, and entered the lino-covered hall. A glass-fronted door faced him and beside it a passageway continued on. He unlocked the narrow door, to reveal shabbily carpeted stairs leading to the upper floors. He went through, locked the door behind him and then mounted the stairs almost silently.

At the first landing he opened the middle door of a line of three and went in. After closing the door behind him he crossed the oddly furnished room and unlatched the big window, pushing it up. He shivered at the blast of cold air but the room badly needed airing. He gazed around at the mixture of old and modern furniture. It was utilitarian; the chairs nondescript but comfortable. In one corner was a D-ended dining table with four heavy Victorian chairs. The fabric of the sofa was torn but there were three reasonably comfortable armchairs, and on a low table was an old television set.

There were two rooms leading off and he entered both in turn, dropping his bag on the double bed in one and then testing the taps of the kitchen sink in the other. He opened more windows. Beyond the bedroom was a white tiled bathroom and he washed before turning his attention to the bedroom. There was one really good piece of furniture against a wall.

The late Georgian chest had an inlay of satin, applewood and ebony above the drawers. The mahogany was well grained. The delightful piece had one obvious flaw. The rear ball feet were what a dealer would call 'married', and had been put on at a date noticeably later than the chest itself.

Hashimi fetched a small car jack from the kitchen, placed it under one end of the chest and levered it up until he could comfortably reach one of the rear ball feet. He unscrewed the foot and when it was free unscrewed a further section at the top which lay concealed when the chest was in its normal position. After emptying its contents, he laid a stretch of plastic explosive along the lack-lustre carpet and very carefully checked its condition – it had lain rolled in its almost air-tight hiding place for some time. Satisfied, he removed a section and re-rolled the remainder in the ball foot which he screwed back on. He raised

68

the other end and extracted some fuse wire and detonators, giving them close scrutiny before putting aside two detonators and fuse wire and returning the rest. He lowered the chest.

He then took out the two, smaller top drawers, and, with difficulty, groped in the top of the cavity behind the frieze and above where the drawers had been. He pulled off the sticking paper that held the objects in place which he now produced and laid on the bed.

The first package was in oilskin which Hashimi unwrapped almost reverently to reveal the plastic butt of a rifle. Removing the shoulder grip he pulled out the two remaining component parts of a long-barrelled rifle. It was in fact an early Armalite, originally designed for the U.S. Air Force, a bolt action which operated a .22 Hornet cartridge. Not normally his first choice it was nevertheless extremely portable and when packed in the butt would comfortably float on water, a virtue which had once proved invaluable to him. It was the AR-5 Survival Rifle, long since replaced by more recent versions but which was well named so far as he was concerned. It had been a good friend and he hoped it was about to become so again.

He removed another, smaller parcel from the cavity in the chest of drawers and unwrapped a World War II Beretta 34, 9mm short cartridge. Again, he would have preferred a heavier gun with a more powerful velocity but it was light and extremely effective at close range. As he examined it he noticed the RM imprinted on its metal frame which denoted that it had been issued by the Italian Navy. They were the only marks left on the gun. He released the safety catch and removed the full magazine and drew back the breech to eject the round in the chamber. Hashimi always kept his handguns ready for instant use.

Back in the lounge he knelt by the heavy window drapes and eased out from the wide hems, three .22 cartridges from each of the two curtains. In the hollow curtain rail which carried the drapes were more cartridges carefully placed so as not to interfere with the free running of the cords when the drapes were opened or closed.

From under the rim of the dining table he untaped a pullthrough, a small bottle of light oil and a cleaning cloth. He started to clean the rifle, removing the thin film of oil from its barrel until it was dry. He then cleaned the Beretta making sure that the movement was still slightly oiled.

He went into the kitchen and had to break open the stale and mildewed loaf of bread into which he had pushed another Beretta a long time ago. When he had finished cleaning that of breadcrumbs and debris he removed the heavier Browning from his waistband and checked it over. Hashimi was preparing for war and this apartment had always been designed for a last stand if ever he needed one.

In the bathroom grenades were taped behind the washbasin pedestal. The strip light above the washbasin did not work because the fluorescent bulb had long been replaced by an image intensifier nightsight of a particularly narrow design, supplied by the Czechs some time ago. There was more plastic explosive under the fixed soap dish above the bath and detonators and fuse wire behind the metal rail of the shower unit. Yet there were no obvious signs that the apartment was a veritable arsenal.

When Hashimi had finished preparing his guns he returned them to the chest without the oilskin covering ready for instant access. As he replaced the two drawers he noticed the photograph lying face down in one of them. He turned it over and Sophie gazed up at him with a wide smile and a challenging expression. Slowly he sat on the edge of the bed and looked at it. In one corner was written, 'With all my love.' It was one of her studio shots and he had forbidden her to put his name on for her protection and his. The bitter wrong of that still hit him hard.

He could not keep the photograph; if found it could provide the motive for what he intended to do. But in any event he wanted no reminder. He went into the kitchen and burned the print in the sink. As the photograph curled at the edges it seemed to him that her face contorted with the pain she must have felt before she died. He could no longer look and left it to burn until only ashes were left. He then swilled the remains down the sink.

He went up the stairs where there were three more large bedrooms frugally but adequately furnished. He opened the trap door above the landing with a latch pole, hooked down the metal ladder and climbed up into the loft, finding the concealed light switch behind the nearest rafter. The huge cavity was filled with old boxes and oddments, even an old mattress.

There was plenty of central standing room and Hashimi climbed across the rafters to the brick partition wall of the next house. Behind a packing case he pulled out some loose bricks to reveal the second skin of wall and then started to remove it. He climbed through the small gap to find himself in the loft of the house next door. It was an escape route he had planned years ago when he was at the height of notoriety.

He drew back into his own section, carefully put back both layers of bricks, placed the empty packing case in position and pulled the mattress forward to partially cover that. Springs protruded from the mattress, flock hanging out in great lumps. Hashimi prodded about inside until he located two grenades and yet another gun. If ever he needed to retreat he had weapons strategically placed all the way. He took the gun down to clean and returned it later. After he was satisfied that his retreat was ready he left the house with the duffle bag, caught a number nineteen bus to Piccadilly Circus, entered the public toilets, found a booth, took his sheikh's clothes from the duffle bag and slipped them on. He returned to the Dorchester with only the Browning and the small quantities of explosive, detonators and fuse wire he had removed from the safe house.

7

Jost Kranz stirred his coffee and gazed quizzically across the small café table at the woman opposite him. He preferred to deal with men. She had been introduced to him as Mary McGanly. Her features were Celtic and her eyes wide spread and grey. She was a very attractive woman with lips that twitched with humour as she noticed his discomfort. Jost did not need the distraction she posed; his mission was too serious. She wore a wedding ring but that could be meaningless like her name.

"Why don't you relax? Don't you like women?" She realised that she had asked too pointed a question.

Kranz glared at her. "What has that to do with anything?" His accent was heavy but he was at ease speaking English. "I expected a man. If I am to stay with you it might raise comment."

"I'm a landlady with other guests; there will be no comment." She was slightly dismayed by his attitude, not towards her, but because he was supposed to be a highly trained professional. He was sallow for a German and before hearing him speak she might have taken him for a Greek; his hair was as dark as her own but his eyes were deep brown and searching and his face looked gaunt as if he had recently been ill. His hands were strong, though, and their movement very controlled. Perhaps it was his hands that she should watch. "How long do you need to stay?"

"I don't know. Not yet. I must wait for news from Germany."

Mary McGanly accepted that he meant the German Democratic Republic although he had come in from West Germany. "I'm sorry the first two nights were rough. But we had two guests who overstayed and it would have been a mistake to force them out. These things happen. You still seem worried. Why don't you come out with it?"

"Come out with it?"

"Tell me what's on your mind."

"You are Irish?"

"Yes. Oh, I see." She smiled and her face softened. Almost

coyly she said, "I'm not on the wanted list. Most of the Irish in Britain lead quite normal lives. Irish does not automatically mean I.R.A. I am not being watched if that's what worries you."

"How do you know?"

Mary continued to smile sweetly. "I find that an insult. If you don't like what's being offered go elsewhere. I'm under no obligation to you, or to anyone."

Kranz slowly gazed round the café. He had not raised his voice at any time and, anyway, the place was almost empty. "I'm sorry. But we do have a mutual assistance agreement. It is to the benefit of both of us."

"It is, of course. But that includes mutual trust. If I say I'm not watched then that's it. The moment I think the position has changed you'll be the first to know. Okay?"

"I said I was sorry." Kranz stared at his coffee as if he had transferred his distrust to it. He drank quickly and put the cup down carefully without making a sound. "A great deal hangs on my being here. The timing of my stay has to be absolutely right."

"I know that. I suppose they are sweating over there wondering what it is you have on them. Good. Let them squirm."

"How do you know that?" Kranz leaned across the table so that his face was close to hers. His eyes looked hard as stones. "Who told you?"

Mary did not move. She stared back at him quite calmly, chin cupped in long fingered hand. "It's bloody obvious, for God's sake. We don't have to be told. There's nothing new about it but that won't stop them messing themselves over there. If they're innocent they'll be wondering what's been cooked up against them. If they're guilty they'll be getting no sleep at all. It doesn't matter whether it's true or false; the public love to believe the worst of politicians and they know it. They thought they were getting off the hook and now the nightmares are all coming back. Nobody has to tell us." Mary glanced about her. "We're past masters at misinformation. Better than the Russians." She chuckled. "We have to hope that the American-Irish never find out, bless their naïve little souls."

"This is dreadful that you should know." Kranz was shaken.

"It doesn't matter. The detail is yours and so is the validity. We're just guessing but we've had a lot of practice." She raised her cup and frowned as she saw that it was already empty. "We'd better go. I'll pay but I'll put it on your account."

When they left the café they walked up the Kilburn High Road towards Marble Arch.

"It seems years since you bought me a drink. Thanks, Spider." Bulman took the glass of whisky and threaded towards the bench seat beneath the bottle window through which could be seen the scurrying shadows of pedestrians outside. "Cheers, old cocker." He gazed appreciatively at his first drink of the day.

"Tastes better when I've bought it, doesn't it, George?" Scott smiled wryly; Bulman wasn't mean where it mattered most. He glanced at the clock behind the bar. They were early; in another half hour the pub would be full.

"Ever heard of a bloke called Jost Kranz?" asked Bulman after putting his glass down on the plastic topped table.

Scott mulled over the name. "No."

"Well, give it some thought. A German."

"German, eh! Just shows. With a name like that I thought he'd be Zulu. Why?"

"He came over here and we're trying to find him. No luck so far. Thought you might help."

"If by we, you mean Scotland Yard, Special Branch, DI5 and all the other networks with the queer names, how the hell could I help where they fail?"

"Because you have a separate network we can't always tap."

"You mean the underworld? You're out of date, George. And you know that you are. That was out of order, old son."

"Oh, I know you've retired, but you still have contacts. You can still pass the word around. There's Rex and Knocker and Bluie and all the rest."

"I'm trying to forget them. So let me. Is this joker a villain?"

Bulman rubbed his nose. "Perhaps not the kind you're talking about."

"Sounds as if you shouldn't be telling me about him."

"Balls. He's holed up somewhere and we want to flush him out."

Scott watched Bulman's gloved hand lift his glass. "Well I can't help. Obviously he'll be staying with a sympathiser somewhere."

"A sympathiser, maybe. But certainly not a known one. We've been through them all, even the fringe element. Nothing. He's deep. That means a sleeper's been activated, or someone who has lived here for a long time and has been careful not to attract our notice."

"What does he look like?"

"Only just got the mug-shot. Five-ten, eleven stone, or as our American cousins would put it, about a hundred and fifty-four. Dark hair, sallow complexion, brown eyes. Nothing really known about him."

"There's plenty like that here in Soho. You've got a job on. What's he done?"

"I don't know that either. Might be a case of what he's going to do."

Scott shook his head slowly. "You're useless as a copper. How do you ever catch anyone?"

"So you won't help?"

"Sorry, George. You have the resources, you use them."

Bulman raised his drink again, avoiding Scott's gaze. He was thoughtful, giving Scott the impression that it was not Jost Kranz he was really interested in.

"What's on your mind, George? You look as if you've nicked the church collection. Is it about Betty Moorcroft?"

"Jesus." Bulman was uneasy. "Everyone knows."

Scott grinned. "Look, I wasn't under the bloody bed." Bulman's reaction was so untypical that Scott realised that he had jokingly hit the nail on the head. He wanted to laugh but Bulman appeared too distressed. "Everyone doesn't know, George. Maggie and I have noticed and you've ranted on about Betty a time or two. I'm pleased for you."

"She's married."

Scott said nothing at first. Bulman had old-fashioned values; his conscience was playing him up. In a way Scott was relieved; it meant that Bulman was serious, but it also meant that he saw complications. It would be a mistake to tell someone like Bulman that everyone was doing it these days; marriages were breaking up all around them. "Why not leave it to Betty? She knows what the form is. She'll never forgive her husband over his attitude to her father . . ."

"I've not entered into this lightly, Spider."

"I know that. And so will Betty. Let it run its course." Scott reached for his drink. "It's time you settled down."

"It's a bad way to start."

"Is that all that's on your mind? You're not hung up over the Arab, for instance?"

It was a good ploy. Bulman's expression changed. "Has he been on your mind, too?"

"It's obvious that he topped Janeski."

"Do you know where he is?"

"No."

"You're a lousy liar. It will get out of hand. I'm dreading it."

"So am I. But there's no way to stop it."

"There is. But we have to find him first."

"How hard are you trying?"

Bulman did not answer the question. Instead he said, "Thanks for understanding about Betty. It helps."

Scott nodded. Whether Bulman acknowledged it or not, Hashimi Ross was tied in with the killers of Betty's father and he could not help but reflect on her attitude to Hashimi's success and how it might affect Bulman.

The lilting music of the Chieftains softly drifted through the hotel suite. Hashimi lay on the bed enjoying the reels and the jigs and thinking that the Irish influence in him was stronger than the Libyan. But he knew that was not really true. The music suited his present mood and his mood could change very quickly. He was weary from having kept a distant eye on Phil Deacon's house. He sometimes drove past, or changed his appearance and walked past, once even on the same side of the street. When he did this he always made sure that Vi was not around. She was the one person in the Deacon set-up who might recognise him even through a disguise. He had also followed her at a distance and had made a note of her bodyguard.

He really needed help but there was no one he could call upon for a non-political mission of revenge. On missions there had always been back-up, someone to help out in an emergency, someone to flee to when necessary. The long periods of solitude could better be endured when there was someone eventually to see or a woman to sleep with. There were girlfriends in London who would welcome him, but the idea somehow seemed obscene when his whole object was to settle a score for Sophie. It was as if she was watching him all the time and demanding that, even in this, his whole commitment was to her.

As he was checked in as an Arab sheikh it was difficult to go to the hotel bars and drink. Muslims don't drink. He knew that this was sometimes nonsense and that particularly abroad it was a case of when in Rome. But he could not afford to put a foot wrong. When he had been approached by other Arab guests it had been quite easy for him to converse in Arabic and to identify himself with Libya. It usually kept other Arabs at arm's length; Libyans were troublemakers and the Saudis and those from the Shiekhdoms kept a discreet distance.

Hashimi was completely on his own. If he succeeded in what he was doing there was no safe place for him. He could, of course, return to Libya, but he had no wish to do so. He had suffered full passport checks before but this time it would be very different; it was known that he was here and that he had already killed.

The tape finished and he heard it click off. Although the radio cassette recorder was within easy reach he made no attempt to change the tape. Rain started spattering against the windows and the room slowly darkened as cloud built up. He stretched out to turn on a bedhead light and turned his thoughts once more to Sophie. There was nothing more he could do now until after midnight except prepare and there was time in hand for that.

Paddy O'Dwyer was a declared anglophile. He was never slow to denounce the small minority of troublemakers among the million or so Irish who preferred to live in the United Kingdom and he was always quick to point out the advantages and the easy going hospitality of their hosts. And he had not backed off from fights to prove his point. Twice, Paddy had finished up in a hospital casualty ward for his pro-British views, for he was proud of being Irish and saw no reason why he should not use Irish pubs even if some of them were the meeting ground for extremists. What he would not do, and he had made the point to the police, was to act as informer for them. He had done it once a long time ago and had refused to do it again on the grounds that he had not liked the feeling of betraying a fellow countryman no matter how violent and extreme. It was a view the police appreciated and understood.

In recent years, though, he had quietened down and had largely faded from the scene. For the last year he had been the close companion of Mary McGanly and the rumour was that they could not marry due to a husband still lurking in Mary's past.

However, O'Dwyer gave no impression of being concerned about a husband as he made violent love to Mary on her bed. They usually finished up totally exhausted; this was no exception. They rolled back panting and pulled up the bedclothes as the cold crept into their naked bodies.

O'Dwyer eventually rolled on to his side and propped himself up on one elbow. He reached for something on the sheet. "Here; your earring fell out." He held the gold stud in the palm of his hand.

"Was that the only thing, now?" she quipped, taking the stud from him and fumbling at her ear. He watched as the clothes fell away from her. She had a fine and firm body and it never failed to rouse him. He stretched out a hand but she elbowed him away until she had managed to get the stud in. They fondled each other and embraced but the main passion had, for the moment, passed.

"I've got guests to see to," Mary suddenly said and swung her legs out of bed.

He ran a finger down her spine and tried to slip his hand under her arm. "You have too many Irish staying here," he commented. "That could raise suspicion."

"I'm Irish. It would raise suspicion if I didn't. I keep a balance. We have that German, for instance. A strange one. I sometimes feel we've lost sight of what we are trying to do. Why do we have to have him here?" She had put on her bra and was pulling on her tights.

O'Dwyer threw back the sheet, at last accepting that love-time was over. "We have to integrate where it suits us. They've helped us on occasion." He stood up, a ginger-headed rangy figure of a man with heavily freckled arms; he could not take too much sun. His almost gaunt face had a slightly starved look. He appeared taller than his five feet ten. When he had pulled on his shirt he asked, "Ever hear of Hashimi Ross these days?"

"Hash? The last I heard of him was when the papers said it was he who blew up Albany prison. I haven't heard from him in ages."

There was something about the way she spoke that made O'Dwyer look back across the bed as he pulled up his zip. Mary was facing the window in front of which was an old dressing table; he caught her expression in the mirror. "He hasn't laid you by any chance?" There was a strong edge to his tone.

"Laid me?" Mary reached for her skirt and her face disappeared from the mirror. "My God, what are you saying? An Arab? I'm a good Catholic girl."

"Not an Arab. *The* Arab. He's quite a reputation with the girls. I wondered if you knew first hand."

Mary turned, her eyes blazing. "Don't ever suggest that again. I find it offensive."

"Your anger's a bit late. You're my girl. Just remember it. Have you any idea where he might be?"

"Why ask me? You're more likely to know yourself."

"Jesus, look at that rain." He stared at the window. "I've lost touch. I want to see him, though."

"Well I don't know where he is. Why do you want to see him?"

O'Dwyer realised that he could not suddenly go secretive on her; he had already made her bristle. The boarding house was too useful in too many ways. "I was only joking about you and him. I mean, he's quite a lad." He could see that she did not believe him as she went to the dressing table to comb her hair. He offered a partial truth. "Sammy Tanner asked me to look for him. Apparently the Vicar wants to see him."

"Phil Deacon? He's a creep."

"Maybe, but he's done us favours. Holed up one of the boys once at a crucial time. He doesn't like the Establishment any more than we do, unlike that nutter Reisen."

"Why couldn't Deacon ask you himself? Why through Sammy?"

"I shouldn't think he knows where I am at the moment. I hope he doesn't. But our grapevine is more likely to find Hash than his."

Mary was not forgiving; the truth about Hashimi had hurt. "Anyway, Deacon was paid for that caper."

"That's not the point. We might need Deacon again. He can be useful."

"And Hashimi? What about him? Hasn't he been useful? He can knock spots off some of our boys. He's better than everybody. And that includes you."

O'Dwyer cursed himself for upsetting her at such a time. "He *was* the best. He's lost a lot of friends, forgotten what it's all about. Nobody will touch him these days."

"They were jealous because he made rings round them. And he couldn't stand their back-stabbing."

For someone who had little to do with the Arab Mary was revealing too much. But O'Dwyer bit back his comments; they could come later. "Maybe you're right. Anyway Deacon wants a word with him and Sammy is trying to track him down. If you do pick anything up let me know. We don't want to upset Sammy. Since the police found those two big arms caches we need him more than ever. Besides, Deacon is willing to pay, and that's another thing we need right now: money."

Mary smiled to herself. Hashimi was running true to form. Nobody could find him if he didn't want them to. And if they did he'd wriggle or blaze his way out. "If I hear anything I'll let you know. But I'm not likely to."

"I'm serious, Mary. It's important."

"So am I, and I know it is."

When he looked at her there was nothing to see but agreement, yet he had the strong feeling that she was mocking him somehow. O'Dwyer decided to be more watchful in future.

Driving alone in London on a clandestine mission was always a chancy business. But Hashimi knew all the pros and cons. Everything was a matter of timing. Too long after midnight could invite the police to stop you. Too soon and there were too many people about. A Rolls-Royce would not be stopped but it would be remembered. An old banger was an open invitation for bored police patrols. So the type of car was important. Travel average; it wasn't foolproof but it was safer.

This was an occasion when he could not wear Arab dress without drawing attention to himself. The only issue on which he could be reasonably certain was that Deacon would not have sought police protection; he couldn't ask for it without losing face and Deacon enjoyed his tough image. Deacon's vanity was Hashimi's strongest ally.

The Ford Escort he was driving was his own but the licence, the M.O.T. certificate and the road tax docket were all in the name of Samuel Baker and would check out with false credit cards he carried if he was asked for additional identification. The legend was watertight.

Once away from central London traffic thinned noticeably. It was nearly one a.m. when he approached the outskirts of Wandsworth. He made sure that he kept within the thirty mile speed limit and the survival instinct of years of being on the run guided him to the quieter streets. In one of these he found a parking slot and he slipped the Ford into the gap where it lost identity in the long line of assorted vehicles.

Hashimi climbed out, made certain the street was as deserted as it appeared to be, up-ended the driver's seat and groped among the springs for the explosive, fuse wire and detonators which were taped to the underside. He also produced an old box of fuse matches. He wound the wire round his waist belt and stuffed the explosive in one jacket pocket and the detonators in the other. He locked the driver's door, then went round the car to open the passenger's side. From under the seat he untaped his Browning with silencer fixed and slipped it into his waistband in the small of his back. He locked the door, checked the street once more, stared along the rows of windows, saw no twitching curtains, and then quietly moved off.

His feet were icy cold in sneakers but he could bear that in the knowledge that he could pick up any other sounds. There were plenty of doorways and basements in these old areas and at the first tread of a policeman's feet he would know what to do. He had left himself the best part of a mile to walk, but his movements on foot were more flexible than in the car.

Hashimi approached Deacon's street and slowed his pace.

The area was dead but the odd light still showed behind drawn curtains. He eased his way round the corner keeping close to the railings. Not even a cat or a rat stirred. It was almost too good, as if they were waiting for him but he was hardened to feelings like that. He moved slowly down the street on the side opposite to Deacon's house, which, with its fresh painted appearance appeared spectral amongst the drab hulks of those either side of it. He stood in a doorway for some time just watching the house until he was satisfied that Deacon had placed no guards.

He went down both lines of cars in turn to make sure they were empty, then returned to the house. Satisfied at last he mounted the steps and lost himself in the shadows under the wide porch. He felt a slight twinge of unease. He had not even heard a distant policeman and the luck seemed almost too good.

He wasted no further time. He pressed a short strip of plastic explosive along the line of the crack by the door hinges and another on the lock side. He placed and taped a detonator into each strip, inserted a measured length of fuse wire, and holding his breath, crimped the ends of the detonators with his teeth. Satisfied that the two runs would hold position he crouched in the shadows to listen. Still there was no sound anywhere. He struck the big bulbous end of one of the fuse matches. It burned like a fuse, resistant to sudden gusts of wind. He lit both fuses with the same match, then ran lightly down the steps, the only distinguishable sound in the street being the subdued hiss of the two fuses behind him.

8

Hashimi was halfway to his car when the explosion rocked the neighbourhood. Lights came on all over the district. Windows opened as people were shattered from sleep. A front door opened and a woman bawled down at him, "What on earth was that?"

It was dark on the streets and the woman was silhouetted against her own hall light but she had seen him, if only vaguely. He called back, "God knows. Sounded like a gas main. You'd better ring the police." He continued on without undue haste.

When he reached his car he withdrew his Browning to tape it under the passenger seat. He was glad now that he had parked so far away from Deacon's house. But he had yet to reach the house in Highbury where he would stay the night and where he had left his Arab clothes so that he could return to the hotel in daylight.

On the way back he veered away from the sound of police sirens and reached Highbury without incident. He found a gap, parked and walked back to the house aware that tonight he had taken risks that he would normally not accept on a professional job. Again he was aware of needing help. There was only one man he knew who had the kind of nerve he required. But he could not ask Spider Scott and even if he did he knew that he would be refused.

He slipped the key into the lock, turned it and pushed the door. A chain prevented it opening more than an inch or two. He stood there and quietly cursed in both Arabic and English. He owned the whole house and had seen to the sub-dividing. To give better impression that the house was occupied he had rented out the lower floor through an agent. A condition had been that no chain should be put on the front door but as many locks as required could be used provided he had a set of keys. The agent had explained to the tenants that the landlord travelled a lot and could arrive at any time. The rule had been broken.

He blamed himself for blundering. He should have noticed

the chain was there. He stared at the door then closed and locked it. It would be a mistake to break the chain, and he couldn't risk entering through a window. He went down the steps and walked back to the car. He could not return to the Dorchester dressed as he was. He climbed into the back seat, made sure all the doors were locked, and curled up. Police had a habit of going down a line of cars to try the doors and sometimes to look for road tax dockets. But he had his papers and would have to accept the risk.

As he tried to get himself comfortable and to blot out the cold he questioned his own competence. Was he losing touch or simply out of practice? A pinprick of doubt remained.

Vi shot up in bed and pummelled the curled bulk of Deacon beside her. "Jesus Christ. What the bloody hell was that? The bloody house has been blown up."

Deacon had needed no rousing. He was awake instantly, heart thumping, guessing something of what might have happened but lying still to gather his senses; he had come out of a deep sleep too quickly.

"We've been blown up," screamed Vi in a shaking voice. To confirm her belief a shower of plaster came down on her.

"Shut up, you silly bitch. Listen." There were voices in the house but two of Deacon's men had been given a room so that help was always near. There was increasing commotion from the street. Deacon climbed out of bed and grabbed his dressing gown. Vi, seeing that he was about to leave her fumbled in her bedside table and brought out the lady's pistol.

Seeing her, Deacon ripped it from her hand and threw it on the bed. "Hide the bloody thing quick. That's the last thing you want to wave around; the fuzz will be here any moment. Use your stupid head and calm down." He left the room still struggling with the knot in his dressing gown sash, then went down the stairs meeting an increasing amount of debris and what seemed to be the strong smell of gunpowder. By the time he reached the lower stairs he was stepping over great chunks of plaster, brick and wood. The banister was covered in thick dust and in part was hanging loose.

As the dust-shrouded hall came in sight he saw his two

minders in pyjamas and they turned to look up as they heard him approach. There was no point in asking what had happened; it was too obvious. The steel backed door had been flung straight across the hall, smashed into the rear wall and the strong wood had shattered all over the place; the steel plate looked like a buckled section of a torpedoed warship. The whole door-frame had been blown out together with huge chunks of brickwork. The hall lights glowed feebly through the dust cloud through which, outside the house, could be seen the vague shapes of neighbours who had been violently woken by the blast and were demanding to know what had happened.

Deacon shuffled through the layers of rubble. Part of the hall ceiling was still coming down and plaster hung in strips. Strangely enough he felt more controlled now that he was satisfied about what had actually caused the explosion. A professional job; just enough to let him know that his house was no longer the fortress he thought it to be. There was no need to call the police, they could all hear the sirens approaching fast. Just the same, it looked better to report the explosion and he told one of his men to call the local station before the police actually arrived.

Deacon had no wish to get involved with the locals and he stayed in the hall but he told the remaining man to go out and pacify them, to tell them the I.R.A. had bombed the wrong place, anything, but to keep them out of the house. When he stepped nearer the great gap where the door had been he could see that house lights were on all over the place. He stepped back inside to await the arrival of the police and prepare the lies he would have to give them. No, he had no enemies and had no idea who would do a dastardly thing like this to him. But he knew all right. The Arab.

They had a family meeting later that day. Deacon had hired a firm of cleaners to clear away the mess and a builder friend was already repairing the brickwork and constructing a new front door. Two electricians were running a cable for two powerful lights to be fixed under the porch and which would remain on all night. At the rear of the house similar work was being done.

Deacon used the dining room as a boardroom, with one of his

85

men posted outside to keep the workmen away. Vi was included because she was now very much involved, her life as much at stake as anyone's. She did not like the idea because she wanted no direct participation in her husband's affairs but she accepted the present necessity; she was scared as she had never been before. Deacon's son, Ted, was also present. In his late twenties, he was a thinned down version of his father, an efficient killer with a sharp memory for detail. His cold-bloodedness showed itself through his bleak eyes and through a persistent indifference to most things, bar the family. There was no visible warmth in the man, no emotional outbursts of the kind his father could produce.

Also present was Charlie Harris, a pale-faced, blond-haired psychopath who had the habit of quietly explaining to his victims how they were about to die. Ted and Charlie had stage-managed murders for Deacon so far with a hundred per cent success rate. They were a deadly team, with otherwise nothing in common. Harris was close to being one of the family in Deacon's eyes. Vi kept quiet on the subject.

A glass of water had been placed in front of each one. The table was really too big for the four of them so they had gathered at one end with Deacon sitting on a carver at its head. He stared at the others in turn. This was a time for calmness and family unity. "He's played into our hands," he said. "The alarms stopped him getting in so he's been forced back on a stupid act of bravado. There was no way he could hang about after setting the bomb so this was no attempt to top us. The question is what do we do about it?"

Ted sat back slowly chewing gum and turning a ballpoint between his short fingers. He had no intention of writing anything down, indeed there was no paper to hand, but it was something with which to fiddle. His gaze suddenly shifted from the table to his father. At times even Deacon felt uncomfortable under his son's scrutiny. "What can we do until we know where he is? And what are we doing about finding out?"

"It's in hand," replied Deacon. "I've got Sammy Tanner on the job. We have to wait for the information but meanwhile should prepare against something like this happening again. As from now, we all live in the house. We entrench."

"That's what he wants," Ted pointed out mildly. "He wants us all here under one roof. Trussed chickens."

"You mean you can't handle it?" Deacon was angry.

"Oh, we can handle it. As long as we recognise what he's doing. The bombing wasn't just bravado. It was to show us that he believes he can get us any time. It was to unnerve us and to group us. He succeeded didn't he?"

"What are you trying to say, Ted? We can't leave here. We'd be the laughing stock of the whole neighbourhood. And that's something which can spread fast. If we lose face we lose money and reputation. We go down the drain, son, and fast." Deacon struck the table flathanded. "Dammit, the berk over the road is already complaining about the porch floodlights we're putting in. He says they'll shine right into his bedroom at night. Before this happened he wouldn't have dared open his mouth. I dealt with him but that's what we're up against. If we move out it's for good and with the cry of chicken behind us."

Ted stopped chewing. "Oh, I agree, Dad," he said softly. "All I'm saying is that the Arab knows all this. He's thought it through. He knows what we'll do next and he's right. What he can't know is what we'll do after that."

Vi sat studying her long painted fingernails, her hands not quite steady. She was fast realising that her practice shooting at the makeshift range was not just for fun, that if anything happened to her bodyguard, she might actually have to use her pistol to shoot at someone. The thought made her shudder. She spoke hesitantly. "What about the fuzz?"

"What about them?" Deacon looked menacing.

"Well, shouldn't they be giving us protection? I mean, this Arab is a wanted man."

Three sets of eyes fastened on her and she knew that she had made a terrible mistake. "It was just a thought."

"Keep them to yourself."

"Then what the hell am I doing here?"

"To get through your thick head what we're up against. It's no game. We'll take the Arab okay, but it needs a bit of planning. He thinks he's been clever grouping us like this. It's a big mistake. We'll draw him in like a magnet."

"Yeah." It was the only word Charlie Harris had uttered yet

it carried a convincing menace. All he needed was to be pointed in the right direction to pull the trigger or to use one of his repertoire of murderous tricks.

"What about the Montaya brothers?" Ted asked, looking up sharply.

"Lonnie and Bix? What about them?"

Ted showed surprise. "You can't have forgotten that we used them to find Scott through the Arab's girl. They actually carved her up. Shouldn't we warn them?"

"Where are they staying now?"

"Brixton. Somewhere off Coldharbour Lane."

"Then they should be safe enough. The Arab can't know that we used them and even if he did he'd still want us. We should keep this among ourselves. The Montaya boys will pester us for daily news. They'll be okay."

Ted tapped the table with his pen. "Okay, let's leave it."

"Right," said Deacon. "I'll chase up Sammy Tanner and see if we can speed up finding the Arab. Meanwhile we'll have someone on duty all night and every night. I'll work out a roster."

The blasting out of Phil Deacon's front door was not given a great deal of space in the late morning edition of the *Standard* as it had happened too late at night for the daily newspapers to run a story, but it was picked up by both Bulman and Scott. Bulman called at Scott's office and they went for a short walk to Trafalgar Square, making for the steps opposite the National Portrait Gallery and towards the fountains being whipped by erratic winds.

"Do you know where he's hanging out?" Bulman asked.

"Who? Hash? Didn't you ask me that before?" Scott stepped back as cold spray spread towards him.

"Yes. You lied your head off. We need to find him before he goes too far."

"He's already done that."

"Look, Spider, we're not the only ones to connect him with last night's blow-out. For my money he can take out the whole Deacon clan and do society a favour but that would still leave *him*. It's not just Deacon he needs to worry about. He should be looking over both shoulders."

"I expect he's doing that. Hash is a real pro."

"Don't you think it's gone too far for you to protect him? He's not doing you any favours is he?"

"You have Maggie's outlook. And I fully understand. But what do you want of me? I can't stop him. I've already tried. I could betray him but I won't do that. We're not the only ones who know what's going on. Your boss will know, and certain people at the Home Office will know. Why don't they do something about it?"

"You know why."

"To save their own lousy skins. They're still scared of what the Arab might blurt out if he's pulled in. It's damn all to do with me."

"Yes it is. He's your friend. You're probably the only one who can stop him."

"There's no way I can stop him. And supposing I could? What would happen, George? Hash calls it a day; then what? They'll kindly escort him out of the country? No way."

Bulman was silent. He turned up the collar of his coat. "It's bloody cold out here. They might."

Scott shot Bulman a sceptical look. "It's a bloody big mess isn't it? I can imagine that there are a few people in the Security Service and at the Home Office who must be sweating blood over this. If Hash finishes what he's obviously set out to do there'll be a lot of mud thrown at the police and they're going to strike back at lack of help from Special Branch and DI5. The public outcry certain politicians are trying to avoid might happen anyway. I'm glad I'm out of it."

"You're not out of it, and you know it. You're in it because you're the sort of bloke you are. And you have a special relationship with Hashimi Ross."

"Not now. It's dead."

"Then we're wasting our time out here. Let's get back." But Bulman was smiling quietly to himself as Scott did not answer.

Scott sat in the foyer of the Dorchester. He had no idea what name Hashimi had used to register. When he had left Bulman he had come straight to the hotel. It was a forlorn action to take

89

and one in which he had no confidence. He could not hang around too long without raising questions among the hotel staff. It was around lunch time and he was beginning to feel hungry. He read the *Standard* through twice, but still no one turned up. It was no use; it had been a foolish impulse.

Scott rose just as the occasional curious glance was being cast at him. He went outside and watched the taxis come and go and it was from one of the alighting passengers that he received a greeting. Hashimi paid off the cab and came towards Scott with a smile; he was in his Arab clothes. "I can guess why you're here but you're wasting your time, Spider. Have you eaten?"

"I'm starving."

"So am I. It's been a long cold night."

When they were seated in the restaurant Hashimi said, "You took a long shot."

"It was a crazy thing to do. I was just giving up."

"Everyone needs a little luck some time. It's good to have company."

"You've created your own isolation cell. What made you do it?"

"The isolation or the bomb?"

"You know which."

"I want them to suffer as Sophie did."

"There's too much against you, Hash. And I don't just mean Deacon. Call it a day."

"That's impossible."

"In that case I'm sorry you confided in me."

Hashimi gave a whimsical smile and then ordered wine for Scott. When the wine waiter had gone he asked, "Why? Are you going to shop me?"

"That's not worth a reply. *But why did you tell me in the first place?* There was no need."

"You're the only one I trust and I need a link."

"You could have had that by making contact without telling me where the hell you are staying."

They ate slowly and thoughtfully. Eventually Hashimi sipped his glass of water and said, "You're the only one I can turn to. Not for help. I don't need that. But you'll listen and you'll understand. *You're there.*"

Scott's hunger had gone. He ate because he needed time to think. "You're placing too much responsibility on me," he said at last.

"Perhaps. But who else is there?"

"Why should there be anyone? You chose this dangerous path, and you should walk it alone. Don't drag anyone along with you."

Hashimi laid down his fork and spread his hands in a gesture. "You've proved my faith in you again. Nobody else would have the nerve to say that to me. You don't toady over my money or fear my reputation. I've been surrounded by such people. I need your solidity, Spider; your reliability. I told you where I am because you are the only person I would trust with the knowledge. If I'm wrong about that trust, if you betray me, then there's nothing anyway. The only girl I ever loved was butchered to death. The only true man friend I have is you. That's all I've ever found in life to matter."

Scott was touched by the simple sincerity. It was no use telling Hashimi that he had discovered his values far too late, that there was no way he could bury his violent past. "I'm not as strong as you think. You do realise that even coming here I had to check for a tail? I don't know how far George Bulman will go to find out where you are but you have to accept that he too is my friend. I owe both of you something, and between you, my position is becoming impossible."

Hashimi waved the waiter away as he came to collect his plate. "Listen to me. For years I worked with terrorist groups. They pulled together but not for each other. It was always the *cause* that mattered. That was the be-all and end-all of everything. If someone wavered he became a pariah and was most likely executed. There was no room for doubt. Friendships flourished only as long as the objective remained unanimous. All the passion, all the feeling was in what we were doing. Life didn't matter. We were bloody crazy, Spider. There was no friendship to be had there. I couldn't have talked like this to any one of them. To express doubts was to invite suspicion. To express strong doubts was to commit suicide. I only need you to be at the end of a distress line. Someone I know who'll be there. Someone who will listen even if he does not agree." He paused, hands clenched with the agony of his emotional outburst. "I have to prove to myself that there's trust somewhere."

Scott did not know what to say. He had never seen Hashimi like this before. The man needed help but would not accept help for he recognised the abyss into which he was falling. Comfort in a recognition of a need was all that was left to him. "I'm not a priest," Scott said hoarsely.

Hashimi smiled. "Which one do I go to? A Mullah? Or the Catholic representative of Jesus Christ? I want somebody I can believe in."

Scott inclined his head numbly. "Okay. It won't worry me what you do with Deacon's mob. But the moment someone innocent gets hurt in the crossfire is the time when I shop you, Hash. Understand?"

Hashimi slipped out of his emotional jacket with an effort. "There you go again. That's what I'm banking on. Your word."

Deacon met Paddy O'Dwyer in a basement club near Paddington Station. O'Dwyer held a membership card and drink could be obtained almost round the clock. As they sat in one of the dark corners Deacon turned his nose up.

"Don't knock it, Phil. It suits me and I can't give the wrong image by going too plush. And the whisky isn't watered. Anyway, with the way things are happening to you, you're bloody lucky I'm seeing you at all, so you are. If I'm seen with you by the fuzz questions will be asked and I could be blown."

"I'm not I.R.A."

"Keep your voice down. You're not Band of Hope either. My image is clean. It's the only way I can operate with safety."

"Okay, so you've put yourself out a bit. You'll need me again some time."

"If you're still around," jibed O'Dwyer. "You're leading a charmed life from what I hear."

"Look, is this a knocking game or will you help me? You weren't so bloody cocky when you needed my help."

"That's why I'm here. You want to find the Arab? I can't help but say this, but he's had no trouble finding you, has he?"

Deacon's mouth tightened. "Everyone knows where I live. The address is in the phone book. I've had just about enough of this. How would you like the whisper to go out about what you really do for a living?"

O'Dwyer's face tautened and his eyes blazed. Before he could speak Deacon pointed to the opposite table where a man sat drinking a beer. "He's mine. There's another one outside. No, he didn't need a membership card. Let's say he has a persuasive manner."

O'Dwyer relaxed. "It's taken me twenty-five years to build my cover, and I don't want it ruined by a private feud. It seems to me that the Arab has gone public. He's leaving a trail a mile wide. You can't expect me to be overjoyed."

"If he's left a trail that size it should be easy enough to track down. Stop quarrelling. Look, I'd do it myself but my hideyholes are different from yours. That's why you were so glad to use one after the Harrods bombing. You have your own system and the Arab is part of that. You're much more likely to know where he's gone. You can pass the word around, pick up a whisper. And forget this business of a private fight. It can affect all of us if he's caught."

O'Dwyer mused over it. "I know the Arab is going it alone. If he's gone public in operation then he's gone private in intent. I don't know what you've done to him but I don't envy you your position. I agree it's best swept under the carpet and to do that we've got to find him. From our point of view he's gone wild and we don't like it in case he talks in his sleep."

"So what was all the aggro for?"

"I didn't say I wouldn't help find him. But I have to weigh it against the risks of exposure."

"The risks will be greater if we don't find him."

"Maybe." O'Dwyer shrugged. "He's not the grassing kind. But he does seem to have gone crazy. Anyway, we can do no more yet. It's a matter of patience. He's gone deep and he always did have an extra trick or two up his sleeve. We'll find him though. Where do I find you?"

"Just give me a straight phone call."

"You might be bugged and my accent is a giveaway. I'll see that a note is pushed through your door."

"You'd better make sure it's bloody daylight or someone is likely to get plugged. Let's get out of this place, it's like a coffin."

Hashimi's disguise was simple. He had left the Dorchester in a casual, Savile Row tailored suit. He wore a hat and carried a small paper parcel. He was trying to spread his risks. He was using the house in Highbury more than he had ever used it before. There were times when he must have been seen.

As he caught a cab to the Marble Arch underground car park he ran through the problems of the previous night. He had awakened in the car to a deserted street and a dripping dawn and had shivered violently for several minutes. He still couldn't get into the house without ringing the bell and it had been too early for that. Eventually he had driven off to find a café where he had breakfast. When he returned the chain was off and he had gone upstairs, had a hot shower and slept for a couple of hours.

Before he left the house he had rung the agent who looked after his affairs and insisted that the chain be removed from the door. He had carried his Arab attire in a grip; to have worn it near the house would have been too conspicuous. Changing in public toilets had become routine.

He shook off the recent memory as he now paid off the cab at Marble Arch to find his car. He climbed in and put on a short beard with the use of the rear view mirror. When satisfied he drove off to Wandsworth.

Thirty minutes later he was passing Deacon's house, took quick note of the work that had been done and noticed the new porch lights to which workmen were putting the final touches of plaster encasing the wire. The door had already been replaced as he had expected. A man sitting on the steps watched him drive past with more than casual interest. But Hashimi had long learned the art of picking up vital detail on the periphery of his vision; he had seen all that he needed to see. He turned the corner and came back down a parallel street at the rear of the house.

Finding the nearest tobacconist, Hashimi bought a magazine then asked the woman behind the counter if there were any rooms to let nearby. She referred him to several cards pinned to a noticeboard and he asked her to recommend one. She gave

94

him the address of a boarding house in the street that ran at right angles to the one in which Deacon lived.

It was a seedy place with nothing to distinguish it from the houses on either side. By over-paying Hashimi obtained an upper room that overlooked the street. It was too much to hope that he would have a view of Deacon's house but at least he had a clear view of the street corner. If Vi, during her escorted excursions, was in the habit of going the other way then he was out of luck. But he had done his homework. The main local shops would bring her along this route. Even if she drove or caught a cab to the West End she would probably come this way. He would not have taken the room had he not believed that the odds were in his favour. He already had some idea of her habits by following her before he blew the door out. He left the boarding house and found a serviceable public telephone.

With the help of Paddy O'Dwyer, Mary McGanly was laying the tables in the dining room when the call came through. The telephone was in a small private office off the hall and had an extension in her apartment upstairs.

"I'll get it," said O'Dwyer who was nearer the door.

"Leave it. We don't want everyone to know that you spend your life here."

"Don't we?" He grinned and gave her a pat on the behind as she squeezed past him.

She went to the office; the telephone was on her desk. "Reception. Can I help you?"

"I hope so, Mary," replied the Arab. "When and where can we meet?"

Her hand immediately tightened on the receiver and her gaze shot to O'Dwyer who had followed her into the office. She recovered quickly. "Hold on while I look but I think we're full at that time." She pulled out the guest book and flicked through the pages knowing that O'Dwyer was eyeing her curiously. She checked the bookings. "I thought so. We're full. Will the following week do?"

"Okay," said the Arab. "Make it the place where we used to meet in Maida Vale. Just slip in a time and be careful how you do it."

"I'm holding one reservation in pencil. He's got to let me know by seven this evening. If you ring back after then you might be lucky but I can't guarantee it." She put the phone down as O'Dwyer moved towards her, returned the book to the drawer and headed for the dining room. "I must finish those tables. I'm running late."

"I'll be with you," O'Dwyer said. But before he went through the dining room door he quickly pulled out the reservation book and searched for a pencilled entry. He didn't find one.

9

"I'm here."

Mary McGanly spun round. She had begun to feel like a prostitute standing under the pool of light cast by a street lamp, and she hadn't liked some of the attention she had drawn from passing men.

"Hash! Mother of God. How long have you been standing there? You frightened the life out of me."

He stepped from the shadows of a doorway as she flew towards him, throwing her arms round his neck and holding him fiercely.

"Oh, Hash. Hash. Where the devil have you been? I've missed you so."

He held her close, stroking her hair and patting her back, laughing a little. "I thought you'd forgotten me. It's been a long time."

She was crying. "It's been well over a year. Why haven't you been in touch?"

Because I fell in love with someone else. Really and deeply in love and all you supplied, my darling, was warmth and humour and a need. But there is no way I could have told you that because it would have hurt you. Hashimi expressed his unspoken thoughts by squeezing her with genuine affection. "You know how it is in our game. I've been on the move a great deal." He glanced round. "Let's get away from this light."

"Have you a car handy where we can sit and talk? Hash, it's so lovely to see you again."

His car was round the corner but he did not want her, or anyone, to connect him with the registration number. Mary had too good a memory. "It's too far to walk to and it's the wrong way."

With their arms around each other, her head on his shoulder, they slowly strolled down Maida Vale towards Kilburn, where she had her guest house. "What was the problem when I rang?" he asked. "Who was there?"

She hesitated. "Paddy. Paddy O'Dwyer."

They staggered against a short wall, recovered and laughed. "We must look as if we're drunk," he said.

"I am, Hash. Drunk with happiness. Somehow I didn't expect to see you again."

"It's a good thought to hang on to. With the life I lead I can't give guarantees to anyone. So what's so bad about Paddy being there? He's solid. I'd have spoken to him had I known."

"I didn't want you to."

He noticed the doubt. "Why not?" When she didn't answer he suddenly laughed. "You two are not . . . that's okay, Mary. He'll be around long after I've gone."

"It's not the same for sure. It could never be. God, I wish there was somewhere we could go to bed."

"You mean your place isn't safe any more?"

"Paddy spends a lot of time there these days. He'll be back later tonight."

"You mean you have to account to him? That's not like you."

"He can be awkward. Short-tempered." She stopped walking and swung round in front of him, encircling her arms round his neck again. "I could deal with it if you're coming back."

"I'm on the run. Don't risk your own cover, Mary. Does Paddy know we used to be together?"

"No. And I don't intend to tell him."

He kissed her as she strained against him and they swayed as one for some time. When they broke away breathlessly he realised that he could be making trouble for himself.

"What else is there about Paddy that you're not telling me?"

"Nothing. He was always awkward under the charm."

"Efficient, too. I don't know him all that well but I can guess at some of the capers he's been behind. Do you intend to marry him?"

"How can I? I have a husband somewhere. Anyway, there's no way that I would."

He propelled her forward again. "I've heard about your husband. Everyone has. I don't think he exists. I think it suits you to have one in the background to keep the wolves at bay."

"Maybe. I'd like to think that you came just to see me, but you want something don't you?"

"There was an old house in South Norwood that you used to use. A run-down place that you battened up and made service-able. Is it being used at present?"

"If it is it'll be by kids. It collapsed, so it did. And the bulldozers moved in."

"A pity. I need somewhere like that."

"There's a much better place. There's an old warehouse in the East End. It's been vandalised something shocking. Anything flammable has already gone; a real wreck of a place. There was a cold store unit inside which has been hacked to pieces; even the door has gone and that took some doing. But there's a basement. The door at the top of the steps down to it has gone but once the dust had settled and the local yobos realised that there was nothing left to smash or burn, we had some of the boys go in to build a new, metal door at the foot of the steps. It's burglar proof. To be of any use to us it had to resist everything bar gelly. Does that sound all right?"

"Tell me all you can."

"We've used it when the heat's become too hot for some of the boys. There are crude but serviceable toilet arrangements. It's a big area. Too big really. But it did enable us to put sleeping bags and an oil cooker one end, with a fair sized store of tinned food, tea and coffee. A forty-four gallon drum of water is always kept topped up. The boys go in with a truck and hose it in at night. All servicing is done at night."

"They can still be seen at night, Mary."

"Sure. But it's rarely used and we're talking about a twice-a-year top up. When it is needed it's invaluable. Air holes have been drilled in the concrete above the door but it does get stale down there. The last time it was used, I later heard that the boys would open the door at the dead of night to get some fresh air, and then sleep by day. Sensible."

"You're trusting me a lot."

"Oh, for God's sake, Hash. I'm the quartermaster, I use my own judgment. What are you going to do? Trot off to the fuzz? We have to scratch each other's backs. Anyway, it's more than that isn't it? We're interdependent. We damn well have to be."

"Can I take a look at it?"

"The keys are back at my place. I can sort something out about you getting them."

"How many sets?"

"Two. One lot is in a safe deposit. I'm given good notice if there's likely to be a need. Logistics want all the time they can get if a caper is on and that's part of my job."

"And Paddy's?"

"And Paddy's." She was aware of hesitating. "Keep away from him."

"Why?"

"Just do."

"I need to know if you can't trust him, Mary. I don't want slip-ups."

"All you need to know is that he does his job and as far as that's concerned he is to be trusted all the way. Beyond that I won't go. He's never been mad keen on inter-liaison; he blows hot and cold on it. How long will you need the place?"

"A few days. I'd like to take a look tomorrow if I can. Any chance of getting the keys now?"

"We'll stop short of the house. You keep well out of sight while I go in. If I come out again I'll have them. If I don't it's because I can't."

"You mean Paddy will be there."

"I don't like to think of you and him at the same time. Can't we fix up something together, Hash? I'm burning for you."

"The problems seem to be your end. You must sort them out and then give me the safe times for me to ring you."

She smiled sadly. "I never expected a phone number from you. I don't think I've ever had one."

"It never stopped us though, did it? Paddy seems to be a new problem."

Mary didn't bite. She hung on grimly to Hashimi's waist as they went towards the guest house. "Just one thing. The area around the warehouse is due for re-development. It's been sold to some speculator. But it takes years for these things to go through. We're looking for somewhere else just in case. Now let's hope Paddy isn't back."

Hashimi was worried by her concern. Mary could handle

anyone and he could not recall seeing her so agitated before. Paddy had obviously become a problem to her.

Bulman did not make the mistake of having Scott followed when he went to search for Hashimi. Scott would most probably have found out and a good relationship might have been ruined even if the friendship somehow survived. It would have been a big mistake. Nevertheless he would have laid odds that, after their discussion about the Arab, Scott would have sought Hashimi out if he knew where he was; Scott cared about his friends whichever side of the law they fell, and he did not forget his debts. But there would come a time, if things got too bad, and he was sure that they would, when Scott would have to stop sitting on the fence.

Meanwhile Bulman was still under pressure from Sir Lewis Hope to find Jost Kranz and so far he had drawn blank. Because of the secrecy Hope sometimes placed round many of his requests there were often restrictions on official nationwide searches instigated by him. Hope wanted it all ways; success without the full usage of facilities.

It was a ridiculous situation and inevitably it led Bulman to wonder what was behind it. When a criminal went into hiding someone, somewhere, knew and could recognise him. But the German seemed to have arrived with no record or even a guarantee that his name actually was Kranz. And even if it was he might not be using it here.

Bulman was in a position of stalemate, and Betty Moorcroft was quick to pick up his mood when they met, and they were doing that more frequently. She was getting to know him and had learned that when George was engrossed as he had been so much lately, something was going to happen. She could only hope that it would be nothing like what had so tragically happened to her father. She did not voice these fears to him but the slow build up in him was like an internal combustion; eventually it would burst out with a roar.

Hashimi drove along the old wharf. There were potholes all over the place as if someone had been having fun with a three inch mortar. Recent rain sprayed from under his wheels as he eased his way along, the springs groaning beneath him. The short row of derelict warehouses was deserted but a little nearer to the river there was activity around some buildings not yet in a state of decay. Life began to appear from that point on. Above the roofline cranes reared like predators waiting for pickings from the river. When he stopped the car he could hear the distant hum of hidden traffic.

Hashimi pulled up and climbed out. The Thames was out of sight and he could hear it slapping against the wharf. He was in a small, reasonably isolated oasis. After the initial vandalising, he guessed that the distance from the nearest dense living area had discouraged vandals from continuing with an over-kill of condemned property.

He walked along trying to avoid the puddles and found the warehouse Mary had described. It was still supported by its original steel frame but was quite clearly deserted. Even the breeze-block walls had been attacked but they had stood their ground and apart from huge chunks hacked out here and there, appeared fairly solid. The corrugated iron roof had not escaped damage and great holes had let in the rain which swilled over the concrete floor. There was refuse everywhere; empty drums and smashed crates. The huge double sliding doors had long since gone, together with the metal runners. It was a dismal, depressing place which reflected nothing but failure. It was ideal.

The steps to the basement were at the far left rear of the site. In the opposite corner the remains of a cold room gaped out in an agony of brutalised concrete and remnants of metal shelves, too twisted to be of use. Again the door had gone. Hashimi went down the chipped steps to a foul smell of animals and humans. There was a right-angled bend in the stairs which placed the door out of sight. Avoiding the worst patches he fumbled for the keys and tried to insert the larger one into a keyhole at the base of the door. The keyhole was bunged up and he spent some time unblocking it with a long bladed pen-knife. He closed his mind to the stench and turned the key. The keyhole at the top of the door was clear. Following that he turned the middle key and pushed the door. It opened more easily than he had expected. The door itself was deeply scratched but whoever had installed it had known their business. It was safe.

The basement hide-out was not as bad as Hashimi had expected. There was plenty of room, with bed rolls neatly strapped, plenty of tinned food and the means to prepare it. There were mugs and plates and utensils in an old dresser. He tapped the water drum which was up-ended on to a crude but serviceable platform. A tap had been inserted near the base. At the far end were screens formed by old crates and behind them was a crude arrangement of washbasins and a chemical toilet.

Hashimi stood in the rough centre of the room and took stock. As a hiding place it was ideal yet there were doubts in his mind. But he knew that he would not find anywhere more suitable in the time he had in mind. Mary had given him a fairly accurate description even though the outside was more neglected than perhaps she knew. Yet the foul approach was probably one of the biggest safety factors. He had hidden in sewers and in hovels far worse than this. But it was not himself he was worried about.

He went round the walls. He needed a chain and a strong wall staple. He would have to get them and return that night. After locking up he went back up the steps and breathed a little more freely once outside. He walked back thoughtfully to the car. Inside he groped under the shelf and produced a radio telephone. It would now play a useful part in what he must do.

Detective Chief Inspector Reeves called on George Bulman late that day. He tapped on the open door and stood there until Bulman called out, "Hello, Jack. How's the bomb business?" Reeves came in and sat down after glancing towards Haldean's open door.

"Everyone looks at that door," Bulman commented drily. "It's giving Haldean a complex. He thinks he's not trusted." Raising his voice, he added, "Better than having the door closed; this way we know he's not listening at the keyhole." He grinned at the flow of expletives coming from Haldean's office.

"He's to be trusted, then?" asked Reeves, catching on.

"Just about. But keep your voice down. Now, what's happening at the Anti-Terrorist Squad?"

"Not a lot. You expressed interest in the Wandsworth bombing. Deacon's place. Any particular reason, guv'nor?"

"There's always a reason."

"I see. Secret Service stuff. I'm never quite sure whether you're still a copper."

"Nor am I, Jack. What've you got?"

"Strange business. Sort of contradictory. I don't think it's really one for the Squad. It's more likely a gangland thing than terrorism, but we were called in because the locals were puzzled. The right amount of explosive was used to blow the door. Not too little, not too much. An expert job. What contradicts it is the use of an ordinary slow fuse. That's odd."

"How do you mean?"

"A terrorist would use a radio control detonation, not a burning fuse."

"It's a built-up area; wouldn't that make it difficult?"

"If he intended to use U.H.F. he'd need a clear passage. Buildings could obstruct. Which means he would have had to be in sight of the place and, therefore, too near for a reasonably safe getaway. If he used a simple high frequency then it would be okay in a built-up area. A bloke who can gauge his quantity so accurately would know about this unless he was dead lucky. Luck when using explosive inexpertly is usually bad luck."

"I'm not sure I know what you're suggesting."

Reeves looked resigned as he said, "He was either a lucky mug or an expert trying to mislead us. I reckon he is so good at it that he was trying not to leave his trade-mark."

Bulman eyed Reeves for a few moments. "Why are you looking at me like that?"

"You have an interest in this which you're keeping to yourself. There's a rumour around that it could have been the Arab."

"The Arab? Hashimi Ross? Where the hell did you get that from?"

"There're a few stories floating. Some from Murder Squad about obstruction from high places. This one's come straight out of Special Branch."

"They must be slack down there. The silly season."

"How can you be so positive unless you know something we don't?"

"I just can't see what the Arab would be doing with Deacon. Can you? I mean, he'd have blown up the whole bloody house."

Reeves uncrossed his long legs and stood up. "Okay, guv'nor.

But you can't expect us to help you. I sometimes think that half of police time is taken up with inter-departmental jockeying."

"God forbid," Bulman retorted. "But thanks, Jack. Appreciate it."

When Reeves had gone Bulman wondered just how long the cloak of secrecy could hang together before it exploded like Hashimi's bomb.

Because of parking difficulties Vi Deacon often used a cab to take her on her numerous shopping expeditions, rather than use the Jag or Merc, even though she was chauffeur-driven. She disliked having a chauffeur or anyone with her on these trips, but what made her particularly unhappy was Deacon's insistence that she now had a double bodyguard. One had been intrusion enough but to have two in the cab with her was almost more than she could bear. Her fear of what had happened just about controlled her decision not to argue about it; provided that when she was free of the cab they did not stay too near her.

Hashimi had learned about the cab, and its use indicated Vi's intent if not her actual destination. He could see the cab go past the corner from his boarding house room and he was now spending more time there than at the Dorchester or the house in Highbury. When Vi went past, Hashimi would rush down to his car and follow, having fixed a parking slot by paying extra to the boarding house proprietor.

It was not always easy. He dare not get too near with two gunmen in the cab on the look-out for anyone following, but over a period of a few days he developed a judgment, once the initial direction was established, which enabled him to drop back to a safer position.

For the last two days Hashimi had felt the time to be right. There had to be certain pointers and, as always, a certain amount of luck. He saw the cab go past towards Deacon's house and instead of waiting he went straight down to the car. It was another ten minutes before the cab reappeared. He pulled out and followed, keeping well back.

There was nothing regular about the routes the cabs took, except for the early stages through Balham or Clapham South from where they could branch north or south for a good selection of shops without going into the West End of London. Today the cab headed up Balham Hill and turned right at Cavendish Road, eventually to cut down Kings Avenue heading south-east towards Streatham. Hashimi was grateful for the choice of main roads. It was much easier to form part of the scene than by using the short cut minor roads which would have exposed him more easily.

The cab continued direct south down Streatham Hill and the wide stretch of Streatham High Road. Vi had not come quite so far south before and Hashimi had to concentrate to hold on without being obvious. At one time he lost her but picked her up again at traffic lights. This, the main London road, was always busy. He tucked in behind a double decker bus for a spell and then closed up a little as traffic speed generally dropped.

When the cab found a gap to do a U-turn Hashimi continued on but used his mirror to see Vi and her minders alight outside Pratts, the big departmental store. Hashimi took the next turning left. He could afford to take the risk of illegal parking because he had false number plates but he still had to find a gap and he had to drive some way before he did. He locked the car and walked down the incline towards the main road. He was wearing his short beard and a hat, and a Burberry over his smart suit. He carried a briefcase.

Hashimi sighted one of the bodyguards outside the main entrance of Pratts and slowed his pace. Approaching from the opposite side of the street he stopped well before he was actually facing the store. There was adequate reason for doing so; both sides of the street were lined with shops and it was possible to place himself obliquely to a shop window to pick up a reasonable reflected image of the bodyguard.

He did not know how long Vi would spend inside but it appeared to be a high quality place so Hashimi took an optimistic view. From previous experience he had learned that Vi extracted the maximum time. He looked around for a policeman and agreed with the old adage that there was never one around when wanted. He moved and then returned, and then joined a bus queue for a spell. But if Vi's man was doing his job properly he must eventually notice the Arab.

When Hashimi finally saw a bobby coming his way he approached diffidently as if not sure of himself. "I don't know how to say this," Hashimi said awkwardly.

"Try it straight, sir." The policeman had already categorised Hashimi as 'well off'.

"Don't make it obvious but take a look at the man waiting outside Pratts. Please don't let him see you."

The constable turned carefully, not knowing how seriously to take the request. "The bloke with the dark brown coat?"

"To the left of him and behind. A blue raincoat and hands in pockets."

"Right. What about him?"

"He's armed."

"*What?*" The policeman eyed Hashimi closely. "You having me on?"

"No. Of course he might be one of your chaps. But he really is armed." Hashimi gave a show of gaining confidence. "I was walking along. That fellow was standing where he is now. The man in front of me bumped into him as he moved across the pavement looking the other way. At the time his coat was undone and it pulled back with his jacket as the other man went past. I clearly saw a gun protruding from a holster. It was momentary but definite. He did his coat up as soon as the other man had gone after a quick apology. I don't think anyone else saw; I just happened to be in the right place."

"Are you absolutely sure, sir? Could it have been a pipe or something?"

"In a shoulder holster? Look, I'm so sure that I've been looking for a policeman ever since. I could have pushed straight on but it would have played on my mind. I'm not a nutter."

"No, sir. Which side was the holster?"

"The right shoulder. He must be left-handed."

"I just hope you're right, sir. Would you mind waiting there." The policeman spoke rapidly into his transmitter, his back turned to the man across the street, and then faced Hashimi again. "A squad car's on it's way. I'm walking back a bit then I'm crossing over. Stay fairly close."

"You sure you need me?"

"I just want to make sure you're not kidding me." They crossed the street further up and well away from the store and walked slowly along until they were about some thirty yards from Vi's minder. Within three minutes a blue saloon car approached, stopped outside the store and two men stepped out. The uniformed policeman with Hashimi hastened forward as he recognised them as plain clothes men from his own station; his description must have been good for the two detectives went straight up to the minder and one of them flashed a warrant card. A few words were exchanged before the minder tried to run for it. The detectives chased and grabbed him but the minder struggled hard. The policeman joined in and the four men attracted a big crowd in a matter of seconds. Passing traffic slowed down as the fight went on.

One of the detectives bawled at the gathering crowd, "Get back, he's armed." Children were pulled away protectively and the crowd widened out spilling on to the street and producing a blast of horns from passing motorists. Having effectively removed one of the opposition Hashimi slipped behind the crowd and into the store. Almost immediately he saw Vi approaching with the second bodyguard behind her. He drifted into the gathering crowd of shoppers who were making their way towards the doors attracted by the commotion outside.

Not wanting to go on to the street again, Hashimi slipped to one side of the crowd now blocking part of the entrance. He watched Vi and her bodyguard who were now lurking at the back of the crowd by the doors. Whether the minder had sight of his colleague or whether he simply gained an inkling of what might be happening outside was impossible to judge but he suddenly whispered in Vi's ear and forced his way through to see what was happening outside.

Hashimi wasted no time. He hastened round the back of the shoppers now pushing forward, and stood close behind Vi. "One scream and I'll shoot your spine out." He thought she was going to faint as she instantly recognised his voice. He put out a hand to support her elbow. "I've nothing to lose and I don't mind shooting my way out. You'll be okay as long as you're not stupid. Now walk back into the store. I'll be right behind you all the way."

As word spread that a gunman was outside, even the ground floor shop assistants were having difficulty standing by their departments. Attention was directed to the front of the shop as Vi and Hashimi headed back searching for the nearest emergency exit.

Outside the struggle had finished but Vi's man had put up quite a fight in the knowledge that the penalty would not be light when the gun was found on him, but he feared Deacon's wrath even more than the law. By the time the second bodyguard had forced his way through his colleague was up against the plain police car, legs and arms splayed while he was searched and disarmed. A gasp went up from the crowd as the gun briefly appeared. The second man took stock, saw his colleague's bloodied face and dishevelled clothes and wondered what had gone wrong. Whatever it was had been nothing to do with Vi. But by the time he had struggled back his charge was nowhere in sight. Feeling sick with fright he scanned the shoppers once more to make sure he had not missed her then hurried back through the store. He wouldn't have put it past her to have gone back to do more shopping just to make it difficult for him. But he was deceiving himself and while he searched for her he somehow knew that he wasn't going to find her. He weighed up the possibility of just opting out rather than report back to Deacon.

The police siren sounded as the blue van screamed through the traffic to pull up behind the police car. By now the gunman was handcuffed and was bundled into the van with two uniformed men and the doors were closed. The van roared away, siren wailing, flasher revolving and the two detectives turned to the uniformed man who had radio'd in and who was now collecting his helmet which had been knocked off in the struggle. One of them patted him on the arm. "Nice work. Your informant was observant. Where is he?"

The officer looked around. "Must have been too much for him. Anyway, he was right."

"Up to a point. I thought you said our man had a shoulder holster; right side. So how come there was no holster and the gun was in his hip pocket?"

10

"Put your seat belt on."

Vi sat white-faced beside Hashimi in the car. Occasionally she nervously glanced at the protruding gun in his waistband. He had very deliberately detached the silencer first, explaining to her that he did not want it to catch if he had to draw the gun quickly. He wanted her to see it to unnerve her for they had a long way to go through traffic.

"I said put your belt on and stop trying to weigh your chances. You have none."

She fumbled with the strap and clicked it on. "You're going to kill me. You won't let me go now." Fear was back in her voice. There was nobody to blame for her being here, not even her attitude to her bodyguards. They had all been outwitted.

"I'll only kill you if you're stupid. Pull yourself together. If you had a hand in killing my girl you'd already be dead. Now cool it and just be a good girl. Where's your shopping by the way?"

Feeling slightly reassured she said, "It's being delivered. Your luck will run out, you know."

Hashimi drove along the back streets as far as he was able. "The only luck I had was when you came in view when you did. But it would have made no difference. I'd already dealt with the one bloke and would have had no problem dealing with the other one."

He was forced back on to the main London Road in order to find direction and he drove silently for some time. They were past Brixton before he said, "Your minders may be quick on the trigger if given the chance, but they have no idea about bodyguarding. They were useless. Phil should send them on a course; there are some quite good schools around. You should not have been left alone in the store."

"One of these days you're going to be too bloody clever."

"Got your nerve back? Then stop your hands trembling.

You've got spirit though, Vi. Hang on to it. You're going to need it."

As they approached central London they ran against the rush-hour traffic heading south.

"Where are we going?" asked Vi, more concerned now that the direction was baffling her.

"The East End."

When they eventually reached the wharf some forty minutes later Hashimi was tired but his vigilance did not ease. He had stopped well short of the derelict warehouse. They sat there until Hashimi was satisfied that the place was deserted, then he said, "Unstrap, pick up your handbag from the floor and pass it to me." He had made her drop it as soon as they had entered the car.

"I need the bag, for Christ's sake. A woman needs things." She groped on the floor of the car.

"You'll get it back."

"May I take my handkerchief from it? I want to blow my nose."

"Sure. Go ahead."

Vi was quick but not quick enough. She managed to get the gun out and had been steeling herself for this very moment. She even got a shot off as he grabbed her hand. The bullet whistled wide of his head and penetrated the roof of the car. Even with a small gun the roar was ear-shattering in the confined space. She struggled but Hashimi bent her wrist back until the gun was pointing at her own face. "Okay," he said. "Pull the trigger again."

She stared at the .22 aperture as if it was a cannon, her eyes widening with fright.

"You want me to squeeze it for you?" he asked her.

"Please don't. DON'T."

"You try to blow my head off and you say don't. Go on, Vi, pull it or drop it."

She released her grip and he carefully took the gun from her, examining it with some contempt. "Now we wait to see if anyone heard the shot. You had better hope that nobody did."

They sat there for fifteen minutes. Vi had her hands to her face and was close to tears. Hashimi sat with his window down listening and apparently paying no attention to her. "You're lucky," he said at last. He took the keys from the ignition. "Out you get and don't be so daft as to run. You won't get far in those heels." He climbed out and came round the other side to help her but she thrust his hand away. He led her towards the shell of the warehouse.

She didn't take real interest until he guided her inside and then she stood still, gazing about her. "What the bloody hell is this?"

"It's an old warehouse."

"I can see that. What are we doing here?" Realisation was dawning slowly.

"Come on. Let's get it done. There's all mod cons."

"Shit. You bastard. I suppose it's all right for you lot; your standards are in the sewer."

"Be careful, Vi. Don't ever forget I'm a man of violence."

He took her arm and gripped it tight when she struggled, propelling her forward to the steps. When they reached them he said, "You can walk down or I can push you."

She turned, her face contorted and he thought she was going to be sick. "I can't go down there. The stench is dreadful."

"Close your mind to it. Get going."

"I can't. It's making me ill."

"Then you've developed a weak stomach since your childhood days. I know your background, Vi. You've known worse. Now move or you'll finish up in it."

She went down with a handkerchief covering her nose. At the bottom she reeled back against the wall while he opened the door.

"It's better inside," he said and pushed her through, turning one of the locks behind him.

The air was stale but better than when Hashimi had first come here. He showed her where everything was and she began to comprehend with increasing horror. "I brought some books in," he said as if the gesture made up for everything else. "And I've also supplied a good gas lamp with spare canisters. There's no heating but plenty of blankets and it doesn't get so cold down here. It's well insulated."

She stared about her with disbelief. "You can't leave me here. It's a bloody pigsty. I would die down here."

"Sit down in that chair there." He pointed to a battered armchair. "SIT!" he bawled. "You're pushing me too far."

When she sat he pulled a thin steel chain from the old dresser and padlocked her ankle while she sat cursing at him.

"Nice ankles." From his crouched position he looked up at her. "Nice legs too, Vi. You've got a good figure."

She stopped swearing and looked nervous. She pulled her legs together. "Oh, God," she moaned. "You wouldn't."

"Don't tempt me. Anger turns me on. Understand?" He had read her absolutely right; she was now more concerned about what he might do to her than where she was. He fastened the chain to the stout staple he had driven into the wall and explained.

"The chain will let you get anywhere you need to go except too near to the door. I don't want you banging on it. There's little likelihood but someone might just hear you if you did that. You can scream and shout as much as you like. The place is virtually sound proof. These walls are solid; that's why they stood up to the treatment they've had."

She glared at him in disdain. "You accuse my Phil of being a killer. What are you then? You're worse. This is torture. Inhuman."

"Torture is what was done to my girl. I've never tortured anyone in my life."

"You've put the fear of God into them. On planes, in embassies. You've frightened them to death."

"You should have done your homework better, Vi. Maybe I should have taken a photo of what they did to Sophie. You'd be sick then all right. You want me to give you the detail?" When she dropped her gaze he continued, "You'll stay here until Phil comes up with who tortured her. If he doesn't then you'll know he doesn't care about you enough. Think about it."

As he walked towards the door and the final impact of being left alone struck her, she leapt from the chair and ran after him. He increased his pace and she flung herself forward so that the tightened chain jerked her leg from under her and she fell on her face.

Hashimi stopped and looked back. Vi was lying with hands

stretched out and he noticed that two of the blood red nails had broken. Her face was sideways on the concrete. She lay mouthing obscenities at him, her lips drawn back like a dog's. As her panting eased she pushed herself up on one elbow and winced as the chain bit into her ankle. She looked down the line of her body. Her skirt was ruckled, showing a long line of thigh, and one shoe had come off. In a half sob she cried out, "Look what you've done to my bloody tights. *Look at them.*"

Hashimi smiled politely and continued to the door. Vi started to scream out, one piercing sound after another, her hands flailing against the floor. Before he left she bawled out, "Help me up, you bastard."

"And get a knee in the crutch? See you. Be lucky."

Hashimi closed the door quickly behind him. Vi was screaming again. He applied all three locks and went back to the car. He drove to Marble Arch, parked the car and removed the beard, placing the radio telephone in his briefcase before he left the underground car park. He walked to the Dorchester feeling he needed freedom of movement. Once back in his room he used the portable telephone to ring Phil Deacon.

A cold-blooded voice answered. Hashimi asked, "Are you Deacon?"

"Yes. Who are you?"

The voice was too young. "Phil?"

"No, Ted. I said who are you?"

"I know you did. Go get your father."

"Just who the hell do you think you're talking to?"

"You just told me. And you very well know who I am. Now go get him."

"You bastard."

"That seems to be the limit of your family vocabulary. Now get him or you'll be one Deacon less."

Hashimi heard the thump of the phone being banged down. Deacon came on, gruff and subdued. "Have you got Vi?"

"You know I have. I want the names of the men who tortured and killed Sophie under your instructions."

"Nobody tortured anyone under my instructions."

"Don't make it difficult, Deacon. Just give me the names and where I can find them."

"I'm not responsible for what he did."

"He? Don't bullshit me. It took two to do what was done to her. One held her while the other one did the knife and cigarette work. If you string this out I'll do to Vi, cut by cut, burn by burn, blow by blow what was done to Sophie."

"I don't know where they are. I need time to find out. It went wrong; why can't you leave it alone?"

"As you would if it had happened to Vi? And it's going to happen, Deacon, if you don't come across now."

"They were casual labour. They're not my boys. Which is why I don't know where they are. Look, I'll see what I can find out. Give me a couple of days."

"You can give me the names now. The addresses by to-morrow."

"I'm not sure what the names are. You know these jokers, they use anybody's name. I'll get them. But don't harm Vi. She's done nothing to nobody."

"Nor had Sophie. Deacon, I know you're lying your head off and playing for time. I'll give you exactly twenty-four hours' worth. The only one it will really affect is Vi. I'll ring this time tomorrow. If you haven't the answers by then I'll send Vi's first instalment to you in the post. First class. She's broken the nails of two of her fingers by the way but you'll be able to see that for yourself. Either way." Hashimi cut out.

Gerald Sanger was very senior in the hierarchy of the Security Service and had direct contact with Sir Lewis Hope. He was a highly efficient career man and had been with the organisation for many years, having spent quite a few of those in the field with DI6 before being put to grass with internal security. He had come to report the result of a protracted surveillance on an American businessman whom the F.B.I. had tipped off as being a highly suspect subversive in the field of under-the-counter trade deals with the Eastern Bloc.

Sanger came behind the desk. He had a sheaf of photographs in his hand which he placed in front of Hope one at a time, giving a brief report on each. A short man of slight build, and receding grey hair, there was a smugness about him as he laid another shot on Hope's desk. "That's particularly interesting," he remarked quite mildly.

Hope gazed at it. "Well we already knew he was staying at the Dorchester."

"Not Spooner. The Arab behind him."

"Is this a guessing game? London is full of Arab sheikhs. That hotel's owned by one."

"A sultan, actually. You don't recognise him, sir?"

Hope came to life. "Good Lord! Can it possibly be?"

"Hashimi Ross. You've got to hand it to him. The Dorchester. You'd expect him to be in some underground doss-house, or staying with unmarked friends."

Hope picked up the glossy photograph and studied it. He smiled slowly. "Well I'm damned. Well that's the way it sometimes happens. Has he been followed?" There was more than a touch of concern in his voice.

"I've only just learned where he is. Our job was Spooner. I don't think anyone else has picked up the significance of the man behind him. I came straight to you as soon as I'd checked with file mug-shots. He wears so many disguises that he's difficult to pin-point physically. But it's him all right."

Hope could not believe his luck. "Good work, Gerald. First class."

"Shall we pull him in?"

Hope jerked in his seat, the smile instantly leaving his face. "No. No. I don't want him brought in."

"But he must be here for a purpose. That man's the most dangerous around."

"I know that. There are reasons. I just don't want him touched right now. The time will come."

Sanger looked doubtful. "He's slippery. Shall we put a team on him?"

Hope thought carefully. "He'd know. It wouldn't take him long to twig a tail."

Sanger agreed. "What then? Keep the hotel under surveillance?"

"No. We were lucky that he didn't spot the photographer."

"Oh, he was in a Telecom van. We must do something or we'll lose him."

Hope swivelled round in his chair, still holding the glossy. "See what you can do inside the hotel. Have a word with the management. All we need to know is the first sign of the Arab checking out. As soon as we know that we'll despatch a team to see where he goes. But the signal must be prompt."

"All right. But it's dicey. He may suddenly pay up and leave."

"There can be a hiccup over his account. Look, book one man into the hotel ready for instant action. I don't want the Arab suspicious at any time. Check what accommodation we have near the hotel. And designate a standby team."

"Right you are, Sir Lewis. He can, of course, do a lot of damage meanwhile."

"That's an acceptable risk. Take all surveillance off Spooner or Ross will pick it up and think it's for him."

Sanger did not argue even though he disagreed. He did not know what was in Hope's mind and on the basis of the instructions he'd received, he did not want to know. To let the Arab roam at will was crazy.

"One more thing," said Hope. "I don't want George Bulman to know about this. Or anyone else. This is between the two of us."

"I have no dealings with Bulman; have never considered him as belonging. But I take your point, sir."

"It could be a vital one, Gerald. Between these four walls. That's a priority order." Hope had thought less of using someone like Deacon against what he considered to be dangers like those posed by Bulman. Belatedly, he had realised that he could fall into the same trap as Murison. Yet the temptation was always there. He began to perceive that there might be another way, more subtle, and ultimately more effective.

Phil Deacon called a meeting with his son Ted and Charlie Harris. It was a tense occasion. The three men sat at the end of the table and Harris listened to the other two swearing and making promises of what they would do to Hashimi once they caught up with him. When they had vented their anger Harris slipped in quietly, "We have to find him first."

It was a reality they had to face, and they quietened down.

"We've got to get Vi back," Deacon said obviously. But it was enough to get them going.

"I take it you've no idea where she is?" asked Charlie.

"No and there's not much time to find out. That butcher starts sending her home in instalments this time tomorrow."

"Will he do it?" Ted seemed to hold doubts.

"He's broken into the house, scared the living daylights out of Vi, and smashed some of my records. He's killed Salter, blown our bloody door in and snatched Vi. He'll do it. I don't see how we'll find out where she is in the time. And he knows it. What do we do?"

Ted, still seething at the way Hashimi had dealt with him said, "We'll have to give him the Montaya brothers."

Deacon scowled. "That won't bring Vi back. He wants us as well. He wants all of us. I don't think he'll let her go."

"Nor do I, but we've got to do it. If we give him the Montayas he'll go for them. We could be waiting."

"He'll be expecting it," Harris said quietly.

Deacon rubbed his face. "I wonder if we should warn them? It would give us more gun power."

Harris shook his head. "They'd be off. We'd be left on our own. On the other hand if we scare them off we could take over their pad and wait for the Arab to turn up."

"Supposing we offer to take out the Montayas ourselves. Guaranteed results. Wouldn't that take him off our backs?"

Deacon and Harris greeted Ted's suggestion with silence. After a while, following the doubtful glances passing among them, Deacon slowly shook his head. The two younger men were cunning and they could handle a situation, but his experience was the greater and in matters like this they listened. "It's not what he wants. He's judge, jury and executioner. He wants us and he wants us to be the last. It won't work but I'll offer it. We've got to be resigned to hand up the Montayas. It'll give us breathing space but let's sort out a trap. There'll never be a better chance. It'll be the one time when we'll know where he's going."

"Do you feel like a cup of tea?"

"Tea?" Bulman stared at the phone as if it had insulted him.

"The pubs aren't open, guv'nor. Coffee then." Detective

Chief Inspector Reeves grinned at his receiver knowing that Bulman couldn't see him.

"Is it worth it, Jack? I can get tea up here."

"There's a place in Victoria Street where they do very good cream doughnuts. Cornwalls I think it's called. I've got to go out. I can see you there in ten minutes. It's on me." Reeves put down the phone before Bulman could answer.

Bulman glanced at his watch. He stood up and bawled at Haldean's door, "I'm going out for tea and doughnuts." He could hear Haldean laughing long after he had closed the door.

The urns were steaming on the counter when he went in and condensation dripped down the plate glass windows. Reeves was seated at a table too small for him but had managed to keep a seat vacant in the crowded café. Reeves ordered two coffees and doughnuts as Bulman wedged himself into the cramped space.

"You must be up to your eyeballs in debt to tolerate a place like this. It's for pygmies," Bulman moaned.

"I thought you'd like it. I have something that might interest you." Reeves bit into his doughnut to keep Bulman waiting but when he spoke again he kept his voice well down. "You still interested in Phil Deacon?"

"Sort of. I'm surprised that you are, though."

"Ah, well, we believe he holed up one or two of the boyos after the Harrods bombing. But we don't believe he's generally into terrorism. Anyway it's reached me that one of his boys was arrested in Streatham earlier today. A beat copper was tipped off by a passing businessman that Deacon's boy was carrying a gun; he'd seen it as someone brushed past."

Bulman glared dully at his doughnut. "So?"

"According to the copper's report the witness couldn't have seen the gun in the way he described."

"So he knew the gunman was one of Deacon's boys and set him up?"

"That's what it looks like. Thought you'd like to know."

"Why? It's not much is it? A kind of gang warfare."

"The witness was sallow. Looked Israeli or possibly Arab. Short beard. Well-dressed and quite well-spoken. Medium height."

Bulman stopped examining his doughnut. "Did he have a very slight Midland accent?"

"The copper thinks he might have had. But the Arab is quite capable of other accents."

"If that's who you think he is he's more your concern than mine. What would the Anti-Terrorist Squad be doing telling me?"

"Because whenever he crops up some bloody funny things start to happen in high places. And I think you know what I'm suggesting, guv'nor."

"Why would he be interested in one of Deacon's boys?"

"That's another reason I've told you. I have a feeling you might know."

"I haven't a clue," Bulman said blandly.

Reeves wiped his hands on a paper napkin. "Look, sir, we can help each other. I've heard on the grapevine that you're looking for a bloke called Jost Kranz."

"Who told you that?" asked Bulman sharply.

"We do have some friends in Special Branch in spite of the terrible cock-up they made over the Harrods affair; we could have had those jokers but Special Branch thought they could go it alone. You've restricted the request to them because there's less chance of leakage. I've just shown you that that's bull. We have a much better chance of finding him for you. Special Branch are too restricted. We can dive into all sorts of alleys which harbour both criminals and subversives. We're smaller than S.B. but I reckon our resources are better. You tell us what the Arab is up to and we'll try to find Kranz. On the quiet. Special Branch can take credit."

"If I told you, Jack, it wouldn't help you. As you suggest there's some bloody funny goings on."

Reeves showed his disappointment. "A pity." He drank his tea disconsolately.

"If I told you, you couldn't use it. We're all in chains. *We're the bloody prisoners*." Bulman looked across the cramped table. "I'll tell you a little. It would suit quite a lot of people, including myself, if Phil Deacon stopped fouling the air we breathe and started stoking coals down below. You read what you like into it. I've said no more than is obvious. Now what can you do about Kranz?"

Hashimi withstood the non-stop abuse from Vi. He had seen fear register in various people in so many different ways. He held a sneaking regard for her; as scared as she was she intended to leave him in no doubt as to what she thought of him.

The lamp threw a weak light in such a large basement and did little more than form a flickering pool of sinister, dark illumination.

"I'll get you another lamp. But it won't be until tomorrow."

"You know what you can do with your effing lamp. How long am I going to be in this rotten dump?"

"That depends on Phil, and at the moment he's not being too co-operative. Maybe he doesn't care what happens to you."

She stood in the middle of the doubtful light bowl, her willowy shadow wavering, while he stood half in shadow on its fringe. "Don't give me that," she spat back at him. "Phil cares. In his thick-headed, off-handed way, he cares. What is it you want from him?"

"You know what I want. I want to know who he used to deal with Sophie."

She walked slowly towards him, her chain tinkling on the concrete. "Look what you've reduced me to," she said as she reached its limits.

"It's a lightweight. Better than being dead."

"Is it? Is this some kind of living? I need a change of clothes."

"You'll have to rough it, Vi. I don't think Phil would let me in to grab a change of laundry for you."

"You clever bastard. If I give you the names will you let me go?"

"I'd have to check it out first."

"Would you let me go for Christ's sake?"

Hashimi considered it for some time, then answered abruptly "Yes."

"Well, I believed you when you said you'd kill me so now I suppose I must believe that you'll let me go."

Hashimi made no reply. Vi was trying to sort herself out. He stood there waiting in the gloom. Terror and intimidation worked. It was of no comfort to him that he no longer obtained satisfaction from the fact.

"The Montaya brothers," Vi said softly. "Bix and Lonnie."

"Spell it for me."

"I'm not sure I know. The names cropped up at a meeting we had after you blew our bloody door down. I won't forgive you for that."

"Montaya. Bix and Lonnie. Where?"

"I don't know exactly. Brixton. Somewhere off Coldharbour Lane."

"That all you've got?"

"That's it. I wouldn't hold anything back after going that far."

Hashimi looked at his watch and then held it close to his eyes in the bad light. "Okay. I'll be back." He noticed Vi's sudden change of expression. "Don't feel bad about it, they're savages. Sorry about the lamp."

Ted tucked the Jaguar expertly into a space and switched off the engine. The three men sat for a while. The street lamps did little to ease the darkness which suited the Deacons and Charlie very well.

"You've a little way to walk," Phil pointed out, "but it's best not to get too close. I'll stay with the car to make sure we've still got one when you come back. Don't hang around, Ted. We need to get away from here."

The Deacons climbed out from the front and Charlie Harris from the rear. Phil moved round to the driver's seat and climbed back in. Just before he closed the door he said to Harris, "See you some time tomorrow. Don't let anyone into the place meanwhile."

Ted Deacon and Harris walked away after making note exactly where the car was parked and putting on some thin nylon gloves. It had been dark for no longer than an hour and the night hawks had yet to show themselves in numbers. They did not hurry and they did not talk. Although they did not always see eye to eye, on missions like this there was never dissent between them.

They knew exactly where to go and it took them about twenty minutes. When they approached the house they did a careful check to make sure that nobody was paying them attention but they had chosen the time carefully; the street was virtually empty. They went up the steps and opened the front door to climb the stairs. At the top Ted groped for the door bell and rang it. It was a short while before a voice called out, "Who is it, man?"

"It's Ted. Ted Deacon."

The door opened and Lonnie Montaya peered out. "Good to see you, man. Long time." He held his hands out flat and they went through the routine of slapping.

Ted said with a grin, "It's a bloody wonder you can see anything up here. If we'd been your colour you wouldn't have noticed us."

"The kids nick the light bulbs, man. You want to see Bix?"

"We've got a job for you."

"Come in. He's playing some Earl Hines down there." Lonnie's expression changed slightly as he caught sight of Charlie but he led the way in and down the long passage to the end room.

They entered what was clearly the living room. Bix had his back to the door facing twin speakers but he rose hastily as Lonnie called out, "Ted has a job for us. We could use one right now."

Bix faced the door where Ted and Charlie remained. "Yeah? What sort of a job?" He was the elder brother and lacked Lonnie's gullibility. He was immediately suspicious when he saw Charlie.

"We want you to stay out of sight for a bit. Something's cropped up."

Charlie smiled and Bix had seen that smile before. He dived for the settee as Lonnie dropped dead from a shot from Ted's silenced gun. Charlie fired at Bix, heard the crash of his body and took his time going round the settee. Bix was crumpled but still alive. There was a blood stain on his shirt. Charlie fired again and Bix fell back with a long groan of pain.

Ted said, "Right, I'm off. Don't let anyone in until we call tomorrow. Then we'll wait for the Arab."

"Bix is holding on. Poor bastard. I think I'll let him take his own time to flake." Charlie grinned happily.

"As long as you know what you're doing." Ted turned to go as Charlie called out, "Look, if I'm gonna stay in here let's move these two jokers to one of the bedrooms. I want to watch telly. Give us a hand before you go."

The Brixton riots had long since passed. Shops had been torn apart followed by thieving and looting, and fights had been rampant.

Hashimi thought back to the most recent riots as he boarded the tube train. To take the car where he was going would be to ask for a stripped-down vehicle or no car at all when he returned to collect it.

By the time he reached Coldharbour Lane it was nearly midnight. It was difficult to know into which tributary he should turn so he took one at random and kept walking up the double line of bay windowed Edwardian houses, so many of them converted for rooming. It was quiet in the street but music of various kinds sometimes escaped from half-opened windows.

The search at first appeared to be forlorn, but people like the Montayas would be known among the right elements and it was on these that Hashimi had to rely and they were more likely to be prowling at this time of night. He heard approaching voices, laughing and swearing and sometimes bawling into the night. He listened carefully; most probably West Indians. He had placed his Browning in his waistband and he now unbuttoned his topcoat ever mindful that he was a stranger in the area.

They did not hear him because he was in his sneakers but they were bound to see him as they drew near. He kept walking. Youths. Once he was spotted their tone changed and they spread out, menacing and mocking him. They were looking for trouble, probably another gang, or better still someone with money. He was already close to the railings so that they would have to go round him but he was at least protected on one flank.

"Hi, fellers. I think you can help me."

They formed a half circle round him as he placed his back to the railings.

"Hi, fellers," parroted the leader, a tall gangly youth. "How much bread you carrying, man?"

"I'm looking for someone called . . ."

One youth strode up and lunged with a knife. He did it inexpertly with the intent of impressing his friends which

Hashimi could now see totalled about seven. Because the knife was badly handled the blade came too near to Hashimi's throat for comfort. In a reflex action he gripped the knife hand, pulled it down, swung round and threw the youth over his back in a 'flying mare'. The youth struck a colleague who fell back but the others came rushing towards Hashimi with hysterical fury. He drew his gun and side-swiped the first to reach him, and then one of them screamed out, "He's got a gun." Before the youth could react further he froze in terror as Hashimi pushed the end of the silencer under his chin. "Back off or I'll blow his head off."

They fell back confused and unsure. Their leader was on the ground moaning with pain. Two youths suddenly broke away and ran off down the street. "Now cool it," Hashimi ordered. They were slowly fanning out away from him and he could see what was going to happen. The youth he had thrown was struggling to his feet but Hashimi barked another threat. He remained down, cursing. And then the inevitable happened. The three who had fanned out suddenly broke up and ran, leaving only two youths – the leader and the youngster who was trying to breathe with the gun stuck at his throat while Hashimi held him in an excruciating finger hold. It was what Hashimi had wanted to happen but he would have to get quick results.

"Where do the Montaya brothers live? Make it quick."

"Hell man, if that's all you wanted to know why didn't you say so in the first place?"

"Because you came at me with a knife. Where are they?"

"Random Road. Thirty-three. You'll need that gun if you're going after them. I hope they get you."

"Where's Random Road?"

"Second left, first right. Top floor."

"Apartment house?"

"Yeah."

Keeping the finger lock on his hostage, Hashimi suddenly pointed the gun at the leader. "You'd better be right, sonny."

The youth tried to drag himself back, his face screwed up with pain. "Why should I lie? What's it to me?"

Hashimi side-handed his hostage and as the youth fell to his knees he spoke to his friend, "You'd better get to a hospital. I could have done some nasty damage to that arm." And he ran light footed up the road to screamed threats.

It took ten minutes for Hashimi to find number thirty-three Random Road. The front door was unlocked; locks were for bunging up or removing. But the apartment doors themselves would be well secured. The hall was pitch dark; light bulbs, too, were for removing. He crept up the stairs to the mixed smell of rancid oil and stale air. He felt his way carefully to the top floor. When he reached the landing he groped for the apartment door, and ran his hands over it.

He risked using a small flashlight. There was an old-fashioned doorknob with the keyhole beneath it. He crouched down and carefully picked the heavy lock. He could hear a radio or television from inside. He slowly pushed the door right back against the wall. He went in and closed the door. The long hall was unlit but sufficient light escaped from a room at the end and from which came the sound of a late night film. First he must check the other rooms to make sure there would be nobody at his back.

The first two were bedrooms, quite well furnished. The Montayas were obviously not on the bread line. In the second of the two rooms, he found two men who he guessed to be the Montayas. Both were on the floor by the bed as if they had been dragged there. One lay awkwardly but was clearly dead with a bloody chest wound. The other had somehow dragged himself up against the wall but was barely conscious. He had a blood covered hand up to his chest and was moaning feebly and frothing at the mouth. He had been left to die the hard way.

Hashimi was tempted to switch on the room light but refrained. He crouched near the dying man and then swung round to face the door as footsteps approached hurriedly up the passage. Deacon had outwitted him.

11

"I don't like meeting like this. There's no need." Baedeker leaned against the parapet to stare across the Thames at the Festival Hall lights. The gentle swell on the water broke up the illumination reflections and scattered them in sparkling clusters.

"I think there's every need," Jost Kranz replied. "I'm out on a limb and out of touch. How long am I supposed to stay here?"

The man from the East German embassy pulled up the collar of his coat against the stiff night breeze sweeping down the river. "Until we think the time is right for you to return to Germany. You must have been briefed before you left. What's happened to make you nervous?"

"I'm not happy with the accommodation arrangements. There could have been a better choice than using the I.R.A."

"McGanly's not known to be I.R.A. Indeed she has a reputation for despising them. You're safe there. We couldn't use known sympathisers in case a search was started for you."

"They're bound to search for me after the political bombshell I exploded before I left. I can understand the softening up, the fears some government ministers must now hold, and it gives leeway for the opposition to make use of it, but too long a wait can be counter-productive. The documents are ready and have been for some time. It's a matter of correct timing. The West German press is sniffing hard for extra scandal and it will be a mistake to keep them waiting too long or they'll lose interest."

Baedeker turned to face the small gardens hiding the base of the Savoy Hotel. There were few people about and the traffic had thinned. Well to their left a small group gathered round a coffee stall and intermittent laughter reached the two men. "We shouldn't lose sight of the fact that the reason you left Germany was because you believed your life to be in danger. It must stay like that."

"It's as much in danger here isn't it? They must know that a lot of our information is old hat with perhaps a few new insignificant revelations, but the whole is mixed with fabricated evidence. Good forgeries, but that will eventually come out. Meanwhile I'm a sitting duck."

"It will take them ages to separate fact from fiction. And by then the damage will be done. You accepted the risks."

"You mean I obeyed orders. Anyway, the true exposure fell far short of total success. True, certain officials were discredited. I think they may be well braced for a second attempt."

"We have to keep trying. Again and again. This won't be a failure. Not total. It can never be that. The backroom boys did a thorough job as I understand it. Have you suddenly got cold feet?"

Kranz shook his head and answered slowly. "No. I agree that they did a good job which will certainly produce a strong reaction. I also agree that my proclaiming a threat against me made the new boys rustle. It was a nice touch. The public love to believe that sort of thing. It's here – this side of the Channel – where it doesn't feel right. Mary McGanly is sleeping with her colleague O'Dwyer and there's something about him I don't like."

"You're not registered under any recognisable name, are you?"

"Of course not. But McGanly has made too accurate a guess as to why I'm here."

"That's the luck of the Irish. She's very sound and there is no one more loyal to their cause. She's been underground for a long time and that develops flair and anticipation. Whoever you stay with will speculate about the reason for your presence. She at least has voiced it aloud, so you know where you stand. Stop worrying."

"She's not the only one who can anticipate. If you pick anything up, any whisper that they're on to me will you please let me know urgently?"

Baedeker threw up his hands. "What a question. Of course. We're monitoring in every way we can. If we find anything it will strengthen our hand and prove you right in Germany."

"Sure. But it might be too late for me."

"Are you armed?"

"I am now."

"Good. It's as well to prepare against every eventuality."

Hashimi rolled under the bed just before the door opened and the light was switched on. Balls of fluff wavered in front of his face. The bed cover did not reach the floor and he could see the feet of the Montaya brothers. And then to one side of them another pair appeared; scuffed suede shoes with faded blue jeans above them. He heard something rustle but the feet remained still until one came out to kick the ankle of one of the brothers. The foot of the victim twitched and Hashimi guessed that it was the man who was barely alive. A low moan confirmed it.

"You're taking your time ain't you, matey? What's it like to die slowly? Come on, it might be your last chance to tell me."

Hashimi quickly realised that he wasn't expected, at least not yet. He did not know who was standing by the bed; he did not recognise the voice. Whoever it was was an obvious sadist who had come back to gloat over his victims. Then he heard a loud munching; the man was standing there eating as if nothing was wrong. Hashimi was at too much of a disadvantage under the bed to move. He could only wait and hope that the heavy dust did not make him sneeze.

The feet moved, coming quite close to him. Then the man sat on the edge of the bed which Hashimi felt push down on him. Very carefully Hashimi wriggled to the other side. If he could get out the seated man would have his back to him but he had to move a little at a time.

"You can't have much time left, Bix. Why drag it out? You're not going to play that bloody trumpet again are you, cocker? You were never any good at it anyway. You only took the bloody thing up because your poxy mother christened you after Bix Beiderbecke. Maybe she was right because you're gonna die about the same age as he did."

Bix Montaya must have responded somehow because the man on the bed suddenly laughed and jibed, "It must have crucified you to try that. Don't do it again or I'll have to deal with you and you could pop off too soon."

Hashimi managed to ease himself from under the bed but he was facing the wrong way. He rolled slowly, gun in hand and a loose board creaked under him. He heard the bed springs go as the man jumped up, and he hurled himself towards the bed head, twisting to come up for a shot. A bullet tore through the blankets and embedded in the floor just where he had been before. Hashimi fired by raising his hand above the bed but keeping his head down.

"Jesus."

Hashimi guessed that his unsighted shot must have gone near but the lights went out and the door slammed. Was the man still in the room or had he left it? Hashimi crept along the side of the bed trying to avoid the loose board and groped for the wall. He stayed down and held his breath. The only thing he could hear was the terrible noise of Bix Montaya in his death throes. He released his breath slowly and crawled towards the door, occasionally pausing. Keeping well down he reached up with one hand to switch on the light. He was alone with the Montayas. He rolled on to his stomach and peered under the bed.

Hashimi rose quickly. There was a gurgling from Bix and Hashimi gazed down at eyes now open but full of pain. "Close them," he said. A flash of understanding touched the eyes, and a brief, agonised look of gratitude. The eyes closed and Hashimi shot him through the centre of his forehead before the lids could so much as flicker. Bix was out of his misery.

Hashimi crouched again to put his ear against the door. He put out the light again and lay flat, clear of the door but within reach of its handle. He pulled the door open slowly and noiselessly. There was still diffused light coming up the passage. He pulled himself forward, and, chin touching the floor, dragged himself sufficiently to peer round the door. There was nobody in sight but the light came from the far door which was clearly open.

He rose to creep along the wall but flattened again near the door before peering round it. It was a little while before he was satisfied that the man had gone and he had to examine the other rooms to be absolutely sure. With gun in hand he went to the front door. It was firmly closed.

He returned to the room where the Montayas lay dead. Keeping the light off he opened the window and peered out. It was too dark to make a useful appraisal and he was reluctant to use his torch.

Hashimi then turned on every light in the apartment. Keeping to one side of the front door he opened it to let the light flood out. The landing was clear. He looked down the stair well. There was little light filtering to the bottom but he would have seen any shape directly at the foot of the well. He ran down lightly, pausing at each half landing. On the last run down he stopped halfway and vaulted over the banisters to land at one side of the stairs. He quickly checked the rear of the hall and then went to the main front door. Dropping prone again he pulled the door back, crawled forward then reached up and shut the door to prevent being silhouetted against the light.

Keeping to the right-hand side of the steps, away from the semi-basement end, he went slowly down them in a crouch to reach the street. He did not believe that the gunman had fled; there were the lines of cars, basements across the street, a mass of hiding places where he could wait out of sight. Hashimi sped across the pavement and tried the nearest car door. It was locked. He worked at the lock, opened the door and slammed it, immediately dropping flat. Running footsteps came from behind him. He rolled, just made out the crouching moving form and fired.

The man spun round but had the sense to hurl himself behind a car as another shot whipped up the street towards him. He'd been hit in the side but his hands were free and he reached round the car to fire back at Hashimi who was rushing forward. Charlie Harris knew he'd been hit but his adrenalin kept him going. He sprinted across the road and turned to fire as Hashimi reached the gap between the cars from where his target had just fled. It was a wild shot and a car window shattered.

It was an uncanny battle. The guns themselves made practically no sound but the shots revealed subdued flashes through the silencers and the bullets ricocheted eerily. Both men knew that the silencers were a mixed blessing; they kept the noise down but in no way helped aim.

Harris felt blood trickling down his side and slipped a hand under his jacket. His shirt was soaked. Hashimi was waiting across the street and trying to work out his next move. It could turn out to be a long battle and unless the shots landed on target tenants were going to ring the police at the sound of ruptured metal or smashed glass. Harris backed away slowly along the line of cars and then broke into a run.

Hashimi did not wait. He realised that it would be a mistake to stay where he was so crept along in the direction from which Harris had come. He dashed across the street and searched the area where Harris had last been sighted. He suddenly slipped and put out an arm to save himself. His hand was wet. He felt the tackiness of it. Blood. He knew his first shot had hit his man but not how effectively. After a while he stood up and looked over the top of the row of cars. A little later he was satisfied that his man had gone.

Even then he took nothing for granted. Hashimi kept his gun in his hand and walked wearily down the street. He didn't tuck his gun out of sight until he reached the main road.

It was almost three in the morning when Hashimi reached the warehouse. He had with him a heavy duty flashlight. As he unlocked the door Vi called out in fear but he noticed that she had kept the gas lamp going.

"It's me. Hashimi." As he looked across to the nearest corner he saw her crawling from one of the bed rolls. She had removed her skirt and now desperately scratched round for it. "I'm not going to rape you but you now have other problems. Phil has knocked off the Montaya brothers. There's now no point in my ringing him. I suppose he had them killed so that they wouldn't get in the way when he laid a trap for me. He had left a nightwatchman there. It wasn't Ted, it wasn't his voice. Who do you suppose?"

Vi hadn't quite shaken off the effects of sleep and the impact of what he had told her had yet to bite. And then, instead of answering him immediately, she crouched like a little girl with her hands cupping her chin. Gradually the long fingers moved to cover her face and she groaned softly behind them. When she looked up she said listlessly, "You promised to let me go. Where do I stand now?"

"Frankly I don't know. This has changed things, for the moment anyway. I don't want to lie to you."

"You'll kill but not lie? That's a comfort."

"We killed because we believed our cause to be honourable.

The guy they left with the Montayas is a sadist. Has he got a name?"

Vi nodded feebly. "That'll be Charlie Harris."

"I plugged him but I think he'll live."

"That's a pity. I can't stand the bastard." She buried her head again, turning from him so that he could not see.

"You could have done better than Deacon," he said.

She shrugged, her back still to him. In a choking voice she answered, "Women like me will always finish up with men like Phil; who else would have us? He's got his good points."

Hashimi didn't answer. He made sure that he had locked the door then went to the corner where the bed rolls were kept.

"What are you doing?" asked Vi nervously.

"It's too late to go anywhere else. I'm sleeping here."

She crept back into her bed roll and watched him strip to his underwear.

"Stop worrying," he called out. "Apart from anything else I'm knackered." He climbed into the roll. "Sleep tight."

Two hours later he awoke as he always did at the slightest sound. He propped himself up on one elbow. Vi was a few feet from him. She was lying face down, one hand stretched out towards his discarded clothes. She was about three feet short and the chain was taut. "You should know better," he remonstrated reasonably. "I know the exact length of that chain. That's why I'm in this corner and you're in yours." He held up the keys. "They are in bed with me. Now go to sleep."

Vi eased back and rose to her knees. "Don't you ever make mistakes, you clever bastard?"

"Certainly I do. And one day it will be my last."

"I just hope I'm there to see it."

"The Arab will probably kill her." Deacon turned viciously on Charlie Harris who was holding his cauterised and bandaged side. "You stupid bastard, you should have got him while you had the chance."

"I was bleeding, for Christ's sake. Wounded. It could have gone on all night and someone would have called the cops."

"Wounded?" Deacon sneered. "A bloody flesh wound. You didn't even need a quack."

"I didn't know that at the time, did I? I wasn't expecting him so soon. It was your bloody idea. Not one of your better ones."

Deacon came round the table like a bull and Ted was quick to dive in to grab his arm. "Cool it, Dad. Cool it. He must have got Vi to talk. She was here when we talked about the Montayas."

"She didn't know where they lived." Deacon was still glaring murderously at Harris.

"She knew near enough. Anyone round there will know the Montayas, or at least, of them. The Arab knew we were stalling. He got there a day too soon. He outsmarted us."

"Maybe he'll ring just the same. We've done his work for him. Maybe he'll lay off cutting her for a bit." Deacon shook his arm free and grasped the edge of the table.

"Stop worrying about Vi. She's given him some information – so there's little point in torturing her now – and he won't top her while she's of some use. If he does that he's got no lever at all."

But Deacon wasn't satisfied. Harris should have used the opportunity. When could they expect another one like it? "Our weakness is not knowing where he is. What's Paddy O'Dwyer up to? He hasn't produced a bloody thing. If I threaten to shop him we might get somewhere."

Ted and Harris exchanged glances; Deacon was overwrought and worried sick over Vi; he wasn't thinking properly. To shop O'Dwyer could bring the I.R.A. on their backs if the word got out and it would if he were openly threatened.

They talked until dawn without finding a solution. One thing remained constant: they had to find the Arab. Everything hinged on that one fact.

Bulman called on Deacon at eight o'clock that same morning. As he stood in the porch he noted the fresh paint work on the new door and observed the plastering where the wiring had been done for the lights above him. The door jamb was new and the whole area of brickwork had been rebuilt around the frame. Nobody answered the bell so he hung on it until he heard someone bawling out for him to stop. The door opened and the younger Deacon stood there, unshaven, and dressed in a badly rumpled suit. Bulman produced his identity card with a great flourish. "I've come to see Vi. Your mother?"

"At this bloody time in the morning? Where's your warrant?"

"You need more sleep, laddie. I didn't say I was arresting her. May I come in?"

"Look, we've all had a bad night. Ate some fish that upset us. Come back some other time." Ted's eyes were red. None of them had gone to bed that night.

"Don't obstruct the police in their inquiries, lad. Go get her."

"Piss off."

As Ted was about to close the door Bulman said, "How would you like a patrol car or two waiting outside here with sirens howling and flashers revolving? Would wake up your neighbours wouldn't it?"

"That's harassment."

"Which is the counter to obstructing the law. I just want a few words with her."

Ted was recovering rapidly. Behind a yawn, he said, "She's out shopping."

"They're not open yet, unless you include the newsagent down the road. Don't make it difficult."

A voice down the passage bawled out, "Who the hell is that? Close that bloody door."

Ted bawled back, "There's a copper here who wants a word with Vi."

"She's at her mother's."

"It's Bulman, Phil. How're you keeping?"

"Shit." Deacon shuffled to the door looking worse than his son. "What the hell do you want with Vi?"

"You two look as if you've been on the booze all night. It's private."

"We had a few jars. Celebration. If it's about my wife it concerns me too."

Ted stood to one side showing no reaction whatever to his father's contradictory statement about the previous evening. It simply didn't matter to him. Bulman wasn't going to get the truth and that was the end of it.

"I just wanted to be sure she was okay. I worry about you people, you know that."

"I have sleepless nights about you too, Bulman. I have nightmares about you still being alive the next day. If she's not here you can't speak to her can you?"

"That's true enough. Where was she snatched? Streatham?"

The change over both men was remarkable. "Where'd you get that crap you stupid bugger?"

"The word is that the Arab is after you for knocking off his girlfriend Sophie. I thought you'd like police protection if your lives are in danger. You should have reported a snatch, Phil. You haven't the resources to find her if the Arab has arranged a kidnap. You know that. Almost every police force in the world is looking for him. Now what chance do you stand? He can get the backing of any terrorist group: worldwide. And he has a terrible reputation with women. Sex appeal. Strange really."

Deacon was speechless, his lips moved awkwardly. Even Ted had tautened. For a moment Bulman thought that Deacon was about to cry and he saw something of the strain the man was under. He smiled. "Well, I'm glad I'm wrong. I hope she enjoys her early morning shopping with her mother. I have a soft spot for her, you know. Sorry to disturb you."

Bulman went down the steps: it had been worth getting up early to get at the truth if only through lies and reaction. Deacon was suffering; he deserved to. But Bulman was less sure about Vi.

His staff had already gone and Scott himself was within minutes of locking up when Bulman tapped on his office door. The craggy face peered round. Scott looked up from his desk. "You're too late. I'm off home, taking Maggie out."

Not put off, Bulman entered the office and sat down wearily. "It's been a long and eventful day," he said. "But this will only take a minute. I was hoping to find you alone."

"You must be on the wagon. Make it short, George."

"The Montaya brothers were found murdered early this morning. Shot."

Scott started to tidy his desk, still intent on leaving. "It wasn't me. I've never heard of them."

"Nor had I until this afternoon. And then only because it is generally known at the Yard that I'm interested in Phil Deacon. He used to hire them on occasion."

Scott closed his central drawer and began to take a mild interest in what Bulman was saying. He glanced pointedly at his watch.

"Hashimi's prints are all over the place. A strange thing, too, is that on one of the Montayas two guns were used. Which suggests that there was more than one man. Forensic don't yet know which shot actually killed him. The obvious one is plumb in the middle of the forehead but it came out at the back of his skull. Two more rounds have been taken out of his guts. The other bloke was killed with one shot straight through the heart."

"You think it was Hash?"

"What I think doesn't matter. I'm not on the case. But there's very strong circumstantial evidence against him. A West Indian youth was taken to hospital by one of his friends. His story is that they were walking along minding their own business when a character of the Arab's description came up to them and demanded to know where the Montayas lived. Sensing trouble, our good citizen said he didn't know and without an excuse me, this character sets about him and breaks his arm and threatens to break the other one if he doesn't come across with the address."

"You believe it?"

"Certainly I do. But not in the way it's been served up. The statement was made to the police after the hospital authorities became suspicious of the youth's story. One had a knife. So they called the police while the arm was being set. At that point nobody knew the Montayas had been done. The other pointer is more speculative; I would guess that there were a gang of youths, and that they ran up against the wrong fellow. Hash could handle that kind of situation."

"Couldn't the youths have killed these brothers?"

"Their dabs have been taken but nothing in the house has matched. Anyway, it was too professional a job for them. The other odd thing was that all the lights in the apartment were left on. The police checked after they'd taken statements from the youths. The Montayas were found about three in the morning."

Scott, now totally absorbed, looked thoughtfully at Bulman.

"It still doesn't sound like Hash. It's queer isn't it? Lights and dabs. He might just as well have left the apartment door open."

"He did. Or someone did. Has it occurred to you that it's not carelessness but that he doesn't give a damn any more? Perhaps he wants to be caught. Perhaps he is simply cocking a snook at the whole bloody lot of us."

Scott shook his head not knowing what to believe. "Do you think these two jokers were hired by Deacon to do Sophie?"

"Well, Ted and Charlie Harris are more refined in their topping jobs. You could be right. But we can't let it go on. I want to know from you where he is."

"I wondered when you'd get round to that. Certainly I'll tell you where he is. Once it's been established that he actually did the murders."

Bulman appeared hurt. "You're carrying loyalty too far."

"Don't be daft. Hope doesn't want him brought in and nor does the Home Office. They won't be pleased if you do it."

"I didn't say I intended to. But I might be able to stop further slaughter."

"Supposing you saw him and he said he didn't do it. Would you believe him?"

Bulman stretched wearily. "I might. But if the Montayas were the two who did Sophie over, then that's what he was there for whether he did it or not. There's another thing. He's snatched Vi. He's got her somewhere and her life must be in danger. I can't see how he can let her float again. We've got to find her."

"Are you sure, George?"

"I'm totally satisfied. That will be how he got on to the Montayas. She's missing and Deacon's in a blue funk. He probably thinks Hashimi will do a duplicate job on Vi. You've got to help me find her. Officially she's not missing."

"I can't help."

"Yes you can. I'm not asking for the Arab this time but for Vi back in one piece. Use your old contacts. Spread the word. Someone, somewhere must know. I can conjure up some snouts but they won't come up to some of the people you can approach. Please, Spider. Get your priorities right."

Scott shook his head reluctantly. "Every damn time I reckon I've shaken off the past, something comes up to prevent me. And of course, it's all in a bloody good cause for everybody but me. Okay, I'll ask around."

When Bulman left, Scott was still seated and staring at his desk. This was not a matter he could raise with Maggie; they simply didn't see eye to eye on anything connected with Hashimi and Maggie's feelings were strong. He realised that by agreeing to help Bulman he had walked into an open trap. Whatever Vi was, whoever she was married to, few would believe that she had even a fringe role in killing Sophie. She had to be found. But to find her for Bulman was simply a backdoor method of handing over Hashimi, and that stuck in his throat.

Sir Lewis Hope was unaware of the connection between the Montaya murders and Hashimi Ross until Bulman felt obliged to point it out to him. Hope, like Scott, had never heard of the brothers; they had been common criminals, albeit exceptionally violent ones, and simply did not come within the orbit of State Security.

When Bulman informed him two days after the event Hope heard the strong peal of alarm bells. If the police were satisfied that the Arab had committed the murders then it would be increasingly difficult to block the police in relation to Hashimi. The pressure on him and the Home Office would be considerable. Hope grasped at straws. "But I understood the bloody man had never been in captivity. So how can they be sure that the fingerprints are his?"

Bulman explained patiently and in some despair. "It's true that he's never had his dabs taken officially. But prints have been picked up at various places where he's been and from discarded weapons he has been known to have used. True, there's a technical problem in law, but that would immediately be resolved once he is captive. Meanwhile everyone is satisfied that the prints are his. Murder Squad want him, sir."

"Well I don't know where he is so why tell me?"

"I thought you'd be interested in anything to do with the Arab, as he's an acknowledged subversive. I also thought the Home Office might be interested."

Hope shot Bulman a frosty look. "Thanks, George. That will be all."

When he was sure that Bulman was clear of the building Hope sent for Sanger. When the door was closed Hope asked, "Everything all right at the Dorchester?"

As he hadn't been asked to sit down, Sanger stood in front of the desk. "He's still registered at the hotel but he's away from it an awful lot of time. He doesn't always sleep there. I must admit that I don't like the loose nature of the surveillance, Sir Lewis. We don't know what he's up to most of the time."

Hope appeared worried. "Neither do I. But if we give him a round-the-clock surveillance I'm convinced he'll very quickly know it. If he has a very loose tail we might also lose him but for quite different reasons. It's a fifty-fifty thing. At the moment I'm more interested in his future plans than his present ones. The time will come when we'll need to know exactly where he is at any given moment. It's a matter of very delicate timing. So bear with me for a while. Meanwhile have we any top-grade marksmen?"

The question was unexpected. Sanger gave it some thought; it was far from a common request. "Our own men or contracted out?"

"Contracted out, I think. Provided they are crack shots and absolutely reliable."

"That won't be too difficult. How many?"

"Certainly two. Perhaps three."

"Are you considering a terminal job or a warning and wounding? It can make a difference as to who is approached."

"Oh, definitely terminal."

"How many targets, sir?"

Hope gazed up speculatively, then spoke quite firmly. "Two. Both are men."

12

The Montaya murders commanded little press coverage as the police did not announce the name of their chief suspect. Already frustrated by being blocked on anything concerning the Arab, Scotland Yard Murder Squad sent out an all-stations call for Hashimi Ross without first consulting C13, the Anti-Terrorist Squad.

This caused anger at C13. Hashimi Ross was a terrorist and, therefore, was very much their concern. The problem centred around the changed M.O. of Hashimi. The Montayas had been criminals; it could be claimed that terrorism was not involved. But C13 saw important side issues. They, more than anyone, knew of Hashimi's skill at disguise. So what description had gone out? The one the West Indian youth had given? As this was the most likely, it could safely be assumed that the Arab looked nothing like that now.

Because the Montayas had occasionally worked for Deacon, he and his son were interviewed later on the same day that Bulman had called. No prints of his or any of his known associates had been found in the house, so the call remained routine. When the Arab was mentioned the Deacons went blank. During the panic of the previous night it had not occurred to them that Hashimi might get the blame for a crime they had committed; they had merely wanted to remove the brothers to have free run of their flat in order to set a trap for Hashimi. When they thought about it they found that they did not want Hashimi brought in; he still had Vi, something which he was not likely to tell the police.

The Deacons faced a tough dilemma. If ever there was a time to swallow pride and for them to go to ground for a while it was now. They needed time and detachment. But to move out was to lose contact with Hashimi and Vi. Whatever the arguments for leaving, Phil Deacon would not budge. His future credibility and way of life depended on solving the present crisis. The only initiative he had so far shown had turned out to be disastrous. But it was not easy to deal with a hardened professional who had the nerve and skill to operate successfully in the open and under the eyes of the police. He needed just one small slice of good luck to point him in the right direction. It would come, he was sure of it.

Martin Holmes decided against calling a cab. It was cold but dry and he elected to walk from the House of Commons to Northumberland Avenue. He had cut short his lunch in order to keep an appointment he had reluctantly made with Sir Lewis Hope that morning.

The two men met too often in the line of duty to shake hands. Holmes plopped his stocky frame on to one of the chairs and came straight to the point. "The police are searching nationwide for Hashimi Ross and there's nothing I can do to stop them. When he blew a hole in the visitors' room of Albany prison we could at least hide behind the vast speculation. There was no direct evidence to implicate Ross. But the finger seems to point straight at him over the Brixton murders. Can't your men get there first?"

"What makes you think we haven't done so?"

Holmes brightened. "Are you serious? You know where he is?"

"I know his main base. He's staying at the Dorchester."

"Good Lord." Holmes showed his surprise. "You must admit that the man has style. What do you intend to do about it?"

"Nothing. Not yet, anyway. The time has to be right."

Holmes looked hard at Hope. There was a smugness about the Security chief that he didn't much care for. Then another, more disturbing thought struck him. Hope wanted him to know. If anything went wrong then there was a shared responsibility. He decided not to fall for it. "As the police come under the auspices of the Home Office I'd better let them know."

"The Security Service also comes under the auspices of the Home Office. Perhaps not to the same extent but of necessity. You must do what you feel best, my dear fellow."

You crafty bastard, Holmes reflected bitterly. "I don't understand that observation. Are you suggesting that there's a conflict of interests?"

Hope smiled. "Isn't there? The police want him brought in and we would rather see him disappear into the blue yonder. Justice can be served either way."

"Sir Lewis, if you talk like that we're in grave danger of falling into the same trap as we did over Murison before he killed himself. He deliberately misled us for what he saw as altruistic reasons. He was wrong and so were we to take notice of him. May I suggest that you are making the same mistake now."

"Nonsense. The present situation is quite different. The Arab is an enemy of the State. Nobody disagrees with that. All that's in question is how the risk he poses is best neutralised."

"Those were exactly Murison's arguments."

"Dammit, man, he went round having people killed for political reasons. He made his own judgments of who constituted a danger to us. The Arab is an international terrorist wanted by every civilised country. There is no comparison. This is not a question of *whether* but of *how*."

Holmes wriggled in his chair. He'd ask for a move to the Commonwealth Office. Hope had already implicated him but he wanted it to go no further. Highly cunning and adept at self preservation, Hope well knew that if the police brought in the Arab it might well prove disastrous to them both. Much of what had been swept under the carpet could fly straight out the other side. "If you didn't want me to pass this on to the police why on earth have you told me?" Holmes couldn't resist asking even though he already knew the answer.

"It's only right that you should know. What happens to the Arab is very much your concern. We know where he is and provided the police don't foul things up we'll move at the right moment. Do you think you can stall them?"

"It's impossible. It's all gone too far. The call's gone out for him."

"But you agree it's best that we deal with him?"

"That depends on what you have in mind."

"Come now, Martin, the last thing I want to do is to implicate you in our procedure. There is no need for you to know. But if you continue to feel that you should inform the police . . ."

Holmes knew that he couldn't. His loyalty stretched two ways but his self interest only one. Hope had called his bluff and had known the weakness of his position from the start. "Provided that you have the matter under strict control and that there is no way of losing the Arab I'll go along with you. But I can't do a thing about the police. We've already laid too many smoke screens."

"I can't guarantee that we won't lose the Arab. He's cunning and quick. But we do hold a very big advantage which we are playing extremely carefully. Meanwhile it is conceivable, isn't it, that you can discreetly play off Murder Squad against C13? A little disinformation might help."

"We'd better go up by the back stairs. I don't want anyone to see you."

Mary McGanly took Hashimi's hand and led the way up the semi-darkened staircase. She gripped him with a man's strength as if she was afraid he might change his mind.

"Are you sure this is a good idea?"

She did not answer but once they were in the bedroom she kicked the door shut, flung her arms round his neck and kissed him with a hungry fierceness that fired him. They fell on to the bed and rolled until they almost fell off it again. It was one of the rare times that Hashimi felt inadequate with a woman but even while they struggled in a crazy embrace he knew that he dare not disappoint her. It was simply that he had not been prepared for such a violent emotional reaction from her. She wanted him like nothing else and intended to leave him in no doubt.

Some time later at a point of near exhaustion he suddenly noticed that the curtains weren't drawn. She felt his body stiffen, noticed the direction of his gaze and chided him in her so soft brogue, "It's all right, sure. The room's not overlooked." She smiled radiantly and kissed him passionately. "Would I be so foolish, now?"

He shook his head, wondering. He hadn't even had time to take in the room. It didn't worry him that Paddy O'Dwyer must have lain with her many times on this same bed. He understood her need and was surprised only that it was more insatiable than he remembered. She kissed him again and then placed her head on his chest. He wondered if, for once, she was being reckless. "Where is Paddy?"

She lifted her head. "Why must you spoil it? He's gone across the water for a day or two."

"Where exactly?"

"Does it matter? Dublin, so. Belfast is too obvious. Don't leave me again, Hash. I couldn't bear it."

He stroked her back. "You of all people should know the name of the game. They're probably crawling all over the place looking for me. I left my card in Brixton."

"Did you do that job? It was clumsy for you."

"No I didn't do it. But I would have done had someone not beaten me to it. And don't ask me why."

Mary raised herself, hovering over him. He held her head between his hands and placed his thumbs under her beautiful, wistful eyes. "We could go abroad," she said. "I'm getting tired of all this anyway."

"Abroad. Here. What's the difference? Only the language and the style of police uniforms. It's a dream, my love. I'll always be hunted."

"We could go to Libya. Even Ireland."

"You'd never settle in Libya. And neither would I. And you've been too long in England to return to Ireland. You're part of the scene here whether you like it or not." He reached up to peck her lips. "How many rooms have you got here?"

"Eight. I can take twelve guests in all."

"What sort of guests?"

"Travellers mostly. A few tourists. The word gets round. Australians, New Zealanders, I've even got a German at the moment."

"Is he a traveller?"

She tapped his nose and smiled cheekily. "Don't ask questions."

"I might need the warehouse for longer than I thought."

"That's okay. Who've you got in there?"

He tapped her nose and grinned. "I must get back." He tried to struggle up but she made it difficult for him.

"One for lost time, Hash. I've missed you so much."

The bedside telephone rang and Mary lazily reached for the receiver, her gaze still on Hashimi. Her expression changed dramatically and she heaved herself from him. "Of course it's still vacant. What do you think I've done with it? See you then." She swung out of bed and reached for her underwear. "Hash, my darling, you must go. Paddy's on his way. He flew back this evening and was ringing from West Ken."

"What's the rush? We must have half an hour."

"No. I'm worried for you, not myself. Come on, love, move it."

He sat up, disturbed by her attitude. "He doesn't worry me."

"I know that. Get your clothes on. I don't want him to see you here."

Hashimi reached under the pillow and withdrew his Browning. She smiled as she slipped on her skirt. "Same old Hash. I didn't even see you put it there. Hurry now."

"There's something you're not telling me. I can slip down to the lounge and wait for him. We can have a drink together."

"*No*," she flared. "I don't want you to see him. Now for my sake hop it fast."

He started to dress. "Just now it was for my sake. Has he been got at? Does he owe someone a favour? Phil Deacon for instance?"

"Hash, I don't even know that name. Now will you get out and give me a ring after three tomorrow. I have my reasons." She was brushing her hair rapidly. "I love you. Just remember that."

She showed open relief when he finally went to the door. She gave him a quick kiss and was tidying the bed before he had closed the door behind him. He went down the stairs, crossed the road and slipped into the nearest doorway.

The porch of the guest house was quite well lit so that Mary's guests could find their way back at night. There was no name to the house. Most who stayed there simply knew it as Mary's. The door had glass panels allowing the hall lights to filter out and increase the outside illumination. The place looked cosy and warm, and had it been twice as big Mary would still have had no difficulty in filling it. Only her dual role prevented her from expanding. The money meant little to her; it was the cause that was all important. And as yet she had shown no signs of disenchantment.

A shadow appeared behind the glass across the street and Hashimi checked that he was well back in the doorway. The guesthouse door opened and a man came out to stand under the porch. Hashimi stiffened. The light wasn't good but there was a familiarity about the man's stance that alerted him. Instant recognition was a survival accessory. He became certain as the man lit a cigarette in cupped hands. Even that small motion tripped the memory, and the flickering light did the rest.

Hashimi recalled the two instances when they had met. One had been outside Moscow about eight years ago, and the other two years later at a camp run by the East Germans in the South Yemen where torture techniques were taught, and which had some Cuban staff. He did not recall the man's name; names were meaningless in this particular game. He watched without moving.

The glow of the cigarette brightened as the man drew on it before going slowly down the steps to the bottom where he hesitated to look up and down the street. He eventually moved off away from the direction of the Kilburn High Road which probably meant he was merely going for a walk along the back streets. Hashimi felt sorry for him; he recognised all the signs of a man on a mission. The waiting was always the worst.

The footsteps were still retreating down the street when a cab rounded the corner and drifted in towards Mary's place. Hashimi stepped to the edge of the doorway, craned forward, then rapidly crossed the street as the passenger was settling the fare. O'Dwyer was mounting the steps as Hashimi called softly, "Paddy? Paddy O'Dwyer?"

O'Dwyer turned, suitcase in hand, and gazed down the steps. Recognition came late but when it did he ran down to hold out his hand. "Mother of God, I don't believe it. Hashimi. It must be years."

The two men shook hands vigorously but O'Dwyer did not invite Hashimi inside. He looked up and down the street. "I'm just back from Dublin. What are you doing here?"

"I wondered if Mary was still here. It must be well over a year since I last saw her. And you."

O'Dwyer lowered his case against the wall. "I thought you might have been in already."

"I was casing the place from across the street. I'm on the run."

O'Dwyer grinned. "So what's new? You're always on the run. Where are you staying? We must get together and have a few jars."

"You didn't answer my question. Is Mary still running the place?"

"Oh, sure. The same old Mary. Nothing's changed."

"Good, I'm glad of that. I was wondering whether I should just bowl in and say hello. Are there many guests around the place? I don't want to be seen by any of them."

"There are usually some. Why don't you ring her first? Or give me your number and I'll pass it on."

"I don't give my number to anyone. Nor my address. You should know better than to ask."

"Come off it, Hash. It's been a long time. I just thought it would be great to talk about the old days."

"Of course it would. But I'm particularly sensitive at the moment. I heard on the grapevine that someone is trying to set me up with Phil Deacon."

"Who the hell is Phil Deacon?"

"I'm surprised you've forgotten so soon considering the help he gave your lot not so long ago. I know who he is. And I shall choose my own time in blowing his treacherous head off. He'd better give up the idea. Fast." Hashimi patted O'Dwyer's arm. "Good to see you. I'll give Mary a ring." He walked away leaving O'Dwyer quietly mouthing in anger as he picked up his case and dashed into the house to the telephone.

Joachim Baedeker closed the door and locked it. The sound-proofed room had been 'swept' only that day, a routine considered unnecessary by some but never to Baedeker. He indicated a chair to the tall, bespectacled man who was with him, and then went round the desk to tidy it before he sat down. In this room, in the middle of London, he preferred to speak his own language. It was a small luxury to him for normally he insisted that English should be spoken at all times by those who worked with him.

"I apologise for the utilitarianism of this office. It was designed for security rather than for comfort." He spread his hands and offered a reserved smile. "How can I help?"

Herbert Keime possessed the precise, dry style of a lawyer. He was not a man given to hasty decisions and weighed each one very carefully before voicing it. Wisps of hair covered his head and his serious expression seldom varied. He considered most issues several times before drawing a conclusion. Baedeker did not like him and he was far from alone in his appraisal.

"We've been over the Kranz papers again and there are weaknesses." This was Keime at his most pedantic.

"There always have been," Baedeker pointed out patiently. "With documents like that there will always be faults. Too perfect a job attracts suspicion from the outset. In these circumstances everyone expects the truth to be exaggerated."

"It's not the truth I'm worried about. There is a way of strengthening what we have without plastering over the cracks too obviously."

"And that is?"

"To kill Kranz. Although it wasn't voiced at the time, that was my original plan."

Baedeker's dislike of the man intensified. "If you had voiced it I wouldn't have gone along with it. Kranz is a tried and faithful hand. He's done some good work for us. This would be poor reward wouldn't you say?"

"You do as you're told, Herr Baedeker."

"Not here I don't. I assess my orders. I obey if humanly possible. But this is my territory; I know it and something of the people who live in it. If a desk man like you starts telling me what to do in the field then I'll go over your head."

"You're over-reacting. You must face the logic of what I say. It would make a great deal of difference."

"You can stuff your logic. There has to be a damned good reason for dispensing with Kranz before I'll even consider it. Do you realise just how much it costs to train a man like that? He's a top professional. It would take years to replace him with someone as efficient and experienced."

"And do you realise just how valuable it would be to bring down the present West German Government and replace it with one more sympathetic to ourselves? Have you any idea what that means?"

"I find that insulting, Keime. Just what do you think I'm doing here? State your case."

"As you know, threats had already been reported as having been made against Kranz before he left Germany. This gives credence to his claims. If the papers we have were stronger all could be well, but it is now thought that there are too many flaws that might come out too soon. How much stronger would Kranz's claims be if the threats against him were carried out."

"You think I haven't considered that? Do you think that Kranz hasn't thought of it? The moment he suspects there's a plot against him he'll talk. And your little scheme will explode in your face and will put us back years. I had a talk with him the other day. He's getting nervous. He's no fool."

"He can still serve us better if he dies."

"Possibly. As long as we get away with it. But we're on foreign soil. The Security Service will know that he's here even if not the exact location. We had to leak that he's on the run to give authenticity to his claims of death threats. If an assassination of this kind goes wrong we'll be in trouble, particularly back home." Baedeker controlled his distaste of the man sitting opposite him. Then he said casually, "If it has to be done, if I'm convinced of the necessity, then why not let the British do it? Think how much more convincing that would be."

"Why should they?"

Baedeker smiled contemptuously. "Dr Max Blaser was over here just after Kranz arrived. He saw Sir Lewis Hope. Now I realise that he would have done that anyway as a matter of courtesy, but it's quite possible that he might have asked a favour. He flew straight back after the visit. Air Force plane; special trip."

Keime hated conjecture and said so.

Baedeker agreed that he was guessing but anticipation was a big part of his job. "I think Kranz feels it too. An experienced professional picks up vibrations. I ridiculed him but I believe he's right."

Keime took his time in thinking it over, his pale eyes focused on Baedeker. "If you are right then Blaser has taken the threat seriously."

"He was bound to do that. The question I can't answer is whether Hope has the will to help Blaser."

"Your surmise is chancy. I deal in facts."

"We can keep Kranz here until we're sure. If I'm right then the British won't want to hang around too long, although these things do take a little time to arrange convincingly."

"You're suggesting we hang on for a while?"

"Yes. It's much better someone else does our work for us and leaves us with a saintly halo."

Keime inclined his head. "So you agree in principle, Herr Baedeker. We are divided only on the question of procedure. Which makes you a hypocrite, I think."

Baedeker smiled widely, his argument won.

It was not until the following morning that Jost Kranz caught Mary alone. O'Dwyer had gone out and so had most of the guests. Mary was preparing the tables for dinner when Kranz approached her.

"Could I have a word with you alone, Mrs McGanly?"

Mary looked round the room. "We're alone here."

"All right." He crossed the room to close the door that led into the kitchen and again to close the door to the hall. The dining room was small, even cramped, but Kranz went to the centre of it to be as far away from the doors as he could get. Mary continued to lay the tables.

"Mrs McGanly, is it possible to have your full attention, please?"

She looked up at him, feeling grim after spending a night with O'Dwyer. She noticed the strain around the German's eyes. "It's serious, is it?" She moved between the tables to be nearer to him. "What is it?"

"It is important that you do not misunderstand me. I am not prying into your private life; it is none of my concern."

Mary was immediately guarded. "Go on," she said hesitantly.

"You had a visitor after dinner last night. Before Mr O'Dwyer came back. I thought I recognised him as an old friend."

Mary felt cold. She was slipping. "How do you know, and what damned business is it of yours?"

"It's none of my business. None at all. I notice things in order to survive. You could call it prying, but for my own protection and not to see who you sleep with. That is absolutely no concern of mine. But this man I think I know. I want to make contact with him."

Shaken, Mary looked round the room again. She could hear movement in the kitchen. Suddenly the small dining room wasn't private enough. She moved nearer to Kranz and put a pile of cutlery down on the table with some napkins. "You bloody snooper," she accused him, but she kept her voice down. "You bastard."

He shook his head apologetically. "Don't be angry. I'm no threat to you."

"You bet your sweet life you're not. Pack your bags and go."

"If you make me do that then I will have to tell Mr O'Dwyer what I saw. I don't want to do that."

"Blackmail is it?" Mary was having difficulty in controlling her voice.

"You force it on me. Wouldn't it be better to listen?"

Mary glared angrily at him. He was showing no emotion at all which made it worse for her. She tried to calm down. "Okay. Who do you think you saw?"

"I haven't seen him for some time but he looked like a man I knew called Hashimi Ross."

"The terrorist? Everyone knows of him. You must be blind."

"A terrorist to his enemies and a freedom fighter to his friends. My sight is good; I don't think there was a mistake."

"Well I bloody well do. I wouldn't have a terrorist in this place, for God's sake. You're out of your mind."

For the first time Kranz relaxed. He smiled and his severity disappeared instantly. It was like looking at a different man and Mary suddenly realised the immense strain he was under. "In your time you have probably housed more so-called terrorists than anyone else in London." His smile widened. "And yet you believed what you said. The illogicality of the Irish." He was on the verge of laughter.

Mary felt her lips twitch and suddenly she was smiling, shaking her head in disbelief at the turn in their conversation. "Well," she said, "as you pointed out, it depends whose side you're on." She sobered up; it was still a serious matter. "But you're wrong. I don't even know him. Why would you want to contact such a man?"

"I approve of your caution. But I mean him no harm. I think he might be able to help me. It's possible that his own circumstances are not too dissimilar from mine. Maybe we can help each other. He is a very experienced, highly trained man but I think I can contribute."

"Contribute to what? Explain."

"If you don't know him it's hardly worthwhile. But if you do, then perhaps we can watch each other's backs."

"He's in danger? I mean, more than a man like that would normally be?"

"I don't know. It's possible. A brief meeting with him would enable me to find out if we are able to help each other. It can do no harm."

As Mary was about to make another denial, Kranz said hastily, "Just in case he turns out to be the man I think he is, will you please think over what I've said. Mention it to him. You never know."

"Is that all you want me for?"

"No. Is it possible to get me another automatic pistol, and I would like a bullet proof jacket."

"I can get a gun. The jacket's not so easy, not without drawing attention. We have a few in Belfast that came our way from the Ulster police without their permission. Are you expecting trouble? Because if you are we don't want it round here."

"I simply want to protect myself. You know how it is. I shall be grateful for any help you can give."

"A gun and a flak jacket. I'll see what I can do. And keep your mouth closed about my private affairs."

"Of course. One good turn . . ." He gave a polite bow and left the room.

Mary leaned forward against the table. She was deeply worried that she had been seen with Hashimi. Kranz had sharp eyes and was obviously a very quiet mover. She wondered what was going on to disturb the German; it was all too near home and the danger signals were flashing. Yet she now saw that there was no way of getting rid of Kranz without stirring it up with O'Dwyer. Then it occurred to her that there was a way if things became desperate . . .

Hashimi Ross, dressed as a sheikh, visited Selfridges in Oxford Street. He went mid-morning before the lunchtime crowds came in, and spent some time in the toy department. He roamed the section until he found the remote controlled toys.

His interest lay in the fact that they were operated by a high frequency band which someone with a little knowledge could fix in a certain way. They could also be operated in a built-up area, unaffected by buildings or other obstructions. He wanted the most powerful unit he could get and settled on a remote controlled aeroplane which he paid for in cash and took back to the Dorchester. There he could work undisturbed on the parts in his room.

It was early evening and still light when he went to see Vi. As he locked the door behind him he said to her, "Tell me about Charlie Harris."

Vi was showing the effects of privation. "Why?" she asked listlessly. "Will he be the first to go?"

13

Vi's clothes were soiled and she had only touch-up make-up in her handbag. There were smudges under her eyes and it was clear that she had been crying. Her head came up when she faced Hashimi; a streak of pride was all she had to fight him with. "And I suppose I'll be the last?"

"Tell me about Charlie," he asked again as he moved further into the cellar.

"You do your own homework. Things have changed. At first I thought there might be some hope of getting out of here alive but I don't believe it any more. If Phil doesn't get you you'll get him. And then what can you do with me? Let me spill the beans? You'll croak me because I can hang it all together. That's the way it is, isn't it?"

"That's not the way I want it."

"It's the way you've got it, mate. The kidnap game is always dodgy; never works out the way it should do, does it? It's all full of cock-ups."

"You seem to know a lot about it, Vi."

"Too right I do. How long does it take? I've had three nights in this stinking cavern. Or is it four? Or five? Alone. No radio or TV and nobody to talk to except when you come to ask my help to kill off my old man. Nothing to do but brood and gaze at these damned walls. Pretty aren't they? It's cold and lonely at night. The place is full of noises and draughts and sometimes when the wind's up it sounds as if the bloody river is coming in. It's primitive and damp and I'm tethered like a goat."

"You're alive."

"For how bloody long? How many do you have to kill before you're satisfied?"

"As many as were responsible for Sophie's murder. What do you want me to do, forget it happened? Have you any idea what she looked like when they'd finished with her?"

"Why don't you shoot me now? Get it over with."

"Do you want any make-up? Face creams, that sort of thing?"

Vi was standing near the chair. His sudden concern confused her. "What's this? A last request before the hanging?"

"Please yourself."

"I haven't got anything to write a list with."

"Here's pen and paper." He produced a ballpoint and a small notebook as he went towards her. She held out her hands and took them from him. "Can I borrow your back to write on?"

"Oh, Vi. What will you try to do?"

She adjusted her skirt, tucking in the blouse which had partially come out. "I can manage." She balanced the pad in the palm of her hand while she still poked the blouse down with the other. "And I could do with some fresh clothes."

"I'll pop in and ask Phil."

Vi finished fiddling with her skirt and raised the pad to write. She lashed out with a desperate speed and caught him round the side of the head with a chair stave which she had pulled from the waistline at the back of her skirt.

Hashimi rode some of the blow as he belatedly saw it coming but his head was ringing as he fell back onto the concrete. Vi came after him and, in a daze he managed to whip her legs from under her and she fell on top of him. She brought the stave crashing down again but he had anticipated it just in time.

Hashimi was operating by instinct as he tried desperately to clear his head. She hammered him again but was awkwardly placed and caught him straight across the shoulders. It was painful enough but he was now beginning to think and act at the same time. Suddenly he threw himself from her as she raised the stave again. He continued to roll and she scrambled to come after him. He kept going until she made a final lunge to find that the chain had run its full extent.

She fell on to her knees and looked utterly dejected. As he lay dazed and breathless, Vi started to strike the floor repeatedly with the stave and sent up great cries of hopelessness. After a while she could strike no more and squatted on her knees, head down as if she was praying. Her shoulders heaved but there was no sound of crying. Suddenly she looked up, her eyes stark and murderous.

He lay on his side looking at her. "Good try, Vi. You were unlucky. Do you want to talk about Charlie now?"

She threw the stave at him and he fended it off with an arm. She was panting heavily but gradually gained control of herself. "If I talk will you forget about Phil?"

He was rubbing his arm where the stave had caught him. "You're asking me to lie to you."

"Does it matter? Maybe I need a lie or two."

"It's obvious you hate Charlie's guts. Does he sleep in the house?"

"I'll tell you if you let Phil off the hook. Charlie can take his chances."

"If I lie now you'll never be able to believe me again. It's all we've got between us. Understanding. It could be important later."

"Why should I act as a sop for your bloody conscience? You're a terrorist who's forgetting how to act like one. But in the end you'll revert to type. When it comes down to it you know no other way. You live by the gun."

"So does Phil."

"If I tell you about Charlie will you at least think over what I've asked?"

"Yes. But don't be hopeful. You deserve a lie, but I can't do it to you. When you've told me about Charlie we can start that list again."

Vi lowered her head so that he would not see her expression and she searched around for the notebook and ballpoint. It was crazy. She was convinced that he was making the little time she had left as bearable as possible.

Maggie noticed Scott's changing moods. He was becoming difficult to live with but she knew the reason. He was trying to sort out his conscience and that was always a torturous exercise for him. As Bulman had once remarked, "A villain is bad enough but one with scruples is impossible." Scott was agonising over Hashimi Ross.

"You want to talk about it?" she asked, handing him his drink. She wanted to put her hand out to him but in his present mood he would probably misunderstand.

"No. We simply don't see eye to eye on the issue."

"Darling, I don't yet know what the issue is."

"You know, love. You know. It's no use discussing it because you'll over-simplify."

"Okay, I should have known better. But I don't want you hurt, Willie. You always get yourself involved."

"I'm not involved this time, am I?" He gulped his drink nervously.

"Well what do you call it? Look at you. You're wandering around as if the business has gone bankrupt. Try me again. I won't pass judgment. Really."

He gave her a shamefaced glance. "Hash has kidnapped Vi Deacon. Phil's wife."

Maggie suppressed instant comment. She was staggered. "That's terrible. Why would he do that?"

"That's the easy part; to flush out Deacon and his boys. It's already been partially successful." He did not mention the Montayas; there was no way he could.

"I don't know what's in your mind, Willie. If it's what I think it is I don't really see a need to talk about it. You know what you should do."

"Sure, betray a man who saved my life. That's what it comes down to."

Maggie did not make the mistake of replying. Her heart went out to him.

Scott drained his drink and toyed with the empty glass. "It looks as if that's what I'll have to do. Vi's kidnapping has made a difference."

"What will he do with her?"

Scott screwed up his face and looked at the ceiling. "I doubt if he knows himself." He lowered his gaze to meet Maggie's. "But when the time comes to decide he won't be soft about it. And that worries me sick."

Maggie rose and crossed over to him to sit on the arm of his chair. "This time, Willie, I won't try to persuade you. You know what has to be done."

"At the Dorchester? You've got to hand it to him. Spider, that deserves a drink." Bulman struggled up from his chair.

"I don't want paying for it." Untypically, Scott was drinking too much. He had grassed and he had to learn to live with it. All the justification made no difference. The only thing that helped was the fact that he had warned Hashimi against involving innocent people or Scott would shop him. But it didn't really help his unease.

Bulman pushed his way back with the drinks. He knew how Scott was feeling. "Get stoned if it makes you feel better." He shoved the whisky across the table. "A treble. From me. That ought to make you feel better so stop feeling sorry for yourself."

Scott raised his glass. "It's not an easy thing to come to terms with."

"I'd feel the same. But it's the Arab who's broken the rules. He shouldn't have snatched Vi. Anyway, telling me isn't grassing. You haven't done it officially and I shan't be telling anyone else; not unless it gets right out of hand. Stop being a silly bugger."

"What will you do?"

"See if I can have a word with him."

"He could easily top you, George. He's obsessed by what happened to Sophie." Scott raised his drink. "And knowing her as I did I really do know how he feels. She was a lovely girl, a threat to nobody. And I can't shake off the fact that she died because of me. It sticks."

"If he feels I'm in the way of what he wants, he might top me. But this is revenge, not a terrorist caper. He's on his own this time." Bulman gazed thoughtfully at the shadows passing the bottle windows. "I don't want to make it official. I can't tell you why but my nose is twitching."

"Shall I see him?"

"I don't think you'll get anywhere. If he thinks there's a good chance of being nabbed he just might respond. I can threaten him with the Montayas. Whether he did them or not he must know that it looks bad for him. Leave it to me. If I get nothing from him we'll have to pull him in."

"Be careful, George. Being at the Dorchester won't stop him shooting his way out."

Bulman telephoned the manager of the Dorchester to make an

appointment for that afternoon. They met in the manager's office at four p.m. prompt.

Bulman kept it short and asked if he could go through the guest list.

"Who are you looking for, Mr Bulman?" The manager was wary.

Bulman gave a full description. "I don't know what name he's staying under. It would help if you could tell me. And the room number."

The manager sat back and eyed Bulman wearily. "You'll forgive me if I'm slightly bewildered. But I think that an organisation like Scotland Yard should get its act together. I've already been asked for this information and have given it. Indeed, we had to do some quick reshuffling of reservations to make a room available to one of your men; he's still staying here."

Bulman was shocked. Ripples of alarm ran through him. "Are you sure it was a police request?"

"Special Branch. Or at least that was the information I received. Credentials were established."

Bulman noted the unspoken question. He pulled out his warrant card and laid it on the desk. "Just in case you are having doubts."

The manager studied it and passed it back. "What's happening?"

Bulman gave an embarrassed smile. "You said it yourself. Lack of proper liaison, I'm afraid. I'm sorry to have wasted your time. Could you just indulge me in giving me the name your Arab guest is booked under?"

Bulman was seething when he left. Someone had sold him short and it was ominous. As he crossed the foyer on the way out he took stock of who was there. It wasn't so much that he wanted to locate the inside man – it did not matter who he was – but that he himself was not seen and reported.

When he returned to Scotland Yard he immediately made discreet inquiries about the Dorchester and came up with nothing. Special Branch had no knowledge, or if they had they had no intention of letting him know. He had enough friends there to satisfy himself that nobody was lying to him. He went back to his office and sat behind his desk, furious and worried.

The whole business smacked of Hope's handiwork and it was clear to Bulman that instructions had been given to exclude him from the project. It left him wondering why. He decided not to try to see the Arab until he knew what was going on in his own department.

Hashimi Ross had left the Dorchester as a sheikh and arrived at the Highbury safe house dressed in jeans and sweater with a topcoat against the increasing cold. He carried a holdall. As he entered the house he noted that the door chain had been removed as instructed.

Once settled in he caught a bus to the West End and once again walked along Oxford Street to Selfridges. The cosmetic department was close to the huge doors in the main hall and he spent some time buying the various creams and beauty aids which Vi had requested. He then bought the largest available bottle of Mitsouko by Guerlain and settled the whole bill in cash. And then he bought copies of *Harpers* and *Vogue*, before restocking on groceries in the Food Hall. When he had finished shopping he walked to the Marble Arch car park and picked up his car to drive back to Highbury.

He stored away his foods and made coffee, drinking it while he examined the contents of his holdall. All that was left of the aeroplane he had bought was the transmitter and the receiver. He took the grip up to the roof space where he kept so much of his lethal equipment, and brought down five rounds of .30 ammunition together with the night sight.

He spent some time cleaning the rifle and then fixed the sight with an expert's precision. With the sight fixed the barrel would not fit into the butt so he wrapped the rifle parts in a dark towel and tied it with string, making a crude but safe carrying handle that would slip over his shoulder. He made sure it was safe then left the house and put on the short beard before driving to the boarding house in Wandsworth where his parking slot remained permanently free. It was evening by the time he arrived and he lay on his bed for a while, his mind fully occupied by what would happen later that evening. It would be the culmination of all his preparations so far.

Deacon's house had become a fortress. When Deacon, Ted and Charlie Harris went out at all they never went alone. Deacon had seven armed men living in and he had selected them carefully. Five had already done time for 'grievous bodily harm' and they were all expert with handguns.

Deacon had the numbers to cope with the Arab if he appeared but he still lacked vital information. After the Montaya murders he had not expected the Arab to telephone the next day and in this he was correct. What worried him was that Hashimi had not carried out his threat to send Vi through the post in instalments. And he inferred from that the worst; Vi was already dead.

They had talked long into the night every night to work out ways of trapping the Arab but they always came back to the same point; they had yet to find him. Touts at many levels were being used but they operated mainly in south London, and extending the search north of the Thames meant using the services of other organisations. That was difficult; Deacon could not, for instance, ask Rex Reisen in Soho, to help. It had to be assumed that Hashimi was holed up beyond the Deacon territory which constantly brought him back to people like Paddy O'Dwyer whose own network stretched throughout Britain.

Deacon had begun to think that O'Dwyer was holding out on him until he received the telephone call to advise him that O'Dwyer had just met Hashimi. In turn Deacon had made some quick calls. Cars from all directions had sped towards Kilburn but were too late. By the time any of them reached the area Hashimi had long gone. But it was at least a near miss and more than had otherwise happened.

All that was left for them to do was to wait for Hashimi to come for them and to make sure that they were ready. They all accepted that it would happen in a matter of days; Hashimi had his own problems not least of which was the police. He might avoid them – as he always did – but they could still limit his options.

Two men were on guard every night using the old military method of two hours on and four off. As soon as it was daylight, one man, covered by two others, would examine the two cars outside the house in case they had been wired during the night. Deacon had considered removing the cars but the three agreed that they might act as a magnet to draw Hashimi into range.

Deacon was convinced that he had taken as many precautions as he could. It was now up to the Arab. All Deacon could do was to busy himself in an effort to take his mind off Vi. He had never before been in the position of victim and he didn't like the feel of it.

Hashimi had noticed that Baker, the boarding house keeper, had cast the odd inquisitive glance at him, particularly at dinner time. It was obvious to him that Deacon would have had his scouts out a long time ago and Hashimi recognised that he hardly constituted the average guest. He paid out too much for the parking space for one thing. And he had paid generously for other favours. He had been too free with his money to stay at a place like this when he could clearly afford better.

After dinner he sought Baker out and asked to speak to him privately in his office which was an over-sized broom cupboard at the back of the stairs. Baker was doing well out of him. The question was that if any of Deacon's men had approached him would he think that he might do better? When the overweight proprietor had squeezed himself behind his tiny desk to give himself some air of authority, Hashimi sat on the kitchen chair beside the desk. There was just room to close the door. Hashimi asked mildly, "Has Phil Deacon or any of his men been in touch with you, Mr Baker?"

Baker paled instantly; he was for trouble-free profit. "Phil Deacon?"

"Come now. Everyone round here knows of him. He's a gangster of some repute." Hashimi flashed a police identity card. "Someone is out to get him and he's not a man to call on police protection. I probably should have warned you at the outset that I'm with Special Branch. It's not Deacon we are interested in, we leave him to the Met, but the man we believe is after him. An Arab if we're right." He noticed Baker's strange look and added with a smile, "It takes one to know one, Mr Baker. Well, I'm only half-Arab, born here, but I always get landed with the terrorist jobs."

"Terrorists?" Baker sounded highly nervous. "I've got nothing to do with terrorists."

"Of course not. But it's important that none of Deacon's boys

163

know I'm here. They don't want the police around. It makes them nervous and Deacon can do what he likes as far as I'm concerned. But I do want this Arab. And this is a good place to wait for him. How much has Deacon offered for information?"

Baker swallowed on his reply which confirmed to Hashimi that an offer had been made.

"Okay, I understand. But you'll have to make your mind up whether you operate for the law or for Deacon. Whatever he's offered I'll double it. I want this man before Deacon starts shooting up the district and blowing people up. I want him quietly."

"He offered two hundred pounds but I'm not interested in that sort of money. I don't want trouble round here. Shootings. My God. Someone's already blown his door off. People were terrified."

Hashimi peeled off ten twenties from a wad he produced. "Half now and half when you tip me off. We can always produce funds for something as important as this. It's more serious than you think."

Baker couldn't believe his luck as he took the money, but greed was still in his eyes.

"Make out a receipt in the name you have for me."

"A receipt?"

"I've got to have something to justify expenses. They'll crucify me back at the Yard if I can't prove I've used the money legitimately."

"Supposing I don't hear anything?"

Hashimi shrugged. "Then you've made yourself an easy couple of ton. I can hardly take it back and I do need your co-operation. It's important that Deacon doesn't know the police are here. He'll get nervous and that could spoil everything."

"He won't know from me." Baker reached for the receipt book.

"Good man." Hashimi took the receipt and waved it. "I'm sure that he won't."

Baker smiled smugly. "I always knew there was something special about you. You're the sly one."

"That's a fact." Hashimi made great play of putting the receipt away carefully. "Mustn't lose that. Wouldn't do if any of Deacon's boys found it, would it? Wouldn't want to land you in it."

Baker's sloppy smile remained fixed on his face as he realised what he'd done. "I won't let them near the place," he asserted. "You can count on it."

Hashimi left the guest house just before ten o'clock that night. He chose a moment when the reception hall was empty and then slipped out carrying his wrapped up rifle like a gunny sack. He took a circuitous route to the street running behind and parallel to the one where Deacon lived. Back garden met back garden and Deacon's was walled all round with solid brick. It was too early for the streets to be clear but there was not a great deal of activity. He reached the corner and waited in the shadows until there was no sound of footsteps at all. He turned to the rain pipe of the end house and started to climb.

His method was not so refined as Scott's but he was light of weight and he used the pipe as he would a rope. He reached the gutter and wedged his package into it before heaving himself on to the slated roof. Retrieving the rifle he slung it over his shoulder and crawled up the slope until he reached the apex which he straddled.

He looked straight across to the opposite row of houses. He worked his way along until he faced the rear of Deacon's place. It was well lit up and the back garden was illuminated.

Hashimi slipped the roll from his shoulder and turned so that he lay flat on the slates with a view over the top. He laid the roll carefully in front of him so that his body would stop it slipping and undid the string to open the blanket with the rifle sections facing upwards to prevent them rolling down. He assembled the rifle and finally screwed on the long silencer. The weapon was now easy to control but his position wasn't good for a downward shot. He tried sighting the rifle on the windows as the night sight picked up every fragment of light.

Through the sight Hashimi counted off the windows, searching for the middle one on the second floor. There was a light on and the curtains weren't drawn. Lights, the great deterrent to a burglar, at this distance worked as a boon to an assassin. A patient assassin.

As time passed the streets quietened down. A hazy cloud of illumination hung over the area to his left indicating the more commercial sections of town, but where he rested the light was dull and in patches below. At one stage he heard a copper's unmistakable tread, followed later by a gang of drunken youths.

At half past eleven he saw movement in the room but nowhere near the window. Some of the other window lights had gone out and curtains had been drawn as Deacon's fortress closed down for the night. But the garden lights stayed on and Hashimi guessed that there would be someone watching the rear. He could see the pale haze of the front porch lights rising above the skyline.

His concentration was now solely on the one window. He adjusted his position slightly, legs splayed, elbow over the apex of the roof to obtain better purchase. He squinted through the ungainly sights. There was still so much light about the house that the magnification hurt his eyes. However, he could see the shape of a man moving about the room and he waited to choose the moment for a shot.

Suddenly, from an awkwardly moving target, everything started to go Hashimi's way. The figure approached the window, growing in size all the time. The light was now behind the target but the silhouette was well defined. Arms reached up to draw the curtains and Hashimi steadied the rifle and squeezed the trigger.

The two arms already reaching up suddenly jerked higher and then the whole figure collapsed from view. The tinkle of glass reached Hashimi across the gap but from his position made less noise than the burp of the rifle. He immediately ducked below the roof line and dismantled the rifle with expert speed. He rolled the parts in the towel, tied it, and slid down the roof to make good his escape.

14

Phil Deacon was in his music room when he heard the crash from upstairs. At first he thought someone had slammed a drawer too hard. But then there was a shout and seconds later it seemed that everyone was bawling at the same time. He jumped from his chair, switched off the stereo tape and ran for the door. Someone was urgently calling his name from upstairs; then he heard Ted's voice shouting for him followed by expletives of disbelief.

He reached the second floor and it seemed that the whole household was gathered round the open doorway of one of the bedrooms. He pushed his way through, saw the body, quickly noted the hole in the window and switched off the light. "You silly buggers," he bawled. "He could still be out there. Keep away from that bloody window and push those curtains across without showing yourselves. Four of you get out on the streets fast. He'll have fired from the roof over there. Stay in pairs and move it." When the curtains were drawn he switched the light back on. "Don't throw a shadow. He'll know how to adjust for that. Keep this side of the light." Deacon touched the huddled form with his toe as Ted hustled four men out, running downstairs with them. His mind was working fast. He looked across at Charlie Harris who was leaning against the wall beside the window. The two men gazed at each other.

"I reckon that was meant for me," said Charlie.

"Maybe. But how could he know you use this room unless he's been on that bloody roof night after night checking us out? He'd have known that Tommy moved in with you to double up."

Charlie looked savage. "Vi could have told him."

Deacon flung himself at Charlie, his face contorted with rage. Charlie backed away as Deacon tried to grab him by the throat. Two men jumped forward to hang on to Deacon's arms but he was in such a temper that he threw them off and one crashed against the window.

Charlie, his way to the door blocked by Deacon, bawled out, "Okay. I'm sorry. *I'm sorry.*" Many years younger, he knew that in this mood nobody could tackle Deacon; the man was acting like an enraged animal.

With an enormous effort of will, Deacon stopped, his hands still held out like steel grapples. He was red in the face and panting. His breathing eased first, then he slowly lowered his arms. He rubbed a hand over his face and looked at Charlie a little sheepishly. Suddenly he patted Charlie on the arm. "Okay," he said, "we're all a bit uptight." He pointed to the window. "It's that bloody bastard out there. Let's look at Tommy."

Deacon knelt beside the body and heaved it over. Two open eyes stared accusingly at him but he did not trouble to close them. There was a little blood on the jacket which he opened to show the expertise of Hashimi. There was a large patch of blood on the shirt and the hole was right over the heart. They stared at it, impressed and a little awed. One by one their gaze switched to the curtained window. If ever they needed confirmation of the professionalism of the opposition then they had it now.

Deacon turned back to the body. "Well at least he never knew what hit him." There was begrudging respect in his voice.

"What do we do?" asked Charlie. In crisis he unconsciously submitted to Deacon's greater experience.

"We can't tell the fuzz, can we? We don't want them crawling all over the place. They'll see the chance to stay on our backs. We'll get rid of him."

"He's married," Charlie pointed out. "What will you tell his wife?"

"We tell her he never came here. We'd better warn the rest of the boys and they'd better keep their bloody mouths shut or they'll go the same way. Go down and check the Jag. We'd better deal with it right now. First thing in the morning take the rest of the glass out and then get a glazier. We want it all fixed up before mid-day."

Charlie ran down the stairs while the other two men pulled the body towards the door. Deacon went over to where the man had fallen. "There's some blood stains here. When you've got Tommy downstairs come back and clean it off. If you can't budge it I'll order a new carpet so let me know. I don't want a trace."

He stood in the room remaining the right side of the light. The Arab would have gone by now but he was more than capable of surprising everybody. The sound of the men carrying Tommy down the stairs gradually faded but Deacon's thoughts were on what Charlie had said: he could well have been right. Vi hated Charlie's guts: she could easily have tipped off the Arab. And that indicated two things; that Vi might still be alive, tortured by the Arab into putting Charlie up for sale. It was the one point on which he agreed with Charlie; the shot had not been meant for Tommy.

Deacon began to think of ways he could get money to the widow without her becoming suspicious. He left the light on and was just leaving the room when two men came up the stairs with a bucket and cloths. Deacon stood aside then went down to find Charlie returning through the front doors.

"The cars have gone," Charlie announced. "Ted must have taken them with the boys. We'll have to wait until they're back."

"I hope they had the sense to sweep the cars before they got into them. I wouldn't put it past the Arab to pull a stunt like this in order to rush them straight into an explosive situation." But in his heart Deacon knew the Arab to be more precise; he would only wire the cars if he was sure that Deacon, Ted or Charlie was going to use them.

He walked over to the drinks trolley, brass framed and glass plated, and asked Charlie what he wanted. It was time to make peace. He just hoped that Ted and the others wouldn't be too long; they had to get rid of Tommy long before daybreak.

Hashimi was standing near the guest house when he heard the cars start up. He started to sprint and raced up the steps as the first car moved off. Deacon had reacted fast; the mobster was understanding the situation better. Hashimi unlocked the front door, the key being the result of another down payment to Baker, and he slipped inside and rested for a while, his back against the door. He regained his breath slowly. He had taken too long coming down off the roof. He went up the stairs, heard a door open behind him and without looking round guessed that Baker's curiosity had been raised to boiling point.

He threw the covered gun on to the bed and turned the door

key. His instincts told him to leave immediately but he could not take to the streets with Deacon's men still on the prowl. To stay was to invite more curiosity from Baker: sooner or later he would make a decision about where his profit really lay.

Hashimi unrolled the blanket, removed the night sight, packed the rifle sections into the butt and tucked the parts about his kit which he now packed. He was ready to leave. He lay fully clothed on the bed and found sleep impossible. His Browning was never far from his right hand and finally he put on the safety catch and stuffed the gun in his waistband. Someone crept along the landing and he waited, watching the door but a little later the toilet flushed and the footsteps returned. As they stopped outside his door Hashimi drew his gun.

It was an old house and most of the boards creaked but whoever was out there had tried to be stealthy. The footsteps moved on hesitantly but Hashimi did not relax. He was sure that it had been Baker and that the toilet flushing had been a ploy; Baker had his own washroom. Unable to settle down Hashimi switched off the light and in spite of the cold, opened the window. He pulled up a chair and sat looking down into the street with the raw air coursing round him. He shivered but forced himself not to move.

It was well over an hour later that the cars returned. They came in from different directions. He saw the flash of headlights first and then the shape of the Jaguar as it cruised past the street junction. The Mercedes' lights illuminated the corner, then cut out. He heard the discreet sound of car doors closing but failed to pick up the running footsteps on the steps of Deacon's house. Still he waited.

About ten minutes later he picked up the faint sound of movement but could not really identify it. A car engine started up again and the lights flashed towards the junction. So it was the Mercedes which he knew to be facing his way. It went past slowly with dipped headlights. Puzzled, he remained there for a while, then closed the window. He had not expected Deacon to call in the police; that would have opened up all sorts of complications, so they must be dumping the body. Two to go, he reflected.

Hashimi was tempted to leave but was still uncertain whether or not Deacon would have posted someone outside the house. He left it for another two hours before he decided that Baker would, by now, be sound asleep. Then he made his move.

He wedged the kit holding the rifle under the rear seat of the car and threw the innocuous gear into the boot. It was four a.m., a bad time police-wise. By five he gauged that burglar time was over and that the police would be more relaxed, particularly as early morning work shifts began to show signs of moving. One or two house lights came on. He wound down the window. There had been no further sound or sight of the Mercedes and he guessed that it had gone deep into the country, with the corpse soaked in whisky and covered up on the rear seat like a drunk. He pulled out and drove off.

By the time Hashimi reached Highbury he felt empty. He was getting too little sleep and in a state of near exhaustion. As he entered the house the street was showing slow and reluctant signs of life. There was a limit to the number of times he could expect to come and go without being seen by somebody, even if careful, and he was always that. A secure house like this one had to be used sparingly or it ceased to be safe, and he was very much aware of using it too often. He had pushed his luck almost too far at the guest house near Deacon's. And he could not stay at the Dorchester much longer, even though he reckoned that it was the best cover of all.

He locked the hall door behind him and when safe in the privacy of the apartment, he taped the rifle inside the chest of drawers and removed explosive and fuse wire from the rear feet. He then returned the four unused rounds to the attic, went downstairs and removed his beard. None knew better than he that it was a sign of nerves when he cooked himself bacon and eggs and made some toast. He ate as if he was starving and washed down the meal with a half pint of Long-life milk. Then, fastidious as ever, he washed the dishes, stripped and went to bed.

Hashimi slept for four hours, showered and dressed then locked up and drove off to the warehouse, stopping once to tank up. On the seat beside him was a big carrier bag. He still felt depleted but his alertness was built in and he lived too dangerously for it to relax. He unlocked the basement door and called out, "Hi! I've brought you some goodies."

Vi was sitting in the chair from which she had torn the stave. She looked as if she had slept no more than he; her features were haggard, but beneath the privation she showed something of the classic bone structure that made her attractive. She lifted her head and lowered it again. "I could use a radio," she said listlessly.

He checked the door locks. "I've considered it. But you might turn it up full volume and slide it over to the door. And there's just a chance that someone will hear it if you did that. Some sounds carry." He stepped nearer to her but out of reach. "You've been finding that out for yourself, haven't you? Your voice is hoarse; you've been screaming your head off."

She glanced up. "What the hell did you expect?"

"Here." He held up the carrier bag. "Will you promise not to crack my head open if I hand this over?"

"No. You can stuff your goodies. I don't believe in making up for my own execution."

He reached into the bag and pulled out a bundle tied up with string; strips of plastic explosive, fuse wire and detonators dangled from his hand together with the modified toy aeroplane unit. He looked inside the bag and then slid it over the floor towards her. "Have a look."

She did not move so he added, "Night creams; Lancôme Progrès and Arden Millennium. None of your cheap stuff. A variety of cleansers and foundations and powder. Everything you asked for. Even lipsticks; colours I thought might suit you. Oh, and there are copies of *Vogue* and *Harpers*. And as a special treat some Guerlain Mitsouko."

Vi showed more interest. She gazed up at him curiously. "Is that the perfume she used?"

He faltered. "Sometimes."

"It didn't do her much good, did it?"

He gazed at the floor, then shrugged. "You'll also find some extra food I bought from Selfridges."

He went behind the row of screens and returned with a sturdy box which he placed near the door. He climbed on to it and started to lay some explosive in the cornice, taped it, jumped down, ran the wire out and then re-aligned the box to lay some more.

"What the hell are you doing?" Vi called out, her voice trembling.

"Exactly what it looks like I'm doing. I'm wiring the place."

"Look, I'm sorry about Sophie. I shouldn't have said anything. It was cruel. You're not going to blow me up just because . . ."

Hashimi turned round sharply. "If I do I promise to shoot you first." He continued working methodically keeping an occasional eye on his prisoner: Vi was well capable of going for him again. He placed the plastic in strategic positions, both sides of the room, while keeping the wire as taut as he could. It took time and finally he inserted detonators and connected the control. He took the box back and returned to examine what he had done.

Her mouth dry, Vi gazed across at him. "Nothing's changed has it? They say that the longer a gunman is with his hostage the better chance the hostage stands. That's bullshit isn't it? You've known all along that you're going to kill me. I just don't understand why you haven't put me out of my misery. This is worse torture than a carving. You want me drivelling with madness first. Well, I promise, you'll have to wait a long time for that."

"I need you as a magnet, a live one."

"I'll tear all that stuff down."

"That would end it quickly for you if that's really what you want. Remove one section and the whole lot goes up."

"You're a liar."

"Try it. But wait until I've gone unless you want us both blown up together." He gave her a long hard look. "I've respect for you, Vi. You wouldn't be a bad one to be blown up with."

She sprung from the chair. "How do you expect me to sleep with that bloody Christmas tree strung all round the room?"

"It's perfectly safe as long as you don't touch it."

"That's why it's there, because it's bloody useless."

"It needs a signal, and I'm the only one who knows the frequency. It won't go off on its own unless you interfere with the sequence. So leave it alone."

As he put the first key in a lock she called out tremulously, "I don't know what to think any more." And then as a sudden afterthought and almost afraid to voice the question, "What happened last night?"

He turned. "Do you want the detail of it?"

"Oh, God. No. Don't say anything. Just let me go some time. Please."

"Wish me luck, Vi, or you could be here for ever." He left her gazing fearfully at the door.

"There's something bloody queer going on." Bulman thumped his gloved hands together while he tried to match Scott's longer stride.

They were walking down the Mall with St James's Park on their left. Straight ahead, in the far distance was the ill defined shape of Buckingham Palace. "I wish this damned mist would lift," Scott complained, but the mist was slight and he was more concerned with Bulman's mood.

"Don't you want to know?" Bulman asked in exasperation.

"You're going to tell me anyway so why don't you get on with it."

"I see. Still got a conscience over the Arab. Hope knows he's at the Dorchester and so far as I'm aware has done bugger all about it. He's up to something."

Scott stopped walking. "We're not calling on the Queen, are we? Let's sit on that bench."

They moved over to the edge of the park, and sat down to face the traffic on the wide avenue.

Scott said, "I never liked that man."

"You've never met him."

"I don't have to. So what's his game with Hash?"

"I wish I knew, Spider. What's so ominous is the fact that he's deliberately kept me out of it. He knows Hash has a suite at the hotel yet he's sitting on it."

"Well he doesn't want to bring him in, does he?"

"If it was that simple he would have told me. There's something he doesn't want me to know. He knows we've all been involved with Hashimi one way or the other. He knows our interest yet he's keeping this to himself. I don't like it. I don't trust his judgment at times."

"Did you see Hash? I mean that was the idea."

"No. It was embarrassing to find out that the department had already been there. As soon as I knew about Hope I backed off."

"If you think it's that dodgy I'd better warn Hash myself."

"Warn him what? Keep out of it. Let me dig around. Anyway there's someone inside the hotel keeping a discreet eye on Hashimi. If you suddenly start draping yourself all over the Dorchester you might be spotted. I could be shot for telling you that."

They sat in silence while Scott wondered if he'd already been seen with Hashimi. Eventually, Bulman said, "Sometimes I think I'm going crazy. All this is far removed from Tom Moody's murder and Murison's suicide yet that's where it has its roots. It's still tied up in some way. And if I'm right then that means we're both in deep – whether we know it or not." When Scott did not respond he added, "I just thought you deserved to be told why I haven't got round to seeing Hashimi after you'd put me on to him. There's something about this caper that scares me. Keep your eyes peeled."

Bulman ran into Detective Chief Inspector Reeves in the hall of Scotland Yard as he was returning to his office. Reeves glanced around nervously – as if he were surrounded by villains. "Can we go outside a moment, guv'nor? Might have something for you."

They went outside and stood back from the jostling stream of pedestrians as Reeves delved into his jacket. "Called at your office. Haldean said he didn't know where you were. He said you never ever tell him." He pulled a note from his pocket. "The German. I took the view that we were concentrating on the London area but I did cast wider. There are a few possibilities but only two that meet the description you gave me. Here. These are the addresses. The Fulham one has only recently been taken over. There's nothing on the new proprietor but there is a guy staying there that tones up with what you gave me. The other one is in Kilburn. Irish girl, good reputation. I know Special Branch have checked her out several times over the years. An anglophile."

"Is that all you've got?"

"It's more than you've had before." Reeves passed over the details. "Of course he could be anywhere in the country but if he needs to move quickly London gives him more options."

Bulman studied the slip. "Would it hurt your feelings if I check these out with Special Branch myself?"

Reeves feigned being hurt. "Why not? If you want to be confused you do that."

Bulman grinned. "You don't like them do you, Jack?"

"Not a lot. I'm unforgiving. I can't stand cock-ups."

"I'll let you know if I get anywhere. Thanks, anyway." Bulman put the note in his pocket and went inside.

Bulman made no mention of Hashimi Ross. Instead, sitting in Hope's office, he raised the issue of Jost Kranz which was the only reason Hope had agreed to see him. Pulling out the note Reeves had given him he spoke as politely as possible. "I need surveillance teams, sir. I can ask the Met to supply them, in which case they will want to know why, or you can detail the head of the watch squad to cough up some men."

"You have a quaint way of asking, George. What have you got?"

"Not a great deal. Both are very long shots but we have to start somewhere. One address in Fulham, one in Kilburn, both are boarding houses and they could both be dead ends. I checked with Special Branch. They have nothing at all on the Fulham place; in fact the bloke has only just taken over and the fellow before him is as white as snow. The Kilburn place has a very good reputation. Run by a woman called Mary McGanly. Irish, of course, which has attracted the odd investigation, but she's lived here at least half of her life and is pro-British as far as we know."

"What does that mean, George?"

"It means she's passed vetting but I've personally never had a great deal of faith in our vetting system. However, it's not the I.R.A. we are concerned about on this particular occasion."

"What name is being used?"

"I don't know yet. It doesn't really matter. But it won't be Kranz."

"So you want a couple of teams. Isn't there some other way?"

"I could just bowl up and ask personally."

Hope wasn't sure whether Bulman was being funny. "I don't

really want anyone else brought into this. It's not just a case of manpower. Couldn't you book a room?"

"If they have one free I could but I'll stick out like a sore thumb. I can do a bit of evening survey. Take the Kilburn address first. Or I can have the places raided on some pretext or other."

"No, no. Low profile for God's sake."

"I have to say again that it is a long shot, Sir Lewis."

"You didn't arrive at it without whittling down a mass of information. Try it. A couple of nights. But don't make it obvious. I don't want him to know."

"So if it's our man you don't want him brought in?"

"Absolutely not. We'll have to think of a way of keeping an eye on him."

Like you've done with Hashimi. Bulman kept the thought to himself then suddenly wondered if there was some connection between the two. "I'll go out there tonight. I'll be in late tomorrow."

"Take as long as you like, George. It's important. Always has been."

So important that you trust me with it but not with Hashimi's whereabouts. Bulman tried unsuccessfully to penetrate the bland expression.

By the time he had cleared his desk and had explained to Haldean that he might not be in until after lunch he was wondering if Scott would help him; a one-man surveillance was hopeless on a matter that Hope maintained was important. He picked up the telephone, first to cancel his date with Betty Moorcroft, then to make contact with Spider.

Bulman stood in the doorway opposite the Kilburn boarding house. He hated surveillance and did not consider himself to be good at it. He became restless and his mind wandered too much. At the back of his mind something about the operation nagged: Hope kept claiming the issue to be vital yet refused to use the many reserves he could call upon. Bulman had the unmistakable feeling that he was in some way being set up by Hope. He pushed his gloved hands in his topcoat pockets and leaned against the side of the porch.

Nothing was happening opposite. There was a limit to how long he could effectively stay on observation so he had chosen the period between eight and midnight. Scott had agreed to help him out the following night; if Hope found out about it there would be hell to pay but Scott's help could prove invaluable.

About nine thirty a woman came out. She stood on the pavement and Bulman could see that she was taking stock. He wondered if she was the proprietor, Mary McGanly. From where he stood in the shadows she appeared to be attractive and he liked the way she walked as she moved off towards the Kilburn High Road. Her silhouette was interesting and for a fleeting moment he was tempted to follow to stave off boredom. She did not look back.

It was almost an hour later when a man appeared who resembled the mug shot of Kranz that Hope had supplied. He too stood on the pavement but more noticeably looked both ways before setting off in the direction opposite to the one the woman had taken. Bulman did not know it but Kranz varied his times for his evening walk, he never set a pattern except for the route itself which enabled him more easily to decide if he was being followed.

Bulman stayed where he was. If Kranz was a professional he would soon pick up the tail. Besides, Bulman's brief was to establish if Kranz was staying there. Nothing more. All he could be certain about was that the description fitted as far as he could judge in the light. Three quarters of an hour later the man reappeared and Bulman had a better opportunity to watch him as he neared the house. It could be the German; all he could do now was to report back to Hope. When he left the woman had not returned; he would check her description with Special Branch.

Vi gazed around the cellar. By now she knew the position of every item in the place. The chair stave lay where it had fallen after striking Hashimi. She picked up the lamp and carried it with her as she wandered as far as the chain permitted. She had become used to the scraping, tinkling noise it made and even to the drag around her ankle. It had been cunningly anchored so that she could not reach the door or the four corners but could reach the far end well behind the screens, and, because the cellar was rectangular with the width shorter than the length, she was able to reach each side.

After Hashimi had left she had rallied and had cleansed and treated her face with the cosmetics he had brought her. It made her feel better and she was annoyed that she had not asked him for some tights. She had ripped off her torn ones and in moments of deep despair had wondered whether she had the strength to use them as a garrotte to throttle him with.

She held the lamp high to examine the explosive he had packed into the cornices. The box Hashimi had used was still there and she dragged it against one wall. She climbed up and held on to the lamp. One batch of explosive was within her reach and she reasoned that if she tugged it away she could then pull on the wire to release the whole chain. As she could not reach the corners where there was more concentration of explosive it would mean that if she could release some and then pull, the rest should fall to the floor.

Vi reached up to grasp the nearest pack. It felt like plasticine in her fingers. She recalled what Hashimi had told her; the system was self-destructive if she tampered with it. She tugged slightly and found some give. The wire leading from it drooped a little. Suddenly she froze. Hashimi was so self assured. So far as she knew he hadn't lied to her but bluff was something different. Had he been bluffing? She didn't know anything about explosive. She had only the man to judge. She withdrew her hand quickly as her nerve failed her. If he was right then the whole concrete block would blow up and if the blast didn't kill her then the massive weight of falling masonry would. She would be buried under the vast weight. Vi climbed down from the box and her hands started to tremble violently.

They met at the side of the Ritz Hotel opposite Green Park. The street narrowed as they walked down it, arm in arm, as lovers do. Since O'Dwyer had returned from Dublin it had become difficult to meet at all and Mary had to seize her moments.

"He's booked in under the name of Roger Kroll. Does that ring a bell?"

"No. Describe him again." Hashimi did not need the description but he wanted time to think.

When Mary had finished he said, "So he claims he knows me and wants to meet. Have you any idea what he's doing here?"

"I was asked to put him up by an East German contact in London. He must be over here because of the Flick scandals."

"Why?" He slowed down the pace preparatory to turning back. He did not want to walk too far.

"The contact for one thing. The timing after the fresh accusations over there for another; there was a threat to someone's life. It could be Kroll. I'm sure he's not over here on a job. He's carrying no demolition gear, no arms except a pistol I supplied him with when he asked for one. He now wants another. He's looking over his shoulder. He's nervous."

"So you went through his things?"

"Of course. I have to know exactly where I stand. He probably knows. He seemed sincere, Hash. He's looking for help and maybe can give some in return."

"Can I meet him at your place?"

"Not with Paddy pitching up like he does. He's suspicious."

"Give him his marching orders."

"That could upset a lot of people. We have to liaise."

"There's still something about him you're not telling me."

"I love you, Hash. But I do have other loyalties."

"Is he trying to find me?"

Mary did not answer but her grip on his arm tightened.

"Let him know about the warehouse."

"He'd kill me for holding out on him."

Hashimi smiled in the darkness. "I thought it was under your control as quartermaster. Don't take any nonsense from him."

"You want him to know? That could be dangerous."

"It's all dangerous. What you're doing is dangerous. You've simply got used to it. There'll be an opportunity to tell him."

Mary pulled him up. "Are you sure you know what you're doing? He's no fool and perhaps could even be a match for you."

"No, I'm not sure and he probably is a match. He's pulled off a few stunts in his time. I've got to take a chance, Mary."

"You realise that you could have the whole Provo movement against you?"

"Yes. But my guess is that he's doing it for Phil Deacon."
When her arm jerked on his he knew that he was right.

"He can still call on the others, Hash. For God's sake be careful. You're running into a bog and you're on your own. They won't read you your rights when they point the gun at the back of your head. Don't do it, Hash, you can't win this one."

"I've got to do it. And meanwhile set up a meeting with Kroll. I'm depending on you, Mary." And when he spoke like that, she couldn't refuse.

15

Unusually for him, Hope left his desk and wandered over to the window. He put his hands in his pockets, open jacket sticking out like a squat tail behind him. "Weather's improved. The river's calmed down."

Bulman read all the signs of indecision but saw no reason to leave his chair because his chief had done so.

"We must find out for sure," Hope said to the window. "We must be positive that the man is Kranz."

"He matches the print you gave me. I don't see how we can be more sure."

"You saw him at night. The print isn't all that good but apparently it's the only one there is. There's not a great deal known about Kranz. He's kept himself well out of the limelight."

"I don't see what else we can do, sir."

Hope turned his gaze from the view. "There are several things. A special camera can be used for a night shot. We can then match up the two prints. We can ascertain when he took up his digs. If the dates match his arrival here that will also help."

"So you'll detail a photographer. The only way we can be sure of the dates is by questioning the proprietor."

"You'll be the photographer, George. All you have to do is press a button. And I don't want any official calls. That could frighten him off."

Bulman rose slowly. "With respect, sir, I am not a camera man. I know nothing about infra-red or whatever they use. And those night shots are notoriously bad. You are talking of a positive identification. I trust my sight more than a camera shot."

"I'd prefer you to do it. There's nothing to it. Can't you use your friend Scott to take a look at the guest house register?"

Bulman was angry. "Scott's not employed by us."

"He's a cat-burglar. Something like that would be child's play to him."

"He's been straight for years. No, I won't ask him. Frankly, Sir Lewis, I find it odd that you are asking me to do a job I'm not qualified for and asking me to persuade a friend to break the law. What's wrong with department B7? Have they all quit or something?"

Hope left the window and returned to his desk. His mood was grim. "Don't dare question me, George. I have my reasons. It should have occurred to you that although we have our differences I'm showing you a great deal of respect and trust. I don't want to bring in B7. I don't want them to know. Not yet anyway. I will happily pay Scott. And you are perfectly capable of handling a camera. I simply want to be absolutely certain that the man is Kranz. I want no mistakes."

"If you say I must do it then I must." Bulman's tone hardened and his voice rose in anger. "But there's no way I'll compromise Scott."

"Don't damn-well talk to me like that, George. You said Mary McGanly went out last night. If she's in the habit of doing that Scott would have more than ample time. I only want the date the man arrived and the name he's booked under."

"How am I supposed to know the name he's using?"

"He's German and will almost certainly have a German accent. It follows that his registration will be Germanic. If you can couple a date to a German name that will be a strong pointer."

Bulman hid his disgust. "I'll do it myself. But I'm still not going to ask Scott for you or anyone. And you've no right at all to ask me. If I'm caught I'll produce my warrant card. It might stir things up but it'll get me off the hook."

Hope's face had reddened. It was a little while before he could speak. "I'm sick and tired of your insolence. And I won't tolerate it. Producing your card would embarrass the rest of us. We can do without that. Just remember your rank when you speak to me. The only reason you're here at all is because I've been willing to suffer you out of respect for my predecessor. *You do as I say. I'm ordering you to ask him. And don't dare question me again.*" In a seething but quieter tone, Hope added, "Now get on with it."

As the two men faced each other both were fuming. Bulman bit back a retort which, had it been uttered, would have left

Hope no option but to suspend him. He swung round and left the office, his fury still barely contained.

Scott laughed. "If it's as easy as he says, I'll do it for you."

Bulman glanced over to Lulu's office as he would if it were Haldean's. "I don't want you to do it for *me*. That's the whole point. I want you to say no. The crafty bastard is trying it on. He's keeping this Kranz character in my court for some reason I don't care for. His reasoning is crazy and he's groping for any chancy confirmation he can get without using the organisation."

Scott tidied his desk. He was still amused by Bulman's concern. "Look, I'll come along for the ride. If it looks easy I'll do it. If it pleases you to tell him I didn't that's okay. I'll meet you at seven. I'll explain to Maggie."

Jost Kranz walked slowly and listened carefully. Earlier that day he had told Mary McGanly the time he expected to take his usual nightly exercise, a step he had never dared take before. Later that day she confirmed to him that the time had been noted. He had learned to live so secretly that even imparting this information had left him feeling exposed and he wished there could have been some other way.

He left the guest house just after seven in the evening. The autumn darkness had already encroached but there was plenty of activity which somehow made him feel lonelier. When there were other people about it was difficult to pick out precise sounds or to establish particular patterns. To make matters worse it had started to drizzle and he turned up his coat collar but maintained his steady pace while others hurried around him.

As he walked further away from the house the streets quietened down and he was better able to concentrate. It was not long before he realised there was someone behind him although he could hear nothing suspicious. He did not look back and the drizzle began to ease. He was forced to turn round as he heard a shuffle and he saw a hurrying shadow. A voice said in English, "Hold on a minute," and Hashimi Ross came up beside him; the man everyone knew as the Arab.

Kranz continued to walk, his pace easy for the smaller man. "You wanted to see me," said Hashimi.

Kranz inclined his head and they turned a corner into a much narrower street. "I recognised you the other night. We met at the Institute and again in Aden."

"I remember. I must be getting careless. I can only score by saying that I saw you the same night. I wasn't waiting for you; I didn't know you were there but I recognised you. Is it possible that someone else might?"

Kranz took the rebuke. "Perhaps we're both getting careless. I know your reputation for disguise but I don't move around so much as you. And I'm not into the gun business. I'm more political."

Hashimi was not fooled. His companion had been a highly efficient hit man, operating largely in Africa, and later in his own country. Perhaps he was slowing down and was now being used in a different way. "You forget that I know that we all had the same weapon training. You don't pass through the Institute without knowing how to use a gun or two." But Hashimi did not mention the guns Kranz had obtained from Mary though he could now see a partial reason why one might be needed. They began to relax and to exchange stories, sometimes using parables to conceal actual, and identifiable incidents. They laughed once or twice but Kranz in particular could not escape the uneasy feeling of being in a foreign environment. Hashimi had the enviable knack of being at home almost anywhere. And beneath the swopping of stories was the need to assess each other, to weigh the trust.

When they had established rapport Hashimi said, "What's your problem?"

Kranz pointed to an alley. "We can turn down here." They manoeuvred between some bollards and walked down the narrow passage which was just wide enough to accommodate them side by side. "I think I've been set up. Possibly by my own people. I'm not sure. I feel like a stationary target."

"Is there any reason why you should be?"

"Not on the grounds of loyalty. My loyalty is unquestioned. But there could be political advantages if I'm killed."

"Here in England?"

"Anywhere. But this is where I happen to be. It could work better for them here. It would bear out a threat made against me in West Germany."

"A serious threat?"

"Of course. But not real. Not at the time. The threat came from our own people but was made to look as if it hadn't."

"So if your own crowd kill you it will appear as if they didn't?"

"Precisely."

"What makes you think I can help? Or would want to?"

"I know your reputation. And I have no one else to turn to. The Irish accept me because of mutual help but they don't want me there and would not support me in a crisis."

"The Irish in the form of Mary McGanly arranged this meeting to help you."

"No. To help you, possibly. I am not her lover."

"What can I do?"

They entered a much wider street and suddenly there were other people. Kranz's voice dropped a pitch. "I don't know. It's a contact. Perhaps you are suffering the same. We could watch each other's backs. I thought I should at least ask you."

"Of course. At the moment, though, we're on different courses. I have a job to finish. It should only take a few days. It's dragged out too long as it is, and the longer it does, the weaker my position. But once I've finished I would be quite happy to make further contact. Then I might be able to help you. That's all I can offer."

"It's as much as I could expect. It has helped to talk about it. I'm lucky to have seen you." Kranz laughed lightly. "Old warriors. Old comrades."

And yet so young, mused Hashimi; I'm not yet forty and Kranz wasn't so much more, yet it was almost certain that both looked well beyond their years.

"It's good to see you again," Hashimi said with sincerity. "At least we know that we've both enjoyed the same training. You must be a very worried man to have made contact in this way."

"I am but I can't duck out. If I did they would have every reason to go after me. I can't defect, it's not in my nature. I can even understand their reasoning; it makes good political sense, but it would be poor reward for what I've done for them over the years. I'm in a trap and there seems to be no way out. If they set up an assassin and I can stop him it would make them think twice. I doubt that they would try again; they'd know that I know

and it would be too risky a second time. They'd cut their losses."
Kranz laughed again but Hashimi could still detect the concern.
"I might even get promotion."

"It's happened. When I've tied up my problems I'll give you
a call. Who do I ask for?" He did not want to indicate that Mary
had already told him.

"Roger Kroll." There was no point in being evasive when he
had arranged the meeting. "I hope I haven't put you out in any
way."

"Not at all. We must help one another. There is always
someone conniving to kill people like us when it suits them.
We're the great expendables. I'll be in touch. Good luck." He
held out his hand and the two men shook on the agreement.

Hashimi dropped back and in seconds disappeared from the
street. Kranz walked on aware that he had bared his soul to
someone he had met only twice and knew largely by reputation.
Yet he felt better for it. And he had convinced himself that his
fears were well founded. Suddenly things were looking up.

By seven thirty that evening Scott and Bulman were in position
but there was a complication. The next door tenants were having
a party, the porch lights were on and the front door was ajar
which let out more light. By keeping well back the two men
could stay out of sight but people were constantly coming and
going which made concentration difficult. There was the additional risk of the door behind them opening and the house had
more lights on than usual. They decided to move to the next
house away from the activity.

From their new position they could not see the front door opposite so could have no shadowy warning of anyone approaching the
door from the hall. It offered Bulman a little less time for his
camera. It was perhaps half an hour later that Scott picked out
the barely audible sound of footsteps approaching the guest
house from the opposite direction to the Kilburn High Road.
Neither man was alerted, it was merely an observation until Scott
said, "He looks like the bloke you described."

Immediately Bulman took interest. As the figure came nearer
and passed under a street lamp he realised it was Kranz. It was
the first indication he'd had that the German varied his times.

He brought the camera up and took two shots before Kranz was beyond them. Kranz mounted the steps and disappeared into the house.

"Thanks," said Bulman. "I nearly missed the bugger."

"No sign of the woman. We'd better hang on. If she doesn't come out I'll do a recce. If she does, nudge me."

They waited and grew colder. The noise of the house party grew progressively louder and it sounded as if some guests, insulated by liquor, were drinking outside on the porch, but it was impossible to actually see them.

Scott had agreed to hang on until eleven after which Maggie would get worried. At ten o'clock Mary McGanly appeared with a tall, willowy man, and they walked off down the street together; they seemed to be arguing. When they had turned the corner, Scott, without consulting Bulman, crossed over to the house.

When he reached the door he peered through the reeded glass panels, saw no sign of movement and went straight in. He stood in the tiny hall and noted the doors leading off. The nearest one had private printed on it and he walked straight over to try the handle. It was locked with a mortice and he had trouble opening it. From one of the rooms came the sound of television. The office door opened as the heavy tumblers moved, and he went in, using his torch rather than switch on the light. There was a small, untidy desk and he crossed to it.

In the porch across the street Bulman waited, watching the guest house but distracted by the increasing noise of laughter and music two doors away. It seemed that Scott had been gone hours but he knew that the time could actually be measured in minutes. From the Kilburn High Road direction came the sound of footsteps and they had a vague consistency that sparked alarm. To his horror he saw Mary McGanly returning with the man. Their mood was no better than when they had left and their voices were raised as their anger increased. Whatever their quarrel they were returning to continue discussions in the house and Scott was still inside.

Bulman didn't know what to do for the best. He could not get in before them to warn Scott. There was an hypnotic effect in the approach of the two and he could only watch and hope that Scott would come out before they entered. As they climbed the steps he came to the edge of the porch but it was a token gesture. Scott was on his own. There was no point in crossing the street but he felt compelled to do so, whatever the consequences.

Inside the office Scott had found what he wanted, but with some difficulty as every drawer had been locked. He was stepping into the hall, closing the door behind him when he heard the front door open. He stepped as far away from the office as he could and just had time to adopt a sloppy smile when Mary McGanly and Paddy O'Dwyer entered the hall. He had caught the sounds of dissent and the Irish accents just before the two appeared. He didn't give them a chance to react or to speak. He threw his arms out wide as if to embrace them and cried out in a slurred voice, "People. Praise the Lord. I was beginning to think the place was empty." He advanced towards them with arms still outstretched and the sickly grin widening.

"Where have you come from you drunken sot?" Mary McGanly, still angry with O'Dwyer, was in no mood for drunks.

Scott looked hurt, his arms drooping sadly. "Don't be like that. I'm from across the road. I've come to invite you over." He spun to embrace the hall and almost fell over, steadying himself against a wall. "Everybody's welcome. Where are they all?"

"Probably in bed where you should be. I've already been invited and you don't live there so push off." Mary took his arm and looked to O'Dwyer for help. Holding Scott between them they got him to the door and on to the porch. Scott broke into a fit of giggling as they helped him down the steps. Bulman, who had been waiting, suddenly walked past as the group appeared.

They steadied Scott on the pavement. O'Dwyer said in contempt, "You sure you can make it across the street?"

Scott shook his arms free. He turned to grin at them. "Come on over."

"Later," said Mary. "Mind how you go."

"Watch me." Scott staggered across the street. Halfway he attempted to steady himself and turned to wave. He continued on, made an effort to straighten, then went up the steps with an effort. At the top the group in the porch moved aside for him, making the odd crack as he entered the hall. Once he was inside Mary returned to her own house. The atmosphere between her and O'Dwyer showed itself again and she pointedly said, "I've got some office work to do." She crossed to the office door not caring whether he replied or not. She took the key out of her handbag and inserted it. When she turned it she knew that the door had been unlocked.

She hesitated only fractionally, aware that O'Dwyer was moodily watching her. She went in not wishing to give him any impression that there was anything wrong. Quickly crossing to the desk she tried the drawers to find them locked. Nothing had been disturbed. There was a deliberate system to the apparent untidiness on top of the desk; she knew exactly where everything had been left. Nothing had changed. She relaxed just a little but she very well knew that she had locked the office. It was an important nightly routine.

Mary switched off the light and went to the window to draw back the heavy drapes. She could hear the sound of the party and the group in the porch were still there showing signs that the cold was getting to them. When she had told Scott that she had been invited she had told the truth. She still had her coat on. She went into the hall and once sure that O'Dwyer had disappeared, she locked the office door and crossed the street. Once inside she estimated that there were about eighty people there. She traversed the two rooms where the guests were drinking and could find no sign of the tall, easy-going, drunken stranger who had been in her house. She was very glad then that O'Dwyer was not with her. She had enough trouble but now she clearly recognised that she might have more.

After Mary had sampled the drink and thanked her hosts she crossed the street deeply worried. Nothing like this had happened before over all the years. She had never taken her cover for granted and had worked extremely hard at maintaining it, but something had gone wrong and she could not put her finger on it. She had better get rid of the German as soon as she could without raising queries within her own organisation. Life had suddenly become difficult.

"I need a drink."

"I need one, too," said Bulman.

They walked for some time before they spotted an empty cab. They did not want to drink in the area of the guest house so went back to the West End with Bulman shouldering the camera case. The cabbie found them a pub and they dropped off. There wasn't a great deal of drinking time left but they squeezed into a crowded bar, obtained two large whiskies and tried to find a reasonably quiet corner.

"That was quite a caper you pulled there, Spider. I was worried sick."

Scott swallowed half his drink. "It's a temporary pull. I didn't have time to lock the office door."

Bulman grinned. "She'll think she forgot. Don't worry."

Scott shook his head. "She won't think that. All the desk drawers were locked. No keys in sight. The office lock is solid. A filing cabinet was locked and it's a sturdy job."

"So?"

"In a place like that it's unusual. There was nothing worth nicking. No cash or jewellery. Nothing. So what is there to hide? The guest book was locked away in the desk. I think I found your man by the way." Scott pulled out a scrap of paper. "That's the date he booked in and there's the name he's booked under. Can't be sure it's him but it's the only Germanic name in the register over the last few weeks. Roger Kroll."

Bulman took the slip, noted the date. "It's probably him. The dates fit." He did not explain why and Scott didn't ask. Watching Scott he said, "What's troubling you?"

"I dunno. But there's something about that house which isn't right. Too much security in the wrong places. Now if it was the silver that was locked away . . . maybe it is. But the security is around information. In a small guest house?"

Bulman thought it over. "It's been checked over often enough. Vetted."

"I'd give it one more time, George."

Mary went into her bedroom and sat thoughtfully at the dressing table. Her quarrel with O'Dwyer had left her feeling bitter and she was worried about the office incident. The intruder could have been an opportunist burglar but anyone who could open that particular door-lock during the short time she was out was more than a casual thief. She should really tell O'Dwyer but at the moment she was not prepared to deal with him. Hashimi's reappearance had raised emotional complications and she was left with the strong feeling that her safety might topple. She had such a friendly relationship with the police that the very prospect of it being upset disturbed her. With her coat still on she sat wondering what best to do.

Her cover had always been sound. She had lived in England for a very long time and had many British friends. She loved the country so pretence had never been necessary. Her quarrel was not with the British people but with successive British governments. It was a convincing I.R.A. indoctrination. False records would show that her father served in the Royal Ulster Rifles during World War II, and had won a Military Medal. Her mother had served in the W.A.A.F.s for most of the war. Supposedly both had been loyal British subjects. And if you are Irish and loyal to Britain, then you are among those who hate the I.R.A. with considerable vehemence.

The truth was that she had been born into the I.R.A. Both her parents were strong Republicans from Derry; the name Londonderry would always stick in her throat. Her real parents were both dead, killed by a faulty bomb meant for their enemies. And one of her brothers had been killed by the British in Belfast; that he had been caught setting a trap for the troops made no difference. Mary had good cause to hate the English.

She looked at herself in the mirror. She was running away from the present problem. She could not tell the police about the stranger who conveniently disappeared. Nothing had been taken and as far as she could judge the desk drawers had remained locked. What had he been looking for? And who should she talk to about it?

The answer came when O'Dwyer entered the room. She saw him in the dressing table mirror as he closed the door behind him. "I thought you'd gone home," she observed bitingly. "And, anyway, knock next time, will you?"

"When have I had to knock before? What's got into you? I came to make it up with you."

She watched him through the glass. "You came to get into bed with me."

"Isn't that making it up?" He grinned widely. "What better way?"

"A better way is for you to piss off and let me think."

He came up behind her but her reflected expression stopped him short. "What the hell's wrong with you? You've changed."

"Leave me alone."

"Look at you. You haven't even got your coat off. Come out with me."

Mary rose slowly, went to the door and opened it. "On your bike. I've had enough of you today."

"You'll feel better in bed."

"Out."

He saw her expression harden. "Nobody can change so quickly. It's the Arab isn't it? He told me the other night that he'd been to see you."

"You're a liar. Get out."

"He's been screwing you hasn't he? You dirty little slag."

Mary went white with rage. She closed the door then lashed out at him, catching him across the face with her nails.

O'Dwyer fell back tripping against the bed. He gripped the bedhead to stop himself from falling. Pulling himself upright he glared hatred at her and slowly wiped the blood from his face. "You bitch. I've hit it right on the button, haven't I? No wonder you've been like a chunk of ice with me. What other favours have you done him?"

She came at him again but this time he was ready and backhanded her with such force that she crashed against the door before slumping to the floor, her eyes glazed. He stood over her, panting partly from rage and partly from the lust that anger could raise in him. He wanted her badly, even as she was, and he still thought he could straighten things out between them.

He bent forward to help her. She took his hand then pulled and kicked him in the crutch. O'Dwyer gasped in agony and doubled up holding his groin. Mary scrambled away from him but he shot out a hand and grabbed her arm and held on tight while he tried to ease the fire between his legs. She struggled to break free but he clung on desperately.

"You're breaking my arm for God's sake. Let go." She hammered away at him with her free hand but he held on doggedly. He pulled her closer and she tried to rake his face again but he was in too awkward a position and she was anchored on one side by his excruciating grip. Remorselessly he pulled her forward while he was still doubled up, then suddenly let go and with the same hand hit her viciously on the jaw. She collapsed at his feet, unconscious.

It gave O'Dwyer the time he needed to recover. But even when he was able to straighten he was still in immense pain. He sat on a chair for a while, bent forward and rocking slowly until he could come to terms with the burning discomfort. "You bloody bitch," he moaned softly. "You bloody bitch." He could see that blood was trickling from the side of her mouth where her teeth had torn her lips but he felt no regret. Everything had gone too far.

By the time Mary recovered O'Dwyer was better able to move but he remained on the chair watching her as she lifted her head. As her mind cleared she brushed away the trickling blood and gazed balefully at him. Nothing would ever be the same between them again and this affected issues other than their relationship. As if realising this, O'Dwyer reached out to grasp her hair to lift her head higher. She cried out with pain.

"Where's the Arab?" he rasped.

"I don't know."

He yanked at her hair again and she tried to rise to ease the pain. "Don't give me that bull. You must make contact. Where is he?"

Mary tried to get her legs clear but he made it difficult. Suddenly he back-handed her again but not hard enough to put her out. She brought up a hand to rub her bruised jaw before speaking. "He rings me here. I don't know where he is. You bastard. You'll pay for this. I'll report you."

"No. It's you who'll be on report. You're the one who's behaved stupidly and lied to me. And you still are. I want to know what favours you've done him. You'd better give it straight, my girl, or I'll knock the shit out of you."

Her face was screwed with pain as he tugged again. She grabbed his wrist and dug her nails into flesh. He relaxed his hold and she tried to scramble away from him but the bed was in the way. Again he struck her round the face. Her lips were badly swollen and her face bore the weal marks of his fingers. "I'm not answerable to you," she spat at him. "What I do with my time is none of your bloody business. Take your hands off me, you jealous bastard. He's twice the man you are any time. You can't touch him."

It was the wrong thing to say to O'Dwyer. He rose to his feet, still holding her by the hair, and pulled her up. She at once tried to knee him but he had turned his body away and slightly pulled one leg up. She clawed at his face but he fended her off easily. Then he started to hit her repeatedly across the face and her head swung from side to side with each blow: she was now too weak to brace herself to the pain.

As O'Dwyer's rage eased he thought that Mary was dead. Her face was swollen and her eyes were red and puffed. Where her lips had split he had transferred red scars of blood all over her face. It was impossible for him to recognise her as she was and he suddenly became scared of what he had done.

He lifted her on to the bed and she showed little sign of life. He went to the washbasin and wet a towel to wipe away the blood. It was not an act of compassion but done merely to occupy himself until she came round. Finally, in frustration he threw a cup of water over her face and then another.

Mary opened eyes that had become swollen slits. He stood over her. "Where's the Arab?" he repeated.

She tried to move her lips but they would not part. He shook her. "Wake up, you bitch, or I'll put you to sleep for ever. Where is he?" When she failed to reply he raised his fist as if to bring it smashing down on her face, but it was his contorted features that finally broke her. "No. Please, no."

"Tell me." He left his fist raised.

She tried to hold back but when his fingers touched her bruised face she cracked and tried to escape his touch. "I don't know where he is but he's using the warehouse."

"The warehouse? You mean the docks?"

She barely had the strength to nod and could feel herself slipping away.

"You gave him the keys?"

She rallied and croaked a yes, and then managed more clearly, "Just for a while." Her eyes had closed again as if she had to shut him out.

"*You raving lunatic!*" he stormed. "Do you realise what you've done? We can never use it again. You've blown it, you crazy idiot. Do you know what he's using it for?"

She shook her head as if she no longer cared and in her fuddled mind it came back to her that Hashimi had told her to let O'Dwyer know, yet it had taken a violent beating to get it out of her. She could not otherwise have betrayed him whatever he had wanted. She knew O'Dwyer only too well. Just before she passed out again she realised that her judgment had been absolutely right. There was no way now that she could protect Hashimi, no way that she could warn him.

O'Dwyer stepped back, absorbing the vital information he had just received. Luck had at last come his way. "The way you look you'd better hide yourself for a few days. And don't try using the phone; I'm putting it out of order." But she did not hear.

Before leaving the room he pulled the telephone wires from their socket and then smashed the socket itself. He searched her handbag for the office keys, went downstairs and wrecked the telephone there. If she relied on the Arab ringing her here then there was now no way he could make contact other than by calling in person. It would give enough time. He tidied himself up and left the house. He was now in a position to make the Arab pay, and he would pay very painfully.

16

When Bulman arrived back at his apartment he rang Sir Lewis Hope on a special number which would reach wherever the Security Chief might be. As a result he was in Hope's office before midnight.

Hope was in a dinner jacket but made no protest about being called back from a reception. He opened a cabinet and offered Bulman a small whisky. Neither man sat down, but Hope raised his glass and said, "Cheers."

Bulman responded and finished his drink in a gulp.

"Who broke in?" asked Hope, standing by the side of his desk.

"Scott. He was almost caught, but extricated himself brilliantly."

"I told you he would help. He loves breaking the law. So you're satisfied that it's Kranz?"

"Registered as Kroll. Perhaps we have something on him under that name." Bulman handed over a written report which he had hastily scribbled out. "The dates match the one you gave me. It adds up. He goes for a walk every night, taking care to vary the time, which suggests he's a professional. To find out what he does during the day you'll need more help than I can give."

"You've done well, George." Hope was studying Bulman's notes.

"And Scott. He did particularly well."

Hope barely glanced up. "Yes, of course. Splendid."

"What happens next?"

"You go to bed, dear fellow."

"Scott seems to think there's something dodgy about the guest house."

"Oh, really?" Hope flicked over a page and frowned as he tried to decipher Bulman's writing.

Bulman started to get annoyed. "Don't you think it's worth looking into?"

"Scott's fanciful. Useful for this sort of thing but he builds up things that aren't there."

"Right, sir, I'll drop it. But if you read on there is mention of it in my report. I'll get it typed out tomorrow."

Hope frowned in annoyance and looked up. "It will be nothing to do with us. Report it to Special Branch if it worries you. But I hope you don't waste their time. Good night, George." He smiled. "A nice one."

"But what do we do? Kranz might leave."

"I've got to think it over. Meanwhile I just wanted to be sure that we've found him."

Bulman left the office feeling disgruntled. He glanced at his watch; it was too late to call on Betty even though he had an overwhelming desire to see her. He went towards the elevator. He could see the strip of light from under the door of the communications room and could hear the telex clacking. Two more offices were obviously in use including the deciphering room. He pushed the elevator bell and when the doors opened stepped inside but wedged himself against one of the doors to stop it closing. Hope's office was at the far end of the corridor but Bulman did not have to lean out very far to keep an eye on it. If he released the door it would close long before anyone could reach it.

Hope was quite obviously still in his office but Bulman waited so long that he was on the point of giving up when he heard footsteps on the upper stairs which were at one side of the elevator. He almost let the door go but Sanger stepped into view and walked briskly away from him towards Hope's office. Sanger knocked, waited and went in. The only way he could have known that Hope would be at his desk at such an unusually late hour was if Hope himself had advised him. It was clear that Sanger had been summoned. Bulman released the door and went down to the ground floor. There had obviously been new developments.

When O'Dwyer left the guest house he felt both elated and angry. His intention was to hurry round to Deacon's place but the taste of blood on his lips persuaded him that he had best clean up first. His hands too, were tacky with blood and with sudden concern he realised that it must be Mary's. His remorse was not caused by what he had done to her – she had deserved that in his view – but in the possibility that he might have gone too far. She had still been unconscious when he had left and the last thing he wanted was police interference.

He went back to his own two-roomed apartment a block away and let himself in. He scrubbed up and changed his blood-spattered shirt. By this time he had cooled down but was still incensed at Mary's treachery; it took a long time to find somewhere safe for emergency hide-outs and the warehouse could no longer be used. Hashimi might be outside the law but he was not in the Provos and these days it was difficult to see where his loyalties lay.

He rang Deacon's number and had difficulty in getting past the stranger who answered the telephone. It was a long time before Phil Deacon came on and when he did his voice was full of suspicion.

"It's me, Paddy."

"Paddy who?"

"Oh, for chrissake what's going on? Paddy O'Dwyer. I've got to see you straight away. I've some red hot news."

"Give it to me now. If it's good I could do with some."

"Over the phone? You're not yourself, Phil. Just be ready for me. I don't want acid through the letter box." O'Dwyer hung up and went out to find where he'd last parked his old Triumph.

The streets were reasonably clear as he cut down towards the Thames, and it was still the right side of midnight by the time he reached Wandsworth. He had to search to find Deacon's place and when he did wondered why all the lights were on. It took a little time to find a slot and when he approached the house the door was already open and two men flanked the porch. He went up the steps and was then bundled into the hall before being searched. He was carrying no arms and he bellowed at the top of his voice for Deacon. When satisfied, the two men escorted him to the music room and Deacon had a large Jameson's already poured out for him.

Before O'Dwyer could complain Deacon said, "Sorry about the palaver but these days we don't know who our friends are. We have to examine every dodge to get in this house. Have a seat. I think you know my son, Ted, and this is Charlie Harris."

O'Dwyer nodded. He vaguely knew Ted but had never met Charlie although he had heard some odd rumours about him. He had yet to touch his drink when he said, "I have some interesting news about the Arab." He looked doubtfully at Ted and Charlie.

Phil said, "They know all about it. They're up to their necks. Have you found the bastard?"

O'Dwyer was not satisfied. "I don't care whether they're up to their necks or not. I don't know what's going on here but what I have to say is for your ears only."

"It's okay, Dad." Ted gave Charlie a nod and the two men left the room.

Deacon shrugged wearily. "We're a bit on edge." He sat in one of the comfortable chairs he used to listen to his music.

"You look as if you're under siege. I know the Arab's causing you problems but they must be worse than I thought." O'Dwyer sat down in the next chair so that they were side by side facing the far speakers.

Deacon did not enlighten him. "It's late, Paddy. We're all bloody tired. What have you got?"

Paddy drained his drink and shook his head as the spirit gripped his throat. "God, I needed that. Do you mind if I have another?"

Deacon reached for the bottle and handed it over. "Help yourself but get on with it."

O'Dwyer poured a generous measure; the Irish whiskey fired him. "I think I have a lead on the Arab."

Deacon had noticed the abrasions on the back of O'Dwyer's hands but made no comment. "You *think?*"

"Well it involves one of our safe places. Once I mention it to you it'll be no use to us. It's a big sacrifice. We'd need to replace it."

"You want me to find a replacement?"

"To point me in the right direction; someone who deals with this sort of thing. I don't want to use our own organisation; it's overstretched. We need something completely outside the orbit."

"Okay. You don't want me or anyone else to know. That's

sound. But I do have the odd place you can use when the chips are down as you already know."

O'Dwyer stretched his legs; the conversation was going his way. "I appreciate it. There's an old warehouse by the docks. It's derelict and the site is due for redevelopment. There's a basement which the boys have made safe. The Arab has been using it."

Deacon sat upright, the weariness falling away from him. He gripped the arms of his chair, his eyes bright and probing. *"You let him use it?"*

"I didn't. I've only just found out. I don't know to what extent he's using it, but the place is equipped for long-term stays."

Deacon's thoughts were racing too fast. Before he could stop himself he burst out, "Could he have Vi in there?"

"Vi? He's got Vi?" O'Dwyer stared at Deacon who was gazing at the far wall in a state of agitation. "Has he got Vi?" he asked again. His mind wasn't on Deacon's wife but the crazy passion that must have driven Mary to let Hashimi borrow the warehouse for such a desperate purpose; it was far worse than he had thought. Mary had got the organisation involved in a stupid caper that could bring a concentrated police action around their heads if they ever found out. His fury against her suddenly surged back.

Deacon spoke cagily. "Now we've both coughed information we didn't want to give. Well now you know. He lifted her in Streatham right under the noses of two of my boys and the fuzz. This warehouse seems just the place. It's typical that he wouldn't use one of his own set-ups. He's a crafty bugger."

"You've kept it pretty quiet," said O'Dwyer, aware that he had to handle this carefully; every new revelation was more disastrous than the last.

Deacon climbed to his feet. "I'll have to let Ted and Charlie know. It can't be helped. I'll need a plan of the place. We've a lot of thinking to do. And we can't leave it too long." He suddenly clapped his hands together and for the first time in days his expression brightened. "We've got him. Whether he's staying there or not, he's dead."

But O'Dwyer's thoughts were following a different track. "If he has got Vi there you'll have to be damned careful." The last thing O'Dwyer wanted was a blood-bath in the warehouse, something which would not go unnoticed in Belfast and Dublin.

Deacon was not put off. He was becoming more jubilant by the second. "Let's go into the office," he said. "You can draw up a location plan. Let's get it right and fix the bastard once and for all."

Kranz usually rose late for two reasons. Playing a waiting game with nothing actually to do, removed urgency. And then there was the fact that he had no private bathroom and he hated sharing. There was one bathroom on every floor and Mary McGanly had her own. Whilst he had his own washbasin and shaver point it was his habit to hang around his room until he was satisfied that everyone else had finished their ablutions before venturing into the nearest bathroom. Breakfast did not worry him and he would go down to the small dining room to have coffee, after all the other lodgers had disappeared for the day. While he waited he would sit at the window of his room and through an earpiece, listen to the morning news from a transistor radio.

This morning was no different. He sat listening and watching people passing below and at the same time reflected on his meeting with the Arab the previous evening. There was a sound at his door and immediately he removed the earpiece and switched off the radio. It had been more of a thump than a knock. He went to the door. "Who is it?"

There was an unintelligible reply followed by a slithering sound as if someone was running a hand over the woodwork. Kranz pulled out his gun from under the mattress and went back to the door. "Who is it?" This time there was no reply: instead he could hear a snivelling sound as if a dog was sniffing at the bottom of the door. He yanked the door open and stood to one side. Mary McGanly fell forward into the room. Kranz stepped over her quickly to make sure that the short corridor was clear. He stepped back into the room and had to pull Mary clear of the door before he could close it.

She had fallen face downwards and it wasn't until he gently rolled her over that he saw the puffed, cut and bruised face. She obviously needed medical attention. The cuts on her lips had congealed to a swollen black mass. Her clothes were stained and the fact that she was wearing a crumpled topcoat suggested that she had been in them all night. He eased the coat off her, pulling her forward while she moaned, and threw it on to his bed. He quickly assessed that she had no broken bones then lifted her on to the solitary armchair with great difficulty.

Kranz had no liquor in the room but he doubted that he could get any past her lips. He wet a towel and delicately bathed her face with it. The cold water revived her a little and her eyes opened as far as the contusions would allow. He could just see the suggestion of iris through the ugly slits. But she was undoubtedly gazing at him and he thought she knew where she was.

"Who did this?" he asked quietly.

She held out a hand and he could see that she was trying to straighten. He helped her sit upright and it seemed to do some good for her movements became more positive. He held her by the back of the head and could feel the sweat matted to her hair. "You need a doctor," he said.

Mary shook her head slowly: she was in obvious pain. "No doctor." The words escaped from lips that could barely move. She made a considerable effort then and gripped one of his hands. "Did you see Hashimi?"

It was the last question he expected. "Yes. Don't worry about that now."

"I must." Every word was an effort but it was clear that she wanted to go on. "Where is he?"

It was an odd exchange. They should be talking about what best to do for her. "I don't know."

"Oh, my God. We must find him."

"Why is it so important? What's gone wrong?" Kranz knew it was agony for her to speak but she had made him anxious. She was silent for quite a long time but he could see that she was now fully aware of what was happening and needed more time to think. Something had gone drastically wrong and he wondered if he might be involved. Yet he would not hurry her. She had clearly been beaten within an inch of death. It was her own strong will that made her hang on. He had seen similar courage before in Aden but that was a long time ago and something he preferred to forget. To jog her, he repeated, "I don't know where he is. If he wants to see me again he'll contact me here."

"We've got to find him. You've got to help him."

Kranz could not miss the irony; only hours ago he had been asking the Arab for help. "I wouldn't know where to start looking."

"I would. Can I have some water?"

He got it for her and waited while she tried to swallow. "Shall I get some brandy?"

She shook her head again. "Tell Zoe that she'll have to fend for herself for a few days. Tell her to hire temporary help. And tell her that in no circumstances am I to be disturbed. If I want help I'll call for it. Will you do that?"

"Of course. Will she take notice of me?" He recalled that Zoe was the cook.

"I'll scribble a note to say I'm not well." Mary sipped some more water then said, "Listen carefully. There's a warehouse in the East End docks which Hashimi is using. I don't think he's staying there and I don't know what he's using it for but it's the only place you are likely to find him." She swayed in the chair and he thought she was about to faint but she rallied quickly. "He's in danger. Someone who wants Hash's blood has found out that he's using the warehouse."

"Are you talking of O'Dwyer? Did he beat you up to get this out of you?"

Mary considered the implications of telling him. Her head was woolly and the pain had made her feverish. But matters had gone so wrong that she had reached a point of no return. And then she was helped by Kranz saying, "If you want my help you had better not hold back. I won't fly blind for you or anybody."

She tried a smile and gasped out with pain, "O'Dwyer owes a favour to a gangster called Phil Deacon. And Deacon wants Hashimi's head."

Kranz did not like the sound of it. This was not the usual sort of problem. "What's the Arab up to?"

"I don't know. I trust him and that's an end of it." Mary found the words difficult to form. "I'm certain that Deacon wants to kill him, though I don't know why."

Kranz was silent for too long.

"Are you going to help or not?" Only yesterday she had been thinking seriously of getting rid of him. How things had changed.

"I'd be happier if I had some idea of what's going on."

"When you met him last night did he ask you what you were doing here?"

"No. You probably already told him, or at least what you had surmised."

"Damn you." Mary tried to struggle up but fell back in the chair. She slowly recovered her breath and continued weakly. "You wanted his help. I fixed a meet. What the bloody hell's wrong with you? Are you chicken?" The effort of anger took it out of her and she closed her eyes, breathing heavily.

"Okay, you've made your point. I'll help him. What am I up against?"

"All I know is that by now Deacon will know about the warehouse and that Hash has been using it. They'll try to lay a trap for him. Go over there and see what's happening. It might take some days. I don't know. I don't suppose they know any more than what I've just told you. Be careful. Try to make contact with him and warn him." Mary had to pause again. "In the bottom of the wardrobe in my bedroom you'll find some binoculars. Take them and the camera in the top drawer of the chest. Look like a bloody tourist. Anyway it will give you something to do."

"What about you? You should be in hospital."

"I know. But I can't go without a lot of explanation. See if the coast is clear and then help me back to my rooms if you will. I'm sorry about this."

He helped her up and she leaned against him. Together they walked slowly to the door where he propped her against the jamb while he took a look in the corridor. He could hear a chamber-maid vacuuming downstairs but the way was clear on this floor. He held her steady and they moved along slowly.

"Not a word of this to anyone," she instructed. "I'll draw you a plan. Nobody knows that area like I do. Nobody. And don't worry about me. I'll be up and about in no time. Just concentrate on getting Hashimi clear. Okay?"

Kranz agreed, but he suddenly felt threatened: the euphoria of yesterday totally gone.

O'Dwyer slept at Deacon's place. He might not have been so eager had he known that Hashimi had shot one of Deacon's men and that he had slept in the dead man's bed. But by the time they had finished discussing what to do it had not been worth returning to his apartment. He rose, borrowed a razor, showered and went down to the large kitchen-breakfast room at the rear of the house to find Deacon, Ted and Charlie Harris already there.

"There's coffee on the hob," said Deacon. "Help yourself. Toast and cereal on the dresser. If you want anything cooked you'll have to do it yourself." It was obvious that the three men, in spite of little sleep, had been up for some time.

Deacon had re-drawn the plan they had made during the night and it was now spread over the kitchen table. "It's a pity you can't give us more precise detail," Deacon complained. "We need more than this."

O'Dwyer poured himself a cup of coffee, heaped in some sugar and sat down to join them. "I've already told you. The warehouse is not under my control. If it gets out that I've told you I'll be on the marked list." He pointed to the plan. "I haven't been there for a long time." He swivelled the plan round so that he could study it. "That looks about right. There's nothing I can add. You'll not get in without keys. The alternative is blowing the door down."

But Deacon was still not satsfied. "What about a spare set of keys? There must be some."

O'Dwyer pushed his coffee away; his mouth felt foul and he was beginning to worry about the state in which he had left Mary. "Stop trying it on, for God's sake. They will be hidden somewhere safe and nobody is going to tell me. You've got all I know and I can't help you any more." He stood up, the scratches on his face dark and angry.

Not once had Deacon passed any comment on O'Dwyer's state. In matters like these he could be astute. He connected the scratches with the information O'Dwyer had given him and the facial wounds had quite obviously been made by a woman. It was best not to remind O'Dwyer that he looked as if he had been pulled through a hedge. He still needed the Irishman on his side. "Thanks," Deacon said. "If this works out I owe you."

"I'm off," said O'Dwyer. "I've gone as far as I can." As he drove back to Kilburn he was strongly tempted to call at the guest house to see Mary. But he resisted: it would be better to keep away.

Deacon used two cars belonging to his men. The Jaguar and the Mercedes would be too conspicuous. He and Ted rode in the first one with two men in the back, and Charlie drove with three other men in the second car. It was still early morning and the peak hour snarl-ups were yet to come.

Deacon felt better now that he had some positive news and was mobile. And he was thinking more hopefully of Vi. They approached the docks and stopped some distance from them. Deacon decided to recce the general area. The second car was to remain where it was in a side street distinguished only by graffiti-covered factory walls.

He became nervous as they drew closer, unable to dismiss the notion that the whole idea might be some elaborate trap arranged by the Arab just to get them there. He drove past the active part of the docks first and then cut back away from the Thames and turned into the derelict warehouse site. He drove as slowly as he dared, gun on the seat between his legs, while Ted and the other two men held their own guns ready for an instant shoot-out.

They learned little from the first recce except that an area of about three large blocks was completely deserted and that the road surface was like a tank trap. It was impossible to miss the forlorn, gloomy aspect of a place which even the vandals now neglected. And yet somewhere in there the Arab had been up to his tricks. "We'll go past once more," Deacon pronounced but a second time round added nothing new to their knowledge. He drove back to the point where Charlie waited.

This time both cars edged to a spot behind and out of sight of the warehouse and within a few minutes' walk of it. They left one man with each car and the remaining six started to walk. They split up when they approached the intersection that would lead them directly to the warehouse, with Charlie leading the way and Ted bringing up the rear to watch the widely spread roof tops.

They approached from both ends of the block and stopped

before they reached the warehouse. Deacon was very much aware that his group could attract attention if seen from the Thames side where road work was in progress. He dispersed his men but kept Charlie with him.

Deacon didn't draw his gun until he was actually in the shell of the warehouse. Charlie came in behind him and then drew level before they stood back to back. There was nowhere for anyone to hide; even a rat would be spotted. They moved towards the stairs. O'Dwyer had not prepared them for the smell. Deacon went down first, wrinkling his nose. At the foot of the stairs he could see that a small area had recently been cleaned and lightly sanded to make a clear path to the door. He looked back at Charlie who was standing on the bottom step.

Deacon located the three key holes and ran his hands over the steel. O'Dwyer had been right; it was an explosives job. But was Vi inside? He put his ear to the door and could hear nothing. Increasingly frustrated he signalled for Charlie to come over. Perhaps younger ears could pick something up. Charlie pressed his ear against the steel and concentrated for some time. Eventually he looked to Deacon and shook his head. He pushed the door with both hands flat, gauging its strength.

Deacon signalled Charlie and they retreated to the top of the steps. "Did you hear anything at all?"

"Nothing," replied Charlie. "Maybe the door's sound proof."

Deacon looked doubtful. "I squinted through the central key hole but I can't see a thing. There might be a cover the other side."

"Shall we bang on it? If there's anyone there they must hear something."

"If the Arab's there he'll know we're outside."

"Sure, but what can he do? He'd be trapped in there. He can't stay there for ever."

"You're not thinking, Charlie. If he's got Vi in there with him he's got his way out. And according to Paddy there's enough food to last weeks. We've got to find a way to get him out or to break in ourselves."

Deacon's nerves were becoming ragged. In a sense they were no better off with O'Dwyer's information. "If I could be sure Vi was not in there we could blow the bloody door off."

"If she's not then you've got to face up to it, Phil. She won't be anywhere else."

Deacon's features sagged. He was so close to knowing yet no nearer a solution. "Let's go round the back and see if there's another way in."

They went outside. Deacon gave a signal to the others to stay where they were, and he and Charlie crossed to the rear of the building. They found the stumps of two door frames at the back but the cellar itself had only the one way in and out.

They went to the front again but remained inside the framework of the building. It was difficult for Deacon to know what to do. So far as he was concerned Vi was the key to everything. Charlie, and perhaps even Ted would sacrifice Vi to kill the Arab and remove the threat from themselves, and he realised that it might come to the point where he was on his own where his wife was concerned.

The long run between the old warehouses was still clear; he reflected that it wasn't exactly a lovers' walk. Seeing Ted peering out from across the street he signalled him over and his son ran to join him.

"All we can do is to stake the place out," Deacon said. He gazed around. "There's reasonable cover. I want two men to stay opposite now and to watch as they've never watched before. The Arab's crafty with disguise. If they see any sign of him and the coast is clear I want him killed and dumped in the river at night. Both men must have silenced guns. Let one of them have the radio telephone so that we can be called at a moment's notice 'f there's any problem. I think the rest of us must find some sort of doss-house nearby so that we're on tap."

"We ought to leave someone in the house at Wandsworth. If he's keeping an eye on the place he'll smell a rat. It must look occupied," Ted pointed out. "There's someone there now. One more will do."

"Then you'd better stay there."

"No, Dad. The Arab wants you, me and Charlie. We've got a solid reason to do it right. We don't want any cock-ups. We three keep in direct contact with this place."

Deacon looked to Charlie who nodded assent. "Okay. The rest of us go back now and one of the boys can return with some grub and coffee for the two who stay. Charlie, dig up some two-way radios. They could be useful, particularly when it's dark. See if you can get some night glasses. Maybe Paddy can help us there. And we'll probably need some gelignite. Anything to add?"

Ted and Charlie gave it serious thought. "How long do you think this will last? Our blokes might be seen. It could be dicey, Dad."

"Then suggest something else." Deacon's tone was dangerous. "If he's in there he's gotta come out. If he's not then he'll go in at some stage. It doesn't matter which as long as he's in our sights. Just impress on the lads that he'd better not see them. If he does they won't be answerable to me; they'll be dead. Get it through their heads, Ted." He saw his son's expression and added, "Look, son. One day, two days. No more. It'll all be over. Let's get bloody cracking."

Like Deacon, Kranz had realised that the earlier he got away the better but he was already well behind the gangsters' movements when he left the guest house in Mary's car. An accomplished driver, he made good time to the warehouse following Mary's very scratchily written and almost indecipherable plan. He came in at the far end of the unused warehouse block, was about to turn in when he caught sight of movement further down. He continued straight on towards the river line, tucked the car away behind the riverside block, and walked back.

He was lucky to have seen someone at the warehouse but wondered if he himself had been noticed. He approached the corner very warily, and crouched low before peering round. He could see nobody. His angle of vision covered only the warehouse area itself. The whole site now appeared to be empty but he was quite sure that he had seen something during the drive between the blocks.

Kranz looked behind him. For the moment he was safe. He decided to wait to see if anything developed. After a while he thought he could see movement in the shadows of the framework of the warehouse and he raised the binoculars. He was right: two men. They disappeared again and later came back in full view. More men joined them from his side of the block and confirmed his initial sighting. When the group started to move towards him Kranz sprinted down the alley and rounded the corner where his car was parked. He risked peering round, and after a while the group reached the corner he had just left but then walked away from him. He guessed that they had parked behind the warehouse and were returning to their cars. One stopped at the corner and looked back in the direction of the warehouse. He lifted an arm in a half salute, half farewell. So someone had been left behind.

Kranz waited until they were out of sight and then reflected on what he should do. If they were the men Mary had referred to, then it was clear that they had not found Hashimi but were waiting for his arrival. He walked towards the river. It was more active here but he cut across a demolished site which looked like a relic from war-time bombing and moved away from the direction of the warehouse. After a while he veered away from the river and cut up towards the original intersection but further away from the warehouse site. It was difficult because life was much more evident in this region and if he couldn't see the action he could hear it; not too distant voices and the clear sound of traffic.

He reached the long stretch leading to the warehouse and crossed to the other side, aware that he might be seen by the waiting man. But he was a fair distance from the watcher and reasoned that his vigil would be more locally confined. He found a gap where double doors had been ripped off a long time ago. He checked the direction of light in relation to lens reflection then raised his glasses again, uncomfortably aware that there was some road work going on close behind him. He leaned against the battered brickwork and scanned the vandalised buildings opposite the warehouse. There was more skin to the bones of the building than the one Hashimi was using, and, therefore, more cover, but patient waiting eventually revealed slight movement. Kranz hung on. His diligence was rewarded; there were two men, not one. He made a mental note of their location and returned to the car.

As he drove off he accepted that there was absolutely nothing he could do in daylight. It was impossible to approach the place without being seen and he had no doubt what instructions the two men had been given. He would have to wait but meanwhile could report his findings to Mary.

She had given him a flat key. Her note which Kranz had delivered to Zoe had contained instructions that she was to be left alone until she said otherwise. She had a kitchenette in her small flatlet and there was adequate food.

He found her almost as he had left her, lying fully clothed on the bed. He wondered whether he should undress her and put some blankets over her but she did not appear to be cold. She blearily opened her eyes as he came in and relaxed when she saw who it was. "You look dreadful," he said in an attempt to persuade her to let him call a doctor, but she knew what he was trying to do and shook her head.

Kranz told her what had happened and promised to go back when it was dark. She showed interest and held out a hand to let him know that she had understood. If anything her condition had deteriorated since he had last seen her and he was deeply concerned. "Is there anything I can get you? Maybe cook you something light?" But again she shook her head. Then she said, "Save Hashimi whatever you do." It was an enormous effort for her to talk.

"Don't worry. I know what I'm up against."

At eight that evening Kranz set out again and parked. He was dressed in dark slacks and pullover and carried a gun in his hip pocket, with a spare clip. He wore canvas shoes and crept up to the intersection without a sound. His earlier recce now paid off. He knew that the approaches along the walls and gaps opposite the warehouse were clear. He hugged the wall and worked his way along.

He reached a ragged gap where he knew the watchers should be positioned, on the other side. It was exactly opposite the warehouse. If nobody was there it would mean that Hashimi had returned and had been dealt with. He went down on his hands and knees.

Someone moved; just the shifting of a foot on grit. Kranz crossed the gap and stopped. Holding his breath he could detect the breathing of a man just the other side of the wall. He knew that the wall continued for a foot or two along the front forming a protection for the man, something to hide behind if he needed to draw back, and the same was true the other end. It seemed to him that, protected by darkness the man was leaning against the front section. It was the only position from which he could have a clear view.

Kranz pulled himself up against the wall, eased out his gun and transferred it to his left hand. He waited, breathing controlled. He gradually reached along the wall until he found its edge. He pushed his hand out further and pulled it back slightly as there was a risk of actually touching the man. He bent his wrist and steadied his hand until satisfied that his angle was right. Then he fired.

The plop was acute in the silence but the falling body and the loud groan spread louder still through the place. Kranz dropped to his knees and fired again as he saw the moving heap. He rolled away as the second man circled deep to investigate. Deacon's man did not fire, well aware that he might hit his friend.

Nothing happened until Kranz heard the buttons of a telephone being punched out. Help was being called. Still on his knees he fired four shots by sound direction alone. The radio telephone crashed to the floor. Someone screamed out in agony and then started to curse in decreasing volume. Two shots were fired and Kranz could just detect the faint powder flashes of the silenced gun. When concrete chips cascaded down from the roof he knew that the shots were the reflex action of a wounded man. He dashed in. The man was doubled forward and Kranz finished it quickly through the back of the head. He went back to make sure the first man was dead then ran across the street to the warehouse, now using a small flashlight to find the steps.

He did not hesitate at the door and hammered on it as hard as he could, shouting, "Hashimi. Hashimi. It's Kranz. They're after you." He did not know whether Hashimi was inside or not but if he was he must hear the shouts. He called again and hammered until his hands were sore. He called out, "If you're there come out now. I've taken care of the watchdogs. It's all clear."

When he finally received a response it was not what he expected. A woman started to scream repeatedly and there was

213

no doubt about the terror in her voice. Kranz could not believe his ears. He sank down, scared now of what he had run into and he covered his ears as the screams grew worse. And then they stopped abruptly.

17

From the moment Hashimi had suggested that Mary McGanly tell O'Dwyer about the warehouse he devised a crude security system to check if anyone had called there. He had cleared a section outside the door and put down sandy grit which he was careful to step over when entering or leaving and which would easily show up if disturbed. He had also bought himself a stethoscope which he plugged over the middle key hole because it was the biggest. He had laid the bait to attract Deacon and was certain that Deacon, once he knew about the warehouse, would not be so stupid as to blow in the door without being sure that Vi was not inside.

By laying a trap for Deacon he recognised that he might well have laid one for himself too. A good deal depended on whether or not he was inside when Deacon called. It meant spending more time there to know what was happening and he had virtually moved in with Vi. He knew that normal conversation would not penetrate the door but he warned her against screaming any time he was there. The rules between them had drastically changed. He could no longer take a lenient view of anything she tried against him. When he warned her that he would shoot her if she made any noise beyond talking he left her in no doubt. Consequently she now spent most of the time in a moody silence.

Vi knew that matters were reaching a climax and could guess that Hashimi was trying to draw her husband in. And she accepted that things would soon be finished for her: Hashimi had gone too far to let her go. When he did leave the basement Vi would wait until she was sure that he had really gone then scream her head off, knowing full well that the Arab was out there somewhere waiting for Phil to enter the trap.

She was happier when Hashimi wasn't there, reasoning that outside Phil had some sort of chance. But if Phil ever forcibly entered while Hashimi was there then she had no doubt that in order to get Phil he would blow himself up too. A change had come over Hashimi during the last two days which she found hard to understand. He carried a gun all the time now and a gadget which she did not realise was a transmitter. Even when he ate, and he was never close to her when he did, the gun and the gadget were by his side. Most worrying of all, his humour had gone, as if he knew that none of them had much longer.

At the time Deacon and Ted went down the steps Hashimi was inside. Neither he nor Vi heard them but Hashimi never opened the door now without first listening at the keyhole with the stethoscope. It was an agonising routine but he never failed to perform it. Several times that morning he had listened at the door. Nearer mid-day he very carefully checked again before opening up.

Vi had become used to these actions over the last two days and had come to realise that he was worried. She watched him crouch at the foot of the door and study the sand he had put down. His hand went out above it and he turned to gaze thoughtfully at her.

"We've had a caller," she suggested, brightening at the very idea.

Hashimi rose slowly, gazed up the steps without moving out, and then closed the door and locked it. He walked slowly towards the far corner where he kept his bed roll and where Vi could not reach him.

"Am I right?" she goaded. The possibility had offered a respite from her deepening depression.

"You might be."

"Then Phil knows I'm here."

"I want him to know."

Her spirits dropped immediately, but it was the Arab who seemed the more depressed at that moment. She studied him as he sat on a box and wondered why his mood had darkened so much. "What do you want for lunch?" she asked in an effort to draw him out. But he only shook his head before raising it to look at her with an expression she had not seen before. Suddenly she felt very cold as if ice was clustering around her heart. She almost burst into tears as a terrible fear welled up, but she managed to hold on.

For a moment she almost felt sorry for him. Usually so relaxed, he now sat on the box, legs splayed and hands clasped tightly in front of him as if confronted with some terrible problem. "You've just come to terms with what I've been telling you all along." Her voice was rough but steady and she felt rather proud of herself. During the days she had been captive her life had changed out of all recognition. She had lost touch with normality and it was sometimes difficult for her to dredge up a physical image of her husband. Suddenly Vi found the courage to articulate her growing conviction of how things would end. "You've finally realised that you've got to do it. You poor, contemptible sod."

She was sitting in the chair she favoured, the stave had not been put back, and she reached for her handbag and took out some of the pots he had bought her. She began to clean her make-up off and all the time he watched as if imposing a self-torture. When her face was clean she began to make it up again. "I want to look my best for my funeral. You should have brought those tights I asked for, but it's too late now isn't it? No time left."

Vi carried on making up and there was a regality about her that had not been evident before. She paused before applying lipstick. "You've been kidding yourself, haven't you? You believed that you had given up the old terrorist lark. A changed man looking for justice for his ravaged girlfriend. Well let me tell you, Hashimi, old cock, you were more to blame for her death than my Phil. It was you who put her on the rack because you are what you are. She would have been in no danger at all but for your capers. You set up the situation, and poor innocent bitch that she was, she did what you wanted. Why don't you bloody well shoot yourself if you want justice?"

Her head was high but it took all her courage to control her terror. "You'll justify knocking me off. You'll do that all right because you have to have a patsy for your own bloody conscience. All this stuff you've bought me. It's not really for me but to make you feel better. There was a time when I thought I understood why you were doing it but I didn't understand half enough. I do now. You'll always be a terrorist. And you'll always justify yourself no matter how many Sophies you destroy. I pity you. But I'll be on your conscience for ever because I had no part in any of it.

Shit on you. You're scum. Like all con men you con yourself more than you do your victims. Remember me, Hash, old son. You remember me well. If you have the guts."

Hashimi remained impassive through her measured tirade. He even relaxed a little as he released his hands and stood up. "You're probably right, Vi. I'm probably all the things you say I am. I doubt that I'll ever find out. Nothing's so simple. I lifted you to force Phil into giving me the names of the men who actually killed Sophie but you gave them to me and Charlie did the job I intended to do. And then I saw the advantage of hanging on to you. It's the way it goes. But it gave me the opportunity to find out a few things about you too, and that came as a surprise. I admire you. Had I known before what you are really like I would probably have left you alone."

"You don't know whether to stay here or piss off, do you? You're not so sure as you were."

"You're right again." He smiled at his own indecision. "It's all a matter of judgment. It always has been. Win some, lose some."

"I've lost the bloody lot. I don't know what it's all about any more. I'm not even religious. I never thought I would envy those who are. I haven't a bloody God to pray to."

Hashimi didn't reply. He was torn between going outside and staying put. It was a matter of timing. If Deacon had been here then he would have left men to keep an eye on the place. Hashimi accepted that there was no way he could leave in daylight and be undetected. Night time was another matter and that would be the time when Deacon would make a move. He was sure of it.

The day passed slowly. Vi could not concentrate on reading and conversation had died. There was nothing left to say. As time passed she grew more edgy, refusing to eat. And when he refilled the lamp it reminded her that permanent darkness was not far off. She cried a little but made sure he did not see her, and even began to pray.

When Hashimi started to check his gun and examine the transmitter which she thought of as a gadget, Vi knew there was not much time left. She had learned that Hashimi was sensitive to events and he obviously thought that one was about to happen.

She had lost count of how many times he had crossed to the door but there was something final about the way he did it now. Her heart began to squeeze in her chest and her breathing became laboured as she watched him. She saw him stiffen as he listened through the stethoscope and could judge that he was weighing up the possibilities of going outside. When the hammering on the door started Vi jumped from her chair and Hashimi tore the instrument from his ears.

At once Vi knew that whoever was outside could raise no hope in her; clearly it was someone Hashimi knew. She could accept that until he bawled out that the coast was clear and he had taken care of the watchdogs. She only just caught the words through the heavy door and they somehow reached her out of context because she was so confused. But the important part to her hammered through her head. She was scared and weary and she put the wrong meaning on part of what was said. She immediately connected the watchdogs with Phil and it dawned on her with increasing terror that he was one of them. What little world she had left fell in pieces about her and the courage she had maintained with so much effort at last deserted her. Phil was dead. She screamed and screamed, releasing all the fear and tension that had built up over the last few days. She was still standing and screaming with all the power of her lungs when the shot rang out. She stopped screaming, stared at Hashimi with an expression of reproach he was never to forget, then collapsed at the foot of her chair without a whimper.

Hashimi crouched at the door looking back at Vi's corpse and put his hands over his ears because the sudden silence was worse than the noise. Screams were life; silence was death. He felt bewildered and empty and was unable to move. He managed to rub his eyes and was glad only that he had finished her with one shot and that she never knew what hit her. Vi more than anyone had made him see himself as he really was. For a terrible moment he thought he had shot her to shut out the image – the accurate image – that she had projected of him and he prayed that the reason had not been so selfish. In truth her panic had partly transmitted itself to him but he could not accept that he could ever panic like that. She had deserved far better. His regret was as delayed as his reaction to her screams had been instinctive.

But it was all too late now and Kranz's repeated calls were demanding reponse. He managed to call back, "Are you alone?"

"Of course. Get out of there quick or Deacon will be back."

"Wait for me at the top." Hashimi picked up the transmitter. He could not look back again. He unlocked the door for the last time and went through. He paused only fractionally before he locked the door from the outside; Deacon would expect it to be locked; it must not appear too easy. He went up the steps with leaden legs. He felt worse than when he had found Sophie dead as though, in killing Vi, he had killed part of himself.

An agitated Kranz was waiting at the top, gun in hand. "What the hell were the screams? You had a woman in there."

"Forget her. What's the form?"

"Deacon had posted two men opposite to make sure they got you either coming out or going in. I had to shoot them; any other way would have been too chancy. Deacon will be back. I don't know when. And there are bound to be reliefs for those two. Let's get out of here."

"You go back to Mary's place and wait for me to call you."

"The phone has been ripped out. O'Dwyer beat her up."

Hashimi gripped Kranz's arm. He felt sick. Vi's accusation raced through his head. Sophie. Vi. Mary. Vi had been right. He created the situations and they paid the price. "Look," he faltered. "There's a place in Highbury. It's almost served its purpose. Go there." He gave the address and then repeated it but Kranz had grasped it first time. "Here are the keys. Front door and inner door. Up the stairs. I'll contact you there but first see if Mary's all right. How was she when you left?"

"Not at all good. But she won't have a doctor. If she takes it easy she should recover but she'll need time. It was she who told me about this place."

"I gathered that. You push off. And thanks. Glad to know you're more political than a gunman."

"It's no time for joking. You can't stay here. You'd be mad."

"I've always been mad. I'm only just realising how much. Get out of here quick."

As Kranz ran between the buildings, Hashimi briskly crossed to where Deacon's men were lying but before he entered the building he heard an engine and saw the erratic beams of head lights as a car bounced over the potholes. He dived to the side of the building and waited. A car approached slowly to the intersection and stopped. It just protruded enough to be seen. The lights were switched off and then on again before the car reversed back, dragging its beams with it. It was obviously a signal.

Hashimi ran round the back of the building and climbed up a half-bricked girder which he had already earmarked. He made more noise than he intended as he scrambled up the corrugated iron roof but the men below him were dead and the others had yet to park the car before returning. He reached an uncomfortable position from where he could see across the gap to the warehouse where Vi lay dead and chained.

Hashimi did not hear an approach until the men were almost below him. A torch was flashed guardedly and a voice cried out, "Jesus Christ. No wonder they didn't reply." Footsteps ran forward and Hashimi strained to listen to what was said in loud whisper.

"Be careful. The bastard might still be around." There was a scraping as the two bodies were brought to the front. "Bring the car round. We can't leave them here."

"Right. Is the phone okay?"

"I'm checking now. They didn't even have time to use their radios. Get moving for Christ's sake, and watch your back. The Arab must move like a snake."

Footsteps sprinted away. Hashimi could not hear the number being punched out but the voice that floated up was just audible. "Lou? This is Charlie Harris. Get Phil quick."

Charlie Harris? It came as a shock to Hashimi that he had shot the wrong man. But he quickly dismissed it from his mind and concentrated on what was being said below. "Phil. Charlie. Trouble. The Arab's done Harry and Jimbo. Stone dead. You'd better bring the boys. I'll wait here. Of course I've got my eyes peeled, they're revolving round my bloody head. Make it quick."

The car lights floodlit the intersection and then turned towards the warehouse. Hashimi pulled his head below the roof level; the lights were blinding in the darkness and the driver, realising it, switched them off as soon as he drew up.

"Get them in the boot, Joe. We'll have to dump them later."

Hashimi listened to the sound of the bodies being loaded and then Charlie said, "Where are those bloody walkie talkies? I've put the phone in." And then, "Christ, what a bloody mess. Phil warned them to keep sharp. How could they have missed him crossing over from there?"

"Maybe he was already out."

Charlie didn't reply. Instead he said, "We don't want the same thing happening to us. You keep that bloody gun in your hand and you develop radar, boy. Let's get right to the back so he can't come up from behind."

"What about the car?"

"What about it? Leave it where it is. The Arab knows we've been watching the place. What difference can it make? Might even give us cover."

The exchange died and Hashimi lay above the two men knowing that he dare not move a fraction on so fragile a roof. The slightest creak would warn them and they would blast at anything.

Kranz drove back to Kilburn. He was in no hurry and he wanted time to think. He was not new to sounds of terror but Vi's screams had somehow upset him. And she had been left behind in the cellar, probably dead. Kranz wondered what Hashimi had got involved in but it was a waste of time to speculate. So much had happened even though it was not yet eleven o'clock as he reached central London. He arrived in Kilburn some twenty minutes later, managed to park close to the house and then ran up the steps. The hall was empty and he took the stairs two at a time. On the top floor he unlocked Mary's door and went in.

When he switched on the light she did not move and she was more or less as he had left her. It was noticeably colder in the bedroom and he decided to undress her and put her between the sheets. He crossed over to draw the curtains then wondered whether it would be kinder to let her sleep on or to wake her and tell her that Hashimi was so far all right. He crossed to the bed. She appeared to be more relaxed than before and he took this as a good sign. Her bruised lips were open and so were the slits of her eyes. It struck him that he was gazing at death.

At exactly what point he realised it did not matter. One moment he was about to put out his hand to gently shake her and the next he knew she was dead. He tested her pulse and her breathing and there was no response. She had been battered to death and Kranz guessed that there might have been a brain haemorrhage resulting from the brutal assault.

As he examined her Kranz considered his own position. Had anyone else been in the room? His instinct was to leave quickly; he did not want to be part of police questioning and it would be inevitable if he stayed. Yet if he left it would look bad and someone might have seen him use her car. It would not have mattered then but it mattered now. Her death should be reported but it was not something he was prepared to do; too much explaining would have to go with it.

First, it was better to leave the room and to give himself a little time to think. He opened the door, peered down the corridor and stepped out just as Zoe the cook came onto the landing. He gave her a nod but it did not satisfy her as she walked towards the flat.

"Is Mrs McGanly all right? I hired the temp like she said but I want to know how long she's to stay."

"As long as you need her." He had blocked the way to the door.

"I must have a word. It's been a very long day coping without her. I've only just finished getting everything ready for to-morrow."

"Didn't the note tell you to leave her alone?"

"Yes, but I need to know how I stand. It won't take a minute."

"She's not well and she's resting. Leave it until tomorrow. Don't disturb her now."

"Okay. But I must know." The plumping Zoe turned on her heel and went downstairs.

Kranz went to his room and packed, slightly trembling at his narrow escape. He crept down the stairs and passed the television room, the sound of music escaping through the door. He suddenly realised that he had left the key in Mary's door but it could make no difference now. He went down the steps to the street and for the first time turned towards the Kilburn High Road in the hope that he would quickly find a cab. Zoe's appearance had decided matters for him and it was not difficult to imagine what would happen next. He was about to be crucified.

A second car stood side by side with the first to enable both to get away quickly. Deacon asked, "You've seen no sign of him?"

"No. He must have scarpered. He can't be inside the cellar."

"Let's go and see. Where've you put Harry and Jimbo?"

"In the boot."

"We'll have to dump them in the river. But first let's get this over. Ted and Charlie come with me, you two stay here, and you stay by the head of the cellar steps."

Four of them crossed over with Charlie carrying the gelignite that Deacon had brought with him. Deacon led the way down, his mood grim and beneath it fear at what he might find. At the base of the steps he spoke to Charlie, "Okay. You're the expert. You've got all you need and you can detonate from the top of the steps as they're dog-legged. We'll leave you to it. Don't overdo it. Just take the door out."

Deacon and Ted went back up the steps and left Charlie to fix the charges and run back the wire from the detonator. There was no longer any point in avoiding the issue. They all believed that the Arab had gone after killing the two men and all that was left to do was to see if Vi was still in there.

On the corrugated roof Hashimi lay as still as ever. The explosion of the door being blasted off reached him quite clearly but was still subdued as the cavity around the door absorbed a good deal of the sound. He balanced himself as he adjusted the position of the transmitter and was ready to send out the signal.

For a while there was an acute silence as Deacon's men waited for the smoke to clear before rushing down the steps. Hashimi strained his ears realising that he should have been nearer to pick the precise moment. Then from the cellar came a great wail of anguish which carried up the steps and out into the open and turned dramatically into a roar of utter fury. Deacon had found Vi. Hashimi sent the signal and it seemed that the whole world exploded.

18

It was like seeing it in slow motion. The outline of the warehouse seemed gradually to lift and the bright flash of the explosion escaped through the gaps it created so that the whole bizarre appearance was that of the building rising on a cushion of flame. When it reached its peak it hovered and then collapsed without seeming to disintegrate. It simply sank down as though on a hydraulic shelf. Halfway down it accelerated at great speed and a tremendous roar spread rapidly in every direction as tons of steel and concrete burst down into the cellar.

The two men who were below Hashimi ran out into the open and then scuttled back again as debris and dust spread through the air. As Hashimi covered his head a great slab of concrete crashed through the corrugated iron roof, tilting it so that he had to cling to the jagged gap to save himself from falling through. He hung by his finger tips and managed to ease his legs over to a safer position. The only reason he was not seen by Deacon's men was because they had balled up to save themselves as the slab splintered on the floor to send reverberations right through the shaky structure.

As the noise quietened down Hashimi heard one of the men call out, "Let's get the hell out of here."

"What about Phil and the others?"

"You want to go down to that tomb and scrape out the pieces? You silly sod, they're pulp. This place will be alive with coppers any minute."

Hashimi, who could not move until they had gone, heard the whole exchange quite clearly. He was at such an awkward angle that he could barely hang on and he willed the men to leave quickly. A car started up and lights came on, and with a scream of tyres it was away, covering the potholes as if they weren't there.

Hashimi moved awkwardly to the edge where he had climbed up. He almost slid down the brickwork and jumped the last few feet. He ran round the building to see the remaining car with its roof dented in and covered in dust and rubble. For a moment he gazed across to the old warehouse. There was nothing to see but a great gap and a ghostly dust pall rising from the huge hole in the ground where Vi, Phil Deacon, his son Ted and Charlie Harris lay buried with one other man. The saga was over. He had done what he had set out to do; he had killed every person involved in Sophie's murder and two innocent people had gone with them.

He felt nothing then. There was no sensation of triumph or remorse; nothing at all. The next moment he was running as hard as he could to where he had left his car. The explosion would have been heard over a wide area and the sirens of police and fire brigade would be wailing through the night at any minute. He headed for the place in Highbury.

When he arrived outside the house he realised that he no longer had the keys. A light was on upstairs and he guessed that Kranz was waiting up for him. He used a five-pence piece to throw at the window and it made a penetrating crack as it hit the glass. Kranz must have realised the situation for he opened the window and saw Hashimi signal for the door to be opened.

Hashimi followed Kranz up the stairs and threw himself into a chair the moment the living room door was closed. Kranz stood looking down at him. "You're covered in dust. What happened?"

Hashimi showed his weariness and a trace of disillusion. "I blew the place up. I've finished my job. I'm at your disposal."

Kranz sank to a chair. He had no idea why Hashimi had blown up the warehouse and he did not ask. But he kept thinking that a terrified woman had been down there. "You want some coffee? I've found where everything is."

"No." Hashimi shook his head. "I just want to ease it all out of my system. How's Mary?"

"She's dead."

Hashimi shed his weariness. *"What?"*

"She was dead when I got back. The beating must have done internal damage. O'Dwyer really laid it on."

Now all three women were dead. Again Vi's words came back to Hashimi; she was already haunting him. "I hope that bastard

226

gets picked up. I never thought I'd see the day when I'd wish the police luck, but I hope they get him."

"It's more likely that they'll look for me." Kranz explained what had happened, adding, "All circumstantial evidence points to me. I took the note to the cook. I used Mary's car. I was seen leaving her flat and I stopped the cook from going in. And it was I who disappeared immediately after. I'm a natural suspect."

Hashimi gazed up at Kranz, trying to take it all in. "So you're on the run?"

"So are you by the sound of things."

Hashimi seemed to come to terms with what had happened. "I suppose we're always on the run when it comes down to it. That's bad though. Bad all round. Did you leave anything at the guest house?"

"It's all here. It wouldn't have mattered though. I've got to make up my mind what to do. Circumstances have ruined my mission here. I can make contact by phone but I won't be helped in getting back to Germany; they wouldn't want the embarrassment of it nor the risks. They wouldn't want openly to cross the British police."

"What do you think they'll do?"

"If they can find me they'll kill me. I'm quite sure they were going to do that anyway: I've simply made it more difficult for them. But at the same time what has now happened will remove any doubt they might have had about the benefit of getting rid of me."

"I reckon this place is about to blow if it hasn't already but we might be lucky. I was banking on you returning to the guest house and to keep you covered from there."

Kranz sat down at last. "I know you were. So was I. It was the way things worked out. But what about you?"

"I have a way out. I've laid my plans. It's not going to be so easy to help you now. That's not reluctance; you probably saved me tonight. But the game's changed."

"I understand. If I can stay here I'll try to make plans to return to East Germany and take my chances there."

"You can stay here as long as the place remains safe. I've got some wigs here, cheek pads, that sort of thing. You can dye your hair. I've got some blank passports but we'll need some shots of you. Maybe I can take them myself. We'll work on it. Meanwhile you stay here. I'll take the keys and get another set cut. I won't stay here because I'm supposed to be on view somewhere else. I've been away too long already. I'll push off in the morning. Let's see if we can get some rest."

Sanger reported to Sir Lewis Hope later that morning. "The Arab's back at the Dorchester, sir. I thought you should know."

"Thank God for that. I thought we might have lost him. Any idea of where he's been?"

"None. It was your policy not to have him followed."

Hope did not need reminding. "I want you to find out anything you can about a gangster called Phil Deacon and whether he is alive or dead. As soon as you can. Warn our man at the hotel to keep in close touch with the situation there. I have a feeling that the Arab's departure might be imminent."

When Sanger had gone Hope permitted himself a smile of satisfaction. It seemed that everything was working out quite well. He had reached a critical point but saw no reason why the rest of his strategy should not work out well. But by three thirty that afternoon he had his first shock, in the unwelcome form of George Bulman.

Bulman entered the office and Hope immediately saw that he bore bad news. "May I sit down, sir?" Bulman sat fractionally before Hope's nodded consent. "Trouble," said Bulman and for once Hope could detect no satisfaction in the tone. "Mary McGanly's been murdered."

"Mary who?"

"The guest house keeper where Kranz was staying."

Hope felt his world slipping away. He found it difficult to swallow and his thoughts were scrambling through his head. "*Was* staying?"

"That's what I said. Kranz has hopped it. Everything points to him being the murderer. She was brutally beaten to death."

"Oh, my God." There was no way Hope could have prepared himself for this. Smug satisfaction had turned into a nightmare. He hated Bulman then; the man was always bad news. "Are you sure about this? Why should he murder her?"

"I didn't say he did, Sir Lewis. The local C.I.D. think he did and there's a lot going against him. Everything points to him. Anyway he's on the run and his description has gone out to all stations. There was no way it could be stopped if that was what you wanted. They are on to Interpol for some mug shots."

Hope's face fractionally unfroze. "I doubt that they will come up with any. We had the only copy and that didn't come from police sources. Special Branch will sit on their copy."

"That's what I thought, sir." Bulman's expression was bland which left Hope wondering whether he had said too much.

Hope stared at his desk and saw only the ruin of carefully made plans. "We've got to find him, George."

"With respect, sir, the whole damned country will be looking for him. I wouldn't know where to start."

Hope was now deeply worried. It was suddenly all going wrong. He groped. "Have you heard anything about Deacon?"

"Phil Deacon?" Bulman realised that Hope was now giving away pointers without even realising it. The man must be crazy with worry but why should Kranz's absence upset him so much? "I've no idea what's going on in the Deacon camp. I've lost sight of him. He's strictly for C.I.D."

"What about the Arab?" Hope asked more shrewdly. He was recovering from the shock news but still had to find direction.

"His whereabouts? Haven't a clue, sir," Bulman lied again. "Are you looking for him?"

Hope did not reply at once but eventually he said, "All right, George. I need time to work things out. Leave it at that for the moment."

When Bulman left he knew that Hope was a badly shaken man.

Both ends of the block had been sealed off and a mobile crane brooded over the police cars and fire tenders. A car was moved to make way for a mechanical digger which trundled forward to hover over the lip of the rubble-filled basement. There was nothing left standing upright and firemen had difficulty in moving around the fractured girders and the mass of concrete, much of which had powdered to leave soft spots for the unwary to fall into. Steel rods which had been embedded into the floor of the warehouse now stuck out like probes to impede and to impale;

they were dangerous, broken and bent in a haphazard array that had to be watched. Firemen with heat-seeking equipment tried to keep their feet as they searched for evidence of body heat to locate victims.

Nobody really believed that there was life under the tons of masonry but people had been known to survive the most terrible disasters in odd pockets where some sort of cave had been formed under the heaviest weight. So the men worked on and the mechanical digger began to remove some of the top layer of debris which offered the searchers a better chance.

The only indication that anyone might be buried there was the damaged car that had been left behind. The two men Kranz had shot were found in the boot. The police traced the owner through the registration number and the answer came quite quickly. It belonged to Anthony Charlton who lived in Balham, the other side of the river. It did not take long for the local police to establish from Charlton's wife that he had been away for a few days. She did not know where; he often went away. Nor did it take long to discover that Charlton had form; he had been to jail twice for armed robbery but had kept out of trouble for some time. With that revelation came a report from the local C.I.D. that Charlton operated for Phil Deacon.

From that point inquiries moved fast. Deacon's house was visited and the two men who had been left behind to occupy it gave no satisfactory answers and were taken in on suspicion of obstructing the police. Recent events came to light, like the blowing down of Deacon's door and the elaborate precautions he had since taken. There were no indications in the house itself and no sign that might reveal detail of the man Hashimi had shot by mistake. Deacon had covered himself well and this slowed things down. There was no sign of Deacon, Ted or Charlie Harris.

However, the wall of silence began to break down when several of Deacon's men were rounded up and interviewed. Some were missing and their wives and girlfriends began to wail about their absence. What clinched matters was when the two men who had fled from the bombed site were found and one of them cracked under pressure. From that point the police were inclined to believe that the whole Deacon family was under the rubble. This news was passed on to Scotland Yard who had shown previous interest in Deacon's antics and in turn the information reached Bulman about five o'clock that evening. This coincided with a report that some human remains had now been found on the site and that work was going on.

Bulman sat thoughtfully at his desk. When Haldean left for the night he barely noticed and failed to acknowledge the ritual farewell. He sat back holding the edge of the desk and gazing at nothing. So the Arab had done it. He had wiped out everyone he said he would, everyone who had played a part in his girlfriend's murder. Walter Janeski who had called himself Salter. The Montaya brothers. Charlie Harris. Phil Deacon, his son Ted, and probably his wife, Vi. Seven people. But how many more might there be? It had been established that one man had been with Deacon in the cellar. There might have been others at some other time. Ross had wiped out the entire heart of a south London gang.

Bulman glanced at his watch. There was just time to catch Scott and he rang the travel agency to arrange a meeting. He tidied his desk, locked his safe and gazed round his office as if it was unfamiliar to him. He locked the door behind him and moved towards the elevator unaware of the odd greeting from passing colleagues. For once he did not know what to do for the best.

They met on the south side of Trafalgar Square and juggled their way through traffic. Too many streets converged at this particular point and at once Scott saw that Bulman was barely aware of what was going on. They went deep into the park and found a damp seat. Bulman had barely said a word and Scott wondered what could have subdued him so much.

Once seated Bulman placed an arm along the back of the bench seat and half turned to face Scott. "Well, he did it. Hashimi. He got the lot."

Scott showed no surprise; he knew the Arab better than anyone. "I've seen nothing in the press about Deacon."

"It's too soon and they haven't scraped out what's left of him yet. Hashimi blew up an old warehouse with them inside. But I'm in no doubt. He's finished the job."

"So what's your problem?"

"You know that I know where Hashimi is hanging out. Or at least his base. My problem is what should I do about it?"

Scott expressed surprise. "If it's a matter of conscience, George, you'd be better off discussing this with Betty. She's a copper's daughter and you two have become close."

Bulman shook his head. "There are angles about this that I couldn't mention to her. I shouldn't mention them to you either but I know they will stop with you and you know what's been going on. You're involved because the Arab saw to it that you were."

"Are you asking me whether you should turn him in? I'm the wrong bloke to ask if that's the case. I haven't got a copper's mind. From my angle he's knocked off a bunch of murderous bastards who would have gone on killing, and we're better off without them." Scott turned his collar up wishing that they'd chosen a less windy spot. "I know the Arab has murdered them but you have to examine his motive. It was not for money or gain but his kind of justice. And with people like them it's sometimes the only kind that works."

"I didn't want a bloody lecture, Spider. I know all that. But I'm a copper and my duty is clear. I know very well what I should do but it's not that simple, is it?" Bulman stopped talking as two young couples hurried past, heads down against an increasing cold wind which moaned through the trees. "In the first place I'm not supposed to know where the Arab is. For some ugly reason Hope doesn't want me to know. To some extent that already absolves me; working for him is security, not police. The rules are different.

"I'm not on the Deacon case. A whole squad will be covering that. I have information that could help them but so has Hope and he won't give it up. And he with his Home Office buddies have withheld it for much longer than the Arab has been on the rampage. If I cut across them I'm in trouble."

Scott was puzzled. "You've already made up your mind. What do you need me for?"

"Because you are in there somewhere. I've thought about it a lot. Hope knows where the Arab is and has done nothing about it. I think he wanted Hashimi to take out Deacon and his mob because Deacon was a link with Murison. And when you mention that name a lot of people in high places still quiver in their silk socks. Now that particular danger has gone he must find it a relief.

"That only leaves two who could be a danger. Hashimi because he broke you out of jail and because he knows about the attempt on your life while you were there. Hope will safely assume that Hashimi knows why it happened, and that threatens him and his pals who helped Murison for whatever reason. If it came out, he could not survive the scandal. He'd lose his job and his power. And so would others. The truth about Murison has never come out; it still remains dynamite and the longer it's covered up the more serious it becomes. And the second man is you."

"Me? I'm no danger to Hope. I could have landed him in it a long time ago had I wanted to. It's not my style. He was guilty of gross incompetence more than anything."

"He conspired, Spider. Whatever his convictions at the time he followed a route that could have got you topped and Murison would still be playing at being God. He knows that. And he doesn't want it hanging over him."

Scott thought it over. "Are you saying that he's trying to do the same as Murison did? Knock off people he considered to be a danger to the State?"

"No. You're hardly a danger to the State. You're a potential danger to him, though. Circumstances change. Something could crop up to make you change your mind about him. He's becoming paranoiac. He's so unsure of himself that he's always looking over his shoulder. I don't know what he's up to but I'll bet my future on you and Hashimi being part of it. I think that's why he's cut me out. I wish I could read his bloody mind."

"So what do you want me to do?"

"One thing's for sure; I'm not bringing Hashimi in. It's not my brief. Whatever Hope's up to could be stopped if Hashimi is warned off. Tell him to get the hell out. But don't be seen doing it. We have at least one man on the inside keeping an eye on him."

"If I was seen doing it Hope could arrange to have me picked up as an accessory. No thanks, George. You do it."

"I can't go that far. You don't have to go. Phone."

"I don't know the name he's registered under."

"Here it is. Memorise and destroy. I'm finished if that got out. Anyway, you're the only one he trusts and he'll know your voice."

Scott took the slip. Sheikh Munir Hashar. "That's not easy to remember."

"Then keep it until you've made the call and then destroy it damned quick."

"You're not sliding out of this, George?"

"No. I wouldn't do that to you. Right now Hope doesn't trust me, if ever he did. My voice is too distinctive and I'm no good at changing it. Your accent is basic London."

"You mean Hashimi's calls are monitored?"

"I don't think so. Hashimi would pick up the signs and the hotel wouldn't be keen to play that kind of game. You are much better and far more practised at playing the old deception game."

"Thanks very much."

"It's a fact. And I would have difficulty in getting over the conscience bit. I am a bloody copper after all; I can't go around telling murdering terrorists to duck out quick even if a mate of mine might be tied in without him knowing."

It was the one argument that Scott understood; he knew all about conscience. "Okay. I'll do it. But I can't do it from home with Maggie there."

"Just one more thing," said Bulman. "The place you cased the other night. You remember the woman who almost caught you? Mary McGanly. She's been murdered. The news will make the evening editions."

Scott had a strong recollection of the incident and of the attractiveness of the woman. "Who killed her? The bloke who was with her? They were arguing like mad."

Bulman raised a brow. "The German is down for it. He scarpered. He would have to wouldn't he? If he's here on a job he wouldn't want police questioning. You might have a point. I'll pass it on for what it's worth but the circumstantial evidence is strong against the other guy."

Scott telephoned from a call box. Sheikh Munir Hashar was out. There was nothing more that he could do except to try later. He could not leave a message because he could not give his name.

On the way back home he bought an *Evening Standard* and found a report on Mary's brutal murder at the bottom of the front page. Mary had been a local character, well liked. There was even a hazy, and obviously early picture of her which did her no justice at all. Scott was appalled at what he read but he had only met her very briefly and she had not been too pleasant then. His main concern was to continue to try and make contact with Hashimi.

Paddy O'Dwyer heard of Mary's death from a friend who knew how close he was to her. O'Dwyer did not have to feign shock; he was shattered to his roots. He somehow got back to his apartment and sat on the bed bewildered, scared, and drained of colour. He had been on his way to the guest house when he had been stopped.

Never in his life of deception and intermittent violence had he felt so full of fear as he did now. This was no situation where his Provo colleagues would want to help him. On the contrary they would want recrimination for killing a trusted area quartermaster, whatever she had done. Her indiscretion with the Arab would not have warranted her murder.

O'Dwyer's concern was self-centred. His small renovation business did quite well and he had two men to help him but he had been absent too often of late and work could suffer. Yet he felt the need to get away again, even though the finger might point. After all his association with Mary was well-known locally. He calmed down a little and decided to think things through carefully. Panic was never the answer. He decided to take a walk and to buy a newspaper to see what was being reported.

Hashimi was washing in his bathroom at the Dorchester when the room phone rang. He lifted the receiver and waited for the caller to identify himself. There was a silence both ends before Scott said, "You'd better get out of there at once. They know you're there."

"Fuzz?"

"No."

"Thanks." Hashimi put the receiver down; Scott had returned a favour. He waited thoughtfully with his hand still on the receiver. His expression did not change as he made up his mind what to do. Fifteen minutes later he left the hotel in his usual Arab dress.

O'Dwyer could not believe his luck. He poured himself a large whisky, sat down and laughed with relief. He picked up the last edition of the *Standard* and scanned what he had already read several times. The description of the German was quite good and it was clear that he was the only suspect. Being interviewed by the police was suddenly less daunting. But he would still prefer to avoid it. He saw the answer; he would put it about that the terrible murder by the German was so upsetting that he simply had to get away for a few days. He drained his whisky, poured another and started to pack. He would fly to Dublin.

He was so elated with his good fortune that he was on his third drink when the apartment bell rang. He opened the door and there was an Arab in full regalia. At first he did not recognise Hashimi and when he did he gave a sloppy smile. "Sorry, Hash. I don't need any oil shares."

"Can I come in? Just a quick word?"

"Sure. I'm trying to drown my sorrows. Did you hear that terrible news about Mary? Holy Mother of Jesus. I hope they get that German bastard; I hope they tear him apart." O'Dwyer had closed the door and he indicated a chair from which he removed some of the clothes he had folded.

Hashimi sat down, pulling his robes around him. "Going away?"

O'Dwyer waved the half empty bottle. "Wanna drink?"

"No thanks. I won't be here a minute. Where are you going?"

O'Dwyer sank to his chair, his face flushed from drink. "I've gotta go. I'm shattered after hearing about Mary. Poor, poor girl. Why the hell would he do such a thing for Christ's sake? I must get away for a few days. I just can't face it." His expression of deep sadness changed as he asked, "How the hell did you find me?"

"It's no secret. Everyone knows you round here. You're a very popular figure. I simply asked around."

O'Dwyer gave an unbelieving grin. "In that gear? Everyone will have noticed. That's careless isn't it?"

"It doesn't matter, Paddy. Nothing much does any more."

O'Dwyer shrugged and spilled a little drink. "So what can I do for you?"

"Well, you can stop lying through your teeth for a start or you'll have a job explaining it all away in the confessional."

O'Dwyer's gaze sharpened. He stiffened as he sensed danger. "What the hell are you talking about?"

"The way you beat Mary to death."

"You're off your rocker. The bad weather's got to you." O'Dwyer realised that he was badly placed: his gun was under a pile of clothes on the bed.

"Did you do it because she loaned me the warehouse? The site's due for redevelopment. It was only a matter of time. Little was lost and I could have used influence in finding you somewhere better. I simply needed a place quick. Or was it because she had begun to spurn you? The jealousy overcame you did it? You had to beat her to death?"

O'Dwyer staggered to his feet. He reached for the bottle. "This is sick. Here, have a drink for God's sake and stop this bloody bullshit."

Hashimi did not move until O'Dwyer hurled the bottle at his head. He threw himself out of the chair as O'Dwyer dived for the gun under the pile of clothes. The bottle struck the back-rest of the chair and whisky shot out over the fabric. Hashimi fired from a prone position and the shot took O'Dwyer in the stomach as he turned with a gun.

O'Dwyer sank to his knees, a hand over his stomach, the other still holding the gun which he raised with an effort. Hashimi fired again and O'Dwyer screamed, blood spurting from just above the bent knee. "Sorry about that," Hashimi said unemotionally. "I couldn't kneecap you in the position you're in; I can't get a shot behind the knee."

O'Dwyer was in agony but still he would not let go of the gun. He struggled to raise it again and Hashimi just waited for it to come up so far when he shot O'Dwyer through his gun hand. O'Dwyer fell back, his legs bent under him.

Hashimi stood up. "I want you to die slowly as she did. She did nothing to merit what you did to her. Mary lasted a full twenty-four hours. You'll be luckier than that. The police aren't going to get you; they're after the wrong man which is one of the hazards of our game. We can't come forward and give evidence."

O'Dwyer reached up with his uninjured hand to grope for the bed. He could not take weight on his injured leg and his stomach was a mass of pain. He met Hashimi's gaze and the hatred in him poured out leaving nothing of the popular image he had nurtured for so long. It was difficult for him to speak and when he did his deep fear came through the quivering voice. He was dying and the bravado of years had collapsed; other people were for maiming and killing, not himself. He was facing what some of them had been forced to face without guilt of crime. "They'll know it's you, you bastard." He doubled up again trying to stem the flow.

"Of course they will. It doesn't matter. I've probably more to answer for than you, but not in the same way. We're a doomed breed, Paddy. Others will come but each time it will be more difficult. One day they'll find a solution to people like us, not perfect but enough to make us keep our heads down more often than we do. Have you anything to say before I go?"

"Like what, you shit? Get a doctor for God's sake."

"I don't think God, yours or mine, had any part in this. The Devil maybe. How about a confession? I'll finish it quickly for you."

"Go stuff yourself. I didn't touch her. There's no way you can know one way or the other." O'Dwyer's voice tailed off in a long moan and he was now bent so far forward that his head was touching the floor.

"The German told me," Hashimi said simply. "He's a friend of mine. And Mary told him."

O'Dwyer lifted his head, his face screwed up as hand, knee and stomach bled copiously. Yet he could still be saved with a blood transfusion and a capable surgeon. He seemed to realise this as he mutely pleaded with Hashimi to go no further.

"Confess," Hashimi demanded. He placed a mini tape recorder on the floor in front of O'Dwyer's face. "It's running. Describe what happened. Or if that's too painful, just admit that you killed her."

O'Dwyer saw the trap. If his confession was passed on to the

Provos, saving him now would not help. He would merely be reprieved for another session. He accepted then that one way or the other he would die. He tried to look up but it was too painful. All he could see was the hem of Hashimi's robe which meant that he never heard the plop of the shot that finally killed him.

Hashimi checked his magazine and replaced the rounds he had used. He made no attempt to tidy up. He left the apartment and caught a cab back to the Dorchester. But as soon as he entered his own suite he knew something was wrong and went for his gun.

19

They came at Hashimi from all angles; two men from the bathroom once he had passed beyond it, two who had crouched behind the bed, and one more who had been immediately behind the bedroom door. His gun was in his hand as they reached him but before he could raise it one man smashed his own weapon down on Hashimi's wrist and the rest smothered him from all sides.

Hashimi struggled madly but his robes slowed him down. He kicked out but the numbers were against him and he was gradually overpowered as he dragged them all round the room. The untidy group fell on to the bed and somehow Hashimi was turned over and his hands forced behind his back while he was handcuffed. When that was done they grabbed his still flailing legs and held on fiercely while they were bound. They left him on the bed and stepped back bruised and panting.

Hashimi lay awkwardly. He said, "You've got to get me out of here first."

Gerald Sanger wiped bloodied lips with the back of his hand and then smoothed down his sparse, ruffled hair. He had lost touch with this kind of violence and realised that he was really beyond it. He said to the others, "Search the place for weapons and then tidy up and wait outside. Don't hang around in a group but stay close. I'll give a shout when I need you again."

When they had gone Sanger holstered his gun but kept a respectable distance from Hashimi's feet. He detoured to the dressing table and wiped his face in front of the mirror, watching Hashimi's reflection and seeing him trying to squirm off the bed. It did not matter. He returned to stand just inside the closed bedroom door. "You have a choice," he said softly. "You can go out as laundry or you can walk out sensibly. Which do you want?"

"You can't expect me to walk out quietly. Why should I make it easy for you?"

"Because we can make it easier for you. We can do a deal."

Hashimi tried to get into a sitting position on the bed. "Help me sit upright. I can't think like this."

Sanger gave a trace of a smile. "Don't be bloody stupid, old boy. What's it to be?"

"What sort of a deal?"

"We can hardly discuss that here but it's one that would get you out of the country."

"Feet first in a box."

"Don't be silly, old lad. We could toss you from the window. Well?"

"I don't trust you. Any of you."

Sanger went through into the small hall, opened the suite door and called softly down the corridor. When he entered the room again Hashimi was standing but swaying uncertainly. Sanger still would not go too near. Two of his men came in and he said, "Laundry basket. Is the van still round the back?" When one man nodded he added, "Give him a jab but gag him first. Get the other two to help you."

Hashimi was on a low bed when he woke up. He felt vaguely sick and when he looked over the edge realised that he had not far to fall, as if he was on a bed reserved for drunks in a police cell. He came round slowly and took stock with barely a movement. The first thing he realised was that he was no longer bound and manacled but had been stripped to his underwear. He sat up slowly.

It was fairly warm in the cell and well lit. But for the bed which he quickly discovered was bolted to the floor, there was no furniture; nothing he could rip off and use as a weapon. Nor were there any blankets and the mattress was horsehair and hard so that there were no springs he could rip out. The ceiling light was behind a bowl-shaped grid and was well out of reach. There were no windows. On the wall opposite the padded door was a washbasin with press-button taps and beneath it a plastic bucket. In two corners of the high ceilinged cell, far out of reach, were two television scanners.

The bed was too low to sit comfortably so he lay down again and said to the walls, "I'm awake. What's the deal?"

He heard a soft laugh from somewhere but made no attempt to trace it. He had been in such cells before but never as a prisoner. This one was at least clean and had a smell of disinfectant as if it had not been used for some time and had only recently been prepared. "I want a pee," he shouted at the walls.

"Use the bucket." The voice appeared to come from all four walls. Suddenly the light went out and the darkness was the deepest Hashimi could recall. He felt he was floating. There was a faint but indistinct noise and when the light came on moments later a cold buffet on a cardboard plate was just inside the door. At one side of it was a paper napkin wrapped round what proved to be some plastic utensils.

Hashimi made no move towards it. He could suffer hunger for long periods. When he gazed at the padded door again he noticed the indistinct outline of a cat door at its base through which the plate had been pushed.

"Why did you have to put the light out?" But he received no answer; they were showing him that every function of the cell was operated by what he correctly assumed to be the Security Service. They were making their presence felt without actually showing themselves. It was an old technique and one which did not influence him. He suddenly felt so relaxed that he fell into a natural sleep.

When he awoke he felt a presence in the room and was not surprised to see Sanger standing inside the door. "How do you know I wasn't faking?" he asked as he sat up with his legs stretched out straight.

"It would have made no difference," Sanger replied easily. "You could probably take me but there's too much for you to negotiate the other side of this door. If you touch me you'll be dead almost immediately. You are on tape and vision all the time. As if you didn't know."

"What's the deal?" Hashimi asked again.

"You seem anxious now. Yet in the hotel you didn't trust me. We found a mixture of foreign currencies in your room, by the way, and settled your account for you. It wasn't cheap."

"So the hotel staff are witnesses to my abduction."

"No. Only that you weren't on view when your account was paid. Don't make anything of it, Hashimi. The hotel won't. And,

242

anyway, you have this massive reputation for escaping. The next time you try it you could be killed. Let's talk business."

"I'm listening."

"We're not sure how many people you've killed during this jaunt of yours. It doesn't really matter; you are wanted for murder several times over but we found you before the police did. We'll give you freedom for one more job."

Hashimi pulled his knees under his chin and wrapped his arms round them. He gazed up quizzically at Sanger. "What's your name?"

"Smith, Jones, Brown. Anything you like."

"Okay, Smith, Jones, Brown. What's your designation?"

"I sometimes wish I knew. But I come with the highest authority. You think I don't carry enough clout to do a deal?"

"How can I tell? My life is on the line. I have to be careful."

"If I say so your life is over. You do a deal through me or you don't do a deal at all. Make up your mind."

"A shooting?"

"That would be preferable. Arranging an accident in these circumstances would be almost impossible; we have to keep sight of you to make sure you do the job. That's reasonable, wouldn't you say?"

"Certainly. But that brings your lot within sight of whoever you want knocked off. So why can't one of your people do it?"

"There's nothing to stop us. There are sound reasons, however, for getting someone else to do it. You're a natural."

"Tell me those reasons."

"For a presently condemned man you're asking a lot. But, okay, if it will help you make up your mind." Sanger glanced up at the central light. His hands were in his pockets and he was relaxed. "First of all you've had far more experience than anyone we have. Training is not the same as the real thing. You have considerable credentials obtained under the most exacting conditions. You won your spurs a long time ago, Hashimi."

Sanger waited to see how his prisoner was taking the proposal but could observe no obvious reaction; the man was as controlled as himself. "And then there's the little fact of our lot not wanting anyone pointing the finger at us afterwards. We want no visible part. There are so many crackpot organisations these days that eyebrows might be raised in certain critical quarters when this character is dead. We've recently been accused of all sorts of diabolical capers and certain sections of the press revel in it. There are many who want to believe the dark side and it doesn't do our image any good. We've even been accused of brutally killing little old ladies."

"And of course you're as innocent as the driven snow."

"No. But that time we were. You know that people like to have a go at us. We just want to avoid a situation."

When Hashimi continued to sit hunched up and silent, Sanger added, "This is a one-off. The opportunity is there to use you. Why risk our own men? And it's a let-off for you."

"What sort of let-off?"

"After the job you lay low for a couple of days in one of our places and then we see that you get out of the country. Before the job is done we go over what you want to do and where you want to go. We'll provide passport, and if necessary, visas, and enough cash to keep you for a few weeks."

"So there's no real cash reward?"

"We're offering you your life. Nobody is going to complain if you're found dead in a dark alley; not even the Civil Rights movement. Anyway, you only need enough to tide you over until you can contact your father." Sanger smiled. "I know you have your own passports but ours stand up to more scrupulous testing. That's the deal."

Hashimi uncoiled and slowly rose. As he saw Sanger stiffen he said, "I'm not going to try to jump you here, for God's sake. As you pointed out, I can't beat the lot of you and you're carrying no gun for me to swipe." He paced the far end of the cell, head down and looking slightly ridiculous in his underwear. He turned to face Sanger with hands on hips. "Who do you want hit?"

"That doesn't matter."

"It will matter to him. And I need to know what the hell he looks like. I don't want to be blamed afterwards for killing the wrong man. Or maybe that's the idea."

"It would be a clumsy way of going about it. A name doesn't matter. I can show you what he looks like. That's all you need."

"Let me see."

"I want to know whether we have a deal first."

244

"It could be my own father. I want to see what he looks like before I make up my mind."

"Have we a deal in principle? You can change your mind once you've seen the print, but I won't show my hand unless you're in all the way."

"And the alternative?"

"We won't hand you over to the police. You've lost touch, and perhaps even face, with the main terrorist groups but you might still have some fanatical friends who would be willing to take and kill hostages if you're sent to prison. We won't stand for that. The alternative is a bullet in the head and a dark alley for a tomb. It's up to you."

"Okay. I agree in principle. Now show me the print."

Sanger looked dubious. He had not liked the way Hashimi had replied.

The Arab lifted his arms. "What the hell do you expect? Do you think I kill just for the hell of it? I kill because I believe in what I'm doing. Do I have to show enthusiasm for this job? I'm in a fix. I'll do it to get out. No other reason."

Sanger still hesitated. He reached for his back pocket and produced a stiffened envelope from which he took a paper print. "It's a copy of the only one we have. We can't improve on it but it's clear enough for your purpose."

Hashimi reached out for the print. His hand did not so much as quiver, nor his expression change by a fraction, as he gazed at the undoubted features of Kranz. But he was shocked and held the print for some time to muster his calm behind the frigid mask. Kranz. My God. The German had believed his own people were after him. It would seem that they were willing to let the British do the job for them. He handed the print back. "What's he done?"

"Why should you care? What's it to be?"

Hashimi was getting a delayed reaction which was in danger of showing. He turned to the far wall and went over to the washbasin, pressed the cold tap and splashed water over his face. "This place is airless," he complained. It would look odd if he delayed too long but there were still some issues he needed explained. "Where is this character?"

"Don't worry about that. You'll know when you need to. We'll draw him out for you to make it easier. He's under close surveillance; he won't escape the net. If by chance he did, then we'll honour our bargain. What's your answer?"

"I'll do it. What else can I do? You absolutely certain that you've got him wrapped up?"

"So far as we're concerned he's in a mobile prison. Get some rest now. There's a lot to sort out. Where we'll put you up meanwhile, the time and place, and the weapon; you'll have a choice of those. We want you to be completely familiar with the rifle you use."

Hashimi nodded slowly. With crowding and mixed emotions he lowered himself to the bed while the door was opened for Sanger to slip out.

Joachim Baedeker had been expecting the visit but not quite so soon. He had sent a signal to Leipzig hoping that Herbert Keime might be elsewhere since his return to Germany, but Keime had somehow found time to catch a flight to London. And he must have done it by the skin of his teeth.

The two men went into the sound-proofed room and the atmosphere between them, never friendly, was now heavy with unspoken recrimination. It was Baedeker who first voiced the ridiculousness of the situation. "Before we start a slanging match let's get the issue clear. None of us is to blame over this latest and most unfortunate development. I don't know what happened but it has no bearing on the way matters have been handled in any way. As soon as I saw the press reports I sent a signal and you've arrived here the same day. So there has been no possible delay. Let's sit down and talk it over sensibly."

Keime sat facing Baedeker across the desk. His rigid expression suggested an unbending attitude and, to Baedeker, revealed yet once again that Keime was a book man; he worked in theories, little understanding the real world and the many unexpected issues that could so inexplicably go wrong.

"Why would Kranz kill this woman?" Keime asked.

"Why must you assume that he did? Because the police are looking for him? Circumstantial evidence seems to point towards him but even if it didn't it would have been unwise for him to stay at the guest house. He had to leave. Police and reporters will question all the guests. It might have finished up with his photograph in the newspapers; inevitably he would have been mentioned as a German businessman. He might have come through it but he would have become too exposed. He was in an impossible situation."

"Has he reported to you?"

"No." Baedeker shook his head. "And I don't expect him to."

"Why not? What's in your mind?" The bad feeling was creeping back through Keime's tone.

"I don't think he was satisfied with the situation as it was. He was never very happy about it and he has had more time to think."

Keime sat stony faced then said, "What do you intend to do about it?"

With sudden exasperation Baedeker replied, "What do you suggest? You're the ideas man."

"And you are the operational executive. The responsibility is ultimately yours."

Baedeker controlled himself. "So it's up to me?"

"Of course."

Baedeker sat forward and intertwined his fingers, his knuckles white with rage. "If that's the case, Keime, just what the hell are you doing here? You could have ignored my signal or sent one back telling me to get on with it. If you see your mission as over go back home."

Keime's lips compressed; he did not quite know how to deal with Baedeker, and he fell back on the official line as he was bound to do. "I shall report your unco-operative attitude to Command. I spent a long time building this up only to see it ruined by you."

"It was a great idea. But you didn't come up with the possibility of a murder. It's your job to anticipate these things."

"The project must be saved at all costs."

"It can't be. It's finished. If we try to use someone else instead of Kranz the whole thing will collapse round our ears as phoney. It's done. Dead. A failure." Baedeker eased back in his chair as he saw Keime facing defeat. "The scheme was ill-conceived. You'll have to come up with something else. You might just as well burn the papers relating to the Flick organisation. Whatever happens to Kranz he is now discredited one way or the other. I'm sorry it was your personal brainchild." But Baedeker could hardly keep the satisfaction from his voice. It was not because of a failed project – he always hated that happening – but because he could not tolerate the man opposite him who had no knowledge of human nature and the strain under which field men worked.

"You can have any rifle you like within reason and provided that it's of Eastern Bloc manufacture. We don't want to implicate our friends in any way. But you'll be well used to those weapons, won't you?"

"In that case I'd prefer a Type 64. They have a built-in silencer which is highly effective. This is an assassination, and Type 64s were made for that express purpose."

Sanger shook his head and sighed. "Look, Hashimi, I know you can use the damned things better than I but don't take me for a fool. We can't use a Chinese weapon for reasons you well understand. Our relations with China are good at the moment so let's keep it that way. Anyway, Type 64 is a pistol; we want better accuracy than that. It won't be a face to face confrontation."

"I was thinking of the sub-machine gun, same number. I couldn't miss with a burst and there would be practically no noise. So the People's Republic is out. I suppose I'll have to settle for a Kalashnikov AKM, but if it's a one-shot situation I'd accept a Hungarian Kiraly. As long as it's accurate what does it matter? Is this to take place at night?"

"Naturally."

"Well, I'll need an image intensifier. Night-firing can be dodgy."

"I've arranged that already. The range won't disturb you. Very short, but we want the velocity and accuracy of a rifle because I doubt that there'll be time for a repeat."

Hashimi smiled bitterly. Sanger was very convincing; lying obviously came easy to him.

Sir Lewis Hope looked drawn. While Sanger seemed to thrive on the increasing activity his superior was becoming more morose. He had virtually reached a point of no return. He could abort but if he did he would be faced with questions he would have difficulty in answering. It had been his own decision to abduct Hashimi Ross while fully aware that all police forces were on the look out for him. If it finished the way he wanted it to then he would be answerable to no one; there would be no need of explanation, and he would have finally won.

He laid down his pen as Sanger entered his office. He rubbed his eyes wearily and listened to Sanger's report. It all seemed to be going fine, at least that part of it. But there was another part. "Any news of this fellow Kranz?"

"None, sir. He's well holed up somewhere or he's managed to leave the country."

"Damn. How long can we hold on without him?"

Sanger went as far as he dared: "That's up to you, sir. I can keep the Arab on tap by telling him that it's taking time to set up. But I wouldn't delay too long. I also had the fleeting impression that he knew Kranz, or at least recognised the face."

"Oh! What made you think that?"

"When it first cropped up. He covered it very well and I could be wrong. Anyway it didn't stop him agreeing to do it."

"Can you trust him? I mean could he be up to something?"

"Of course he could. If he sees an opportunity to escape he'll take it. He's quick witted and has guts. But I've sewn him up as tightly as anyone can. We've selected the house. When it's time to move his food and drink will be spiked and if he doesn't eat or drink we'll forcibly inject him. Once he's in the house the problem is almost over. If you still want to take a chance on Kranz turning up why don't we get Hashimi into the house so that he's already where we want him to be to do the job? If we have to do without Kranz then an instant decision can be made."

"The Arab is safer where he is."

"He's got to be removed some time." Sanger had the impression that Hope was afraid to change the present situation.

"Yes. Well do what you think best."

Sanger did not much care for that. "I'd rather have your direct order, sir. I've so far succeeded because your orders have been precise, and if I may say so, absolutely right."

Hope shrugged. "I'm surprised that you prefer to avoid responsibility. All right, move him." As Sanger was about to go

Hope signalled him back. "Sit down. There's another matter to link with this one. And I can assure you that on this occasion my orders will be very precise indeed. But you must listen very carefully and memorise well. Everything depends on it."

Hashimi woke up with a slight headache and a stale taste in his mouth. He was slow to come round and his thoughts were woolly. He knew that he had been drugged and had been expecting it to happen. He realised that he was on a bed similar to the one in the cell and he slowly rolled off it. He pushed himself up and stood unsteadily while he scanned his new prison.

The room was much larger than the cell. The furniture was shabby but nevertheless offered all basic comforts with armchairs and a slightly worn carpet. He walked unsteadily to a door and found a fairly large kitchen with everything he could need, even though all the cutlery was made of flimsy plastic: nothing here could be used as a weapon. Another door revealed a bathroom and shower. When he crossed to what must be the front door he was not surprised to find it locked. The first window he tried opened quite easily but when he looked down there was a fifty-foot drop to the street and iron railings stood between a narrow basement and the pavement. It was clearly an old building in a quiet district and he noticed one or two 'For Sale' notices across the street. He wondered from how many windows he was being watched. If he so much as lifted a leg outside he had no doubts about what would happen.

He now had blankets but even if he knotted them together to try to lower himself from a window at night he knew that he would be picked out by night glasses and shot; they would not risk losing him. And to jump would be suicidal. The room was high ceilinged as these old houses invariably were and the ceiling lights were well out of reach some fifteen feet up, and, like his first cell, were protected by heavily secured steel mesh. There were no wall lights. His extra freedom was a myth, his boundaries had been only slightly extended.

His denims were crudely folded on the floor on the other side of the bed and with them was a change of underwear and a clean shirt and socks. This clearly meant that they had collected all his belongings at the Dorchester. Still in his underwear, Hashimi sat in one of the armchairs and tried to clear his head.

After a while he went into the bathroom to find that only the cold water taps worked. He showered and the icy water made him gasp but it removed the residue of his sluggishness. When he was dressed he went round the place; there must be some method of keeping an eye on him whether by sight or sound. But much could be concealed in the hideous pattern of the wallpaper, particularly high up where he could not reach.

He had no watch and there was no clock. He could only gauge the time by the encroaching darkness and once it was finally dark there was little to do. There were no books to read and time passed very slowly. Hashimi found he had too much time to think. Images of Vi would taunt him and he knew that in a way he was as much to blame for the deaths of Mary and Sophie as he had been for hers. It was strange that it was Vi, the over-made-up wife of a mobster, who always came to mind and not Sophie. But Vi, with her homespun philosophy still echoing round his head, was the one who had understood him better than any of the others.

Sanger called some time later. There was a reverse spy hole in the door and Hashimi had no doubt that it was a special job with a huge fish-eye focal coverage. When he heard the tumblers turn in the lock he guessed that Sanger would not enter without first looking into the room. And he accepted too that Sanger might enter alone but there would certainly be more men outside. He suspected that the Security Service owned the whole building and probably a few more about the area.

Sanger gave a bright smile as he shut the door. He did not lock it but the sound of it being double locked from outside was clear as he crossed the floor with a golf bag over one shoulder. He threw the bag down on the bed. "One AKM rifle with image intensifier," he said cheerfully. "Do a good job and you're on your way. You'll find five 7.62mm cartridges in the pocket. That should be more than enough."

"When's it to be?" asked Hashimi cautiously.

"Within a day or two. We won't keep you waiting; we don't want your nerves stretched. Just a couple of details to sort out. Takes a little ingenuity to set up a target in a precise place."

"So you still have the target in your sights?"

"Absolutely. Dare not slip up now."

"I'll need another look at the photograph; I don't want to slip up either."

Sanger produced the envelope again. "I'll leave it with you. In a couple of days none of us will need it. Study it until it's imprinted in your mind."

"I will." Hashimi took the envelope but did not open it.

Sanger looked round the room. "Sorry about the spartan accommodation. I'm sure you've had worse. Anyway, it won't be for long. Got everything you need?"

Hashimi inclined his head. He placed the envelope on the bed by the rifle.

Sanger took stock once more, gave a tap on the door and disappeared through the gap as it was opened. When he had gone Hashimi picked up the golf case and slid the rifle out. He noticed at once that it was in beautiful condition. He held the weapon and groped in the pocket to produce a small plastic bag which he emptied on to the bed. He picked up one of the rounds and thoughtfully weighed it in his hand. Grim-faced he suddenly closed his fingers over it, and muttered something under his breath.

20

Bulman read the copy of the internal report. Remains of Phil Deacon had been identified and what had been found of a female corpse could only be Vi. He had already been sure of who would be under the rubble but there were probably other bodies to find. He did not need confirmation of identity but the routine and grisly task nevertheless had to go on.

The press were making a meal of it and Bulman gathered up the newspapers he had been reading at his desk and bundled them into a corner near the safe. What concerned him most was the complete lack of news on the Arab. Scott had told him that he had managed to warn Hashimi but since then there had been a blank. Bulman had checked with the hotel and there was no doubt that Hashimi had left. But he could not, during a telephone call to the hotel, ask some of the questions he wanted to ask for fear of them getting back to Hope. He needed, for instance, to know whether Hashimi had settled the hotel account personally.

As officially he was no longer involved there was nothing Bulman could do. But he felt that something about the whole affair was not quite right and that he was somehow still tied up in it.

Confirmation of his suspicions came mid-afternoon when Gerald Sanger walked into his office after a gentle knock.

Bulman gazed up without enthusiasm. "What can I do for you? You seem to have lost your way."

"I certainly had a job finding you. Nobody seemed to know where you are."

"That's because they don't want to know. I'm one of the great untouchables. And I'm not listed on any board. Bulman, the big secret."

"May I sit down?"

"Feel free. The chairs won't object. Hope might, though."

"Ah, yes. Well, that's why I'm here at this particular time. Sir Lewis is away this afternoon. Even so, what made you say that?"

"It's best that I don't tell you. I'm not his favourite person at the moment." Bulman winced at his own observation. "That was a fatuous remark; I've never been his favourite person. So what's your problem?"

Sanger glanced towards Haldean's open door as Bulman said, "He's out on a job. Nobody trusts that open door."

Sanger wandered over to Haldean's office and went in. He looked around and even bent to peer under the desk while Bulman watched on, fascinated. Sanger returned, made sure that he had properly closed the main door and sat down. Even then he gazed round the room as if he was looking for bugs. "You want to take the phone apart?" asked Bulman sarcastically.

"I'm sorry." Sanger gradually unwound.

"This must be serious," said Bulman, his interest now fully aroused.

"I would liked to have come sooner but, as you intimated, Sir Lewis would not be too pleased. I'm not at all sure that I'm doing the right thing now, but I have to do something."

"Why the hell don't you get on with it?"

"We're holding Hashimi Ross." It was blurted out as if Sanger had to get rid of it quickly.

Bulman's nerve ends kicked. For a moment his mind was in a whirl as the danger signs congested in his head. "You mean the Security Service?"

"Of course. We picked him up at the Dorchester. Quite a handful, I can tell you."

"Well he would be wouldn't he? Why are you telling me?"

Sanger took a long slow breath. "I have a feeling that you strongly object to me. You must have your reasons. We've never worked together, though, have we? We've hardly seen one another. Is it because you were working on the Arab case and were then taken off while I was put on to it?"

"I had no idea you were my replacement," Bulman lied. "Why should that upset me?"

"Well, suspend judgment on me until I've finished. We all have to do things we don't care for; that's the name of the game. I don't know why you were taken off any more than I know why I was put on. It's the way it goes. But I don't like the way it's developed."

"You've just said we have to do these things."

"Right. But there are limits sometimes. This needs talking about."

"But why to me?" Bulman cut in. "As you say, we don't know one another."

"That's one of the reasons. The second one is that you are still on the fringe of the service rather than a full blooded member and are a very experienced man. I can't turn to my immediate colleagues can I? That's asking to be put on report to Sir Lewis. The last reason is that I know you've been involved with the Arab and might throw some light on the whole business. If you accept those reasons as valid I'll continue."

Bulman sat back, wary and alert. "You're taking a bloody big chance with me aren't you? How do you know *I'll* not put you on report?"

"I don't and I agree that I *am* taking a colossal risk. But from where I sit you're still my best bet."

"So what's crucifying you so much that you have to come to me?"

"I'm sure that Sir Lewis intends to kill the Arab."

"A lot of people would say good riddance. Why should that upset you so much?"

"I'd probably say good riddance, too. But I object to the way it's being done. The Arab has been set up to do a job for us on the promise of his release and safe passage to wherever he wants to go. I don't much care for the trade-off but I wouldn't quibble about it. What I don't like, and what has been haunting me, is that we are going to kill him once he's fulfilled his part of the bargain. It isn't necessary and brings the service into disrepute."
Sanger held up his hands as Bulman was about to speak.

"I know what you're going to say; that I'm naïve and it's a dirty game we're in. Of course. But the whole affair has been put in my hands. I've hired the assassins and I've set the Arab up. I've done the convincing and the persuading and the trussing and it will be me who takes the can back when it's over. Sir Lewis has detached himself very carefully which is his prerogative but I'm left with a conviction that the sell-out will not stop with Hashimi Ross. At some point I'm going to be accused of exceeding my orders in order to protect the Director."

"What makes you so sure?" But Bulman understood Sanger's fears; he'd had personal experience of Hope's cover-ups.

Sanger hesitated as he groped for an answer and Bulman detected a tremor in his hands. "He wants it done yet he's somehow absolved himself. It's difficult to explain. He's told me so much but not enough. I know that can be argued as part of security but there's something definitely not right. It will not stop at the Arab's death. Too much has been left unexplained. Believe me, Mr Bulman, I would not be here if I was not wholly convinced that I'm about to be dropped right in it. It was a very difficult decision to make."

"You shouldn't be surprised. All this is normal for him. I've said it before and I'll keep saying it until someone listens; he's not fit for the job. Who's the target?"

"That's part of it. I don't know. I'm supposed to let the Arab know, yet I don't know myself."

"Well you have to be told some time, for God's sake."

"I have the feeling that I'll never be told. I'm increasingly convinced that there is no target."

Bulman watched Sanger closely. "Are you trying to tell me that the whole business is a ploy to get Hashimi under wraps so that he can be quietly killed as and when convenient?"

"I'm convinced of it."

"But if you knew Hashimi was at the Dorchester, you could have knocked him off any time. Why this palaver?"

"Sir Lewis gave strict instructions that we were not to follow as long as he was still booked at the hotel. This is one of the things that I don't understand. I think that was when you must have been taken off the case; when the Arab was found to be staying at the Dorchester. Why were you taken off?"

"I'm buggered if I know. I wish I did. It was obvious that Hope didn't want me to know too much of what he had in mind."

"Precisely. And by the same token I'm convinced that someone other than myself has been receiving orders. I think I'm to become the scapegoat for what Sir Lewis is about to do. Why he needs one I don't know, but then I've no idea of his final plan. He's clearly up to something, and it's something that he knows to be unacceptable to government."

Bulman was confused, yet he understood Sanger's fears. "Any other reason for thinking there's no target?"

"Yes. The rounds have been tampered with. A rifle and five rounds have been issued to the Arab to complete the job which is supposed to take place during the next day or two. In my view the balance of the rounds doesn't seem right. I'm guessing, but I would gamble that the cartridge cases have been opened up, most, if not all, the powder removed, and the cases refilled with something else. They might even have been designed to create a blowback to kill. The other point is that the rifle issued is an AKM."

"What does that mean?"

"It's a very fine Russian weapon, possibly the best assault rifle ever produced. But that's exactly what it is; an assault rifle. It's not a sniper's rifle and it is not silenced."

"It will do the job though, won't it? And the use of a silencer depends on where the action is to take place. Anyway, I'm told they upset the balance of a weapon and therefore affect the aim. And if the rounds have been tampered with Hashimi is experienced enough to know, isn't he?"

Bulman was beginning to pick holes but Sanger kept his nerve. "He might well do so but he's in a no-win situation. If the rounds are good he could shoot me as I enter the door but it won't achieve an escape. Too many men are on the job. With a man like that extreme safety precautions have to be worked out. But I don't think the rounds *are* good and I don't believe I am in any danger in that direction. That's another thing; I'm the only one allowed to go near him."

Bulman suddenly slumped in his chair, as if it was all too much to take in. "Well, what do you want to do about it? You've told me but where does it get you?"

"It means that I've shared my fears, at least. If I'm proved to be right I at least know that one other person is au fait with the situation. But what I would actually like to do is to spring the Arab and let him take his chances. Even a terrorist is entitled to be tried under the law. And frankly I think that's the best course; it warns others who might try the same. But that's not going to happen."

"Basically you're afraid for your own skin aren't you?"

"I'm not ashamed of it. Yes. I've done nothing that warrants any form of betrayal."

"Then let him go."

Sanger shook his head. "I can't. There are too many others. The house is watched from across the street day and night."

"Are there scanners in the room?"

"No. High up are dummy recesses which he has probably located, but there's no way of knowing them to be dummy without taking the wall down. There's no need for bugs; he's on his own."

"Can he get out of the windows?"

"Yes. But there's a drop of fifty to sixty feet. He's on the top floor at the front of the house. The windows are under permanent observation. There are no back windows so that he can only go one way."

"You've got yourself a problem. There's nothing I can do to help you."

"It's helped me to offload. There's one other thing. I've been repeatedly warned to tell you nothing or communicate with you in any way. Until now that's been quite easy as our paths have never crossed. But what is it he's trying to keep from you? Even now. This is another reason I called; I hoped that you might have some idea."

Bulman shook his head. "I only know what you've just told me. What do *you* think is going on?"

"I've racked my brains. I think he's looking for fall guys for whatever he has dreamed up. And I'm one of them. You could be another. Is he trying to wipe some sort of slate clean that nobody knows about? Or is he simply getting paranoiac?"

"Where's Hashimi banged up?"

"It wouldn't help you to know. And I couldn't tell you anyway, you know that."

"Bullshit. What you've been saying is enough to get you beheaded at the Tower. And now you've incriminated me. If I went to Hope with all this he would have to drop whatever he's up to. That might be the best way; land you in it and get off the hook myself and fix a trial for Hashimi, or let him go. Hope would have a job explaining why he's hanging on to him when the police are going bananas searching nationwide for the same man."

"If I thought for one moment you'd do that I wouldn't be here. All right. In for a penny in for a pound. It won't help the situation anyway."

"I don't care what he's done," observed Scott. "He deserves better than that."

"Come off it," Bulman rejoined scathingly. "You've been set up yourself without having done a thing wrong."

They were sitting in the reception area of Scott's agency. The staff had long since gone home and Scott had rung Maggie to tell her he would be late. They were facing each other across a low table covered with travel brochures and drinking ale from cans. Scott leaned forward to tidy the brochures. Beyond the sheet glass window with the agency name printed on it, hurrying pedestrians were clearly in view.

"I feel like a bloody goldfish," Bulman commented drily, "but at least we're not being gawked at."

"They're all in too much of a hurry. You're really worried about this aren't you? You wouldn't be telling me about it if not."

"You're the only one I trust. And you understand." Bulman gave a self derisory grin. "I'm beginning to sound like the bloke who confided in me." He had not given Sanger's name in relating what had happened in his office.

"Can you trust him?"

"I don't really know him. It could be a pack of lies. If it is then there's a definite purpose. On the other hand there were some obvious truths. He could have given me a cocktail of truth and lies. If he did he should get an Oscar."

"If he did," said Scott lowering his beer, "he's expecting you to do something about it." He idly watched the condensation trickling down the can.

"Well I'm not calling on Hashimi, that's for sure. He's asked for anything that happens to him. I don't like it but I don't feel sufficiently strongly about it to do anything. Anyway there's nothing I can do. What concerns me is what the hell is Hope up to and what part does he see for me. He's laying a trap of some kind."

"I could go take a look."

Bulman jerked. "A look where?"

"To see if Hash is where they say he is."

"What good would that do?"

"It would solve whether or not you've been fed a load of rubbish. And if you have you can nail the bloke who fed it."

Bulman's reaction was slow. He carefully put the can down. His gaze hardened, his expression was grim. "I'm a fool. Thick, because I should have known. You've just supplied the answer. It's not me they want but you. Hope knows we're close and he knows that you are friendly with Hashimi. The chances were more than even that we would discuss this and that, with your record, you'd come up with that sort of suggestion. It's not all that much a long shot. From Hope's point of view there would be nothing to lose by trying it."

"You mean he wants to get rid of Hash and me?"

"He always has. Have you any more beer?"

"Sure." Scott went through the rear door to his office while Bulman thought it through.

When Scott returned with two cans Bulman pulled the ring and said, "What you've underrated all along is Hope's need to get rid of you. Both you and Hashimi have always been a real danger to him. It's not the way you see it but the way he does. And he's everything to lose. Nobody can predict how Hashimi will react if he's taken to court. He could land Hope right in it if he knows enough. And that's the crux. Nobody's sure what he knows about the Murison business or how much he has guessed. He remains a constant menace to Hope and so do you. Hope is strung up by his own inadequacies, and if he can solve his fears by getting rid of the pair of you he'll sleep a lot better at night. No one will complain about topping a terrorist of Hashimi's calibre. All he needs to do is to tie you in. He's going for the grand slam. And if he succeeds Murison's spectre will be banished for ever."

They faced each other in uneasy silence for some time, occasionally sipping at their beer. At last Scott said, "If you're right it's a crafty move; it's obvious that we simply can't leave it like this. We've got to do something."

"No we don't. We leave it. There's nothing Hope can do then."

"So we'll never know for sure what he's up to."

"I can live with that."

"I can't."

Bulman stretched out his legs. "Hope has a basic cunning. He sometimes shows a certain shrewdness which can surprise. For instance, he insisted that I approached you about entering the house in Kilburn. He reckoned that you would find a way and would be unable to resist. He was right, wasn't he? He's relying on the same logic for this. Don't go near the place, Spider. In any event it's under round-the-clock surveillance."

Scott moved restlessly. To suggest something was impossible was like facing a red button with a do-not-touch sign; the urge becomes increasingly irresistible. "I'd need some night glasses."

"Forget it. You're being stupid."

"I've still got a lot of my own gear."

"For God's sake this is just what he wants, Spider. Be your age. This isn't a challenge, it's a death sentence."

"I won't attempt to contact Hash, although he deserves to be warned. If he's being that closely watched it *would* be stupid. But there's no reason why I shouldn't find out from where the house is being watched or whether it's all baloney. That would be easy to do and there'd be no risk."

Bulman stared at his toes. "You could be falling into the very trap Hope has set."

"Not if I don't go too near the place."

"You'd have to go near to find out those sorts of things."

"You know what I mean. I suppose you do know where he's supposed to be?"

"And you'd promise not to try an entry? Just do a general outside check. No more?"

"I'm not going to attempt to climb through windows under view. I mean, use your loaf. Anyway the place is bound to be bugged inside if he's there."

"Actually it's not. But that might have been said as enticement to enter. I don't like this idea, Spider. It's dodgy. You're taking it too lightly."

Scott was solemn-faced as he replied, "I never take any sort of job lightly. You should know me better. Trust me." And when Bulman did not reply he added, "We do need to know, don't we? If it is a set-up it needs exposing and Hope needs defrocking. We can't hide round corners all the time, George. We've got to get him off our backs for good."

"As long as you know the risks and don't take chances. Just be bloody careful, cocker."

It was in Lambeth. There was so much of Victorian and Edwardian London still standing that a stranger could be forgiven for thinking that so many of the residential areas looked the same. This part of Lambeth had sizeable buildings that were too big for modern families and had either become guest houses or had been converted into flats. As Scott drove along he noticed several 'For Sale' notices, made mental notes and drove on between the usual lines of parked cars. There was not a lot of activity in the area but children would still be at school and mothers had not yet set out to collect them.

He emerged at a T-junction, stopped and asked the way to Suffolk and Langley, estate agents. Half an hour later he was driving back down the street and searching for parking space. He parked, locked the car and walked back in the direction he had come. He was wearing the suit Sophie had bought for him before Deacon's mob had caught and murdered her. It was a very smart business suit and he wore a trilby hat and carried a heavy briefcase to complete the image.

He went up the steps of a house for sale almost opposite the one Hashimi was supposed to be occupying. He let himself in with the keys the estate agent had loaned him, made sure that the house was empty, room by room, and finished on the top floor. He entered the front room. The windows were filthy and he wiped down the upper pane.

He had placed his briefcase on the mantelshelf of an old iron fireplace, and now crossed over to it to take out a pair of binoculars. Standing well back from the window he surveyed the house across the street. The angle wasn't too good but he could see into part of the room through the gap in the net drapes which were pulled back at each side.

It was half an hour before he saw anything move and then it

was too fleeting for identification. There was a limit to how long he could stay and examine the house both from the point of view of the agent and the danger of being spotted by Hope's men. His luck changed fifteen minutes later when someone came to the window, opened it, gazed up towards the roof and then down to the street, before facing a point somewhere to Scott's left and raising two fingers in a deliberate sign of contempt. It was Hashimi.

Scott found himself smiling; considering Hashimi's hopeless position the gesture was typical of the man. He felt a wave of nostalgia for what might have been but Bulman was right; the Arab had gone too far. Nevertheless, the man across the street had saved his life not very long ago. There would always be something between them, and Scott would always have reason to remain thankful for the Albany caper.

He put away the binoculars, closed the case, put his hat back on and went down the bare-boarded stairs. As he returned to his car he realised that he had been lucky to spot Hashimi so quickly. Perhaps the rude sign had become a ritual. One thing was clear; Hashimi had located the precise window from which he was being observed and he wanted Hope's men to know. As Scott drove off, he was satisfied with that part of his operation. The real test would be after dark and what he had in mind he had not dared to tell Bulman.

To climb over the wall of the end house and land in the small yard was no problem. And to test the nearest rain stack and to climb up to the roof also presented few difficulties to a man who had done it so many times before. He was slower and panted a little but his movements were sure. He reached the gutter and swung over, lying there to regain his breath before moving up to a mid-way position on the old slates. He moved along on in a sitting position which was slow but safe.

The night glasses formed an uncomfortable bulk on Scott's chest in his zipped-up track suit. He kept going with his gaze fixed on the row of houses that lay at the rear. He doubted that there was surveillance at the back for Bulman had said that Hashimi's apartment had no rear windows. After a while he stopped and unzipped to remove the binoculars.

He scanned the windows of the rear line of houses but could pick out nothing suspicious. The time had been chosen carefully and it was now just after half past one in the morning. He moved on. The nearer he crept to his target the finer tuned became his nerves.

Judging his position he climbed up the roof to survey the other side where he knew Hope's men were on duty. He pushed the glasses back in his suit and crept up to peer over the angle. He rolled sideways to get at his binoculars again and placed the strap round his neck. He located the blank window which was almost opposite Hashimi's but he could not pick out the men in the room because his angle was too acute. Ducking below the roof line he edged further along and then tried again.

He picked out the reflection of lens behind the window glass and then the shadow seated behind it. The man was well back from the window. Without doubt there was a round-the-clock surveillance.

He dropped below the roof line again. The binoculars would be mounted if observation was constant, and the angle of view would be fixed on the windows below him. Without adjustment the roof was too high to be included in the view and so far he felt safe unless he had overlooked anything from behind him. He peered over again; this time without the glasses. It was now all a question of correctly assessing the angle. He judged his position and moved along a few feet then checked over the roof line again. He did this once more and stopped.

He worked his way down the roof, stopped near the gutter, put away his binoculars and started to loosen the slates. He had to break the first two in order to get purchase but once he had removed them the rest was comparatively easy. It was slow work, however, and each slate he removed had to be spread along the guttering so that there was little risk of them falling. When he had cleared a sufficient number he groped for the roof supports; they were solid and more generous in these older houses. He punched through the felting and the lathes that held it in place and then explored the gap by touch. He lay flat then wriggled through, taking pressure on his arms so as not to dislodge the fringe slates.

Scott located the run of rafters. Every move had to be by

touch; he could not use his torch with a hole in the roof behind him. He crawled across, passed the centre point and then groped as the roof closed in the other side, forcing him to crouch again. The ballcock of a water tank was hissing somewhere to his left. Again judgment had to be right as he kneeled across a rafter. He produced a long, sharp pointed tool like a giant bradawl and started to work at the thick and ancient plaster.

There would come a point when the plaster would fall into the room below, and he could not anticipate what Hashimi's reaction would be once he heard what was going on above him. After a while he had bored a small hole right through and he called softly through it. "Hash." Scott put his ear to the hole.

"I'm here."

Scott barely heard him. "It's Spider."

"Who else would come in by the tradesman's entrance?" The loud whisper was clearer.

"I'm coming down. Grab a sheet and catch the plaster. It's heavy stuff."

Scott gave Hashimi time to act then used his foot to send great chunks down below. When there was enough gap to peer through he saw that Hashimi had folded blankets to deaden the sound of falling plaster. When Scott was satisfied he unrolled a nylon rope from his waist, secured it round a rafter and swung down through the narrow gap.

Hashimi was quite calm as Scott landed and immediately gave a signal for Scott to keep his voice down. His own voice was at normal pitch as he said, "Nice of you to drop in, Spider," but his quip was contradicted by an expression loaded with warning. "You're just the company I need. But I should be out of here soon. Out of the country." He was still shooting warning glances as he continued, "For God's sake look at the state of you; you're covered in plaster and dirt. I'll run a shower. It's cold but it'll get rid of that lot."

Scott followed the drift. "It will have to be a quick one."

"Leave your clothes in here. I've got a dry towel." Hashimi led the way into the bathroom and ran the shower, leaving the folding door of the cubicle open. He signalled Scott to squat near the bath and they sat facing each other close together with the sound of water cascading down nearby.

Hashimi's attitude changed at once and he leaned forward, his head close to Scott's. "I don't know how long we've got. The place is bugged. They know you're here and now I can see that it's what they've been waiting for. You're the last link." As Scott was about to say something Hashimi snapped, "For Christ's sake listen. Don't interrupt, we're up against the clock."

Scott nodded, finding it difficult to hear against the gushing shower.

"They've banged me up here on the pretence that in exchange for knocking off a guy they'll get me out. It's a fix. The man they want me to kill is on the run for a murder he didn't commit. He's holed up in one of my places. By now he should know that I won't be back and he's on his own. Hope's crowd don't realise I know him let alone that I'm protecting him. So they had to settle for me on that pretext. To complete the illusion they've given me a rifle with a filed down pin and the rounds have been tinkered with. Otherwise I'd have shot my way out by now, believe me."

Hashimi was speaking very fast and was obviously animated with the urgency to get it all out. "So why am I still waiting? When you arrived I knew why. I don't know what you've been fed to get you here but you've got to go straight back out. This all goes back to the last caper, doesn't it? They don't want me in open court and you still know too bloody much. They'll be moving in for the kill right now, Spider, so get the hell out of here and thanks for the thought."

"I came to warn *you*. It's finished up the other way. Okay, let's go. I'll help you over the roof."

Scott began to move but Hashimi caught him by the arm. "I can climb up the rope. That's no problem. You go first and wait for me at the end of the terrace. Which end will you use?"

"Left end facing the main street. Why can't we go together?". Scott had sudden doubts.

"Don't look so suspicious. There's a little surprise I want to leave for them. I couldn't fix it before because someone calls daily and I was waiting to see what would happen. It won't take long but don't slow it down by waiting. Just a minute or two. Okay? Oh, and use the back roof if you haven't already. All the apartment windows face the front. They know I can't reach the back other than by the door and that's a Fort Knox job. Now get cracking. I'll be right there."

Hashimi seemed to be nervous as he rose. "We'll beat the buggers yet. I hope you've got a fast car. I'll tell you where to go once we're on the move."

They hurried silently into the living room, with the shower still running. Hashimi signalled impatiently as Scott hesitated. He came close and whispered urgently in Scott's ear, "Do what I damn well say or you'll cock everything up. I'll be right behind you."

Scott climbed back into the roof cavity feeling uneasy but knowing this was not the time and place to argue. Hashimi would know exactly what he was doing. At the gap in the slates he considered waiting but that could cause congestion when Hashimi arrived; it took careful manoeuvre to get through the gap and it could not be done quickly. He followed Hashimi's advice as far as the end of the row of houses where he waited and looked back. There was no sign of Hashimi.

Worried, Scott climbed up to the apex, looked over, could see nothing so pulled out his glasses. He focused on the front door of the house the surveillance team occupied. There was a suspicion of movement; he thought he saw someone signal but whoever was there used the shadows well. Then he heard someone move below and out of sight; the slightest shuffle. It was impossible to decide how many men were there.

Unexpectedly, out of the silence, came the distinct sound of a window being pushed open. Scott could not see below the roof line of the building he straddled but the sound had come from his side of the street. He raised the glasses to scan the observation window opposite. He suddenly felt sick as he saw the muzzle of a rifle protruding. For a moment he lost his balance as the shattering truth struck him. He checked his slide flat-handed just as a terrible yell of anguish gushed into the night. Hashimi screamed out, *"I'm coming, Vi!"* The silenced rifle flashed twice and a prolonged gasp floated into the darkness followed by the sickening crunch of a body being impaled on the railings. Scott vomited on the spot as he slowly slid down the sharp angle of the roof. In his sick agony he realised that Hashimi had drawn attention and had sacrificed himself so that he should get away. But as he lowered himself on to the drainpipe, dazed and tearful, Scott guessed that there was more to it than that. Hashimi had tried to make amends in the only way that he could, and had consequently died as violently as he had lived; aged thirty-six.

Bulman solemnly entered Sir Lewis Hope's office and remained standing in front of the desk.

"Sit down, George." Hope appeared to be quite cheerful.

"No thank you, sir. This won't take long. You'll be pleased about the Arab being killed when everyone else has failed to get him. Saves a long trial and the taxpayers' money."

Hope sat back as if warned by Bulman's unusually conciliatory tone. "I'm glad he's out of the way, certainly. But it took another extremist group to do it. So, as much as I would like to, I can take no credit. Haven't you read the full reports yet?"

"Oh, yes, sir. About Hashimi being holed up in one of his safe houses and a revenge killing by a supposed Libyan group who got him as he tried to escape through a window. I gather they fled so quickly that they left the rifle behind; Russian I believe. One out of three is not a very good score, though, is it, sir?"

"What on earth are you prattling about, George?" Hope's fingers started to tremble as he realised it was by no means over.

"When Hashimi took Scott into the bathroom he scribbled a note for Scott to take out with him. That note has been copied together with Scott's own statement and is safely lodged preparatory to being taken to the Prime Minister. One of the many mistakes you made was in not realising that the man you wanted Hashimi to kill was a friend of his and was on the run for a murder, which he did not commit by the way. Hashimi recognised your lie because he had given the man Kranz a safe house."

"Shut up, you idiot. You've gone mad."

Undisturbed, Bulman continued, "You wanted all three initially. I don't know why you wanted Kranz but that went wrong, anyway. You settled for Hashimi and Scott. It almost came off, too. But men like those two thrive on crisis. Hashimi died for his friend and perhaps for an increasing conscience that became too difficult to live with. They could both have escaped."

Bulman was almost hypnotised by the increasing tremor of Hope's hands, but could feel no compassion as he continued, "To save you voicing it I've already written out my resignation. Not just from this department but from the force. If your resignation is not in by this afternoon, Sir Lewis, I shall immediately release the two statements I have plus my own evidence. You are a very lucky man. You will be able to resign with a dignity you in no way deserve. Goodbye, sir. I doubt that we'll meet again."

Scott stared round the room. "What the hell's happened? This was a pigsty the last time I saw it. Even the bed's been made. And you've changed the three-piece." Scott lowered himself carefully into one of the armchairs as if afraid to spoil it. He still gazed round in wonderment. "Big improvement, George. It must be Betty's influence."

"Shut up and grab that." Bulman handed over a tumbler half-full of whisky.

Scott looked up at him unbelievingly. "You've killed your mean image in one stroke; it's all too much."

"I need this." Bulman returned from the drinks tray with his own glass charged and sat opposite Scott. "Cheers, old mate. Get it down you."

Scott raised his glass in salute. Behind his cheerfulness he was worried about Bulman, and he was also trying to hide his personal sadness. He sipped his neat drink. "Are you serious about leaving the force, George? Is this what we're drinking to?"

"We're drinking to friendship and how valuable it can be. You and Hashimi were friends. He was arguably the most successful terrorist of present times, a baddie par excellence. Yet he saved your life twice when he need not have troubled."

Scott nodded sadly. "He did. But he also killed Vi and I shall never really understand why."

"You should. He was obsessed by wiping out all those involved with Sophie's brutal murder. Not all his plans worked out but he was a great improviser, never lost for an idea and never afraid to follow them through. And I'm quite sure he wanted to let Vi go. But if he did he would have lost Deacon and Ted and

Charlie. It didn't happen the way he hoped. He either backed out or he went all the way."

Bulman took a long swallow of his drink, leaving little in the glass. He shook his head at the impact and gazed over to the drinks trolley. "They found enough of her to establish that she was already dead before the explosion. One shot. I reckon he saw the blowing up of the warehouse as his last effort. He had to lure Deacon in and he couldn't have Vi on the loose to do that. But he did not want her to go the way the others did. I would guess he shot her when she least expected it."

"It doesn't make it right. It's the one thing that sticks in my gullet."

Bulman inclined his head. "He paid the price. Voluntarily. And got you out of a hole at the same time. He'd lost his way, Spider. A highly successful terrorist no longer wanted by the others because he was so good at what he did. There are jealousies and envy among the groups just like anywhere else. Perhaps more. He'd left a bloody trail behind him but it wasn't much of an age to go for a man who once fervently believed in everything he did. I don't excuse him. But I think I understand him just that little bit more. And you understood him well enough before that or you wouldn't have been so concerned. Don't discard him now."

"I was trying to say the right thing."

"I know that." Bulman drained his glass. "You didn't fool me." He stood up. "I'm going to get pissed. I've broken loose from that pontificating bastard, Hope. That's worth celebrating, don't you think. You going to join me?"

JAMES CARROLL

PRINCE OF PEACE

A love so great, a price so dear . . .

Michael Maguire – athlete, scholar, ex-POW, and
ordained priest – is a man with a mission. A mission of
peace. Confronted with the horror of America's presence
in Vietnam, his revolt is absolute – a reaction that will
have tragic consequences. Personal courage and deep
faith – and the love of his friends Frank and Carolyn –
sustain him on his lonely, perilous journey. But it is a
journey that will know danger, jealousy, betrayal and
despair before culminating in a compelling reaffirmation
of faith in human nature and in the redeeming power of
love.

A Royal Mail service in association with the Book Marketing Council & The Booksellers Association.

Post-A-Book is a Post Office trademark.

OTHER TITLES FROM
HODDER AND STOUGHTON PAPERBACKS